MASTER OF THE TEMPLE

*Books by Eric Ericson available
from New English Library:*

THE SORCERER
THE WOMAN WHO SLEPT WITH DEMONS
MASTER OF THE TEMPLE
THE WORLD, THE FLESH, THE DEVIL:
　　A Biographical Dictionary of Witches

MASTER OF THE TEMPLE
Eric Ericson

NEW ENGLISH LIBRARY

A New English Library Original Publication, 1983

Copyright © 1983 by Eric Ericson

All rights reserved. No part of this publication may be reproduced or transmitted, in any form or by any means, without permission of the publishers.

First NEL Paperback Edition March 1983

Conditions of sale: This book is sold subject to the condition that it shall not, by way of trade or otherwise, be lent, resold, hired out, or otherwise circulated without the publisher's prior consent in any form of binding or cover other than that in which it is published and without a similar condition including this condition being imposed on the subsequent purchaser.

NEL Books are published by
New English Library,
Mill Road, Dunton Green,
Sevenoaks, Kent.
Editorial office: 47 Bedford Square,
London WC1B 3DP

Typeset by Robcroft Ltd, London WC1
Printed in Great Britain by Cox and Wyman, Reading

0 450 05559 0

Contents

Prologue		SAND DEVILS	1
Chapter	1	HANS-MARTIN FRICK	11
Chapter	2	ADVICE FROM A MASTER	28
Chapter	3	BUSINESS DINNER	46
Chapter	4	THE ROSE AND CROSS	59
Chapter	5	TO BE A GOD	75
Chapter	6	SAUNA AND SIBELIUS	92
Chapter	7	THE EARTHLY TEMPLE	105
Chapter	8	TIME BOMB TICKING	119
Chapter	9	THE BOTTOMLESS PIT	128
Chapter	10	TOWER STRUCK BY LIGHTNING	146
Chapter	11	SEVEN MILES HIGH	163
Chapter	12	THE SACRED MOUNTAIN	182
Chapter	13	A DEAL	196
Chapter	14	A MEMORIAL ON THE MOON	207
Chapter	15	UNVEILING	220
Chapter	16	A VIEW OF HOLLYWOOD	240
Chapter	17	EARTH AND SKY	253
Chapter	18	AN ARMY WITH BANNERS	269
Chapter	19	RED AND BLACK	279
Chapter	20	GOOD OLD BOYS	300
Chapter	21	GATEWAY IN THE MIND	312
Chapter	22	CHILDHOOD MEMORIES	327
Chapter	23	OLD PHOTOGRAPHS	344
Chapter	24	THE SACRED ALIGNMENTS	358
Chapter	25	THE SCALES	385
Notes			412

PROLOGUE
SAND DEVILS

In the North African desert, towards the end of the year 1909, Aleister Crowley invoked to his own destruction the evil force known to the ancient Egyptians as the god Set.

Crowley was a man obsessed by the need to find God. He had this from his parents but he turned away from their restrictive and fundamentalist Christianity to look for God elsewhere. He was convinced that their beliefs were wrong headed. Christianity, with its insistence on sin, guilt, penitence and damnation was in his view a *crapulous creed*, fit only for slaves. He enjoyed the pleasures of the world and of the body and had no time for a belief system which required him to regard himself as a miserable sinner.

Estranged from his pious mother, he lived in London after he left Cambridge University on money left to him in his father's will. He learned of the existence of the Hermetic Order of the Golden Dawn, a secret group of initiates, and he readily embraced their teaching as a pathway to God. His considerable intelligence soon absorbed their doctrines and ceremonies until, after a few years, he found them too slow for his eagerness, too timid in their explorations of the hidden world. He struck out boldly on his own, mingling with their very English methods a version of tantric sexual worship he had learned in India on a big game hunting expedition. He knew where he was heading – towards union with God. He could not foresee the manner of the union or its outcome.

With a disciple named Victor Neuburg, Crowley left Algiers and marched south towards the desert. At night they slept in any convenient shelter or under the stars. They bought food as they went and carried it in rucksacks, living rough. Crowley was then thirty-four years old, a big framed man just starting to run to fat but still athletic. To accentuate his commanding appearance he shaved his head completely. His *chela* Neuburg was in his mid-twenties, not long out of university and with some claims to being a poet. He was a thin and small young man with a slightly twisted spine that made him carry one shoulder higher than the other and gave him an awkward walk.

On each day of their journey south the two men paused to explore one of the Aethyrs, a difficult and dangerous operation. The thirty Aethyrs, or Realms, were first discovered and described by Dr John Dee, a learned mathematician who became Court Astrologer to Queen Elizabeth I in the late sixteenth century. Dee was assisted in this work by Edward Kelly, a medium who had suffered the indignity of having his ears cut off by the public executioner for the crime of forgery. A description of the Aethyrs and the means of reaching them was compiled by Dr Dee in a work he called *Liber Logaeth*, printed after his death and still preserved in the library of the British Museum.

Dee wrote his work in a non-human language which he named Enochian, taught to him through Kelly by intelligences he believed to be angels. If by angels he meant messengers, then they were angels, but in no sense could they be regarded as angels as the Christian Church understands that term. Because of its complexity, Dee's work lay ignored for nearly three hundred years until the head of the Order of the Golden Dawn, an adept named Samuel Liddell Mathers, came across it in the British Museum and put his keen mind to work on it. While he was a member of the Order, Crowley studied Mather's translation and determined to follow the unimaginable track which Dee had charted three centuries before.

The exploration of the Aethyrs is not a task to be undertaken lightly. The time and place must be propitious, without distractions, and the explorer must be in a suitably heightened state of mind. Crowley began in Mexico City in

1900, his mind ablaze after a ferocious session with a raddled whore.

To retrace the footsteps of Dr Dee the pilgrim does not start with the First Aethyr and continue to the Thirtieth, but with the Thirtieth, proceeding backwards to the First. In Mexico City Crowley explored the Thirtieth and the Twenty-Ninth and found them of such interest that he made up his mind to continue at some future time when circumstances looked right.

In the eleven years that passed from the day Crowley was accepted into the Order of the Golden Dawn to the day he stood with Victor Neuburg in the desert, he had hacked his way deeper and deeper into the hidden world, as if he were chopping his way through a jungle with a machete. His intellect, enthusiasm, energy and courage were formidable and they sustained him and kept him going even after he lost his way. On his journey he encountered concepts and entities, within and without, which would have reduced a lesser man to gibbering idiocy. But Crowley continued undaunted and, through his endeavours, attained a remarkable level of illumination. At a price. He developed a blazing contempt for all morality and a total disregard for the rest of the human race. These were things to be used for his own purposes, nothing more.

In those eleven years he married Rose Kelly, a parson's daughter and sister of another member of the Order of the Golden Dawn, Gerald Kelly the painter. Kelly eventually became President of the Royal Academy and was knighted for his services to art. Crowley sired two children by Rose; took part in a disastrous attempt on Kangchenjunga, a then unclimbed mountain in the Himalayas; crossed South China with Rose and her first child on horseback and riverboat; received a vision in Cairo which he interpreted as God speaking directly to him; drove Rose into alcoholism by his flagrant promiscuity; experimented with homosexuality and became hooked on drugs. At thirty-four, with all this behind him, he felt that he was ready to attain union with God.

A hundred miles south of Algiers, Crowley and Neuburg

left the oasis village of Bou Saada behind them and headed into the real wilderness. They were still working their way through the Aethyrs at the rate of one a day. At Mount Dalleh Addin, after exploring the Eleventh Aethyr, Crowley was inspired to make an offering of himself to a god he believed to be the Pan of the ancient Greeks, though in this he was mistaken. Together he and Neuburg made a circle of stones on top of the barren hill, and in the centre they built an altar of stones and sand. On this altar Crowley lay naked and, while Neuburg sodomised him, prayed to Pan and dedicated the offering to him. The offering was himself and it was accepted, as he was shortly to discover. Fortified in spirit by what he had done, Crowley prepared the next day to explore the Tenth Aethyr.

In Dr Dee's account, the Tenth is called ZAX and it is an accursed place. Dee perceived the Aethyrs as dimensions of being, with strange geometries of their own. They have real existence, but not in our space or time. They are, in Dee's description, *realms*, and they are guarded against intruders from our space-time continuum.

When Crowley made his way into the Thirtieth in Mexico City, he found it to be an immense crystal cube surrounded by a sphere. He was challenged by four guardians in black robes but they were benign and admitted him into this fantastic non-place as soon as he satisfied them that he knew a word of sufficient power. They let him progress from the cube, which was the Watch Tower, into the sphere. But simple though the geometry of the Thirtieth might be, Crowley saw there a fearful vision of the destruction of all things, not unlike the Revelation of St John. Heaven and earth passed away and all things were confounded in destruction.

The Tenth, which he was now ready to tackle, has only one guardian and he is not easy to pass. Dr Dee recorded his name as Choronzon and said that he was a great devil.

Knowing this, Crowley and Neuburg took elaborate precautions. With the point of a dagger they traced in the sand a large circle inside a circle and between the two circumferences they wrote three holy names of God. This has always been the method used by those who call up unseen forces, the tradition being that inside the circle they will be secure from the fury of the thing they summon to appear. The best and fullest details of how to construct a circle are given in a manuscript called the Key of Solomon the King. It was translated into English in 1888 by the head of the Order of the Golden Dawn and Crowley had studied it carefully. The Key of Solomon recommends that two squares be drawn about the circles, one outside the other, with their corners to the four points of the compass. At each of the outer corners of the squares small circles should be drawn and, in each of these, another holy name of God inscribed – in the east EL, in the west YAH, in the south AGLA and in the north ADONAI. Crowley dispensed with the squares and small circles, considering that his basic circle was sufficient. In this, as in other things, he was overly optimistic.

Outside the circle of protection but close to it, Crowley drew a triangle in the sand and along the sides of it he scratched with his dagger three more of the many names of God. This too is standard procedure. The force to be called up will materialise in the triangle and will be caged there by the holy names. Within the triangle he wrote in the sand the name Choronzon.

He had made Neuburg buy three live pigeons in the market-place of Bou Saada. One after the other, he slit their throats, holding each fluttering bird by the legs so that its blood ran down to soak into the sand within the triangle. During this act of butchery, he intoned a form of words based on the Key of Solomon.

'By these most holy names and the other names of power which are written in the book of the heavens, I conjure thee, Pigeon, that thou assist me in this work. Almighty Adonai, be my aid so that this blood may have power and strength in all that I wish and in all that I shall demand.'

So far, all had been done in accordance with long established traditions, though the circle of protection could have been made stronger. Crowley's next actions were arrogant to the point of madness and brought their own retribution. He positioned Neuburg in the circle, where he could observe and record all that happened in safety. Then, wearing a thin black robe from his rucksack, Crowley seated himself inside the triangle where he had spilt the blood and written the name Choronzon. He was risking attack in order to get past the guardian of the Tenth. From inside the black robe, the hood pulled over his face, he told Neuburg to begin.

Victor Neuburg started by performing the banishing rituals of the pentagram. That is, with the point of his dagger he traced in the air at the four points of the compass – east, south, west and north – five-pointed stars to banish any evil or disturbing influence that might be in that place. The stars must be traced in a special way to be effective. With one point upwards, as Neuburg drew it, the five-pointed star is a symbol of man created in the image of God. The pentagrams of earth, air, fire, water and spirit, traced in the correct order and manner, are judged sufficient to dispel any malign influences that may be lurking. On this great occasion Neuburg took the additional precaution of tracing a six-pointed star to the four quarters as well. This sign carries a wealth of meaning for the initiated. Seen as two interlocking triangles, one pointing down and one pointing up, it can mean on different levels the jewel in the lotus; the lingam in the yoni; god in man; spirit in flesh and many other potent concepts.

Neuburg then repeated his tracings in air, though in a different manner, and these were the invoking pentagrams to summon good influences to protect him in his circle. That done, he recited in a loud voice the Exorcism of Pope Honorius.

'O Lord, deliver me from hell's great fear and gloom . . . '

Pope Honorius the Third started life as Cencio Savelli and was elected to the Throne of Peter in 1216. He was reputed to know more about the secret arts than any Vicar of Christ reasonably should. After his death, Pope Innocent the Sixth caused to be burned in public a manuscript thought to have belonged to Honorius: a collection of rituals, invocations and instructions that could only be operated by an ordained priest. A copy survived and in 1629 it was printed as a book in Rome, in secret for fear of the Inquisition. Since then it has been printed in many countries under various titles, but usually as the Black Book of Honorius.

The form of Exorcism described in this book is a long prayer for the protection of the summoner of evil spirits against their malice. It was originally written in Latin but Crowley had translated it into English verse to make it more easily memorised by those unfamiliar with the language of scholars and churchmen. Certain at last that he was secure in body and soul, Victor Neuburg sat down on the sand with his notebook and pencil, ready to record in shorthand whatever might occur. What he expected was that Crowley would slide mentally into the Tenth Aethyr and describe what he saw there, while his body remained in the triangle. He had not been present in Mexico when Crowley visited the Thirtieth and saw its curious cube and sphere spatial relationship. Or at the Twenty-Ninth, where a sky spangled with golden stars arched over a flat green landscape. But he had recorded the description of the Twenty-Eighth to the Eleventh and was eager with anticipation.

Inside his bloody triangle, buttressed by the three names of God scratched in the dry earth, Crowley squatted, a shapeless bundle in his long black robe. With all his powers of concentration he pronounced the Call. In the Enochian language it begins:

'Madariatza das perifa ZAX cabisca micaolazoda saamire . . .'

But to memorise it would be beyond the powers of most men and Crowley used the English translation:

'O ye heavens that dwell in the Tenth Aire, ye are mighty in the parts of the earth and execute therein the judgment of the Highest. Unto you it is said: behold the face of your God . . .'

The Call is a long one and in spite of its pious reference to

God at the beginning, it becomes very threatening and dark in tone as it proceeds. It builds to a climax in which the Aires, or Aethyrs, are commanded:

'Open the mysteries of your creation and make us partakers of the undefiled knowledge.'

As the powerful vibrations of the Call rang through whatever impossible dimensions of non-being link this world to the Aethyrs, Crowley stared into a large golden topaz set into a wooden cross painted bright red. It was in the depths of the jewel, as in a mirror, that he caught his first glimpse of the Tenth and began to describe it to Neuburg. He found it hard to put into words, for the Tenth is a shapeless place, full of drifting and changing forms. And before he could resolve it clearly, the guardian of the Tenth peered at him from out of the topaz. Finding him unprotected in the triangle, the guardian slid into this world and took possession of Crowley; mind, soul and body. It spoke through him. Neuburg scribbled the words down, not yet alarmed because he did not realise what had happened.

When Dr John Dee first explored the Aethyrs and left directions for those who dared to follow him into these wild and dangerous spaces, it was from his house in Mortlake by the river Thames in the then green and pleasant fields of Surrey. Even there, amidst the gentle English landscape, the guardian of the Tenth appeared to him as a mighty devil. In the desolate wastes of North Africa the guardian manifested himself as Set, the lord of darkness of the ancient Egyptians; the murderer of his brother Osiris. The Egyptians saw Set in the sand storm and the arid desert which kills travellers. They named him the spirit of drought and disease, of impotence and death.

Set had no real form of his own, being the essence of destruction and madness working through man and nature. The walls of Egyptian temples and tombs are covered with portraits of the great gods; their statues stand everywhere – Osiris the Good, who civilised men by teaching them the mysteries of agriculture when they were only Stone Age savages; his sister and wife Isis, mother of all living, who protected men and women in this world and the next; their mighty son Horus, glorious as a falcon soaring in the noonday sky. But the statues of Set were smashed during the twenty-second dynasty when the once mighty Egyptian empire was crumbling into chaos and anarchy, nearly three thousand years ago. His portraits were erased, his name scratched out of inscriptions, as if the Egyptians had come to realise the depths of the evil overtaking them and tried to blot out all trace of it from their world.

In forgotten tombs some representations of him survived. Before the prohibition on naming or depicting him, the early Egyptians had shown Set as a creature that has never existed on this earth – a man-beast with a thin and curving snout, square jackal ears and a stiff, forked tail. That is, he had no shape of his own and could only be portrayed by parts of unclean animals stuck together.

In the possessed Crowley's naked body, his black robe ripped off and thrown away, Set reached out over the triangle that was supposed to contain him and clawed at Victor Neuburg. The names of God written along the sides of the triangle were not powerful enough to hold him. At the top of his voice – or rather, at the top of Crowley's voice – he raved that he was 'the terror of darkness and the blackness of nights, the deafness of the adder and the tastelessness of stale water, the black fire of hatred . . . not one but many things.'

Alarmed at last, Neuburg tried to banish the insane creature back to the Tenth Aethyr by reciting the holy names inscribed about his protective circle. He received an instant and daunting answer:

'I FEED UPON THE NAMES OF THE MOST HIGH, I CHURN THEM IN MY JAWS AND VOID THEM FROM MY FUNDAMENT . . .'

Neuburg was frightened, even as he jotted down the ravings of the guardian. Before the situation became any worse, he ritually commanded Set to depart to his own place, using the correct formula of words he had been taught. Far from departing, Set broke into a torrent of obscenity and threw sand from his triangle onto Neuburg's circle, breaking the barrier and creating a way through. Neuburg was still furiously scribbling in his notebook when Set, in Crowley's body, slithered into the circle and attacked him. Not manlike, with his hands, but beast fashion, trying to rip his throat out with his teeth.

In mortal fear Victor Neuburg gabbled out all the names of God he could remember, protecting his throat with one arm while he slashed at his assailant with his dagger. His life hung in the balance for some minutes but he defended himself with the desperation of fear. Eventually, at knife point, he drove the raging creature back into its triangle and quickly repaired his circle while Set screamed at him. That done, the nervous and frail young man found from somewhere inside himself the courage to start recording again the words of hatred roared across the desert:

'I have prevailed against the kingdom of the Father and befouled his beard . . . I have prevailed against the kingdom of the Son . . . '

Victor Neuburg had won a mighty victory in preserving his life and sanity in the face of such malignity. It may be that as he squatted on the sand recording in fast shorthand the blasphemous ranting, there passed through his mind the Egyptian legend that the god Horus had sought out Set in revenge for the murder of his father Osiris. In their struggle Set blinded Horus in one eye by spitting venom into it, but Horus had finally overcome Set by snatching his testicles and ripping them off. In his extremity of terror, when Set had almost overwhelmed him, Neuburg had called upon Horus to aid him, using another of his many names.

In time the power of the pigeons' blood that had been shed on the triangle was used up. The manifestation of Set faded away, leaving Crowley and Neuburg, both exhausted, facing each other across the sand.

Whatever Neuburg thought, Crowley was not at all sure that Set had left him. He insisted that before they rested they must purify the place with fire. They rooted about for whatever would burn and lit a fire over the patch of sand where the triangle had been. Later on, Crowley noted in his diary that in the Tenth Aethyr, 'there is neither beginning nor end, for it is all hotch-potch, because it is of the wicked on earth and the damned in hell.'

From the time that Set manifested in Crowley and found him to be one of his own, Crowley became a man possessed for the rest of his life, a monster of destruction, bodily and spiritual, his own and others. From that day on, no man or woman who had any close contact with him escaped with sanity whole or life unwrecked. Disease, madness, ruin, drug addiction, murder, degradation, despair and suicide walked in his shadow until he died in a Hastings boarding house nearly forty years later, perplexed by his own life.

The sand devil had come at Crowley's bidding. Whether he came from the searing desert or the Tenth Aethyr or from the depths of Crowley's own unconscious mind is not a question worth considering, since all three are identical, but seen from different viewpoints. Crowley achieved his long sought union with God, but from error or malice he chose the wrong god. To initiates the god-forms are cosmic forces personified and to be made one with a god is to become a channel for a cosmic force. The force that poured through Crowley rolled across Europe and then across America like a tidal wave, sweeping many away to destruction, even today.

CHAPTER 1
HANS-MARTIN FRICK

AT OSLO on a fine spring day, Jonathan Rawlings boarded a Scandinavian Airlines jet bound for Stockholm. The only English language newspaper he had been able to buy at the airport bookstall was the *Daily Express*, not the *Financial Times* he wanted. He took a window seat in the first class section of the plane, fastened his seat belt and skimmed through his newspaper while the cabin crew bustled passengers about, stowed their hand luggage for them and made sure they were strapped in. Jonathan was too experienced a traveller to require that kind of attention.

The newspaper reported that yet another British army patrol had been ambushed in Belfast, one soldier killed and two more injured. A widow of seventy-four had been raped and beaten in Doncaster. Ten more people had been executed in Iran by firing squad, eight for political offences and two for adultery.

The plane rolled out slowly to the end of the strip and wheeled to face down into the breeze. There was never anything of interest to look at in aeroplanes, Jonathan thought. Ahead of him were two rows of empty seats and then a blank bulkhead. Through the window he had a view of tarmac and green grass as far as the airport perimeter. He turned back to the newspaper as the engines revved up to full scream and the plane launched itself down the runway.

The Israeli airforce had strafed a guerilla camp in retaliation for a grenade attack against a bus in Tel Aviv. The New York police were holding a man they believed to be a multiple murderer of homosexual adolescents. In Paris, a Middle East diplomat had been gunned down on the pavement outside a restaurant.

The SAS jet lifted off and slanted its nose upwards. Through the window Jonathan watched the ground below fall away sharply as the undercarriage rumbled up into its housing. The newspaper had lost whatever little interest it had for him. The only useful item he had found was towards the back pages – the value of the pound sterling against other currencies. That at least had some bearing on his journey. He discarded the newspaper with its catalogue of human hatred and suffering on the empty seat next to him, reflecting briefly on the complexity of endeavour that had gone into producing this printed comment on the state of the world. His black leather briefcase was stowed under the seat in front of him. He put it on his knees and opened it, knowing that there was more advantage in the sheafs of business papers it contained than in the newspaper that day.

The plane bumped a few times as it climbed up through wispy cloud to its cruising height. Then it was in clear spring sunshine and the seat belt sign went off.

From Oslo to Stockholm is a short flight, only about forty-five minutes when everything goes to schedule. An SAS stewardess leaned over the empty seat to ask Jonathan if he wanted a drink from the bar and smiled at him. She was tall and thin in her uniform; white shirt and blue-grey skirt, her face attractive in an angular way. She wore no makeup and her straw coloured hair was pulled back from her forehead and fastened at the nape of her neck. He ordered coffee, it being only ten in the morning.

Most women smiled pleasantly when they talked to him, probably without even realising it. He was thirty-eight, all but a few weeks, red haired and muscular, not particularly good looking but interesting. To the stewardess he was a man who travelled first class, wore a well made business suit and had an air of purpose. She brought the coffee and leaned further across the seat in front of him. In his mind's eye, Jonathan pictured her without her clothes. Long neck, prominent collar bones, small breasts, a dip below her rib cage to a flat belly and narrow hips above long, lean thighs. He put her age at twenty-six or seven. As he thanked her he touched her wrist very lightly with his fingertips. Pale blue eyes stared for a moment into his and he recognised a look almost neurotic in its intensity. Women like that were precious to him. At another time he would have developed the acquaintance easily and confidently. But on that particular day he had too much else to think about.

Two topics vied for place in his mind, both of great importance to him; one business and the other a personal concern. His business was a sales tour of the Scandinavian countries for the company he worked for, Dovedays Limited. To those not engaged in it, manufacturing industry appears to be one of the least interesting fields of human endeavour. To those in the higher reaches of it, this attitude is a cause of frequent surprise. Dovedays was in the food processing sector, more specifically it was one of the three largest biscuit making companies in Britain. Its sales that year were running at well over £100 million, equivalent to about a fifth of the total British output of biscuits. Jonathan looked through the sheaf of papers in his hand as he sipped coffee, knowing all the neatly typed figures by heart. The reason for his trip was to improve upon those figures and the pressure to succeed was considerable. Not that his future was at stake in any way. Business to him was a game he intended to win, the product was immaterial, whether biscuits, baby carriages or buildings. The tokens in the game were pounds sterling, francs, marks, dollars, kroner – any of the world's legitimate currencies. The rewards for winning the game were money, esteem and control of his own life.

That apart, the hard facts for biscuit makers were that British consumption had peaked and levelled off to a plateau twenty years ago. In the intense competition between manufacturers, new varieties were developed and poured out of factories in quick succession – sweet, digestive, chocolate, salted, flavoured, plain, fruited, unfruited, ginger, as fast as they could be devised – but the overall consumption stayed about the same. The only way to increase sales substantially was to develop overseas markets. Dovedays had been doing this for a good many years, to the point where nearly a quarter of its total output was exported. Scandinavia was a good market for them. The Danes, Norwegians and Swedes had taken to biscuits and in the course of a year they ate nearly half the quantity that Britons got through.

A more urgent factor for the consideration of those responsible for managing biscuit companies was the never ending need for capital investment. To make a worthwhile profit and stay competitive, faster, newer and better machinery must be installed as soon as it was developed. To fall behind in this race was to risk trouble. Dovedays had just completed the replanting of two of their factories at a cost altogether of over ten million pounds. Capacity was up by nearly a third, as planned. Since there was no way of selling the extra tonnage in Britain at a profit, there was a pressing need to step up overseas sales quickly.

Jonathan's immediate boss was Derek Braithwaite, the company's director of overseas sales. He was not an easy man to work with and he kept a tight rein on his department. Normally he made most of the overseas sales visits himself, taking Jonathan along from time to time to familiarise him with the main distributors. This year there were problems. The installation of the new plant had run into engineering troubles and then into labour troubles. The engineering trouble had been resolved and the gleaming production lines were at last ready to run when the labour union called its members out on strike until a new rate for the job had been negotiated and agreed. Between the engineering designers and the workers, some months had been lost and the projected overseas sales drive, planned to start in January, was only now just on the way.

Braithwaite had taken Jonathan along on a rapid sales tour of the company's distributors in Holland, Belgium, Germany and France. Then, since he was preparing for a tour of the United States, their biggest overseas market, Braithwaite grudgingly allowed Jonathan to do the rounds of the Scandinavian countries on his own. The target was to persuade the distributors in all these countries to step up their sales by at least ten per cent before the end of the year and by another fifteen per cent the following year.

The stewardess came back to refill his coffee cup. As she moved away up the gangway he noted that under her straight skirt her buttocks were small and high, giving an almost boyish appearance.

The sales tour was working out reasonably well so far. In Copenhagen he had impressed on Jorgen Christensen the importance of all-out selling and got a solid commitment to the year's increase and a cautious agreement that next year would be even better. Jonathan had made some small concession on price, since Christensen was a hard headed man. In Oslo it had been a different though not unexpected story. Oskar Egeland was a small and precise man, eternally pessimistic; most unlike the rumbustious Christensen. He argued and haggled and insisted that it was all impossible, refused to drink more than one glass of wine at lunch and made the whole business as difficult as he could. When Jonathan left him, Egeland promised to think the matter over carefully and write to him in London. That was the Norwegian's way. Jonathan knew that there would be a letter on his desk when he got back to the office in which Egeland would detail what he thought he could achieve. It would not be as simple as ten per cent followed by fifteen per cent. It would be something more precise, perhaps eleven and a half per cent and fourteen per cent. The numbers didn't matter so long as Egeland was motivated.

The Stockholm visit should also run to plan. Jonathan had met the company's Swedish distributor before in London. Nils Bohman, a quiet man in his late fifties, pleasant to talk to and, like most Scandinavians, a football fanatic. Jonathan had taken him to a First Division match and Bohman enjoyed it so much that he sat and drank neat whisky in his hotel for hours afterwards while he analysed the game in expert detail. Football had little interest for Jonathan, but he admired the skill and understanding with which Bohman dissected the game he had seen.

Apart from Bohman there was someone else Jonathan had arranged to meet in Stockholm, quite unconnected with his business trip, just as there had been someone besides Christensen he had met in Copenhagen. This had to do with his personal interests and would be utterly impossible to explain to Braithwaite or anyone else at Dovedays, in the unlikely event that it came to their attention. There were two distinct sides to Jonathan's nature and life. There was Jonathan Rawlings the business executive, the career elitest climbing the ladder of promotion, the man in a functionally handsome office causing things to happen which produced a financial profit for the company that employed him, who enjoyed expense account living, jetting from city to city with briefcase and credit card, a man committed to the simple commercial values. That was the public man, envied by many.

The other Jonathan Rawlings was a high ranking member of the Noble Order of the Masters of the Temple, an organisation so secret that only its initiates knew that it existed. And in this part of his life he exemplified the saying: 'His door stands closed and he is not known to rulers. His inner life is hidden and he moves outside the ruts of the recognised virtues. He moves about the world buying and selling. Even in the market place he looks for enlightenment.'

The Noble Order of the Masters of the Temple had been established under that name for less than forty years, but its traditions and teachings were of much greater antiquity and its pedigree was long and instructive to initiates. Its immediate ancestor was the Order of the Temple of the Orient, founded in Germany at the end of the nineteenth century by Karl Kellner, a wealthy businessman. That Order had flourished from its foundation and had Lodges not only in Germany but in France, Switzerland, Britain, Denmark, Sweden and America. One of its best known initiates was Rudolf Steiner, the educationalist, though he became ashamed of his connection after a time and left the Order to found his own system. Kellner's inspiration was derived from an earlier Order, the Knights of the Temple, set up in Paris in 1705 with the Duke of Orleans as Grandmaster. The head of this Order at the time Kellner was born was Bernard Fabre-Palaprat and by then it had Lodges in England and in Santo Domingo as well as in France. In turn, the Knights of the Temple took their origin in an earlier Order, the Strict Observance founded in Germany by Karl Gotthelf, Baron von Hund, which established Lodges in Germany, France, Switzerland, Italy, Hungary and, after it formed an alliance with the organisation led by Johann August Starck, in St Petersburg in Russia. Von Hund's source for his Order was an even earlier one, and so the line went back in a kind of apostolic succession to the original Knights Templar, a pan-European military organisation created by Hugues de Payens in the days of the Crusades.

From his experience of many women, Jonathan could predict the degree of sexual response he could elicit from the air stewardess who had brought his coffee. He had looked into her eyes and learned something of her soul. A naked encounter between them would in a sense be like a stage drama in which he had often played. Half of the cast would be changed, the staging would be new, the plot and the action would be the same, though with different nuances. To the uninitiated, sex is physical, love is emotional, God is spirit, for they are unaware of the unity of body, mind and spirit. He pictured himself with her on a bed. The Swedish woman would use her thin body energetically and consciously at first. Then under the expert touch of his hands and mouth she would lose control and twist about to offer every part of herself to his attentions. When at last he slid deep into her, through her blaze of lust a premonition would seize her that the experience to which she had casually committed herself was not merely the ordinary friction of skin and sexual parts but a steady and irreversible climb towards an unknown ecstasy. He would cause her fervour to soar to immeasurable heights until, at the last, she would explode with the incandescence of a star going supernova. Afterwards, as she lay gasping, her straw coloured hair plastered to her face with the sweat of her exertions, she would stare at him dumbstruck for a moment or two before she slid into the dreamless sleep of fulfilment.

She might well be a suitable candidate for membership of the Order, if he had read her aright. He decided to find out her name and pass it on to his Swedish colleagues to follow up.

The Noble Order of the Masters of the Temple owed its beginning to an expatriate German named Hans-Martin Frick who took up residence in London in 1939. Frick was born in Cologne before the turn of the century, the son of a businessman. In those days there were strong commercial and cultural links between Imperial Germany and Sweden and so after Frick had graduated from Heidelberg his father sent him to the University of Uppsala in Sweden to learn the language and the way of life of that country. The long range plan was that he should in due course open and manage a branch of the family business in Stockholm. Before anything could come of this intention, the 1914 war erupted. Hans-Martin Frick, just under thirty years old, joined the German army as a matter of duty and was commissioned into an infantry regiment.

The strategy of the German High Command was to invade France through Belgium and hold a defensive position to keep the Allies pinned down while another force went eastwards to smash the vast but ill-equipped Russian army. With Czarist Russia out of the war, the whole German military strength could be thrown into France and when that was overrun, England would be isolated and compelled to agree to peace terms.

The plan worked very well. By this time Frick reached the Western Front in early 1915, the Germans were dug in and the stalemate of trench warfare had begun. Frick survived the years of mass slaughter by rifle fire, machine gun, bomb, shell, gas and bayonet. He was sustained by a saying of a French adept, Eliphas Levi, that 'fear attracts the bullet and courage deflects it.' By the time he was promoted to Captain, Frick had seen death and suffering on a scale that changed his view of life and directed his attention towards God, though not the Christian god whose priests blessed the bayonets of his men before they went into combat.

About the time that the Bolshevik revolution of 1917 took Russia out of the war, Frick was promoted to Major and decorated a second time for gallantry in action. But by then the Americans were about to enter the war, and only a few months later the German lines were breached by the British army and the war was virtually over. When Frick returned to Germany he found the chaos that accompanies a lost war – civil disorder, armed insurrection, councils of workers and soldiers on the Bolshevik pattern and the abdication of the

Kaiser. The Germany of Frick's youth was dead and buried and a new Germany was struggling to be born out of hunger and desperation.

The Swedish stewardess might be utterly unsuitable for membership of the Order, Jonathan reflected. A candidate was tested in many ways, physical, moral and spiritual, over a period of months, and was required to learn by heart a substantial body of secret doctrine. And then, to demonstrate that it had been properly understood and its implications grasped, expounded it orally to two appointed Inquisitors, neither of whom could be the original sponsor. If that was satisfactorily achieved, the candidate was given the title of Pilgrim to indicate that there was a long and arduous journey ahead, beset with danger. But for those who had the determination and stamina to follow where the path led, there was the promise of a shrine of grace and illumination. The Swedish woman might not be capable, or even ready, for any of that, whatever her carnal potentiality. If, however, she managed to convince the Inquisitors that she was worthy in every way, she would be admitted to membership of the Order as a Neophyte, the name of the First Degree, in a ceremony that was uplifting and enlightening. From then on she would receive much assistance and encouragement and be assigned to a personal teacher. Jonathan had been received as a Neophyte at the age of twenty-one, the earliest age at which the Order would accept anyone. It had taken him over ten years to advance to his present exalted status of Seventh.

Though Hans-Martin Frick survived four years of carnage, his father did not. Old Heinrich died of a heart attack in 1917, leaving everything to his son. Frick took a hard look at defeated Germany when he was out of the army and decided that his future did not lie in the country he had fought for. He realised as best he could his father's assets and was grateful that the old man had prudently transferred a fair amount of his wealth out of the country through Switzerland early in the war. He made his way to Stockholm, as his father had always intended, settled there, refounded the family business and, over the next fifteen years, he prospered. At forty he married a Swedish shipping heiress nearly twenty years younger than himself. It was a contented marriage and they had three daughters.

His business contacts with Germany were strong and from time to time he visited his homeland. He observed with pity the pauperisation and humiliation of the people and could see how the National Socialist Party had an appeal to them. The rantings of its leader, Adolf Hitler, convinced Frick that he had been wise to move to Sweden, since it was clear to him that Hitler was hell bent on a war of revenge against France. As the years passed and the Nazis grew stronger, Frick began to wonder about the safety of Sweden. He thought it possible that when the Nazis extended their empire from the Atlantic coast to the Black Sea, as he was certain they would, then Stalin would retaliate by taking the whole of Scandinavia. In the mid-thirties Frick concluded that it was time for him to move on before the Bolsheviks arrived in Stockholm with guns and tanks. He was well into his fifties by then, a man of substantial wealth, having friends and business interests and contacts in many parts of the world. He considered going to America to live, a country he had visited several times, but he was too European to feel entirely comfortable there. He decided upon England, for he had an old-fashioned respect for the institutions of the country. He did not doubt that England would be involved in the approaching war, but he felt certain that it would survive reasonably intact. He made his arrangements and through the network of international banking, which he understood well, he transferred large sums of money to England and to other parts of the world he regarded as stable. The abortive Munich Agreement between Hitler and Neville Chamberlain of 1938 accelerated his winding up of his affairs in Sweden. Officially sanctioned and vouched for by any number of influential English businessmen who had known him for years, Frick, his wife and their three young daughters took up residence in London in early 1939.

Events proved him wrong about Scandinavia. When the war came, Sweden was able to remain neutral and it was the Germans who occupied Norway and Denmark. Only Finland fell under Russian domination.

Reichsführer Hitler's war strategy was the reverse of the German High Command's in 1914. His intention was to overrun France first, force England out of the war and then turn his major attention to the destruction of Russia. The first part went according to plan – France was beaten and occupied rapidly. But England, though isolated, refused to make terms and opened up new theatres of operation outside Europe. The Russian armies in the east retreated before the German onslaught, extending the German supply lines to breaking point. And at Leningrad they dug in and fought off the Germans for two and a half years, while Josef Stalin drafted and trained new armies to push the Germans back to Berlin.

Frick's contacts throughout Scandinavia and Germany made him useful to the British authorities when they turned their attention to economic warfare. Through his interests in insurance, banking and shipping Frick knew a lot about where factories of importance were sited throughout Europe, what they produced and what they could be set up to produce. He was well acquainted with the potential of various merchant fleets, port installations and other useful matters. He had no allegiance to Hitler's Reich. For him it was not the true Germany. He made his information and contacts available and was useful to more than one British government department as a result.

In front of Jonathan the Fasten Seat Belts light came on. The stewardess bustled up the aisle removing empty glasses and cups.

'Tell me your name,' he said to her. 'Perhaps we might meet in Stockholm.'

'Karin Wikstrom. You can find me in the telephone directory.'

He nodded and smiled and she went off with her loaded

tray. In a minute or two her voice came over the cabin speakers, first in Swedish and then in English, telling the passengers what they already knew – that the plane would be landing shortly in Stockholm. Down below the wisps of cloud Jonathan could see the green of fields and of trees, the glint of water, brown earth and buildings no larger than toys. The plane banked, one wing tip up into the blue sky, the other down towards the ground, levelled and was slanting down the glide path towards the airport.

In the years before the 1914 war when Hans-Martin Frick was learning the family business in Germany he became a member of the Order of the Temple of the Orient. Karl Kellner, the founder, died in 1905 and was succeeded as Grandmaster by Theodor Reuss, under whose guidance it enjoyed a modest but steady expansion. Reuss's mother was English and by profession he was a music-hall singer. He was also secretly employed as an agent by the German authorities who were concerned by the spread of Marxist socialism. Kellner had been a careful man who fully understood the significance of the Order's maxim; Dare, Know, Will, Keep Silent. Reuss was temperamentally different. By 1912 the private publication of the Order, called *The Oriflamme*, was hinting at the sexual nature of its teaching and this journal had a wider distribution than the membership of the Order. In the same year Reuss visited Aleister Crowley at his apartment in Victoria Street, London and was hugely impressed by the daemonic energy in him. He invited Crowley to accept membership of the Order and to establish a Lodge in Britain. Crowley was sufficiently impressed by the broad chested visitor with the big handlebar moustache to go to Berlin and be installed as Master of the new British Lodge. Reuss failed to recognise the destructive nature of the power that possessed Crowley and by admitting him to the Order he was condemning it to annihilation. Some of the other German members had serious misgivings about Crowley when they met him, but they had taken an oath of obedience to the Grandmaster and were unwilling to break it.

Theodor Reuss suffered a stroke in 1922 which disabled him permanently. By the time he died two years later it was agreed between the German members that Heinrich Traenker should become Master of the German Lodge. That left the Grandmastership of all the Lodges throughout the world vacant, as Reuss had held both offices. After much intense thought and appeals for divine guidance, Traenker nominated the Master of the British Lodge for the supreme office. A well-to-do member, Karl Germer, who was a publisher, paid the expenses of Crowley's visit to Germany, for in the ten years that he had been British Lodge Master, Crowley had squandered his entire inheritance and was living in dire poverty in Paris. With Crowley came his tattered entourage, two drug-hysterical American women and an obsessed Englishman who had abandoned his university teaching job to become a disciple. Crowley's election as Grandmaster split the Order, for by then much more was known about him from his own publications and from newspaper revelations of his activities in Sicily, from whence the Italian government had deported him in 1923. Some German members and some Lodges outside Germany refused outright to accept him as Grandmaster and went their own way.

When Frick emigrated to Sweden in 1919 he took with him a charter from Theodor Reuss to establish a Stockholm Lodge of the Order of the Temple of the Orient. He worked diligently to find suitable members and had a fair measure of success as he was in a position to meet influential people on equal terms. He was one of those who regarded Crowley as inappropriate as Grandmaster and, being a methodical man, he went to see for himself. He found Crowley and his hangers-on in Leipzig, the guests of Martha Kuentzel, a woman who was convinced that Aleister Crowley and Adolf Hitler were incarnate gods. Frick invited Crowley to an expensive dinner in the city's best restaurant and listened intently to all that he said. In private he talked to the two women, Leah Hirsig and Dorothy Olsen, and pitied them in his heart for what Crowley had made of them and damned them under his breath for allowing Crowley to do so. He too had felt the power of the sand devil that spoke through the new Grandmaster and knew that flight from it was the only sensible action.

Without disclosing his intentions, Frick made his way to Sicily to see the Abbey of Thelema which Crowley had told him about. In an old single storey farmhouse near the village of Cefalu, Crowley set up his strange shrine to his god and lived with his ill-assorted menage of followers. It had been left on Crowley's deportation in charge of another of his victims, Ninette Shumway, a young French widow who was caring as best she could for her two children, one of which was Crowley's. Frick inspected the building carefully, from the altar in the largest room to the pictures Crowley had painted on the walls. In the main bedroom was a nearly life size mural of Crowley standing between Leah and an unidentified man. All three were naked. The man was sodomising Crowley, who was ejaculating onto Leah Hirsig's belly. Frick pondered the symbolism of the picture briefly. Over the food and wine he had brought with him, he asked Ninette Shumway about the 'great days' of the Abbey.

Because he was a Lodge Master she talked to him freely. And because she disliked Leah Hirsig she took pleasure in describing the goat ritual. In this, Leah had crouched on her hands and knees under the blue Sicilian sky, naked and surrounded by a small group of worshippers – Crowley, Ninette and two friends of Crowley's visiting from Paris. With solemn incantations Crowley had induced a young he-goat to mount Leah's rump. As it began to tup her, he slashed its throat with a sharp knife so that its scarlet blood poured down upon her back. Ninette was not sure to which god this offering had been made, but Frick had no doubts.

His mind troubled, Frick walked down the hill to Cefalu and took the train to Palermo. In a hotel room he put himself through the most elaborate ceremony of purification he could devise, and only when he was satisfied that no malignant influence from the Abbey clung about him did he cross to the mainland and make for home. In Stockholm he called a full meeting of the Lodge and solemnly reported on what he had heard, what he had seen, and how he interpreted these things. He said that he was utterly unable to accept Crowley as Grandmaster and that if the Lodge wished to do so, then he would vacate the office of Lodge Master and leave the Order. The issue was never in doubt. The Swedish members were stunned by what they had heard and voted unanimously to reject Crowley and to become independent. Frick remained Lodge Master until he left Sweden for England fourteen years later.

Even so, Frick knew in his heart that the Order would die through the choice of Crowley. In 1937, two years before Frick's second emigration, the Nazi government suppressed all Lodges of the Order of the Temple of the Orient in Germany, those which had accepted Crowley and those which had rejected him. Karl Germer, who was still supporting Crowley financially, was rounded up and put into a concentration camp. He managed to survive until the Nazis decided that he was harmless and released him. As soon as he could, he emigrated to the United States to promote the Order there. There was already a Lodge at Pasadena and he had high hopes.

Hans-Martin Frick gave much thought to the future of the Order during his last years in Sweden and recognised that it had become corrupt past redemption. When he had been settled in London for a year or so he established a new Order, the Noble Order of the Masters of the Temple. He saw it as a return to the pure springs of Templar tradition, unpolluted by the poisons that had entered and fouled the stream since Kellner's death. In the emotional and intellectual turmoil of wartime London conditions were good for his foundation. He recruited very carefully, testing each step of the way, accepting only men and women of character and influence. He intended to have no more persons of poor judgment like Reuss and Traenker to unbar the gates to destructive forces. His choice was from his fast spreading circle of acquaintances, senior government officials, high ranking service officers, a few members of Parliament from near the front benches, successful businessmen, university teachers, lawyers and eminent physicians.

During the war years when Frick was laying the solid foundations of his new Order, Aleister Crowley was still alive and resident in England, though now approaching seventy. He died in 1947, almost destitute, in a boarding house and was succeeded as Grandmaster of the Order of the Temple of the Orient by Karl Johannes Germer, then already in his sixties. Germer was an energetic man, but the Lodges were divided and pursuing their own ends. His role was more that of executor than executive. When he died in 1960 the original concept of the Order as a worldwide organisation teaching the hidden truths for the illumination of humanity died with him.

Frick's new Order grew and flourished as the old Order withered away. In the post-war years, when travel became possible again and aviation made it faster and easier, he was able from his base in London to establish Lodges in Germany, Scandinavia, Holland, Belgium, France and the United States. He lived to be seventy-three, active to within a few weeks of his death and lucid to the very end. As he lay dying at his country home near Salisbury he assessed his life and his achievements and was satisfied. He had kept faith with his father by developing the family business though he had been compelled twice to transplant it, first to Sweden and then to England. He had served the country of his birth at peril to his life in the trenches of the 1914 war. He had served the country of his adoption by the use of his information network in the 1939 war. He had lived in harmony and mutual esteem with his wife for over thirty years and, though he had no son, his daughters had married suitably and well in England. Above all, he had created out of the bitter ashes of the old Order the new Order of the Masters of the Temple to continue the ancient teaching and traditions. The office of Grandmaster was about to pass into trusted hands.

He died to this world at peace with himself. To the Order he did not die; he made the transition to another plane of being, from where he continued to guide the Order wisely.

Through the cabin window Jonathan watched the threshold of the runway skim past below. Seconds later the wheels smacked the strip and the jets roared in reverse thrust to check the big bird's headlong rush along the ground. Then it wheeled ponderously off the strip and trundled towards the terminal. He had arrived in Stockholm.

CHAPTER 2
ADVICE FROM A MASTER

FROM ARLANDA airport Jonathan took a taxi into the city. It proved to be further than he had expected but the big Mercedes made good time and by noon he was settled in the Grand Hotel. His first telephone call was to London to advise his office that he had arrived and could be contacted at the hotel. He intended giving Braithwaite a summary of his meeting with Egeland in Norway but Braithwaite's secretary said that he was out at a meeting. She would tell him on his return that Jonathan had checked in.

He put the phone down and reflected for a moment or two on the frustrations of working for a grudging and ungrateful man. More than once he had debated with himself whether to leave Dovedays and had once gone as far as attending an interview for a job with another company. They made him a good offer, which he turned down after some hard thought. There was the possibility of doing great things at Dovedays if he could break through the barriers that Braithwaite threw up against his advance – that was the lure that kept him there. On the other hand, a man who intended to achieve big things ought to be well on his way by his fortieth birthday. That didn't give him much time and his experience suggested that if he was still second in command then he would never get anywhere worthwhile during the rest of his working life.

His next call was to Nils Bohman, the company's Swedish

distributor. He too was not available, but he had left a message to say that he would collect Jonathan from his hotel at seven and take him to dinner.

The third call was to the number he had been given as a contact for the Order's Stockholm Lodge. A girl answered in Swedish, switched effortlessly to English when he spoke to her and told him that Mr Ullsten was out of the office.

Booby prize, Jonathan thought wryly, three misses in a row. Not an auspicious beginning in Sweden.

'My name is Rawlings,' he said, 'Did Mr Ullsten leave any message for me?'

'Yes, he said you might call. Have you a pencil – he left a number for you to ring.'

'Hold on,' said Jonathan, fumbling in the jacket he had thrown onto one of the two beds in his room, 'Right.'

She read out the number for him.

'Is that in the city?' he asked.

'Yes, it is a city number, but I don't have any name or address for it.'

'Thank you.'

When he tried the new number an old man's voice answered.

'This is Jonathan Rawlings. I have your number from Mr Ullsten's office.'

'Yes, I was expecting to hear from you today. Ullsten had some urgent business and asked me to look after you. Where are you now?'

'At the Grand Hotel.'

'Are you free now?'

'Until seven this evening.'

'Good, we can meet. I will be with you in half an hour at the most. Please be my guest for lunch.'

'Thank you. I'll be in the lobby.'

Jonathan had been given messages of greeting by the Grandmaster in London to deliver to the Lodges he planned to make contact with on this trip – Copenhagen, Stockholm and Helsinki. He was particularly eager to meet members of the Swedish Lodge because it had been founded from the former Temple of the Orient Lodge which Frick himself had established and led. After forty years there would be no one who went back to those days, he guessed, but some traditions might linger on.

In Denmark he had been the guest of honour at a dinner given by the officers of the Copenhagen Lodge. Besides himself there were eight men and six women present. In his words of welcome the Lodge Master said that many more members would have been there if they could have been given more notice, but they understood the urgencies of businessmen. It was a very good dinner and Jonathan enjoyed himself. At the end of the evening he was expected to choose one of the women, and with the discretion that went with his high status he told the Master that on such short acquaintance it was impossible for him to choose between the illustrious ladies at the table. By asking the Master to make the choice for him he offended no one and assured himself of an interesting partner, since the Master naturally wanted to impress his guest. As a result, he went home with a lean, dark haired woman of about his own age, Annemarie Agerbak.

Conventional religion rejects the bodily union of man and women as the least worthy of human activities and claims that God is to be served in spirit and in truth. Man is seen as a spirit trapped in a gross body and salvation is achieved by ignoring and denying the body's appetites until death releases to pure spirit. The Noble Order's perception of the natural differed very sharply from the conventional view. Sexual union was regarded as the most instinctive and creative expression of man's relation to the world outside himself. It insisted that God was to be served in spirit, in body and in truth and that carnal union between men and women of the Order was to be seen as an outward and visible sign of an inward and spiritual grace. This was the way in which he and Annemarie Agerbak approached each other.

There was no Lodge in Oslo for him to visit during his stay in Norway. A falling out over business matters some years before had been allowed to spill over into Lodge affairs, a most unpardonable error. The Norwegian Lodge had never been a large one, so when about a dozen members ranged themselves alongside the Master and the rest against him, the position was impossible. The Grandmaster appointed a council of enquiry of two members from each of the other Scandinavian Lodges to meet in Oslo and hear the evidence of both sides. The evidence took a day to hear and the council deliberated for another two days. Its final conclusion was that the witnesses had been contradictory and confusing and that not one of them could be surely believed. It recommended that the Oslo Lodge should be closed down for a period of years sufficient for the main members involved in the quarrel to die, after which a new Lodge could be established, free from the shadows of the past.

Accordingly, the Grandmaster dissolved the Oslo Lodge, sending to each member personally a written command which used the form of words Pope Clement the Fifth had pronounced against the original Knights Templar in 1312. It described the Lodge as corrupt beyond the hope of remedy or reform and declared it to be absolutely and entirely suppressed. To the Oslo members this was as emotionally and spiritually annihilating as the Christian formula: 'Depart from me, ye accursed, into everlasting fire.' In matters of discipline the Order was inflexible. This was due not so much to Hans-Martin Frick's Teutonic upbringing as to his determination from the very beginning that no rotten apple should ever be permitted to taint the whole barrel, as had happened to the Temple of the Orient in his own lifetime. 'If thine eye offend thee, pluck it out' was a saying he understood very well.

Jonathan washed his face and hands and made his way down to the lobby to tell the receptionist that he was expecting a visitor. He found a comfortable chair and sat down to wait, watching people pass in and out of the hotel, guessing at their country of origin. The Japanese travelled in groups, that was easy enough. Americans, Germans, British, French – they could mostly be identified by the style of their clothes or their gait.

The voice on the phone had been steady and assured and it was that of an oldish man. Jonathan had little doubt that he would be able to pick him out on sight, though he had never met him or spoken to him before. After a time an elderly man came in from the street, casually dressed in dark grey trousers and a tweed jacket over an open necked shirt. He glanced once round the lobby and made straight for Jonathan. He was tall and spare, bald on top, with grey hair clinging to the sides of his head like lichen to a weathered rock.

'Mr Rawlings.'

It was a statement rather than a question. Jonathan stood up and held out his hand. It was grasped tightly for a second or two.

'Anders Turesson,' the old man introduced himself. 'Welcome to Stockholm.'

'It's very good of you to come here,' said Jonathan, 'I'm honoured.'

He meant it. He knew that Turesson was the name of the Master of the Stockholm Lodge. First contacts were usually made at a less exalted level.

Turesson chuckled.

'It's nothing,' he said, 'the young men are constantly running about with their business in the day. They ask the old-timer to do things for them. I am retired, you see, so my days are my own.'

'Can I offer you a drink?'

'Thank you, but not here. I want to take you to the Old Town for lunch. A little walk will sharpen the appetite.'

They left the hotel and strolled side by side in the spring sunshine.

'A wonderful day, Mr Rawlings. I like this time of the whole year best. The sky is blue and clear and there is a refreshing breeze from the sea. Stockholm looks perfect. When I was working all day I saw little of this. I was in my office or travelling in a car or in a plane. Since I retired I have spent many hours just walking about the city, enjoying it. There is much to be grateful for, I find. Is this your first visit?'

'To Stockholm, yes.'

'Good. I will try to make you see it with my eyes. A city is not just an assembly of buildings with streets in between. It is a work of art, like sculpture almost. It is the collective expression of many people's lives and aspirations over a long time. When you see a city for the first time with a fresh eye you understand what sort of men and women live in it now and in the past. Some cities are beautiful, some are ugly. Some are alive, some are dead. The city is its own people's verdict on themselves. Do you understand this?'

Jonathan nodded appreciatively.

'You know that Stockholm is built on many islands,' Turesson went on. 'The sea flows through it in many channels. Over there in front of us is the bridge that goes across to the small island of Helgeands Holmen and then on further to the bigger island which we call the Old Town. That was where Stockholm was first built, when the capital of Sweden was moved here from Uppsala.'

As they crossed the long bridge, gulls wheeled and squawked overhead in the clear light.

'There on the right,' said Turesson, stopping to point, 'that building with the tall tower on the promontory, that is the Stadhuset – the city hall, you call it. It is worth a visit to see the inside if you have the time.'

'I'll remember that, though I have to go on to Helsinki.'

'I had a telephone call this morning from Copenhagen about you.'

'The Lodge there was very kind to me.'

'They liked you. The Master said that you were very English and a very worthy member. So when Ullsten had to go about his business today, I came to meet you myself instead of sending another.'

The streets of the Old Town were narrow and cobbled between tall, old and close packed buildings. Many of them, once houses, had been converted to expensive boutiques, art galleries and antique shops, Jonathan noticed. Even though it was a weekday there were plenty of people strolling about. Turesson led him to a restaurant which looked full, but where the waiter immediately seated them at the best table. They ordered drinks and looked at the menu.

'Leave the ordering to me, I know this place well,' said

Turesson. 'You will like Swedish food.'

He spoke at some length to the waiter and sent him away, before asking Jonathan about his business trip. After listening carefully, he said,

'I don't know personally this man you have come here to meet, Bohman, but if I can help you in any way, you must ask. I still have a certain influence here from my days in banking, if that is of any use to you.'

'Thank you. Were you in banking until you retired?'

'All my life. I was president of the bank for the last ten years I was working. Do you know anything about it?'

'Only as a customer.'

The food started to arrive, two waiters bringing dishes and serving. It was good and plentiful, in the tradition of hospitality which the Order fostered, and there was plenty of wine to wash it down. The two men warmed to each other as they ate and drank and were soon on first name terms.

'Banking is very interesting,' said Turesson. 'People do not understand that. They see only young men and girls sitting behind counters and older men sitting in offices. They do not understand how the wealth of a whole nation flows like a river of gold through these banks so that it can be used to bring prosperity, to make goods, to make employment for thousands, perhaps millions, of men and women. The coloured pieces of paper we call kroner or pounds or dollars can make food grow in deserts and bring oil from under the sea. They can build factories and houses and theatres and hospitals and libraries. Money is like blood, it must circulate properly or the body grows weak and will die. A bank is a heart, moving the life blood about.'

Jonathan enjoyed the old man's enthusiasm.

'The Templars were the first bankers in Europe,' he said.

'You are correct,' said Turesson. 'Kings and nobles and merchants deposited gold and treasure with them for safe keeping because of the security of their temples in all the lands of Europe. And this gold they lent at interest to other kings and princes to pay for armies and palaces. The Templars also had their firm hand on the land routes and the sea ports of Palestine and so they could import silks and spices and other wonderful commodities from the East that were in demand in Europe. This was good business.'

'We shall rival them one day in riches,' said Jonathan, 'And in influence.'

'I have no doubt. We have large investments already. But of that I cannot speak to you. Tell me about Copenhagen – my friend Jonsson made you comfortable?'

'He arranged a magnificent banquet in a private room of the hotel I stayed in.'

'And he found for you a good woman, or so he told me when we talked on the telephone. Did he tell me the truth?'

'He did. He chose a dark haired woman named Annemarie for me.'

'I know her. I used to travel often to Copenhagen. I still go there once or twice a year to see my friends. What did you do with her?'

Jonathan glanced round. It was after two o'clock and the restaurant was emptying.

'She took me to her apartment,' he said, lowering his voice. 'We celebrated the revels of Queen Esther.'

'In which way?'

'A manifestation of the Great Queen in Annemarie.'

'It was good?'

'Yes,' said Jonathan softly, enchanted by the memory. 'She spoke to me through Annemarie.'

Queen Esther is a Jewish title of the goddess Ishtar. After the Jews were conquered by the Babylonians and carried away into slavery in the fifth century before Christ they turned to the worship of Ishtar, who was demonstrably more powerful than their own god Jehova and whose rites were far more attractive. A memory of this is preserved in the Old Testament, though the priest who wrote the book of Esther three hundred years after the event disguised the truth out of fear of the stern god of Moses. He wrote his account as if Esther had been a virtuous Jewish princess who saved her people from genocide by sexually enchanting King Ahasuerus. In fact, the kings of Babylon went through a form of sacred marriage each year with Ishtar and performed the sexual act with her in the person of her chief priestess, to ensure the fertility of the land and the people.

In Copenhagen Jonathan had evoked Queen Esther in the person of Annemarie Agerbak; that is, he drew down into her the presence of the goddess. Or summoned up the goddess from Annemarie's unconscious, for the two are the same. He had spoken to her, been blessed by her and had enjoyed her sexual favours in Annemarie's body.

Gods and goddesses, he knew, are created by man as personifications of the cosmic forces within himself. From the beginning men have in this way personified different aspects of God under various names – Ishtar, Apollo, Jesus, Bran – each with specific attributes. In this sense all god forms have real existence for those who call upon them, for they are aspects of the one God. And therefore the god forms are created by God as well as by man and all gods are the same god.

The revels of Queen Esther were a long and dignified act of adoration, taught to members of the Order when they had advanced to the Third Degree. If she is properly and graciously summoned she will appear, either in a crystal placed on the altar, in which she will be seen, or in the physical body of a suitable woman like Annemarie. Or, most difficult of all, she can be persuaded to manifest herself in semi-material form. To pass to the Fourth Degree of the Order, one of the many exacting requirements is that the candidate should evoke an appearance of Queen Esther, by that name or another, in the presence of two appointed Inquisitors.

'I am sure that the experience was delightful and filled you both with grace,' said Turesson. 'At my age, though, the rites of obligation are enough.'

A rule of the Order was that the Grandmaster and all Lodge Masters must be capable of the physical act, as was the way with sacred kings in ages gone by. Unlike sacred kings, they were not required to die if their potency vanished through age or illness, only to hand over the seals and badge of office to a younger man and thereafter to continue as an elder councillor. The rites of obligation were a form of check of the incumbent's ability. Four times a year, on the days of the turning points of the sun, a woman member of the Lodge was chosen by lot and became his partner in the ceremony. Her report and that of the witnesses to the rite determined whether he remained in office or not.

'You're not so old,' said Jonathan, 'I'd put you at about sixty-five.'

'Sixty-eight,' said Turesson, 'old enough to be your father. What does your father do?'

'He's a schoolmaster.'

'In London?'

'In Worcestershire, up in the Midlands.'

'I was in Birmingham once, maybe twenty years ago. From there I made a journey to Stratford on Avon to see the home of Shakespeare. Is it near there?'

'That's the right part of the country. Worcester is south of Birmingham and west of Stratford. Did you go to the theatre there?'

'I saw a performance of *Macbeth*. It was very well done. There was a lesson for me in it at the time.'

'What sort of lesson?'

'In the play, Macbeth has a promise of greatness through contact with the hidden world. But then he took the wrong way to achieve the promise and so he lost everything and died miserably. In my own life then I was in a similar position. I took the lesson of the play to my heart and did no wrong. As you can see, the promises were fulfilled.'

'I've never thought of *Macbeth* in those terms. So you are grateful to William Shakespeare for keeping you on the right road?'

'Yes, it was a very personal thing for me. How long will you stay in Stockholm?'

'That depends on my meeting with Bohman. I'll certainly be here tomorrow and probably leave the day after that.'

'If you are free tomorrow evening I would like to invite you to attend a meeting at our temple.'

'I'd like that. Is it a special meeting?'

'We are raising a member to the Fifth. He has completed the necessary work some time ago and has satisfied the Inquisitors that he is ready for this step.'

'I'd be honoured to be present. I've nothing with me.'

'That does not matter, we can lend you what you will need.'

'What time will it be?'

'At seven. I will send someone to your hotel to show you the way soon after six.'

'Thank you. The ceremony will be in Swedish, of course.'

'Naturally, but you will be able to follow it. The words are different but the meaning is the same and you must know it by heart in English.'

Turesson paid the bill and they walked back the way they had come through the Old Town and across the bridge.

'Walk with me for a while,' Turesson suggested. 'I will show you a little of the city.'

Five or six minutes brought them to a large open square with a modernistic fountain in the middle.

'Our best department store is along that way if you wish to buy presents,' said Turesson, pointing to one of the streets off the square. 'We will cross here and sit on the benches on the other side.'

They made their way to the north side of the square and sat on a bench in the pale gold afternoon sunshine.

'I often sit here. This is the heart of the city. Everything goes past if you watch for a while. Yesterday a military band marched past playing.'

'I was interested in what you said about *Macbeth*,' said Jonathan. 'Like you I am facing a personal problem to which I can see no easy solution.'

'In your work?'

'The man I work for will not let me do the things I know I can do. His methods are old fashioned and useless. He cramps me badly.'

'Cramps? I do not know this word.'

'He restricts me. My plans are better than his but I have to do what he says.'

'You have discussed your problem with the members of your own Lodge?'

'They are doing what they can, through the network, but it may take a long time. You know how carefully these things are managed.'

'You are young enough to have time. Something will be arranged, you may be certain. We are all pledged to help each other, especially in matters of worldly success and business achievements, as in spiritual affairs. You are asking me for advice?'

'I suppose I am.'

The Swede ran a hand over his bald pate, thinking.

'I will give you the best advice I know – keep faith with the Order. You see your own position in the most pessimistic light and you are in error. You must change this attitude at once and take care not to fall back into it. I say this to you very seriously as your superior.'

'I accept the reproof,' said Jonathan quickly, using the appropriate phrase for a member who had committed a fault.

'As you must. Let me also remind you that the Order teaches us to give only good and to expect only good. You are not a man standing alone against many enemies. You are a high member of a great organisation that has the influence and power to change events. Is this true?'

'True.'

'Let me speak to you not as a superior but as a friend. I have given you the advice I gave myself years ago after I was at Stratford and then when I went to London to be the guest of the Lodge there.'

'Obviously it worked out well for you, Anders.'

'As you say, though not in the way I was expecting. You must consider that the job you want may not be the one you should have.'

'It's still the one I want.'

'Sometimes we want the wrong things. I wanted something

else and I was wrong, because by keeping faith with the Order I eventually became president of the bank I worked for and Master of the Stockholm Lodge. I did not expect either. If you will consider, what you really want may not be to get this other man's job but to be moved away from his control so that you can display your ability. Perhaps that is being arranged even now. Or, as you feel so strongly about this particular job, then perhaps it is being arranged for this other man to be moved out of your way.'

'As you say, all I can do is wait.'

'I see that you are not convinced. Then if you have the time I will tell you about a man I once knew, Karl Krafft.'

'Krafft? I know the name but I can't quite place it.'

'He was an expert on Nostradamus and other things.'

'Of course, I remember reading a translation of a book by him that had been published during the war. He claimed to interpret how Nostradamus had predicted the future of European history. It was wholly inaccurate.'

Jonathan knew that as much nonsense had been written about Nostradamus as about the Great Pyramid. The facts of his life are ascertainable, the significance of his writings is speculative. He was born in France in 1503, the son of a Jewish family which converted to Catholicism, hence the name Michel de Nostredame, *Michael of Our Lady*. He was trained as a doctor, developed an interest in astrology and became an adept in the secret arts. Because of his reputation his advice was sought many times by the Queen Mother of France, Catherine de Medici. From 1550 onwards Nostradamus published an annual volume of visions he had seen and written down in four-line verses composed in a tangled mixture of French, Provençal, Greek, Italian and Latin, almost impossible to understand clearly.

From the first, Nostradamus's books created intense interest and were published widely in Europe. How he interpreted his own visions cannot be known. He induced them on the surface of a bowl of water and he had seen, as if on a television set, boars and lions in combat, Europe aflame, doomsday and beyond. Since his day generations of students have interpreted particular verses as prophecies of political events – the rise of Napoleon Bonaparte, the battle of Waterloo, the advent of Adolf Hitler, the outbreak of the 1939 war – though these correspondences have always been discovered after the event happened.

Members of the Noble Order had no belief in prediction of the future, knowing it to be unformed. They were interested in visions, however received. Jonathan had glanced at Nostradamus and passed on to other things, feeling that the subject had no relevance to him. Visions are essentially personal experiences with private meanings, as are dreams.

'There were good reasons for Krafft's book being incorrect,' said Turesson. 'Do you know anything about his life?'

'Nothing at all. He was German or Austrian, I suppose.'

'He was a Swiss, born in Basel in 1900. His father was a businessman – he was a director of a brewery.'

'You knew Krafft personally?'

'I met him in Berlin when I was there on business. He was married then to a Dutch woman and he was at the peak of his success.'

'What sort of man was he?'

'Small, dark haired, always very intense. He was very impatient with people he thought less intelligent than himself. That is not a good way to be in life.'

Sitting in the warm spring sun, watching the traffic go round the square, Turesson unfolded for Jonathan the story of Karl Ernst Krafft's busy life and miserable death. Jonathan listened intently, under no illusion that the older man was merely reminiscing idly.

'Karl studied at several universities. He was a mathematician with a great interest in statistical probability. First there were the universities of Basel, Geneva, and finally London University. He was working to establish a statistical foundation for cosmic influences on human lives.'

'A sort of scientific astrology, you mean?'

'He called it cosmobiology. His ideas were a little before their time, since others have followed his work in France and have demonstrated connections between birthdates and times and subsequent choice of careers on a big enough scale for other scientists to take them seriously. There is a man named Michel Gauquelin who has published several books on this subject.'

'I've read them in English and was impressed by his findings. Krafft was pioneering in that field?'

'Yes, but unhappily he was a difficult man to deal with and he quarrelled with many, until his father told him that he must end his studies and work for a living. He would have been twenty-five or twenty-six then. He got a job in a bank in Zurich and continued his studies privately. Naturally his interest in what he called cosmobiology brought him into contact with many people interested in the hidden world, including some members of the Swiss Lodge of the Temple of the Orient.'

'That would be the time of the great split, when Hans-Martin Frick and some others refused to accept Aleister Crowley as Grandmaster.'

'You are well informed. The Swiss Lodge remained faithful to Crowley. The Swiss are great traditionalists and perhaps they did not personally meet Crowley then. However it was, Karl fell out with his employers and lost his job and at about the same time his father died and left him money. He was in a position to resume his studies full time if he chose, but his short period at the Zurich bank had made him over confident in financial matters. He tried to turn a modest fortune from his father into a big fortune on the Zurich stock exchange and lost it all in six months. After that he made his living by lecturing on cosmobiology, in Zurich, Lausanne and Geneva at first and then in Germany. About 1937 he married Anna van der Koppel, the Dutch girl who had been living with him for some years. Then he went to live in Germany.'

'Presumably to get a wider audience than Switzerland could provide.'

'There was more to it than that. He was fascinated by Adolf Hitler. His studies told him that Hitler was a man of great destiny who would change the face of Europe. He went to live in Germany to be nearer to him. One of the Temple of the Orient members he met there was an elderly woman named Martha Kuentzel who preached that Hitler was an incarnate god. Karl agreed with her, I think. When the war began in 1939 he chose to stay in Germany instead of going back to neutral Switzerland.'

'He followed his star, as one might say.'

'To the very end. He had such a reputation from his lecture tours that early in the war he was offered employment by a branch of the German secret service to write them a monthly prediction of the likely course of the fighting. Poor Karl foresaw a great future for himself from this small beginning in the service of the Nazi government. It is easy to guess his dream – he wanted to be at Hitler's right hand advising him. At the beginning he was dealing only with minor officials, but he thought he would get through to the top if he demonstrated his ability.'

'How far did he get?'

'You will see. In one of his regular monthly reports he predicted the possibility of an assassination attempt on Hitler's life. Naturally, it was filed away by some clerk without any attention. Then only weeks later there was a bomb attack on Hitler in a Munich beer hall. That would be towards the end of 1939, I think. When Karl read of this in the newspaper he sent a telegram to Hitler reminding him of his prediction. Within hours the Gestapo arrested him.'

'They thought that he was on the fringe of the plot, of course?'

'Of course. He was able to convince them that he was not and after that he was taken much more seriously and offered another and better secret job. He moved to Berlin with his wife and this is when I met him at his home. He told me a great deal about himself. You could say that he boasted about himself.'

'Even though you were not members of the same Order at that time?'

'There was no Temple of the Orient in Germany at that time because the Nazis had suppressed it before the war. Nor do I believe that Karl ever went beyond the first step in it, if that. But he had met the important German members and they had praised his work. So we had enough in common to be able to talk.'

'What was he doing when you met him in Berlin?'

'He was arranging his own downfall, though he did not see it. He was prostituting his abilities for propaganda purposes. That was what they paid him for.'

'In what way?'

'When I look back now it seems difficult to understand, but the German ministry of propaganda had a project to publish a selection of the writings of Nostradamus to prove that Germany was destined to win the war and rule Europe. They used Karl's expert knowledge to produce fake verses. Then these fakes were translated into other languages and published in various European countries.'

'Did anyone really think that such a thing could influence the course of the war?' Jonathan asked in surprise.

'Who can tell what they thought? Hitler was a man possessed by a demon and he led the German nation into collective insanity in those years. I can only tell you what I know. Karl's book of fake predictions was published in French and in Portugese. He sent me a copy of the French edition and it said in it that it was shortly to appear in English, Spanish and other languages. Whether it did, I cannot say.'

'He sent you a copy?'

'It was not yet published when I met him in Berlin. He mailed it to me later with a friendly inscription. Sweden was neutral, you must remember, and we could communicate with each other. When I read his book I was dismayed to see how far he had strayed from the path of truth in the service of the Nazis. He was prepared to do anything to climb higher in their esteem. At a reception at his home when I was there Martin Bormann and Rudolf Hess were amongst the guests.'

'Did he get to meet Hitler?'

'Events dictated otherwise. In which year were you born, Jonathan?'

'In 1942. Why do you ask?'

44

'A year before you were born Rudolf Hess, who was deputy to Hitler, took a flight by himself and landed in Scotland. The reason has never been clear. Many people take the view that he was deranged. Hitler saw it as an act of treason and ordered the Gestapo to round up everyone Hess had ever known and question them. Karl spent a year in solitary confinement in a Berlin prison while they interrogated him about his relations with Hess. Even when they saw that he had nothing to do with political plots, he was not released. They kept him locked up and put him to work again.'

'More Nostradamus?'

'No, this time they used his science of cosmobiology. He was given information on British and Russian generals and told to prepare assessments of the cosmic influences on their lives and the course of action each would be most likely to take in certain circumstances. Anna was permitted to visit him occasionally and it was from her that I heard about this period in his life. Karl came to see at last that he was only a slave chained to an oar and he sank into a kind of mild melancholic insanity that rendered him useless. They moved him to the Oranienburg concentration camp near Berlin. This was not a death camp, just a dumping ground for people the Nazis did not want at liberty. Anna was also permitted to visit him there, twice I think, in a year and a half. On her last visit he was so ill that the guards carried him into the reception hut on a stretcher. She, poor woman, knew that he would not live much longer and there was nothing she could do. By then the war was lost for Germany, the Allies were on the Rhine and the Russians were well into East Prussia. She did the only thing she was able – she went back to Switzerland.'

'And Karl?'

'In 1945 Anna was told by the Swiss government that they had been officially informed by the Germans that Karl had died in Buchenwald concentration camp. They must have transferred him there soon after she saw him the last time. His end in that terrible place can only be imagined.'

The story finished, the two men sat in silence for a while,

each busy with his own thoughts.

'You either went to see Anna in Switzerland after the war or you corresponded with her,' said Jonathan, 'and you must have had a good reason for going to Berlin during the war to talk to him.'

'I was there on bank business in Berlin and I looked him up because I was interested to meet someone I had heard about.'

'You were also in touch with Hans-Martin Frick in London during the war, I would think.'

'These are not public matters,' said Turesson. 'Official secrets should remain secret. I did not tell you about Karl Krafft to arouse your curiosity about what various people were doing during the war.'

'I understand. Tell me one thing, how do you interpret what happened to Krafft?'

'There is only one interpretation. Many have committed sins against themselves which have led to disaster and the motive has usually been ambition. You should think about this.'

Turesson looked at his watch.

'I must leave you now. Do you know the way back to the Grand Hotel?'

'I think so. Down that street and turn left at the bottom by the Opera.'

'Good. I will see you tomorrow, Jonathan.'

CHAPTER 3
BUSINESS DINNER

WHEN HE picked up his room key from the hotel desk Jonathan found two messages waiting for him. Both said: 'Telephone Mr Braithwaite.' One was timed two-thirty and the other three-thirty. The clock over the desk indicated ten minutes to four.

He rode up in the lift, hung his jacket in the wardrobe and splashed cold water over his face to wake himself up before asking the operator to get him London. While he was waiting for the call to go through he opened his briefcase and took out a note pad in case there was anything of importance to record. The telephone buzzed and he was into the familiar and irritating ritual of trying to speak to Derek Braithwaite.

'Dovedays, good afternoon,' said the professionally cheerful voice of the distant office exchange operator.

'Hello, it's Jonathan Rawlings. I'm calling from Sweden. Put me through to Mr Braithwaite please.'

'Yes, Mr Rawlings, right away.'

The next voice on the line was that of Braithwaite's secretary.

'Mr Braithwaite's office,' she said sharply.

'Hello, Nancy, it's Jonathan Rawlings.'

'Mr Rawlings, I've had to ring you twice this afternoon because you were out. Mr Braithwaite is most anxious to speak to you. Hold on while I see if he's free now.'

Silly bitch, thought Jonathan. The seconds ticked past while he waited, costing Dovedays money all the time. Eventually she came back on the line.

'I'm putting you through now,' she said in the tone of someone ushering a sinner into the Last Judgment.

'You've taken your time,' said Braithwaite's voice. 'I've been trying to get you all day. What's going on there?'

'I phoned before lunch but I couldn't get *you*,' said Jonathan. 'Is there something urgent?'

'What do you mean? Everything's urgent. I want to know what's happening. I'm supposed to be responsible for what you do. Where the hell have you been all this time?'

'I went out for lunch and had a stroll through the town.'

'Do you mean to say that you haven't been in touch with Bohman yet? You've been there all day – what are you playing at?'

'I rang Bohman as soon as I got here from Oslo. He's tied

up until seven and then we're meeting for dinner. I shall be in his office all day tomorrow if you want me.'

Jonathan gripped the telephone hard and spoke slowly to keep himself calm under Braithwaite's pointless aggression.

'What happened in Oslo. Did you make Egeland commit himself?'

'It went as expected. I impressed the importance of the new targets on him and he's doing his sums, as usual. There'll be a letter in the post from him by the end of the week telling us what he can do.'

He could visualise Braithwaite sitting in his habitual pose, jacket off and sleeves rolled up, one elbow on his desk and a black and fuming pipe clenched between his teeth.

'You don't seem to have achieved much in Oslo, then.'

'I'm sure I have. You know Egeland's way of working as well as I do.'

'I've known him a damned sight longer than you have,' said Braithwaite. 'He needs pushing all the time, otherwise he'll sit fiddling with figures till he proves that all he can sell is five per cent of damn all. It sounds to me as if you didn't push him at all. I've told you before, there's only one way to do business with these people – you've got to get your foot on their throat.'

'Egeland will come through. He'll write it all down in black and white and mail it to us.'

'We're in business to sell biscuits, not do sums.'

Braithwaite was clearly in a thoroughly sour mood. Either someone in London had annoyed him or perhaps his ulcer was giving him trouble. Jonathan resigned himself to the niggling and hoped it wouldn't last too long. One day when Braithwaite was being more bloody than usual, Jonathan would lose his tightly controlled temper and say things which would make it impossible for them to work together any longer. More than once he'd wondered if that was Braithwaite's ploy.

'I sold biscuits to Christensen in Copenhagen. He's solidly with us.'

'And you gave him an extra two and a half percent discount. Of course he's with us. Anybody can get business by giving money away.'

'We agreed the extra contingency discounts before I left London. An extra five percent was the top figure and I got Christensen for two and a half.'

Braithwaite switched his attack.

'Why couldn't you see Bohman this afternoon? Didn't he know when you were arriving?'

'Yes, I confirmed from Oslo yesterday by phone and he had my letter a week ago.'

'And he's ducked the meeting? I don't like the sound of that. Something's up.'

'I don't read anything ominous into it. Something came up at short notice in his office, that's all.'

'You're backing your judgment against mine, are you?'

'I've always found Bohman very straightforward in the past.'

'Because it suited him. You'd better ring me first thing in the morning before you go to his office and let me know what he's up to. Got that?'

'Right.'

The line went dead. Braithwaite hadn't even troubled to say goodbye.

Jonathan put the phone down and thought about his boss. Braithwaite was not particularly stupid, not more than averagely malicious. He suffered from ingrained mistrust. He had reached the top at Dovedays the hard way and in the process he had lost any shred of respect for others he may have started with. He came from Sheffield, the son of a small shopkeeper, the eldest of five or six children. He was brought up in the poverty of the pre-war years and with the goad of unemployment to urge him on he had worked hard at the local grammar school and done well. The 1939 war started soon after his eighteenth birthday and he volunteered for the army at once. To him the army and the war were opportunities to advance himself. He managed to become commissioned in the Ordnance Corps and was shipped out to India.

The narrowness of his background both helped and hindered him. He despised his fellow officers because he thought that they looked down on him. He despised the men under his command, being convinced that they were shirkers who would get him into trouble, given a chance. He stuck doggedly to his job, worked hard at it and reached the rank of captain by the time the war ended. Naturally, he had no friends.

Back home he used his school and war record and his evident capacity for work to get a job as a management trainee at Dovedays' factory in Yorkshire. He built a reputation as a salesman and as an area manager, bludgeoning his way through, utterly regardless of everyone else. When the company began to build up an overseas sales department he applied to join it, was accepted on the strength of his record so far and transferred to the London office. Once there, he really sweated to force his way upwards. Though his vision was restricted, he had the energy of two men and it served him well. By long hours, attention to detail, willingness to go anywhere at any time and sheer bulldog persistence he progressed over the years to the position of overseas sales manager and, a few years later, he was appointed to the board of directors.

The general feeling towards him was neatly demonstrated at a head office Christmas lunch soon after Jonathan joined Dovedays. There was a shipping clerk in overseas sales named Bob Thornton, a big and cheerful twenty-year-old. Though Braithwaite had made it to the top there was no detail too small for him to bother with and no employee too insignificant to feel the weight of his tongue. After only a few months of being picked on, Thornton found himself another job and gave notice to leave at the end of December. Braithwaite's attitude was *good riddance*.

Dovedays' London office employed several hundred people and the Christmas lunch was a lavish buffet, almost Dickensian in its array of cold meats, poultry, turkey, hams, puddings, mince pies, Christmas cake and general good cheer. During the chatter and celebration, Thornton ambled up to Braithwaite with a glass of red wine in his hand. Braithwaite was standing in conversation with the managing director and a couple of others, a plate in one hand and a small glass of white wine in the other.

Smiling amiably, Thornton raised his voice to attract the attention of as many people as possible.

'Merry Christmas, Mr Braithwaite!' he bawled.

As Braithwaite turned to scowl at him, Thornton hooked a finger in the top of his victim's trousers, pulled the waistband away from his paunchy body and neatly tipped the glass of wine down between trousers and shirt.

There was an instant of amazed silence, then a roar of laughter from all those close enough to have seen the incident. Faces turned from all parts of the room to peer over shoulders at what was going on. The laughter grew louder and longer when it was seen that Derek Braithwaite was the butt, and it had a hard edge to it.

Bennett, the managing director, waved his arm for silence.

'Get out,' he said to Thornton, 'That was unforgivable. You are no longer employed by this company.'

'You can't fire me, I've already resigned,' said Thornton, still beaming. 'But before I go, I'd like to give Mr Braithwaite his Christmas turkey.'

From his breast pocket he fished out a monstrous leg of roast turkey and sidled round Braithwaite as if he were about to rape him with it.

'Out!' Bennett shouted, 'Now!'

Before Thornton had time to react, Braithwaite turned and half ran out of the room, his trousers stuck clammily to his belly and legs. There was more laughter and a quick cheer from those furthest away from Bennett as Thornton ambled away, waving his drumstick in triumph.

Jonathan quickly composed his face as Bennett's eye fell on him.

'What was that about?'

'Thornton has a grievance against Braithwaite,' Jonathan replied.

51

'I guessed that much. Was he drunk?'

'He gave notice some time ago. That was his farewell gesture.'

'Hooliganism is intolerable, whatever the motive,' said Bennett, frowning. 'You've met the chairman of the board, of course, haven't you?'

'Briefly,' said Jonathan, shaking hands with the tall man next to Bennett. 'I hope you won't think that Dovedays is a madhouse, Mr Innes.'

'Not a bit, I know it to be a very well managed company. Your name's Rawlings, isn't it, and you work in Braithwaite's department.'

Jonathan was faintly surprised that the chairman remembered his name. George Innes was a non-executive chairman, an outsider from the world of banking and finance, who chaired meetings of the board but otherwise played no part in the management of the company. About sixty years old, Jonathan thought, sizing him up; well cut grey hair, straight back and wearing an expensive banker's dark suit.

'Yes, I'm number two in Overseas Sales,' he said.

'Why does that young man dislike Braithwaite so much, do you suppose?'

Jonathan shook his head, unwilling to get involved in office personalities with someone so far removed from the day to day running of the business. Innes grinned at him.

'That's the problem for an outside chairman,' he said. 'No one wants to tell you what's going on.'

'George, you know more about the workings of Dovedays than I do,' said Bennett at once. 'Now let's forget the whole unpleasant incident.'

But Bob Thornton's parting shot was the talk of the Christmas lunch and for a long time afterwards. For Braithwaite it was merely further proof, if he needed any, that nobody could be trusted.

In all, Jonathan detested Braithwaite. He was a grudging and tiresome man, but there was more to him than that. There was something secret about him that Jonathan could not fathom. By the system of numerology he had been taught the number of Braithwaite's first name, Derek, was nine, indicating that he was likely to be an achiever, strong willed, egotistical and intolerant. That was true. The number of his surname was five, indicating that he enjoyed travel, new people, different surroundings. That was plainly true, too. Five was also an indication of strong sexuality. That was out of character. Braithwaite had been conventionally married to the same woman for nearly thirty years and had four grown children. Jonathan had met Mrs Braithwaite and dubbed her completely non-sexual.

This aspect of five might have been dismissed as a quirk to the system. But the number of his whole name, Derek Braithwaite, was the sum of nine and five, fourteen. Fourteen was one and four and added back to five. No less than four of the letters in the name had the value of five. So many fives could not be dismissed. The man had to be a raging volcano of lust. Jonathan was convinced that Braithwaite was rabidly active in unorthodox sexual ways, but he could find no clue.

The telephone conversation with London had irritated Jonathan sufficiently to make it impossible to take the nap he intended before his dinner date with Bohman. He took off his shoes and tie and lay on the bed to read for a while. He had packed only one book and it opened at the marker he had put in it.

'To find the clue we must go to the originator of modern occultism, Madame Blavatsky . . . .'

Untrue and boring, Jonathan thought. He read on.

' . . . inspired other esoteric revivals such as the Order of the Golden Dawn, which included W.B. Yeats among its members, as well as the fantasy writers Algernon Blackwood and Arthur Machen, and the notorious neo-magician Aleister Crowley . . . .'

The telephone was ringing. He started up, feeling chilled. The light in his room was fading, his book lay on the floor. He had dozed off. His watch showed five minutes to seven.

'Tell Mr Bohman I'll be right down.'

In the lift he rubbed his hand over his chin and wished there had been time to run the electric razor over it.

Nils Bohman was sitting in the lobby with a well dressed woman of about fifty.

'Good evening, Jonathan. You haven't met my wife Camilla before.'

'How do you do, Mrs Bohman,' said Jonathan, taking her hand. 'Please forgive me for keeping you waiting. I ought to have been here waiting for you.'

Camilla Bohman had a rangy, outdoor appearance. Golf, thought Jonathan, then corrected himself; *sailing*. Swedes loved small boat sailing on their waterways. She was a handsome woman, blue eyed and with short brown hair.

'You must not apologise to me, Mr Rawlings. I have to apologise to you for preventing your meeting with Nils today. But it was very important. Our daughter had her first baby this morning and I insisted that Nils come to the hospital with me.'

'That was far more important than business,' said Jonathan, smiling at her. 'I congratulate you, though you look too young to be a grandparent.'

'No, I have been a grandmother for two years already. Our son and his wife also have a baby.'

'You must have been a child yourself when you married Nils. We must celebrate this event. The bar is over this way.'

'I am sorry about postponing our meeting,' said Bohman as they crossed the lobby, 'but you see how it is. I cannot disappoint the women in my family.'

'You were absolutely right. Is the new baby a boy or a girl?'

'A boy. Now we have two grandsons.'

Jonathan ordered a bottle of champagne, pleased by the turn of events. Being on hand to share in the Bohman family happiness could only stand in his favour when they talked business the next day. A waiter set glasses on the table and fussed with the bottle cork. It came out with a satisfying pop.

'Has the new baby got a name yet, Mrs Bohman?'

'Please, you must call me Camilla. The baby is to be called Olof, because that was the name of Nils' father.'

'Then here's health, wealth and happiness to Olof,' said

Jonathan, raising his glass, 'and to his mother and his grandparents.'

The standard of spoken English he encountered in his dealings with Dovedays' Scandinavian contacts never failed to arouse in him a feeling of gratitude. He had been through crash courses in French and German and could cope in those countries, though the prospect of an entire evening speaking another language than his own usually brought on a feeling of inadequacy. He had even picked up enough conversational Dutch to be able to exchange polite small talk. On his present trip the question of using anything other than English had never arisen.

Derek Braithwaite, who spoke no language but his native tongue, had been pushing him lately to go on a four week course in spoken Arabic. So far he had been able with some justification to claim that he was far too busy to devote a whole month to such a project. After Arabic, what? Japanese? It was all too likely a part of some stupid Braithwaite plan to frustrate him to the point where he would resign.

The evening with the Bohmans was an enjoyable one. They drove out to a restaurant Nils had chosen and dined well and at length. Camilla talked about her home and her family and invited him to stay with them the next time he visited Sweden. Nils, usually a reserved man, became talkative and would have turned the conversation towards business if his wife had not headed him off once or twice. For that Jonathan was grateful. They had all the next day for that.

After brandy and coffee Jonathan insisted on paying the bill, even though the invitation had been from Bohman to him.

'No, it's a memorable day for you both,' he said. 'You deserve to be guests.'

He tucked the receipted bill into his pocket, thinly amused by the prospect of seeing Braithwaite's unbelieving stare when he saw the amount of it. Eating out in Sweden appeared to cost about twice as much as in London.

They drove him back to the hotel at about eleven, declined

his offer of a last drink, shook his hand warmly and left. Jonathan was well pleased with the evening as he went to bed. The book he had been reading in the afternoon still lay on the floor. He picked it up and glanced at the page, then turned off the light and composed himself to sleep.

That author has an odd way of presenting the Golden Dawn initiates, he was thinking as he lay waiting for sleep to overtake him. Yeats and Blackwood and Machan get a mention because they were writers, though who reads either Blackwood or Machan now? Crowley rates a mention because he was a bogeyman. Not a word about Brodie-Innes, the Scottish lawyer, though he wrote a novel about the Aberdeen witch, Isabel Gowdie. And he collected pornography. Most of the members of the Golden Dawn had the usual nineteenth century hang-ups about sex. Florence Farr didn't. She experimented with George Bernard Shaw, who starred her in one of his plays, but he wasn't very much interested in bodies. She experimented with Willie Yeats for a long time, but it seems that he wasn't very good at it either. She knew Aubrey Beardsley, who was rumoured to be living incestuously with his sister. I wonder if Florence tried with Aubrey – he was very interested in sexual games. And there's not a mention of Moina Bergson, who married the head of the Golden Dawn. He had the same hang-ups until Moina found out in Paris how to draw the goddess down into herself and then he had no choice. Crowley claimed that she became a sexual vampire and sucked away his strength. But somewhere else he said that Mathers prostituted Moina to other men in Paris. Crowley knew them both well, so where's the truth . . . .

When Jonathan slept alone after a convivial evening of food and drink he always dreamed vividly. He was flying in an aeroplane, a big one, from which all the seats had been stripped out. He was lying on his back on the grey carpet and he could feel the vibration of the jet engines through the floor of the plane.

Camilla Bohman sat beside him, completely naked, holding his stiff part in her hand. On her skin above her breasts she had drawn in blue a lattice with numbers in each of its squares. He tried to add them across and down but they were too blurred. Camilla sat as still as a statue, staring thoughtfully at the erection in her hand.

'It's the wrong square,' he said. 'It won't work. It's nothing like the square of Venus – you'll have to wash it off and start again.'

She turned her head slowly to look at him and it was not Camilla Bohman at all, it was Karin Wikstrom, the air stewardess on his flight that morning.

'What square is it, Karin?' he asked, puzzled.

Her clasped hand was sending pleasurable tremors through him.

'I'm not Karin,' she said. 'I'm Moina Bergson.'

The aircraft banked steeply and sent him sliding across the carpet on his back. Camilla-Karin-Moina held on firmly to his upstanding part and was dragged with him until the side of the plane stopped him. She lay sprawled face down, legs apart, then lifted her head to look at him.

'You can't go without me,' she said. 'The captain would punish me.'

That was all Jonathan could remember when his morning call on the telephone woke him at seven-thirty. He lay for a while trying to get back as much detail as he could.

The Masters of the Temple attached considerable importance to dreams. Initiates were taught to recall them on waking and to interpret them, before they vanished into the depths of memory. During their probationary period as Pilgrims they were required to write their dreams down and submit them, with what they made of them, to their teachers. Not that the Order believed that dreams foretold the future in any way. They believed that in dreams the unconscious mind tells the dreamer something of importance to him, often in a confused and symbolic way. The wise man listens to the voice from his inner self and tries to understand his own nature.

The square on the woman's chest had only four boxes across and four down, he remembered, though he had not been able to see the numbers in the boxes. Though the dream had ostensibly been sexual, the square of Venus has seven numbers across and seven numbers down. Seven has been the number attributed to the goddess of physical passion for as far back as history is recorded. The great king of Sumeria, in times so far back that even ancient Egyptian civilisation had not yet flourished, built in his city of Adab a temple to the goddess under her title of Nintu. The temple had seven gates and seven doors and when it was completed he dedicated it to her with an offering of seven times seven oxen and sheep. But the significance of seven is older even than Sumeria and has its sexual connotation because of the moon. The moon's cycle of waxing and waning has four phases, each lasting seven days. The rhythms of life are governed by sevens, each stage of human life being completed in seven years. Above all, the cycle of women's bodies, their sexual receptiveness and their reproductive powers are governed by these sevens and the moon.

But it had not been the seven square he had seen, as would have been appropriate for a dream relating only to sexuality. It had four figures across and four down and so it had to be the square of Jupiter, which adds each way to thirty-four and signifies wealth and material success. During the day his unconscious had picked up a clue of success, something his intellect had missed. It could only be his business with Bohman, since he had interpreted the female figure holding his penis as Camilla at first. She had shifted into the air stewardess as an indication that it was his journey to Stockholm that made this success possible. Why she had then transformed herself into Moina Bergson, an adept of the Golden Dawn who had died fifty years ago, was harder to understand. Perhaps it was no more than his mind jumbling into the dream a person he had been thinking about when he fell asleep. That seemed unlikely. From his experience, dreams had a logic, jumbled though at times it might be. The wealth and material success his unconscious already knew to be coming his way would flow not only from his business with Bohman but also from his own membership of a secret Order.

Jonathan climbed out of bed and took paper and a pen from

his briefcase to draw the square and so fix its significance in his thoughts. It was going to be a good day for him, he decided. He phoned down to room service for breakfast and headed for the shower.

CHAPTER 4
THE ROSE AND CROSS

THE STOCKHOLM Temple of the Order proved to be no more than ten minutes drive away from Jonathan's hotel. A woman in her thirties, who introduced herself as Britt, picked him up in the lobby just after six that evening in a new Volvo. He was rested and ready, shaved and bathed, having left Nils Bohman's office a couple of hours before. His company business in Sweden was very satisfactorily concluded. Now that he had Denmark, Norway and Sweden aligned with the new sales targets, a final trip to Finland would complete a successful tour and even Braithwaite would find it difficult to be critical.

Britt was an attractive woman in the tall and big boned Swedish way. Her hair was cut in a pageboy style, covering her ears and just touching her collar. Her cheekbones were broad, her mouth wide and, under a green woollen dress, her bosom looked impressive. She talked easily and fluently as she steered the big car through the early evening traffic. There were no rings on her hands, he noted. She asked him if his business in Stockholm was finished.

'Yes, it went very well. What do you do for a living?'

She told him that she was a doctor specialising in children's diseases. He was not in the least surprised. The Order recruited as many suitable professional people as it could to all of its Lodges to prevent itself from turning into a wholly business oriented organisation.

She turned the car off a long straight thoroughfare, up a narrow and rising street, and into a square of old stone buildings. She found a parking space halfway round the square and locked the car carefully after taking a leather shoulder bag from the rear seat. That would contain her Lodge regalia, Jonathan knew. For men it was not quite so simple – they usually turned up at meetings carrying a briefcase. Though one eccentric member of the London Lodge, he remembered with a grin, was in the habit of arriving with his regalia in a plastic carrier bag with *Safeways* printed on the side. He mentioned this to Britt as they walked across the square, but she did not find it funny. Different sense of humour in Scandinavia, he thought.

The Temple was in one of the corner buildings. From the street there was an archway through into a stone flagged courtyard and, across that, an entrance to a spiral stone staircase leading upwards. On the first landing Britt rapped on a solid looking door.

Inside there was a narrow entrance hall where Britt signed the big leather bound book lying open on a table and handed the pen to Jonathan. He looked down the new page where the book had been opened. At the top, the name of the ceremony and the date had been neatly lettered. Below that there were nine or ten signatures, the first being that of Anders Turesson. According to the ways of the Order, Britt had signed her name in full, followed by the number and name of her Degree. She was a Fifth, Jonathan noted. On the next line down he wrote his own name and, after it, Seventh.

The member acting as Custodian inspected their signatures before allowing them to pass from the entrance hall into the robing room. To Jonathan it was very familiar, because Temples everywhere followed the same plan. The robing room looked like a golf club changing room, with lockers and benches. Faces turned towards them as they entered and Britt called out a greeting in Swedish. For Jonathan's benefit she added in English that they had a visitor from the London Lodge with them that evening. There were murmurs of welcome, the two or three people nearest him shook his hand, then they went back to their preparations.

Britt opened various lockers, none of which were ever locked, pulled out garments and held them against Jonathan for size. Tonight's ceremony being an upgrading to the Fifth, only Fifth and higher Degree members could be present. In consequence, there were plenty of absent members' lockers to choose from in order to equip Jonathan.

Around him were members of ages from about thirty to over sixty in different stages of undress; men and women. Jonathan watched the women without any great show of interest as they chatted away and stripped off, discarding brassieres, tights and briefs of varying colours and styles. From time to time the door from the entrance hall opened as more members arrived.

Ceremonial dress for Lodge meetings was the same in every country. It had been designed by Hans-Martin Frick himself to resemble as far as was practical the fighting gear of the Knights Templars of the Crusades. Without the least embarrassment Jonathan stripped completely naked, knowing full well that the women present would run their eyes over his body as he had theirs. He kept himself in good trim by playing squash and by swimming and, though approaching forty, he still had muscular legs and a lean belly to go with his square shoulders. The women inspecting him would, he was sure, be fascinated to see that his pubic hair was the same dark red colour as the hair on his head.

He took the long sleeved tunic of dark grey which Britt had found for him and pulled it over his head. It came to his knees and represented the chain-mail coat of the Crusaders. Over it went a sleeveless surcoat of white linen, open sided and also kneelength. The Crusaders had worn a large red cross on the front of their surcoats and the Knights Templars had reduced this to a small red cross over the heart. The Masters of the Temple wore a different emblem – on the left breast of the surcoat, picked out in scarlet, was the Greek letter *Phi* – a circle bisected by a vertical line.

The first meaning of this symbol was formally explained to

Neophytes during their acceptance into the Order, though by then they had mainly worked it out for themselves. The upright line through the circle signified the union of male and female. Other layers of meaning became apparent to members as they progressed up through the Degrees.

Jonathan sat on one of the benches to pull on the black leather knee high boots that were part of the parade uniform. The pair Britt had given him were tighter across the toes than he could have wished, but not unbearably so for the hour the ceremony would last. He stood up and buckled round his waist a black leather belt with a scabbard attached, in which was a cross-handled steel short sword.

During his dressing he had glanced from time to time at Britt. He was right about her figure. When her dress came off he was afforded a view of a fine and full pair of breasts that needed no brassiere. The rest of her body was in keeping – well shaped and strong, long thighed and of pleasing proportions.

Men and women wore the same ceremonial dress, both sexes being regarded equally as soldiers in the service of the Order. In this matter Frick was far sighted when he established the rules, particularly for a man born in nineteenth century Germany, where a woman's place was traditionally held to be in church, the kitchen and bed. With her sword belt cinched tight round her waist, Britt was an imposing figure.

There were several long mirrors round the walls of the robing room. Jonathan stood before one of them, combed his hair and inspected his appearance carefully, as required. He eased his belt a trifle to the left in order to centre the brass buckle and decided that he looked suitably impressive. His own equipment back home at the London Lodge would have been better, but he was pleased enough by his reflection. Britt touched his arm.

'It is time for us to go in,' she said. 'Here is your badge to wear.'

He turned from the mirror to face her and ducked his head to let her flip over it a broad ribbon striped in scarlet and gold on which hung what she had called a badge. It was the insignia of the Fifth Degree, a beautiful and costly example of the jeweller's art, almost as big as the palm of his hand.

'I didn't expect to wear this,' he said, setting it centrally on his chest. 'How is it that you have a spare?'

'A friend who cannot be here tonight owns it. He is a colonel in the army and he was called away on duty today. I asked his permission to let you wear it.'

'Please tell him how grateful I am when you see him.'

He meant it. Lodge jewellery was very personal, very costly, carefully guarded and seldom lent.

'You look good,' said Britt.

'You look pretty good yourself,' he said, smiling at her.

From the robing room a heavy wooden door painted black led into the Temple. It was guarded by a fully equipped Knight of the Order holding his drawn sword upright in front of him. Following protocol, Jonathan stood back and waited while the Stockholm members went through. The Knight Sentinel scrutinised each in turn and spoke in a formal challenge. Each member put his lips close to the Sentinel's ear and whispered his answer before being allowed to pass. One member was not attempting to pass. He sat alone on a bench, his face thoughtful. Jonathan held out his hand to him.

'You are the postulant tonight?' he asked.

The man stood up and shook hands briefly.

'Bengt Johansson,' he introduced himself.

'This is a great day for you,' said Jonathan. 'I am glad to be here.'

'Thank you. You must go in now.'

Jonathan nodded. The robing room had emptied. He approached the Sentinel, waited for the challenge and, in a low voice so that Johansson could not overhear, he spoke the word of the Fifth Degree and received a nod of acceptance.

After the dullness of the robing room's green metal lockers and brown benches, to pass into the Temple was a delight, as it was intended to be. It was a fair sized room, about thirty by forty feet. At the far end, the east wall, was the sanctum, a semi-transparent veil drawn across to screen it. Dimly through the veil could be seen three seated figures wearing the same uniform as the Knights. Down both sides of the Temple were ranged rows of heavy wooden chairs and to the high back of each was fixed a tall staff carrying the brightly coloured banner of the Knight or Lady whose seat it was.

Jonathan made his way to the chair bearing a white banner with the scarlet *Phi* symbol on it – the seat traditionally reserved for visiting members from other Lodges. He was the last to be seated. In a moment or two the Knight Sentinel came in from the robing room, closed the door and bolted it top and bottom before standing with his back against it, his sword still drawn.

While the Knights and Ladies sat in silent contemplation, readying themselves spiritually and emotionally for the ceremony, Jonathan counted the chairs swiftly. There were three rows of fifteen on each side, all but six with banners, which gave him the present size of the Stockholm Lodge. Besides himself there were eleven other men and twelve women on this side of the veil. With three in the sanctum and the Knight Sentinel at the door the Lodge had twenty-seven members in its Fifth, Sixth and Seventh Degrees. No, twenty-eight, he remembered, Britt had told him there was one absent who qualified to be here. Not a very large Lodge, but promising for a city like Stockholm.

Britt was sitting on the opposite side of the Temple under a banner showing a gold crown on a dark blue field – a representation of her surname in heraldic terms, as all the banners were. Then Jonathan stopped busying his mind with such things and let the atmosphere sink in. It was a brave sight, Knights and Ladies sitting upright and still, the reds, greens, blues, whites and golds of their banners ablaze against the white painted and windowless walls. Overhead the high ceiling was coloured blue-black and spangled with tiny silver stars in their proper constellations. On the open floor between the rows of chairs the smooth green carpet had woven into it in gold the six-pointed star that was the Seal of Solomon, fully nine feet across.

From within the sanctum came five heavy knocks that signalled the beginning of the ceremony. The Knights and

Ladies rose silently to their feet as hidden speakers sent music coursing through the Temple, a thunderous and menacing roll of drums, creating a feeling of tension. The drum roll faded and an orchestra continued with a disquieting theme. It took Jonathan a second or two to recognise the music as the opening of a Balakirev overture, a piece of music not in use in the London Lodge, though eminently suitable for a Fifth Degree ceremony.

Over the music Anders Turesson's voice came from behind the veil, speaking slowly and commandingly in Swedish. From the other end of the Temple the Sentinel answered him. Without knowing a word of Swedish, Jonathan could easily understand the exchange. The Master of the Lodge was asking the Sentinel whether the Temple was secure and seeking an assurance that none was present who should not be. The Sentinel vowed in ringing tones that the gates were barred and that all present were of appropriately exalted rank.

The Master spoke again and this time he was answered by a woman's voice from within the sanctum. It was a firm contralto, thrilling to hear. When the woman finished, the Master pronounced the words that declared this sacred chapter of the Rose Cross open and, as he did so, the veil across the sanctum slid smoothly away. There he sat on a high backed, gold painted throne, a coronet on his head. He held the sceptre that denoted his authority as Master, ornately carved, two entwined serpents along its length and an eagle with raised wings at the top. To his left stood the woman who had spoken; dark haired, hawk nosed, about fifty. In both hands she held a richly ornamented gold chalice. To Anders' right stood the Marshal. He too held a rod of office, an ivory baton a foot long, tipped at both ends with gold and finely carved. Behind the three of them, almost covering the rear wall of the sanctum, was displayed the scarlet *Phi* symbol and lettered around it in golden capitals the Latin words *EX DEO NASCIMUR*, which in English signified *From God are we born*.

At the drawing back of the veil the Knights applauded their

enthroned Master, until he at last gestured for silence. They seated themselves to the rattle of scabbards against chairs and waited, while the unsettling music eddied around them. After a while there was a knocking at the door from the robing room and, with the Master's permission, the Sentinel unbolted it, enquired who was there and reported back.

All the details of the Order's ceremonies had been thought out with care and were followed to the letter. The postulant must himself, or herself, come asking permission to enter the Temple. Only when that had been done would the Order help. The Master instructed the woman on his left, whose office was Guardian of the Grail, to bring into the Temple whoever sought admittance. She walked gracefully down the length of the Temple between the rows of seated Knights and brought in Bengt Johansson, leading him by the hand. The Sentinel barred the door again and the Marshal left his place beside the Master and went to meet them, timing his advance so that he stopped Bengt with a touch on the chest of his ivory baton exactly in the centre of the six-pointed star on the floor. He waited while the Guardian offered Bengt her golden chalice and made sure that he drained it.

Jonathan knew that drink. It was a rich red wine, laced with a measured dose of juice of henbane, a common enough plant. But the active ingredient that occurred naturally in the plant was hyoscyamine and it would produce in Bengt a sense of detachment from his surroundings, a feeling of unreality which would make it harder for him to acquit himself well. It was therefore a test of his self control and determination. As a Fourth, Bengt had no knowledge of the ordeal required to pass to the Fifth, though his own insight would have warned him of its general nature.

The Marshal returned to his position beside the Master. The Guardian of the Grail positioned herself a step behind Bengt, to his left. If the postulant had been a woman, the Marshal would have stayed with her and the Guardian would have returned to the sanctum.

Bengt Johansson was a strongly built man in his late thirties. To have attained the Fourth and to have prepared himself for admission to the Fifth must have taken him ten years, Jonathan reflected. This moment was of supreme importance to him. To fail now in sight of triumph would be an unthinkable humiliation.

There began a series of questions and answers between the Master sitting on his golden throne and Bengt standing in the star, to confirm his readiness. Jonathan pondered the meaning of the ceremony and recalled the day, years before, when he had stood in the place of the postulant, seeking admission to the Fifth. The experience was one no person ever forgot.

The symbolism of the set words and actions carried deep meaning to those taking part. Just as in a theatre the audience is caught up in the drama on the stage, so the Knights in the Temple were totally involved in what was being enacted before them. To Bengt the involvement ran very deep. Over a long period he had achieved a certain stage of spiritual enlightenment and was in effect asking for this to be recognised by those who had reached that stage before him. In the Order's words, he had completed the levels of the five points of the pentagram – earth, water, air, fire and spirit. If he received recognition of this and the Fifth Degree was conferred on him, he would be a Lord of the Threshold. In Latin, in the Order's records, that would be *Dominus Liminus*, a title of great significance.

When Bengt had satisfied the Master that he was possessed of the insight necessary to become a Fifth, there came the first high moment of the ceremony. He was asked to recite the Profession of Righteousness. He took a deep breath and his voice rang out. The words were Swedish, but Jonathan recited it in English under his breath.

> 'I have done no wrong;
> I have not been covetous,
> I have not stolen,
> I have killed no man,
> I have not given short measure.'

It was a very old form of words, taken from the Egyptian

Book of the Dead. The ancient Egyptians held that after death a man's spirit stood before the god Osiris and was required to give an account of his life, while his heart was weighed in the balance for truthfulness.

> 'I have done what is pleasing to the gods;
> I have given bread to the hungry,
> And water to the thirsty,
> And clothes to the naked,
> And a passage to those with no boat.'

The Profession of Righteousness was held in great esteem within the Order. Postulants for every Degree and candidates for every office had to repeat it before the other Knights and stood the risk of being challenged by any of them if they did not believe him.

There was a long pause after Bengt had completed it, but no challenge came. The response to the Profession was not quite so ancient, but ancient enough, being one of the psalms of King David. Anders spoke it.

> 'Blessed is the man that walks not in the
>   counsel of the unrighteous,
> Nor stands in the way of sinners,
> Nor sits in the seat of the scornful;
> He shall be like a tree planted by rivers of water,
> Bringing forth his fruit in his season,
> His leaf shall not wither,
> And whatsoever he does shall prosper.'

Again there was a pause, then Anders said,

'It is good. You shall be admitted to this sacred chapter of the Sovereign Princes of the Rose Cross. Draw your sword.'

Even though the drink was beginning to take effect on Bengt, a look of surprise crossed his face. Jonathan knew what he was thinking – 'Is that all I have to do?' If only he knew.

Bengt drew his short sword and held it upright in front of his face, his movements slightly slowed down.

'Repeat the oath after me,' said the Master.

It was a long oath, sworn in the sight of the gods and in the presence of the Princes of the Rose Cross. Bengt's voice came slower and slower until he realised what was happening and visibly squared his shoulders and forced himself to speak boldly through the creeping languor in his mind. At the end of the oath, sworn to everlasting obedience to the Order and eternal silence on its mysteries, he was told to kiss the blade of his sword.

A fanfare of trumpets rang out, clear and triumphant, signalling the taking of the oath. Another question was put to Bengt, who answered ponderously, forcing himself to stand straight.

The central mystery of the ceremony was approaching. The Master's question had been what titles and honours Bengt held in the Noble Order of the Masters of the Temple. With pride, Bengt listed the names of the four Degrees he had attained, in their proper sequence. He made no claim to the Fifth, for though he had taken the oath, the Master had not yet conferred the title upon him.

When Anders spoke again, Jonathan formulated the words in English in his own head. Bengt was being told that his titles and honours were as nothing – worse than nothing, for they were stumbling blocks, empty names that blinded him to the truth. He was told that his pride in such vain observances must be humbled before he was fit to stand in the presence of the Knights of the Fifth Degree.

The startled Bengt was led away by the Guardian, the veil slid across the sanctum and the light behind it faded, until the Master on his golden throne and the Marshal at his side could no longer be seen. The lights in the body of the Temple also dimmed and the music, different again, sighed around the Knights, heavy with foreboding.

Old though the building was, like all the Order's Temples it contained some very advanced electronic equipment to create effects during ceremonies. The controls, Jonathan knew, were concealed in the arm of the Master's throne, so that the brush of a fingertip could bring music crashing or sobbing through the Temple, change the lighting, draw the veil and a dozen other things. Yet while he knew how these effects were brought about, the impact was just as great as if there had been a live player at a great organ or an entire symphony orchestra and massed choir in the Temple itself.

The lights had faded slowly until Jonathan could no longer see the row of seated Knights on the other side of the Temple. Only a tight beamed overhead spotlight picked out on the floor the Seal of Solomon the King.

The Guardian of the Grail brought Bengt back into the Temple. He was naked, blindfolded and his hands were tied together behind his back. Instead of leading him by the hand she pulled him along by a rope round his neck, fashioned into a hangman's noose. She stood him in the centre of the star and took her place behind his left shoulder. Bengt was swaying, his mind disoriented, the rope hanging down his chest. He looked abject and humiliated.

Through the sound system a voice boomed out, not the Master's but another, louder and harder. The questions and answers translated themselves in Jonathan's mind as they were spoken, for they were known by heart by every member of the Order.

'Who are you?'

'A man,' Bengt answered.

'Who is your father?'

'The sun.'

'Who is your mother?'

'The earth.'

'From whence do you come?'

'From God.'

'Where do you go?'

'To God.'

And in a voice that he was struggling to control, Bengt added the last part of the Order's creed:

'What then shall I fear?'

Immediately there was a bellow of harsh laughter through the Temple, then mocking words. Jonathan followed the Swedish version in his mind, enthralled by the drama of the ceremony.

'You who aspire to be a god,' the voice grated, 'know that all gods die.'

The Guardian stepped forward and flicked away the blindfold. Bengt blinked at the figure that loomed up before him out of the darkness surrounding the small circle of light in which he stood, bound, naked and helpless.

Robed full length in flowing black, the tall figure held a painted mask before its face, a mask of the features of a darkly handsome young man, contorted in pain and shock. The words came with a hollow ring through the mask's open mouth.

'I am Tammuz, the beloved of the great goddess Ishtar. I was a god in Babylon, until I was cut down and trampled, as the corn is cut down and trodden. So shall it be with you.'

Surprised by the apparition, Bengt swayed backwards, but before he could step out of the centre of the star, the Guardian slashed across his bare shoulders with a whip to steady him.

Tammuz faded back into the darkness and another tall figure took his place. The mask was of a man of middle years, wearing a high crown, his beard slender and bound crossways with cords.

'I am Osiris the Good. When men and women were as animals hunting their food in the wilderness I taught them the arts of civilisation and made them human. I was a god in Egypt, but my brother Set killed me and hacked my body into pieces. So shall it be with you.'

Again the Guardian cut Bengt across the back with her whip.

One by one the slain gods appeared, each with mournful words. After Tammuz and Osiris came Adonis, his fine face lined with pain.

'I am Adonis, who was loved by the goddess Aphrodite. I was a god in Greece, but on the mountain a wild boar ripped my sacred part from between my legs with its tusks and tore open my belly. So shall it be with you.'

Then came Attis, lover of the great goddess Cybele, who in his frenzy of adoration for her castrated himself with a flint blade and bled to death under the mountain pines. After him came a bearded and ascetic face.

'I am Jesus, son of Mary. I was a god in Galilee. They nailed me naked to a wooden plank and hung me up to die in the scorching sun. So shall it be with you.'

He moved back and was lost in the dark, to be replaced by another and another; Llew the Strong, run through by a keen bladed spear; Balder the Beautiful, killed by an arrow; Bran the Blessed, beheaded – all gods and all slain. Bengt shook under the cut of the whip on his back as each god foretold the same fate for him. When the last of them had gone back into the darkness, the grating, bodiless voice spoke again, icy with contempt.

'You asked what you shall fear. You have been answered.'

The Guardian's arm now rose and fell furiously, flogging Bengt without mercy, until he sank to his knees within the star. In the darkened Temple the only sounds were the crack of whip on flesh and Bengt's laboured breathing as he suffered and struggled to break through the fog in his mind and to free himself from the terrors of the dying gods.

Slowly he raised his bowed head to stare into the encircling gloom. Sweat was trickling down his face, as blood was trickling down his back. His voice came thin and clear:

'The sun my father,
The earth my mother,
From God am I born,
To God I return;
What then shall I fear?'

The flogging stopped at once; the Guardian stepped backwards out of the little circle of light and was gone. Bengt was alone, on his knees, naked and bleeding. With great effort he began to struggle to his feet, almost falling, but utterly determined.

On the eastern wall of the empty sanctum, from which the throne had gone, there was a faint gleam of light. Through the Temple sounded a rising call of trumpets, followed by a crescendo of drums. The light on the sanctum wall grew quickly, as hidden projectors threw on to it a staggering sunrise of red and gold. Across the entire wall was the dark rim of the world with the sun climbing above it, the radiance growing in intensity until the whole Temple was flooded with light from the enormous dawn on the eastern wall.

Bengt, up on his feet at last, stared at it wide eyed, an inner light dawning in him. He had attained the Fifth Degree, he understood the underlying harmony of all things, the significance of slain gods who rise again, death as the gateway to a new life.

The sunrise was complete, the marvellous image on the wall irradiating the Temple with an almost unbearable red-gold glow. The Knights turned their faces from Bengt and rose to their feet to face the sun in adoration of its maker. A magnificent contralto voice rang out from the speakers. Jonathan repeated its words in English under his breath, caught up in the drive of the worship:

'The skies declare the glory of God,
And the earth reveals his handiwork;
He has set a tabernacle for the sun,
Which is as a bridegroom coming forth from his dwelling
And rejoicing as a strong man to run a race.
His going forth is from the end of the sky
And his circuit is unto the ends of it,
And there is nothing hidden from the strength thereof.'

During the anthem, the Guardian untied Bengt's hands and rubbed his wrists, removed the halter from his neck and threw a long cloak of rich purple about him. As she led him from the Temple there were tears of emotion running down his face.

As the sun glow faded into ordinary light, the Knights seated themselves and waited in silence until the Guardian brought Bengt back into the Temple past the Sentinel. He was wearing the uniform of the Order again and if his back smarted under it, he gave no outward sign. As she led him between the rows of chairs the veil slid back to reveal the Master on his throne and the Marshal standing beside him, holding out his ivory baton to command total silence.

The Guardian halted Bengt in the six-pointed star and went forward to take her position beside the Master.

'Worthy Knight,' said Anders Turesson, 'you have passed through the ordeal and have conducted yourself with courage and dignity as befits you. Approach this throne.'

Bengt advanced beyond the central star for the first time, walking slowly, until he stood before the crowned Master and looked him squarely in the face.

'No Knight or Lady of this Order ever kneels to another man or woman,' said Anders Turesson, 'yet, if it please you to do so, kneel now.'

Bengt went down on one knee. The Master reached forward with his golden sceptre of office and touched it lightly to Bengt's left shoulder, right shoulder and left shoulder again.

'By the powers and authority vested in me by the Noble Order of the Masters of the Temple I create you, now and forever, a Sovereign Prince of the Holy Order of the Rose Cross. Rise, Prince.'

The Master stood as Bengt stood. From the Marshal he took the insignia of the Fifth on its striped ribbon and slipped it over Bengt's head. It was identical to that worn by Jonathan and all the others present, a rose with twenty-two petals mounted on an equal armed cross, all in bright red and gold.

Bengt touched the insignia with his fingertips for a moment before turning to face the assembled Knights proudly. The Guardian drew her short sword and stood behind him, the sword over his head. A beam of light flashed off her rapidly twisting blade so that golden fire seemed to play about Bengt's head. Meanwhile the Marshal advanced four steps and proclaimed the new Prince in a loud and sonorous voice, giving him his title of Lord of the Threshold. When he had finished, the Knights rose and saluted Bengt, shouting their acclamation. He had won through his ordeal and was one of their own, an illustrious Prince in an army with banners marching towards the limitless light.

With his ivory baton held in front of him, the Marshal led Bengt from the sanctum to his chair in the Temple. Music swelled up, triumphant, majestic and stirring. Sibelius, thought Jonathan – the same piece that we use in London, last movement of the second symphony.

The Master on his throne was flanked by the Guardian with her chalice and the Marshal with his baton and on the wall behind them appeared the scarlet *Phi* symbol of the Order with the Latin words around it that had been there at the opening of the ceremony. The music sank into the background as the Master pronounced the solemn words which closed the Chapter of the Rose Cross. The veil slid across, the music swelled up again and Bengt led the assembled Knights out of the Temple, all by custom deferring to his newly acquired status.

CHAPTER 5
TO BE A GOD

AS BEFITTED his eminence, Anders Turesson's house was large and stylish. It stood a little way outside Stockholm, a three storied building in its own grounds, the façade painted white, the roof steeply slanting. This was the setting for the banquet after the elevation of Bengt Johansson to the Fifth.

There was no place in the Noble Order for anyone unable to achieve an above average standard of life. To be poor indicated that a person probably lacked the innate intelligence or energy to understand the Order's teaching. And, on another level, it cost a fair amount of money, in dues towards the upkeep of Temples, in contributions to the Order's investments and to afford the personal equipment and regalia worn in the Temple itself and for private workings outside. When Hans-Martin Frick founded the Order he had been of the opinion that in all societies and at all times there were the few who led and the many who followed. In this he was in total accord with the rulers of all nations, from the United States to the Soviet Union. Frick would only recruit those who had demonstrated that they were of the few or, if they were young, could show promise that they would with a little assistance become so.

On the drive to Anders' home, Jonathan learned from Britt that the old man's wife had died three or four years before. He lived alone and in state, tended by several servants.

'What does he do with his time?' Jonathan asked, 'He tried to tell me that he drifts about the city all day long, but I find that hard to believe.'

'He travels a lot. He still has business interests, though he is retired. He goes to visit friends in Denmark and other countries. He has four children, all married with families, and he goes to visit them when he has time. He gives much of his time to running the Order here, of course.'

'He must have known Hans-Martin Frick personally.'

'I have been told so. They knew each other before the war, I think, and then afterwards. They had business together, I believe, besides establishing the Stockholm Lodge in those days.'

'I wish I could have met Frick, but he had been dead for ten years before I became a member. His influence on our lives is so strong that it shapes our characters and destinies. I sometimes think that it's like Paul and Jesus.'

'I do not understand what you mean,' said Britt.

'Paul never met Jesus, yet he constructed the Christian church and its beliefs on what other people told him about Jesus. He even had a disagreement with Peter over it, and Peter had known Jesus personally. But in the end they met the same fate, Paul and Peter were both executed in Rome, whether they agreed or not.'

'I know very little about the history of the Christian church.'

'Then you have that in common with the vast majority of those who claim to be members of it. I think that Christianity was invented by Paul without much regard to Jesus.'

'Why?'

'Evidently he needed to find God, as we do. He lived in a time when slain and risen gods were worshipped all about him. He took the memory of a wandering preacher and elevated it into the concept of another slain and risen god.'

'He should have been an adept, like us,' said Britt.

In Turesson's house the banquet was laid out buffet-style in the dining room. A long table was covered with platters of cold meats, cold salmon, salads and different breads, cheeses, whole roast birds, food for twice the number present. By the wall another table held bottles of red wine and white wine in silver coolers. It was, thought Jonathan, a sumptuous spread in the best traditions of the Order. He took a glass of chilled wine and drifted round the room to meet people, while Britt went off to speak to her friends.

Finding himself alongside the man who had acted as Marshal in the ceremony, Jonathan held out his hand.

'I'm Jonathan Rawlings.'

The other man nodded.

'Olof Linder,' he introduced himself. 'I am pleased that you were with us this evening in the Temple. Did our language give you any problems?'

'None at all, I recited the words in English in my head all through. The ceremony was most impressive, particularly the way you and Anders played the slain gods between you.'

'Thank you. I confess that we did rehearse a little this afternoon.'

'The masks were very well made. Are they old or new?'

'About thirty years old. They were made soon after the Lodge was established here.'

'By a local artist?'

'Yes, the first Stockholm Master knew a young artist with a promising reputation and paid him well to make them. He did not tell him what they were to be used for. But, would you believe it, the young man was so inspired by his own work when he had finished it that he asked to join whatever organisation he had been working for, though he knew nothing about its purpose and not even its name.'

'Was he accepted?' Jonathan asked. 'He must have been, after that.'

'He was accepted after two years, when the Master was convinced of his sincerity.'

'What was his name?'

'Olof Linder. Have you ever heard of his work?'

Jonathan laughed at the way he had been led on.

'You are a very fine artist, Olof, if that's what you could do thirty years ago. Is there any of your work in London I might have seen?'

'Most of my work is in private collections. Like the work of your English artist, Austin Spare. Do you know of him?'

'I own a drawing by him. I'm pleased to see that you are having more material success than he did. The last twenty years of his life were lived in poverty in the slums of South London. I expect you know that he died of cancer in 1957.'

'What is the subject of the drawing?'

'One of his favourite themes – an elderly woman projecting a young and beautiful image of her inner self into reality to copulate with a young man. The drawing is so infused with energy that I am convinced that Spare performed one of his private sexual ceremonies to give it the life it has.'

'I would very much like to see the drawing.'

'Come to London and be a guest of the Lodge, and you can stay with me and see it. I'd be very interested to hear your opinion of it. And when I am next in Sweden I'd like to visit your studio. I'm a collector in a small way.'

'It would give me great pleasure to show you my work. And to sell you something. What sort of things do you collect besides pictures?'

'I've one or two Indian figures and one I think is Tibetan,

though you know what thieves gallery owners are when they want to make a sale. I've a couple of good German wood carvings from the sixteenth century. And other bits and pieces.'

'I really will visit London soon to see all this. Now, you must start eating before everything is gone. I know these people – they are like wolves when there is food on the table. We can start with some cold salmon and mayonnaise, yes?'

Jonathan loaded a plate and nibbled as he talked. Eventually he found himself face to face with the woman who had been the Guardian of the Grail earlier that evening. Her jet black eyes stared boldly at him over her hawk nose. She was wearing a loose emerald green top over a long black skirt, and both her wrists were laden with heavy gold bangles.

'Come and talk to me,' she said in good English, 'I like to meet new people. I'm Greta.'

In one hand she held a used plate, in the other a near empty glass and a cigarette. Seeing her close, Jonathan put her at just over fifty.

'You were magnificent in the ceremony,' he said, smiling at her.

'Thank you. Your plate is empty. Come and fill it at once.'

She sailed through the people helping themselves at the long table, like a ship through flotsam, and piled cold roast beef and salads onto his plate.

'More?' she asked.

'Enough – I'm trying to stay slim.'

'Nonsense – look at me. I eat everything and stay slim.'

He glanced at her wiry body and nodded.

'Your metabolism is well adjusted, Greta. I have to exercise constantly to keep my shape.'

'Well, I didn't have a chance to see your body when you were in the robing room, which is a great pity because my friend over there has told me that you are well developed and strong.'

'You were in the Master's robing room, of course.'

'Anders has told me that you are a Seventh,' she said. 'I wish you could come to my house with me tonight. We do not have enough young men and women Sevenths here in Stockholm yet.'

While they were talking she led him into a large living room where people were talking and eating, perching on chair arms. Greta waved two of her colleagues away from a sofa and took a place on it, Jonathan beside her.

'You have more Sevenths in the London Lodge, naturally,' she said.

'Yes, but not as many as we would like. The way is a long one.'

'How many women Sevenths do you have?'

He thought for a moment.

'Seventeen.'

'Of what ages?'

'Two or three just under forty. One in her sixties. The rest in between. We have quite a number of women Fifths in their thirties.'

Greta was sitting close to him, her thigh pressed against his.

'I am sorry that you are not available tonight,' he said, putting his empty plate on the floor so that he could touch her hand, 'but this is Bengt's day.'

'My obligation is clear. I hope that you will visit Stockholm again soon.'

'So do I. Bengt did well tonight,' he answered, looking round the room for him. He was standing near the long windows in a little group of friends.

'He will reach the Seventh in time,' Jonathan added. 'I am sure of it – there's something about him.'

'I believe so, but it will take some years yet. He learns slowly and never forgets anything he has learned. Sometimes I think he lacks humour.'

'Tonight was not an occasion for humour.'

'No, but I mean in general. If he is assigned to me to teach after he becomes a Sixth, I shall teach him how to laugh, even if I have to stand on my head naked in the public square to do it.'

The party continued long after the food had vanished from

the tables. The flow of wine was uninterrupted, the conversation grew appreciably louder. Jonathan relinquished Greta to Bengt when he came to collect her to take her to his home for the private ceremony in celebration of his attainment. By midnight Britt was back by his side.

'I think it is time to leave now, Jonathan. Do you wish to come with me?'

He put an arm round her waist and squeezed hard.

'I would like that very much. Let's say our goodnights and be off.'

From the moment she had picked him up at the hotel he had been certain in his mind that she would make the offer. The Order's hospitality extended beyond food and drink. Britt had been chosen and sent by Anders for that reason. Only if she had found him personally unacceptable would she have informed the Lodge Master so that he could make other arrangements.

Anders was in the hall, saying goodnight to departing guests.

'Thank you for a marvellous evening, Anders. I hope you will be in London soon so that I can repay your kindness.'

'It has been a pleasure for me. We do not have visitors from your Lodge often enough.'

'When we had lunch together, it didn't occur to me that you knew Hans-Martin Frick personally. Next time we meet I want to ask you about him.'

'It will be my pleasure to talk about him. In the meantime, I hope you won't forget the things that we talked about after lunch.'

'Krafft? Your cautionary tale?'

'*Macbeth*. Take him away, Britt. Goodnight.'

On the drive back into the city she asked Jonathan if he was a Shakespeare fan.

'Only moderately. Anders meant something else.'

'A secret?'

'A warning against impatience.'

Britt's apartment was spacious and comfortable. In the living room there were colourfully woven rugs scattered on wooden floors polished to the shade of honey, and leather upholstered chairs on tubular chrome legs. One wall was covered entirely with bookshelves filled to capacity. She suggested that he sat down while she checked that her son was asleep.

In a few minutes she was back with a bottle and two glasses. She sat beside him on the long sofa.

'French cognac. Do you like it?'

He nodded and she poured large measures. They clinked glasses together.

'Very nice,' said Jonathan. 'Smooth and strong – a good combination. Who looks after your son when you are out?'

'I have a girl living here with me. She is from America.'

'How old is the boy?'

'Six years.'

'Were you once married?'

'No, I've never wanted to be with one man all the time. I have my job and I like to be free. A husband would complicate my life. When I had my thirtieth birthday I decided that I should have a child.'

'Why?'

'Because I have something of value to pass on – my view of life and how it is to be lived, perhaps. I had been a member of the Order for some years then, you see.'

As he sipped the brandy, she continued.

'For most Swedish people religion is not important, you understand. We are mostly busy trying to create a just society here on earth, according to the best humanitarian and social democratic principles. This is good. I want to be a useful member of our society, but I need more than that – some kind of spiritual development, some personal achievement in a different dimension. I had no Christian background to inhibit my thinking and so when an older friend began to sound me out about the Order, I knew it was the way for me.'

'I suppose that is how most of us came to it. So there you were, thirty years old and on the path to enlightenment and you wanted to have a child. How did you select a suitable father – was it the friend who recruited you into the Order?'

'No, he was a good lover and a good friend. You have seen him tonight at Anders's house. But thinking scientifically, I decided that I could do better.'

'What were the factors?'

'A strong and healthy body and a good and active mind. Those were two things I could myself give to a child and so the father must do the same. I found the right man amongst my professional colleagues at the hospital. He was married but that was not of interest to me. I made myself attractive to him without telling him of my purpose. We were lovers for about three months, until I knew that I was pregnant. Then I ended the affair. I didn't want him to feel that he had to look after me or have any responsibility to the child when he was born.'

'Does he know now?'

'Not from me. I think he may have guessed, as he is no fool. We are still friends and we have never discussed it. Are you married, Jonathan?'

'My life has been so full that there's been no place in it for a wife so far.'

Britt's soft woollen dress was fastened at the back of her neck by a large green button. She reached casually over her shoulder and undid it, then set her brandy glass down on the low table and shrugged her shoulders out of the dress. It fell forward and slipped to her waist. She picked up her glass again and leaned back on the sofa, her plump breasts fully exposed. Jonathan stared at them in open appreciation.

He looked up to her face to see the amusement in her brown eyes.

'I didn't invite you here to talk about my life,' she said, smiling at him. 'You are a Knight of the Seventh Degree, far above a Princess of the Rose Cross like me. I do not even know the name of so exalted a rank as the Seventh. But you are here to enlighten me – how do you intend to do it?'

Jonathan smiled back as he cupped a breast in his hand.

'I've been thinking about that since I met you. I was in Copenhagen a few days ago with a Third. We enjoyed the Revel of Queen Esther together. But you are a Sovereign

Princess, a Mistress of the Threshold, and you must have performed that ceremony many times.'

'Very many, always with pleasure. But from you I expect more, Jonathan.'

'The marriage of Shiva and Shakti – have you heard of that?'

Britt's eyes were half closed, like those of a cat, as he fondled her heavy breasts.

'I have heard of it.'

'From whom?'

'From Greta.'

'What did she tell you about it?'

'Only the name. She said that when she performs this ceremony she is unable to speak for hours afterwards. That surprises me, because normally she never stops speaking.'

'It has that effect. We must be undisturbed – an unexpected interruption could hurt both of us.'

'My bedroom is at the other side of the apartment, away from the others. I have never been disturbed there. Will it be noisy?'

'No, very quiet.'

The ceremony Jonathan was proposing was one of great antiquity, a re-enactment of the creation through sexual union. The root belief of the Noble Order was that only by co-operation between man and woman can either advance spiritually. They fulfill and complete each other, so that every sexual joining, however casual, could be seen as a dim shadow of the cosmic act of creation. Performed by adepts, the union of male and female approaches more closely the primal act and partakes of its divine nature, which was seen as continuous and continuing, not once and for all. This point of view is very different from the Christian one, which holds that the creation of the universe by God occurred at some definite point in time past.

In the large bedroom, Britt and Jonathan stripped and stood in contemplation of each other without touching. Both were sexually aroused, but their intention was far from the ordinary human response of getting onto the bed and dispersing their gathering energies in an act of banal copulation.

'You are like Shakti,' said Jonathan. 'Big breasted, narrow waisted, broad hipped. I chose the ceremony well. Show me your circle.'

She moved away a large woven rug to reveal on the floor beneath it a six-pointed star within a circle. He moved to the centre of it and nodded to her to continue. From a chest of drawers beside the bed Britt took an incense taper and a small crystal bottle of water. She lit the taper and joined him in the middle of the star. Again he nodded to her. With the taper in her right hand giving off its sweet smelling smoke, she walked slowly round the circle, speaking aloud in Swedish. And then again, sprinkling from her bottle a few drops of water around the circle, consecrating it to their use, sanctifying the space within it so that no harm should befall them.

When she was beside him again and both were facing to the east, Jonathan pointed with his finger at the six-pointed star, turning slowly as he traced all of it.

'The power of the Seal of Solomon the King flames about us,' he declared forcefully. 'Into it shall come no evil thing.'

The power to shut out all harm was in their minds; the consecration of the circle and the tracing of the star were physical actions to arouse the power that was in him and in her. He faced Britt and took her hands while he spoke of the nature of the ceremony they were embarked upon, his voice full of confidence.

'The marriage of Shiva and Shakti is a tribute to the great goddess from whose womb and by whose wisdom all things in the universe are made manifest in Time. The cosmic act of creation is continuous, the union of man and woman is a representation of it. In this marriage you will become the goddess Shakti and I shall become the god Shiva. Do you understand this?'

'I understand your words but I cannot understand what will happen.'

'When the goddess enters into you you will understand.'

He positioned them both facing east, side by side again, raised his hands, palms upwards and called sonorously on all the forces of the universe to aid him.

'Powers of the Kingdom
Be beneath my left foot and within my right hand . . . '

The prayer named and summoned the manifestations of God, from the Kingdom, which was the earth itself, up through the spheres to the highest emanation of God the human mind could envisage, which was addressed as the Crown. By putting his whole will and thrust behind the ancient form of words, Jonathan was setting in motion within himself and outside himself powerful vibrations which stirred and rippled through all creation, seen and unseen. His voice grew more powerful as he felt the strength surging up inside him, so that when he reached the last lines of the prayer, he seemed ablaze with energy.

'Powers of the Kingdom
Conduct me between the two columns
On which the Temple stands;
Victory and Glory strengthen me upon
   the cubical stone of the Foundation;
Understanding be my love, Wisdom be my light;
Be that which you are and that which you will
   to be, O Crown!'

He ended and waited, feeling the great surge of the words he had energised, reaching outwards to the furthermost planes of being. From the corner of his eye he saw Britt make the sign of the Cabalistic cross on her body and heard her words in her own language, knowing what she was saying. As she touched her forehead, her navel, her right nipple, her left nipple, her words meant 'The Crown, The Kingdom, the Power and the Glory' and as she pressed her palms together at the level of her lips, 'in all eternity.'

They turned to face each other. Following Jonathan's

gestured instructions, Britt sank to her knees and the two of them knelt a yard apart. Between them, on the wooden floor, Jonathan traced the outline of a large equal sided triangle, its base line towards himself and its point towards Britt.

'In this sign we see the oneness of Shiva and Shakti,' he said, 'for from your side you see the representation of the female parts and from my side I see the representation of the male parts, though there is only one figure.'

He clapped his palms smartly together three times and moved forward to sit cross legged within the imaginary triangle he had traced. The soles of his feet were upwards on opposite thighs in a yoga position it had taken him much practice to achieve easily. By westerners, yoga is mistakenly thought to be a system of physical exercises to keep the body supple and the mind calm. But the meaning of the word yoga is *union* and the system was developed by eastern adepts to assist them to attain union with the source of all being.

He showed Britt what to do. She rested her hands on his shoulders, her legs straddled outside his thighs. He took her by the hips and held her while he kissed her belly above the neat triangle of clipped brown hair. Then under the guidance of his hands she lowered herself until he was able to kiss her breasts in veneration, then lower still, and his fingers were between her widely parted thighs, opening her. She sat across his lap at last, fully penetrated, her arms and legs clasped behind his back.

They were still Britt and Jonathan, a man and woman joined sexually, waiting for the transformation that would take place when their bodies and minds were ready for it. They sat straight backed, Jonathan's arms round Britt's waist, supporting her and holding her close, looking into each other's eyes. The ceremony Jonathan had chosen was a lengthy one, not to be hurried by impatience or lust. Two Sevenths together could prolong it for the traditional period of an hour and thirty-six minutes, but that, he knew, would be asking too much of Britt at her level of Fifth.

The position they had assumed prevented any thrusting of sexual parts, as it was meant to. The sensations that formed slowly within each of them came not from the conjunction of their physical parts, not even from the subtle pressures inside their bodies caused by the way they were seated, but from the male and female sexual polarities in contact. Jonathan showed Britt how to follow his breathing pattern and then to let the rhythms of her breathing become automatic, in time with his. Correct breathing was part of what they were doing, to affect the chemistry of the blood stream and so bring about a change in the internal environment of their brains. Gradually a feeling of warmth suffused them both, followed by a sense of detachment. Their conscious egos were moving away to make room for the divine power. A tingling made itself felt through their bodies and became a deep inner vibration, a rhythmic pulsation of gathering energy within them as the gods came closer.

Time no longer had any meaning. They saw nothing but each other, were aware of nothing but each other. Their breathing had slowed in unison and their whole beings had withdrawn into the double unit formed by their bodies. Britt's internal muscles had begun to clasp and unclasp Jonathan's deep planted erection in a slow rhythm that she was unaware of. A deep level of herself had been stimulated into action and they were ascending together a long and gentle slope, unhurried and in complete harmony, to where the gods waited for them. Jonathan's entire awareness was a vision of Shiva and Shakti locked in their embrace and the words for the moment came from him unbidden.

'Eternal Shakti is supreme, her nature is unoriginated and undisturbed joy, everlasting because she transcends the divisions of time; she is incomparable and indescribable, the source of all that lives and moves, the radiant mirror in which is revealed the form of Shiva to himself.'

Britt's arms held him tighter and her mouth found his. They were lost in sensation, oblivious to their surroundings, the room, the building, the city, the whole world about them – all ceased to exist. Britt trembled as the orgasm began in her body and at that moment they were no longer Britt and

Jonathan but Shakti and Shiva, two aspects of the reality which contains male and female within itself and is the source of all.

After a subjective eternity, the exaltation dimmed. Britt unwound her arms from Jonathan's neck and leaned back to look at him in wonder. Though they were still linked sexually, she had become aware of her own separate existence. Jonathan looked at Britt and saw her as a part of himself that he had projected outwards into an existence of its own. She was beautiful and his mind was full of the marvel of what he saw.

He felt her unfold her legs from his back and move gently away until they were parted. She was still staring at him and she was still Shakti, newly aware of herself as a distinct being after the ecstasy of union. She stood up slowly and, without consciously willing it, twirled round the inner edge of the sacred circle to experience the pleasure of movement, her body twisting sinuously and her full breasts swaying in time with a distant music in her head.

The dance of Shakti wove the fabric of the world. At first Jonathan saw only Britt, Shiva saw only Shakti, but as she moved round him he became aware of the room and the objects in it, then of the city and the world outside the room. He was aware of himself and his own body again and it seemed to him that he was isolated inside his own body. They had reached the point of the ceremony – to show that everything men and women imagine that they experience, the course of their lives through the world, is generated for them by the dance of Shakti and the sense of separation and distinctness is illusion, for all things are one and all things are God.

Britt realised what she had done and was pervaded by a sense of her own aloneness among a multiplicity of forms and beings. She shuffled to a stop and looked forlornly down at Jonathan. He raised his arms and she took his hands quickly, to be pulled down towards him. He was still hard erect, for the power of Shiva was in him. Britt sank gratefully onto his lap and sighed in relief as he penetrated her again.

'I was frightened,' she said in Swedish and from her tone he understood her.

'You are Shakti,' he said. 'You and I are one. The sense of separation is illusion.'

'You are Shiva,' she said. 'We are the same.'

Her legs clasped his hips and her arms were about his neck. Jonathan stroked her long back lovingly to calm her. He was slightly surprised that she had reacted so strongly to her first orgasm, but that evidently was her nature. More usually the separation and slow dance manifested itself after the third. A reason why only advanced adepts performed the ceremony together was that, unlike ordinary sexual congress which left the partners with a temporary sense of well-being, the sudden awareness of aloneness after the heightened orgasm of the ceremony could give rise to negative and harmful feelings in those unprepared for it.

They sat together, linked by their sexual parts, until Britt was comforted. In his mind Jonathan held an image of the union of Shiva and Shakti derived from one of his icons at home – an Indian carving of the condition of enlightenment, the god and goddess seated just as he and Britt were. It was carved in wood, stood about a foot high, and was overlaid with gold leaf. The god wore a golden headdress and arm and leg bands set with coloured stones. The goddess had semi-precious stones woven into her long black hair and a jewelled harness about her waist and loins. The expression on both their faces was one of unearthly tranquillity.

When Jonathan became aware once more of the clasping and unclasping action inside Britt, he identified himself and Britt with the two divinities. He projected himself into the form of Shiva and projected the image of Shakti onto the woman pressed against him. He spoke again to her.

'Here is given true insight into the great goddess. He who gains this insight is released and becomes one with her.'

The ceremony, he knew by then, would be curtailed. Though in ordinary coupling for pleasure Britt could no doubt perform the sexual act half a dozen times before satiation, the forces released in her by the psychodrama they were enacting were too strong for her to sustain long. With a woman of his own Degree Jonathan would have expected to extend the marriage to its full length, in which time his partner would have attained orgasm the traditional seven times. Britt had much training ahead of her before she reached that level. He guessed that she would shortly reach the end of her ability to sustain the ceremony and so he decided to let her take him with her into the final act. No harm would be done. They would both have experienced the inner joy, though only a limited part of it.

Britt's orgasm when it came this time was overwhelming and Jonathan went along with it. Each spurt of semen was like a garden fountain flinging its sparkling water upwards into the bright sunshine, until the jet broke and fell in shimmering rainbows. He was one with Britt again and deep in himself he knew that the superhuman ecstasy was shared. As if with his own body he experienced the deep contractions of delight in her belly; through her he could feel the strength and firmness of his own gushing penis, as if she were the man and he the woman.

The ecstasy remained, not fading in seconds as in ordinary human copulation. Time had stopped, the universe was uncreated.

With a woman Seventh astride him, Shiva and Shakti would have remained coupled, but Jonathan was brought back to earth by the realisation that the light had dimmed in Britt. Her arms slid from his neck and her legs trailed loose. She had fainted from sheer pleasure prolonged beyond her limit of endurance.

He held her by the shoulders while he disengaged their sexual parts, then lowered her gently to the floor backwards. Sitting cross legged between her parted legs, he contemplated her naked body, waiting for her to recover. It would have been a grave mistake to try to rouse her. Her mind had blacked out under the stress of the overload on her nervous system and should not be hurried back to awareness of this world. The deep unconscious wisdom of her body would let her recover in its own good time.

Her wetly open vagina brought into his thoughts a quotation from the Babylonian Talmud: And Bathsheba went in unto the king in his chamber. Rabbi Judah said 'On that occasion Bathsheba dried herself thirteen times.'

The words meant that according to the law of Moses, Bathsheba washed and dried her parts after each orgasm and therefore King David had known her thirteen times that day, an even mightier performance than that required by the full ceremony of the marriage of Shiva and Shakti. With such parents it was no strange thing that their son, Solomon, had maintained a harem of seven hundred wives and three hundred concubines. Or when, after David slept with his fathers and Solomon was king in Israel, he rose up to meet Bathsheba and bowed himself before her and caused her to sit at his right hand.

Britt's long legs twitched and her head rolled to one side. Jonathan got up and stretched, then knelt beside her as her eyelids fluttered open. He stroked her face until she mumbled in Swedish, then picked her up and carried her to the bed and got in with her. She was more fully awake by then. Her mouth found his in a brief kiss. He took her in his arms and she sighed once or twice and slid into deep sleep.

CHAPTER 6
SAUNA AND SIBELIUS

THE THERMOMETER on the pinewood wall of the sauna registered a hundred and six degrees centigrade. Jonathan sat naked on the middle step of the long wooden bench, sweating freely. His host, Tuomo Rantala, leaned forward to throw a dipper of water onto the heated stones. It vaporised instantly into hissing steam.

Tuomo's wife, Lilsa, flicked at her bare shoulders with a birch switch.

'We say in Finland that sauna cures the body and the mind,' she said in good English. 'What do you think, Jonathan?'

'Who am I to argue? I'm much too relaxed to even consider it.'

'That is good. You should take a whisk and beat yourself with it.'

'Later, perhaps.'

He had flown into Helsinki that morning from Stockholm on the last leg of his trip, despatched his company business swiftly and had the rest of the day free. He could have taken an evening flight to London, but it had been a busy week and he felt that he deserved some time off. He telephoned the number he had been given for the Helsinki Lodge and was invited to spend the evening and stay overnight with the Master. A taxi ride took him to the address on the outskirts of the city, an area of lakes and trees. To his surprise, after meeting Tuomo and his wife, he found himself stripped and inside their private sauna.

Tuomo was a small and muscular man of about fifty, round headed and with grey streaks in his black hair. His wife was about the same age, equally dark-haired. The years and child bearing had elongated and flattened her breasts, though she was slender and wiry. The thick bush of hair exposed as she sat with her legs sprawled in the sauna was as black as the hair on her head.

'What have you been doing in Helsinki?' she asked.

'I had a business meeting this morning as soon as I got in from the airport and then lunch with my company's distributor here – Eino Jarvinen – do you know him?'

'Yes,' said Tuomo, 'I have met him. He is well known.'

'Over lunch I gathered that he is an active Christian.'

'Yes, and through that he is involved in some charity work

here. That's how I first met him. He is a good man, in his way.'

'He's a good businessman too. After lunch I went out to see Sibelius's house at Jarvenpaa.'

'Of course,' said Lilsa. 'It is one of our national shrines.'

She used the dipper to pour water over her shoulders. Jonathan watched it course down between her breasts and over her belly until it was lost in the thick fur between her legs. She smiled at his interest.

'Social nudity is part of our sauna culture. You do not have this in England, I think.'

'Not in the same way. Social nudity is practised by nudists and it seems to be getting more popular. I've never understood the point. England is not a very sunny country, so there's no great physical pleasure in it as there is along the Mediterranean coast. English nudists pretend that sexual attraction does not exist, as they have no ritualistic use for their nakedness. They say that their health benefits in some way from nude tennis and nude swimming, but with our climate that is an obvious rationalisation. Displaying their bodies to each other must satisfy some inner need, but I'm not sure what.'

'Many Swedes are enthusiastic for naked sunbathing,' said Lilsa. 'It makes little sense to us in the Order.'

'What do you think of Sibelius's house?' Tuomo asked.

'Naturally I am an admirer of his music – that's why I went. I'm not sure what I expected to find. From the grandeur of his composition I would not have been surprised to discover a huge marble palace with colonnades and statues of gods.'

'Then you were disappointed?'

'No, that would be to fit him into my concept instead of trying to see what he was really like.'

'So how do you see him now?'

'A house which a man has built for himself and lived in for a long time must give some insight into his nature. I began to appreciate how Finnish he was, though his music is international. The pine trees growing up the little hill to the house, close together and dark, and the house itself, not large but massively built of stone and timber. It was less like the work of a man than a natural outcrop from the earth itself. In winter, with thick snow about, he must have been like a bear hibernating in its cave, dreaming its dreams and waiting for the spring.'

Tuomo spread his sweaty body full length on the top step of the sauna.

'When Hans-Martin Frick lived in Sweden,' he said, 'he often came to Finland. He had business here, of course, but he went whenever he could to visit Sibelius. He wanted the old man to write some music for the Order and he would have paid well for it.'

'That would be in the thirties, when Hans-Martin was Master of the old Templar Order in Stockholm, not our Order?'

'Right. But Johan had given up composing by then. He was in his sixties.'

'Why do you call him Johan?'

'Sibelius was christened Johan Julian Christian. Later on he took the French form of his first name and called himself Jean. I don't know why. His last statement in music of his beliefs was *Tapiola*. You know it, of course, since you took the trouble to visit his house.'

'Do you think that he ever wrote the legendary Eighth Symphony?'

'I am sure of it. He spoke of it to several people who visited him before the war, including Hans-Martin Frick, who told me. But he was not pleased with what he had composed and so he had destroyed it.'

'A great loss to those of us who love his music,' said Jonathan.

'I do not think so. A man must be allowed to judge his own work. If it fails to please him, then he has the right not to let others judge it.'

'True, I suppose. Do you use any of the John Ireland music in your Lodge?'

'Not any more. We tried it when it was first sent over from

England, but it was not right for us. Do you use it?'

'Not really. There's a fanfare that's sometimes used, but not often.'

When Frick established the Noble Order in London he had looked around for suitable composers to write original music for the ceremonies. He had commissioned John Ireland to write some pieces, but the attempt had not been successful. Ireland's vision had been channelled for too long into a Christian view for him to break out of it into the larger world of the Order.

'In the end,' said Jonathan, 'we always come back to a handful of composers; Sibelius, Brahms, Bach, Mendelsohn, Wagner, Richard Strauss, Mozart – you could count them on the fingers of two hands.'

'If the Order had been founded in his day, Mozart would have been a member,' said Tuomo. 'He was looking for the way. After he discovered the inadequacy of Catholic Christianity he went to the Freemasons for enlightenment. He learned more from them than they taught him, if you understand what I mean by that.'

Wolfgang Amadeus Mozart, the prodigy of European musical composition, was initiated into the Masonic *Crowned Hope* Lodge in his late twenties, after he had married and settled in Vienna. This aspect of his short life has always been ignored by his admirers, who have always regarded him as a music-writing machine – a man who could compose three different symphonies in his head at the same time and put them down on paper only when he had thought all three right through to the end. But Mozart put his talents to work for his Lodge by composing music for their ceremonies. During his final illness he wrote the *Little Masonic Cantata* for voices and orchestra. The words were by another Mason, Emmanuel Schikaneder, a theatrical impressario.

It was Schikaneder who wrote the words for one of Mozart's best known operas, *The Magic Flute*, often described as a pantomime with superb music by critics who do not understand the symbolism of the action, the human search for unity of the conscious and the unconscious parts of the psyche, the intellect and the emotions. The magic flute which guides the questing hero represents the erect penis, the power of sexuality which enables him to unite the divided parts of his soul.

In spite of his tremendous outpouring of enduring music, Mozart was hard pressed to support himself and his family. For the last ten years of his life he survived by borrowing money from another member of his Masonic Lodge, Michael Puchberg, a banker, who knew well that the money he advanced would never be returned. But Mozart's involvement with the hidden world went back before his initiation into the Crowned Hope Lodge, to the time when he was a child prodigy at the keyboard, touring European capitals with his father and sister to give concerts. In Vienna in 1768 he came to the attention of Dr Franz Mesmer, a fashionable doctor who gave music evenings for his friends in his mansion on the Landstrasse, overlooking the Prater park. Mesmer was already exploring psychiatric therapy nearly two centuries before Dr Sigmund Freud followed the same path in the same city. He commissioned twelve year old Mozart to write a short opera that could be performed in his drawing room and it was greatly admired. So began an acquaintance which lasted many years, during which Mesmer became an adept, going far beyond Freemasonry towards the ultimate reality.

'Mozart looked for the way and found the Masons,' said Jonathan. 'Alexander Scriabin found Theosophy, and out of that came some wonderful music too – his *Fire Poem*, for example.'

'We use that in our First Degree initiations,' said Lilsa, pushing her slack breasts upwards to wipe away the sweat collecting beneath them. 'The ascent from darkness into light is very appropriate.'

'Gustav Holst is also a musician who found the way,' said Tuomo. 'If he had added more to the *Planets* he would have set the whole Tree of Life to music. Had you ever thought that?'

'Often. His family came to England from Sweden, I think.'

'No,' said Tuomo, 'from the eastern shore of the Baltic.

His grandfather emigrated from Riga in Latvia. Riga was owned by the Swedes for nearly a hundred years after they took it from the Poles and before they lost it to the Russians. But it was founded by Germans and it was German for at least three hundred years. Before Holst shortened his name for English ears he was Gustavus Theodor von Holst. The family may have originated in Germany and therefore it is possible that its founder was one of the Teutonic Knights.'

Jonathan knew something of the history of the Order of Teutonic Kights, since it had for a while run parallel with that of the Order of the Knights Templar, to which mighty organisation the Knights of the Temple claimed to trace back their pedigree. Like the Templars, the Teutonic Knights were founded in the Holy Land as a military force to keep open the pilgrim routes to Jerusalem for devout Christians. But whereas the Templars accepted noblemen of all European countries into their ranks, the Teutonic Knights accepted only Germans. Not more than a dozen years after its establishment, the Grandmaster of the Teutonic Order, Hermann von Salza, saw that there was no scope for his Order alongside the Templars and in the campaign of 1210 he and most of his Knights were killed in combat. Twenty years later the Order launched a crusade of its own under a new Master, to conquer the infidels of Eastern Europe, take their lands and christianise them by force. Twenty knights and two hundred foot soldiers fought their way from the German homeland into the plains of East Prussia, at that time inhabited by Slavonic peoples who were non-Christians. The drive to the east lasted generations and in conquering East Prussia and Livonia the Teutonic Knights exterminated most of the population by lance, sword and fire. Behind the military advance, the devastated farms and villages were settled by German farmers and traders. With its success, the Order grew in size by attracting more and more knights from Germany by the prospect of the spoils of war.

The port of Riga on the east coast of the Baltic Sea was founded by a German bishop, Albert von Buxhoevden not long after the Teutonic Order was established in Palestine.

To defend his trading post against the heathen Lettish nation, to whom he intended to bring the blessings of Christianity, the bishop set up a military force called the Knights of the Sword. In its first year the Order had only ten knights but its numbers grew steadily as it built outlying fortresses and started to collect protection money from the local farmers. When the Knights of the Sword heard of the gradual eastwards advance of the Teutonic Knights, they appreciated the territorial and spiritual advantages to be gained by merging their small local Order into the larger one approaching them.

Successive Popes approved and blessed the military exploits of the Teutonic Knights, partly because they were carrying Christianity by fire and sword to the heathens of Eastern Europe and partly because the Order handed over to the Catholic Church one third of all the lands they conquered. While the western arm of the Order was pushing steadily through Livonia towards Riga, the Riga chapter, formerly the Knights of the Sword, were busily stamping out all resistance in the plains about their city to create the principality of Latvia. As in East Prussia, so in Latvia, the Knights held the incontrovertible belief that an enemy defeated and spared could come back to fight another day, while an enemy defeated and killed gave no more trouble. This served them well for two hundred years, until the Poles and the Lithuanians combined against them. At Tannenberg in Poland the Order of Teutonic Knights went down in bloody and final defeat.

'You think that Holst, one of the most English of composers, may have sprung from that stock?' Jonathan asked.

'It is very possible. Did you know that the Order still existed nominally for two hundred years after its defeat? The last Grandmaster was Duke Albert Frederick, who ruled over what was left of the Order's territory in Prussia. He married his daughter Anna to the Elector of Brandenburg and at his death the last of the Order's lands were swallowed up by Brandenburg and the title of Grandmaster died.'

'You are well informed about European history, Tuomo.'

'Mostly the history of the Baltic countries. In Finland we

know that small nations like us are always taken over by bigger nations – Germany, Sweden, Russia. All the lands once held by the Teutonic Knights are now ruled by Russia.'

'If history tells us anything at all, it is that foreign conquest is only rarely final. But we were talking about music, not war. You are the first person I've met who shares my interest in musicians who were also adepts.'

'I am interested because Hans-Martin was interested. You know the work of Erik Satie, I suppose?'

'Yes, he's enjoying something of a revival at present. He was an initiate of the Order of the Catholic Rose Cross in Paris and wrote music for its ceremonies. Do you know Cyril Scott's work?'

'No, is he an English initiate?'

'He was an initiate of something, but I've never discovered what. He died in about 1970. He may have been a member of the Order of the Temple of the Orient. At one time he was hailed as the English Debussy, but his music is not much performed now.'

'An English name I know is Peter Warlock, who died young because he went further into the hidden world than his powers could protect him.'

'He took his own life,' said Jonathan. 'He was a lawyer's son named Philip Heseltine, an ineffectual man incapable of earning a living. He existed on a small monthly allowance from his mother and a few pounds a week he was paid as music critic on a daily newspaper.'

'He discovered the Book of the Sacred Magic of Abramelin,' said Tuomo.

'Yes, he used its knowledge to transform himself from a seven stone weakling into a roistering, brawling, wenching adventurer. He signified the change by re-naming himself Peter Warlock.'

'Was his music from himself, do you think?'

'The potentiality must have been within him all along and he used the Abramelin NAGINAH process to release it. But along with the creative powers, he freed from his own depths destructive forces he was unable to control. He became haunted by visions and terrors. He was in his mid-thirties when he turned on the gas taps in his Chelsea flat and lay down on his bed to die and escape his obsession.'

'I seem to remember reading that he was once married.'

'When he was very young, but it lasted less than a year. When he became Peter Warlock he was able to attract women indiscriminately and bed them insatiably.'

'He made use of an Abramelin Square,' said Tuomo. 'I have sometimes wondered which one he used.'

'There is no record, but I have always assumed that it was the CASED Square.'

'I think so too,' said Tuomo, nodding.

'It is not good to talk of such things here where we are unguarded,' Lilsa complained. 'I shall make the banishing pentagrams if you speak any more of this.'

'Too late,' Jonathan gasped, spreading his thighs and leaning back.

The heat of the sauna, he told himself, or the proximity of Lilsa's naked body. But he knew better.

Lilsa stared at his erect and pulsing penis.

'You formed the Square in your mind and activated it!' she exclaimed.

'By accident, without thinking,' he answered.

She stood up and faced east, her arm raised to begin tracing the five-pointed stars that drove away disturbing influences. Tuomo spoke to her quickly in Finnish and she left what she was doing to squat between Jonathan's parted legs. As she reached out to touch his straining part, he recognised a familiar name in what Tuomo had said. It was from the ancient Egyptian creation myth. The god speaks and says: 'I took my member in my hand, I copulated with my fist, my heart came to me in my hand, I ejaculated into my own shadow . . . .'

Tuomo was suggesting that instead of succumbing to the blind lust he had unwittingly evoked, Jonathan should ascend to a higher spiritual plane by assuming a god form. Lilsa looked up from his throbbing erection to his face waiting for consent.

'Per manus dominae,' said Tuomo to Jonathan, phrasing delicately in Latin the English equivalent of *by the hand of the lady*. Jonathan nodded, and her hot palm slid up and down his fleshy shaft.

The CASED Square he had involuntarily pictured in his mind when answering Tuomo's question about Warlock consists of five words of five letters each, set beneath each other so that they can be read across and down the same. Like a legal contract, it is only words until it is activated, a contract in a court of law, an Abramelin Square in the depths of the unconscious mind, both requiring due formality and process. Mathers, who translated Abramelin's book into English interpreted this particular Square to mean 'the overflowing of unrestrained and devouring lust.' That certainly is its effect when activated. Orgasm does not dissolve its force; the person in its grip is driven on and on by an insatiable frenzy until total physical exhaustion brings about his collapse.

Jonathan blotted out that unpleasant thought by figuring himself as the god Atum, shining in his golden magnificence, creator of all things. Under Lilsa's deft manipulation it was only seconds before he knew himself to be at the point of no return. With massive concentration he prayed aloud as his ejaculation began, speaking in the name of Atum.

'I sent forth issue as Shu... I poured myself out as Tefnut... mankind came into being from the tears which came forth from the eye of my member... there came forth Osiris and Isis from my belly...'

As his body shook with the force of each spasm, he heard the mighty voice of the god speaking in triumph through his mouth. Then it was over and he completed the words in his own voice:

'... and they brought forth their multitudes upon the earth.'

Lilsa wiped his chest and belly with a damp towel and he kissed her long breasts in gratitude before rising to his feet to make the signs of the banishing pentagrams to the four quarters, to impress on himself that the force of the Square had been dispelled. He sat down again and splashed cold water over himself from the dipper in the tub.

'Are you in control again?' Tuomo asked.

'Yes. When I accidentally pictured the Square it was as if I had touched a live electric wire. The current went through me and I couldn't let go.'

'I knew that the pentagrams would be too late from the expression on your face. Your lips were pulled back to show your teeth, like a dog snarling. It seemed to me that the way of Atum was better. Now let us not speak of this any more.'

'You are right. Let's talk of something else.'

'You said before that Sibelius was very Finnish. Yet you cannot know what it means to be Finnish. Do you know anything of our history?'

Jonathan reflected for a moment.

'No, nothing at all.'

'Our country is about the same size as Britain, but there are only five million of us. Three quarters of the land is still covered by forest and only a tenth is cultivated for farming. For six hundred years we were a province of Sweden, with no independence of our own. Then at the beginning of the nineteenth century we became a province of Imperial Russia. We achieved our independence only in 1917 at the time of the Russian revolution, when the Russians were so busy killing their own people that they had no soldiers to spare to keep us under their control. In 1939 they invaded us again. We fought them for six months in the Winter War until their size overwhelmed us. We managed to come to an agreement and stay independent, but since that time we have lived uneasily under the Russian shadow.'

'I've always believed that Sibelius grew up in a time of rising nationalism here,' said Jonathan, 'but I can't see him as a political figure.'

'No, I didn't mean it that way. Just as there was a revival of Celtic culture in Ireland in the late nineteenth century, so there was a new appreciation here of the value of traditional Finnish culture. Yeats, an adept of the Golden Dawn, was important in the upsurge of Irish drama and poetry, Sibelius was important here. When he began to produce music like

Finlandia in his thirties, the people heard this new voice and recognised it as their own. He was only thirty-two years old when the Senate voted him a life pension so that he could give up teaching and concentrate all his energy on composing music – and that was before he had written his First Symphony.'

'An act of astonishing discernment,' said Jonathan. 'Governments very rarely rise to such heights. But he still does not seem to me to be as nationalistic as you suggest.'

'Not nationalistic in a political sense. The old Finnish gods spoke through Sibelius, at a time when everyone thought they had been killed by centuries of Lutheran Christianity. Or if you prefer the modern terms, he expressed the collective unconscious of the Finnish people.'

'I know nothing of the old gods of Finland. Weren't they the same as the old gods of Scandinavia – the Teutonic god forms that Wagner revived in his music, Odin, Thor, Freya?'

'Finns are not the same people as Swedes and Germans. Our language is different, our beliefs are different, our experience of the world is different. You are English and so you are related by blood to the Scandinavians and the Germans. I am a Finn – though that is your name for us, not ours – and I am not related by blood to them.'

'How different were the old gods of this country?'

'Before the coming of Christianity the old Finns knew that everything was alive and had a spirit in it, trees, lakes, animals, fields, crops, everything. And therefore everything which existed was worthy of respect and God was in it. You know what Thales the Greek philosopher said, I am sure.'

'He said that everything is full of gods.'

'He was of another people and another time, but he saw the same truth. When the Finns hunted a bear for food, they buried its bones as carefully as if it had been human, to pay respect to its spirit. Before trees were cut down for building, there was a ceremony to be performed, to honour the trees. When water was drawn from a well, two drops were poured back, to preserve the life and spirit. Sibelius had this knowledge inside himself, that he was a part of all created things, a part of God. This is in his music. Those who hear only the dark forest and shining lakes are not listening hard enough.'

'You believe that he was a natural adept?'

'Without question. I also believe that when Hans-Martin Frick asked him to write music for the old Templar Order, Sibelius saw no point. In his own way he had been writing such music all his life.'

Lilsa glanced at the clock on the wooden wall and interrupted.

'We must go out of the sauna soon. Our other guest will be arriving,' she said.

'Thank heaven there's no snow to roll in,' Jonathan joked. 'That's what you do in the winter, isn't it?'

'When it is practical,' she answered. 'Here we have something else instead.'

The alternative to rolling in the snow proved to be an ice cold shower just outside the sauna. Jonathan watched as first Lilsa and then Tuomo stood under it with no expression of discomfort on their faces. When his turn came, he gritted his teeth and walked stoically under the cold jet. His heated body cooled quickly, leaving him gasping for breath. Lilsa held a large towel out to him and he wrapped himself in it thankfully.

'We will dress and drink cold beer to put back the liquid we have sweated away in the sauna,' said Tuomo. 'Then Eila will be here and we will eat.'

CHAPTER 7
THE EARTHLY TEMPLE

BESIDES HIS visit to Sibelius's house, there was something else that Jonathan had done in Helsinki that afternoon which he had not mentioned to his hosts. After lunch his business contact, Eino Jarvinen, had taken him to see the city's largest department store. Every weekend, Jarvinen explained, train loads and plane loads of Russians arrived to shop for the things they could not buy in their own stores.

'It's much the same in London, only we get Arabs,' said Jonathan, grinning.

'Arabs have more money to spend than Russians,' said Jarvinen, 'but for this store it is good business. And for the hotels and restaurants. Almost every restaurant that has music has Russian music. Everywhere you go – balalaikas and folk songs. Only the young get away from it with their American music in discos.'

After they parted, Jonathan found his way into a large bookshop in the city centre and browsed around. There was a display of prints, one of which caught his eye – a black and white drawing of a woodland scene. Two naked women sat on the ground, one holding a cauldron between her knees from which steam escaped upwards. Behind them an older woman raised her skinny arms skywards and, above the trio, another young and naked woman flew through the air on the back of a goat.

Jonathan recognised the scene and looked for the author's signature. It was on a small square plaque hanging from the branch of a blasted tree, the linked HB which stood for Hans Baldung. The scene was the preparation for a witches' sabbath, as imagined by a sixteenth century artist with no personal knowledge of what witches did or believed. Jonathan knew that Baldung had made a set of three drawings on this theme in about 1514. What he was holding was a modern copy of one of them. He bought it to give to his aunt Judith, who would be amused.

The reason for not mentioning the incident to his Finnish friends was the arms-length relationship between adepts and witches. Neither side had much time for the other. Witchcraft had never completely died out in England or anywhere else in Europe. The church-inspired persecution that began in the Middle Ages and killed uncounted men and women had only driven witchcraft underground and thinned out its adherents. The great revival was brought about by Gerald Gardner in the 1950s, after the repeal of the last Witchcraft Act in England. From this source flowed a stream which had swollen to a cascade and irrigated not only Britain but France, Germany, Scandinavia and, above all, the United States.

However the rites varied from country to country and from century to century, the basis of witchcraft, as Jonathan knew well, was the worship of the male and female powers of generation, incarnated in the Queen of the Coven and the horned god in their ceremonies. The marriage of Shiva and Shakti he had taught to Britt in Stockholm could be used by witch covens, if they knew how to perform it, as a dramatic representation of their beliefs. That being so, there would seem to be little reason for the divide between witches and adepts, yet the rift could be traced back at least to the Renaissance, when the rediscovery of classical learning in fifteenth century Italy re-established the ideals of humanism. For fifteen hundred years the Christian church had insisted that men and women were wicked and sinful from birth – even from conception. The Church ideal was the celibate monk or nun, who renounced the world and the flesh to devote themselves in self-abasement to the worship of their slain and risen god. The much older, pre-Christian view that the world had been created to be enjoyed and that life was a gift of God to be used to the full, was kept alive underground by witches, feared and hated by the Christian establishment.

The unearthing of the art and thought of ancient Greece and Rome created a new ideal – or restored an older one – by forcing a reappraisal of man's worth and potential. There arose the concept of the 'universal man' who appreciated and valued all aspects of his own nature, who dared to explore and experience everything and who strove to excell in as many aspects of life as he could. The new learning was spread across Europe by the invention of the printing press and it created a new intellectual elite. The adepts who emerged – Marsilio Ficino, Pico della Mirandola, Heinrich

Cornelius, von Hohenheim, John Dee, Robert Fludd, and many others – were university educated in a time when the vast majority of people could not read or write their own language. So there came about the division between adepts and witches, though both were journeying along parallel paths into the hidden world.

Gardner gave witchcraft a new impetus but could do nothing to bridge the chasm. After his death in 1964, most of the covens that took their origin from his teaching continued in the old way of faith and ritual and only a very few set themselves to assimilate the learning of adepts into their belief structure. Jonathan had no prejudices about witches, old style or new style. He could readily sympathise with Alex Sanders, a successor to Gardner in Britain, who complained that, 'Aleister Crowley said he was writing to help the grocer, the factory girl, the mathematician and everybody, and then put whole paragraphs of his rituals into classical Greek'. In fact, Crowley had written the most secret parts of his Order of the Temple of the Orient teaching in Latin, not Greek, but the principle was the same.

Jonathan's aunt Judith was a woman of spiritual discernment and fulfilment, though she had no aspirations beyond the witch ceremonies she had learned as a young girl in the English countryside. He intended to have the Baldung print framed when he got home, knowing that she would appreciate the irony.

He was dressed and drinking cold beer with Tuomo and Lilsa in their sitting room when the other guest of the evening arrived, Eila Saarto; a dark haired and strongly built woman of about thirty, broad faced, short necked, big bosomed, wide hipped. Her command of the English language was not nearly as good as that of her hosts, but her manner was lively. Jonathan was sorry she had not been with them earlier in the sauna; her bulk would have offset Lilsa's leanness.

'Eila was a Pilgrim for nearly a year,' said Tuomo by way of introduction. 'She was admitted as a Neophyte in February. I invited her tonight because it will help her to talk to someone as advanced as you.'

'It's good for all of us to meet members from other countries,' said Jonathan. 'It shows us that we are part of a large and international Order, not just a local group.'

Over the meal Lilsa served, Eila chatted away happily, sometimes lapsing into her own language when the strain was too great, then catching herself and struggling back into English. She was, he gathered, part owner of a dress shop in Helsinki.

'I am doing all the talking,' she said eventually, 'but you know so much more than I do. Tell me the things I want to know, please.'

Jonathan smiled at her eagerness.

'What would you like to know?'

'Tell me about the Masters, please.'

'Lodge Masters, you mean, like Tuomo here?'

'No, the Masters of the Temple.'

'On that subject you know as much as I do.'

'I have been told that our Order is guided by Masters we do not ever meet or know,' she said. 'Is that true or false?'

Lilsa spoke in Finnish what was obviously a rebuke.

'Let her ask,' said Jonathan. 'It is good to question things. We are taught many things we have to take on trust until our own experience either proves or disproves them. I've thought often enough about the Masters myself.'

'Tell me what you think, then,' said Eila.

'As you know, the Order is managed by Lodge Masters locally and by the Grandmaster of the Order above them. But as you said, we are taught that it is also guided by other Masters who have crossed the Abyss. Adepts who achieve that crossing and remain sane are called Masters of the Temple and they are beyond our concepts of good and evil because they have attained true enlightenment. The Abyss, as we name it, lies beyond the Seventh Degree.'

'But we do not call them Eighth Degree members, I believe,' she said.

'No, because that would suggest that the Order can teach you how to attain it. But there is no such teaching, nor can there be. Sevenths have to find the way for themselves, if they can. Masters of the Temple are self created.'

'It sounds impossible,' said Eila.

'And perhaps it is. Yet our tradition says that it has been done. Look at it like this – the Order trains each of us to the limits of our individual ability. An army trains its soldiers, yet each soldier must fight his own battle. If he finds it within himself to go beyond what is required of him, he may be honoured and decorated. But no one can teach him to be a hero.'

'These Masters of the Temple were once of the Seventh,' said Eila, 'so they must be known by other people.'

'Except that you have to remember that if anyone crosses the Abyss, he withdraws from all active participation in ceremonies and in the management of the Order and guides it from a distance in ways only he or she knows. They have vanished from the life of the Order – those who knew them assume whatever they like. And in a big and active Lodge, they are soon forgotten. That's all I can tell you because that's all I know about it.'

'Was the founder of the Order a Master?' she asked.

'He was Grandmaster of the Order,' Tuomo answered her, 'but he was not in his lifetime a Master of the Temple as we understand that title. He had much to do in establishing the Order. He made the road for others to walk on.'

'Then how can we know if there are any Masters living now?' Eila persisted.

Tuomo looked at Jonathan. Jonathan grinned.

'We can't know for sure,' he said, 'though it is said that there are seven in the world at present. But that may not be true. The only way to find out is to become one yourself.'

As Eila opened her mouth to ask something else, Tuomo interrupted.

'These are useless questions because we do not know the answers, Eila. While Jonathan is with us you would do better to ask him about things to do with your own Degree, so that he can help you.'

Eila said something in Finnish.

'In English you say *I accept the reproof*,' Tuomo told her.

Jonathan nodded and smiled as she repeated the Order's time honoured words.

'I have been in the Order only a few months,' she said. 'My teacher is working hard to make me understand. Can I ask you one simple thing, Jonathan – why is the Order called the Masters of the Temple?'

Jonathan laughed at her pursuance of the same question in a different form, even after the rebuke. He liked her for it.

'The simple answer is that we trace our line back to the Order of the Knights Templar, who named themselves after the Temple of King Solomon. But if you want an answer that will bring you enlightenment, then I must first ask the Master of your Lodge for permission. It's not a matter of answering you with a few words of explanation, you see. The answer to your question is a whole learning experience, which should come from your appointed teacher.'

'If you wish to teach Eila this thing,' said Tuomo, 'then as Master of the Lodge of Helsinki I say that you may do so.'

'Thank you. What's your teacher's name, Eila?'

'Matti.'

'When you next meet him, you must tell him about this evening so that he can ask you questions to make sure that you have properly understood.'

Tuomo spoke in Finnish to Eila and to Lilsa and then in English to Jonathan.

'Lilsa is going to prepare the robes and the chapel. I have told Eila that normally she and Matti would be alone for this lesson, but that Lilsa and I will be present in case she has difficulties with the English words.'

'That sounds very sensible.'

The private chapel in Tuomo's house was on the ground floor, at the back. Outside its unpainted pinewood door, Lilsa handed robes of deep blue to Tuomo and Eila and kept one of the same colour for herself. To Jonathan she gave a white robe to indicate his status of preceptor in the ceremony.

The four of them stripped naked and threw their clothes over a wooden chair. Lilsa's lean body was familiar enough to Jonathan after their time in the sauna. In respect he touched the tips of his fingers to his lips and then lightly to the dark nipples of her slack breasts, and she smiled at him. Meanwhile, Eila had untied the belt of her orange dress and pulled it over her head to stand before them displaying a white cotton brassiere encasing her fat round breasts and white cotton briefs stretched across her broad hips. They too came off and she pulled the dark blue robe over her head, hiding her solidly fleshed body from sight.

'Since Eila is of the First Degree,' said Tuomo, 'I will perform the opening so that it is within her understanding. Then I will hand over to Jonathan. If there are language difficulties, Lilsa will translate. When Jonathan has finished, I will take over once more.'

He was neither suggesting nor asking. As Lodge Master he was telling them how it was to be. He led the way through the unpainted door into his private chapel. Its floor was of clear-shining unpolished pine, its ceiling was painted dark blue and spangled with tiny golden stars. But where the walls of Jonathan's own chapel at home were covered with symbolic pictures, Tuomo's walls were adorned from floor to ceiling and from corner to corner with huge colour photographs of a pine forest. To stand in the room was to receive the impression of being in a small clearing in a northern forest by night.

In the centre of the room stood a double cube altar and round it a circle painted on the floor. Within the circle glowed the six-pointed star. On the altar and at the cardinal points of the circle Lilsa had already set and lit tall beeswax candles. Tuomo closed the door and switched off the electric lights.

When all four were grouped around the altar, Tuomo took a sword and traced its tip round the circle that contained them, speaking commandingly in his own language. Without knowing a word of Finnish, Jonathan understood what he was saying and in his own mind repeated the consecration with him, willing the circle to be a boundary between the world of men and the realms of the gods. Then, with masterful flourishes of the sword, Tuomo described the banishing pentagrams to the four quarters, the sacred sign dispelling any unwanted influences that lurked either in the room or within their own minds. He returned the blade to the altar and positioned himself just inside the circle at the eastern station, facing outwards. Automatically Jonathan took the western station, while Lilsa steered Eila to the southern one and then placed herself at the north. For a while they stood in silence, back to back, spaced around the consecrated circle. In the candlelit chapel, Jonathan felt that the images of trees on the wall in front of him were taking on solidity and depth and that he was indeed in a forest clearing. He let the feeling permeate him, enjoying its unfamiliarity. Tuomo had constructed a chapel of nature, very different from Jonathan's own private chapel, but undeniably effective in emptying the mind of petty considerations and preparing it for what was to come.

Tuomo spoke clearly and confidently, using English.

'Lord of the Watchtowers of the East, I summon you to witness this ceremony and to guard our circle.'

After a pause and a whispered prompt from Lilsa, Eila spoke in English, but with some difficulty.

'Lord of the Watchtowers of the South . . . I summon you to witness this ceremony . . . and to guard the circle.'

'The words are correct,' said Tuomo, 'but there is no force in them and no virtue. Speak in your own language, Eila, and use your inner vision to make the Lord of the South appear before you. You will see him taller than a mountain, making the trees at his feet seem tiny. He will wear a robe of scarlet and in his hand he will hold a sword. His face I cannot describe – you must see it for yourself.'

Eila tried again in her own language, her voice louder and bolder.

'It is good,' said Tuomo.

It was Jonathan's turn. He intoned the words to summon the Lord of the West, keeping carefully to the level of wording which Tuomo had judged suitable for Eila's understanding. He visualised the Lord as a giant figure in a blue robe, standing near a waterfall the size of Niagara and dwarfing it. The candles fluttered for a moment, as if a breath of wind had rustled through the forest about them. Lilsa summoned the

Northern Lord in her own language, completing the circle.

'The Guardians have heard us and are present,' said Tuomo, with complete conviction. 'You may proceed with the mystery of the name, Jonathan.'

Jonathan went to the altar, where Tuomo helped him lift the heavy double cube of wood and move it to the eastern side of the circle, so freeing the centre for use. When Tuomo was back in his eastern station, alongside the altar and facing inwards, wrists crossed on his chest, Lilsa took Eila gently by the hand and led her to Jonathan in the middle of the circle.

A good many years had passed since Jonathan had been a Second Degree member with a First Degree pupil to teach this lesson to. He himself had originally learned it from his own first teacher in the Order, fair haired Dorothy Mawson, ten years his senior, in a room in her apartment in West London. She had fitted the words and actions to herself as a woman teacher with a male pupil; Jonathan had adjusted them to the reverse roles when it was his turn to pass on the lesson to a woman. It was all still in his head because of the impression it had made on him at the time, as it was intended to.

He spoke formally, making his voice carry through the chapel.

'Eila, Lady of the Most Noble Order of the Masters of the Temple, ask and it shall be answered. What is the question you put to me in the world outside this holy circle?'

The music from the hidden tape recorder which Tuomo had activated surprised Jonathan at first. It was Maurice Ravel's *Pavane*, slow and stately. On reflection he approved, though it would not have been his own choice.

Eila wet her lips with the tip of her tongue before speaking, making him wonder whether she was too nervous to understand him later on. But Lilsa was only a short step behind her shoulder, ready to translate if it became necessary.

'Why are we called the Masters of the Temple? What Temple are we Masters of?'

'We are the Masters of many Temples, according to our level of understanding. As a Neophyte of the Order, the meaning for you is that your body is the Temple and you must become Master of it. Later on, in higher Degrees, other meanings will be revealed to you. And when at last, in this life or after it, you cross the Abyss that lies beyond the Seventh, the universe itself will be the Temple and you will be Master of it.'

He paused to let her absorb his words and the ceremonial music filled the silence gently.

'A temple is a place of worship,' said Eila. 'How is my body a temple?'

'Not just a temple, but *the* Temple,' he answered, and waited while Lilsa translated the words quietly. When he was sure that Eila had understood, he gestured to her to take off her robe.

She pulled the loose blue garment over her head and handed it to Lilsa. Jonathan put his hands on her shoulders and placed her exactly on the small five-pointed star painted on the floor that marked the precise centre of the circle, now revealed by the moving of the altar.

In the soft candle light he studied her from head to foot. Naked, she was not plump but large and strongly built. Her round head sat on a short neck and that on square shoulders. Her width of shoulder was balanced by the solid weight of her breasts and again by the breadth of her belly and hips, all in proportion to the muscular columns of her thighs and legs.

Unbidden, Lilsa handed him a small bowl of clear oil from the altar. He dipped his fingers into it and anointed Eila on the forehead, the insides of her wrists, between her breasts, and then, reaching round her, the base of her spine between the meaty flare of her buttocks. He rubbed the oil well in at each point. Its base was oil of almond, he knew from preparing it himself many times in the past, but in it were small amounts of tincture of wild celery, poplar, nightshade and wolf's-bane. Absorbed through the skin, it would produce a pleasant languor that would make Eila receptive to his words.

'As a Neophyte you know the significance of the five-pointed star in your Degree. We say figuratively that we are made of five elements, and for you that is the meaning of the star. We are made of earth, air, fire, water and spirit.'

He waited while Lilsa repeated his words in Finnish. When that was done, he took Eila's hands and guided her down to the pine wood floor, placing her with her head to the west, her feet to the east and the small star on the floor immediately beneath the parting of her thighs. Then, handling her with reverence, he stretched out her arms to the level of her shoulders and separated her legs widely, so that she was a larger version of the small star beneath her and a smaller version of the bigger star within which she lay.

'The pentagram flames about you,' he said. 'This is the sign of God in man.'

He knelt to kiss her on the forehead, the right knee, the left shoulder, the right shoulder, the left knee and back to her forehead, so that he had traced on her body in an unbroken line the symbol of the star.'

'Neophyte of the Most Noble Order, Lady Eila, your body is the Temple and your spirit, which is the spirit of God, inhabits it, as signified by this pentagram which I have sealed on you with my lips.'

Lilsa was kneeling behind Eila's head, close, but not touching her. She murmured Jonathan's words in Finnish. Eila's dark brown eyes were intent on Jonathan's face as she listened and took in what he said.

Tuomo spoke from the altar behind Jonathan.

'If you do not make yourself equal to a god, how shall you apprehend God, for like is apprehended by like.'

While the words were being spoken, Jonathan knelt between Eila's spread thighs. The touch of her skin by his mouth and the sight of her naked body, arms and legs stretched wide so that the lips between her thighs were pulled open within the dark bush of her pubic hair, had made him erect and ready under his white robe. He spoke again, his voice confident and joyful. The form of words was from a scroll written in Egypt two thousand years ago.

'Eila – open your eyes and you will see that the way has been opened and the world of the gods lies within you.

Rejoice in this vision, draw the divine essence into yourself and fix your eyes on the great light.'

He paused while Lilsa translated rapidly in a hushed voice.

'When you are ready,' he continued, 'say *Approach, lord*, and with these words the light will shine upon you. As you gaze into it you will see a god, young and well formed. His hair will be like the sun and his tunic as white as snow.'

In time with his words, Jonathan rose slowly to his full height, his red hair gleaming in the candle light.

'I see him!' Eila breathed, staring up at him. 'Approach, lord, approach!'

Ceremoniously he stretched his arms over her and blessed in forceful words.

'*Tibi sunt regnum et potentis et gloria per aeonas.*'

In English the words meant: yours are the kingdom and the power and the glory forever. This ancient formula was tacked on to the end of the prayer which Jesus taught his disciples by whoever wrote Matthew's gospel. As Lilsa whispered the words in Finnish, he sank slowly to his knees again and hitched up his white robe to his navel to display his hard standing part. As Eila stared in fascination at it, he said:

'From the east the god approaches you, even as the sun shows himself to us each morning.'

'*Approach, lord*,' Eila repeated, her voice almost a sob.

'On earth my kingdom is eternity of desire,' said Jonathan, speaking in the person of the god. 'My wish incarnates in the belief and becomes flesh, for I am the living truth.'

He lay forward and covered her, hearing her gasp as he slid easily into her. The music faded out and seven solemn chimes sounded as Tuomo struck the bell on the altar to signify that a god was present. Lilsa held out her arms towards the east and announced:

'The god has entered his temple.'

Eila lay unmoving beneath Jonathan as he rode her slowly and ponderously, but her sighs told him that she was losing herself in pleasurable sensation. In his experience, big bodied women needed longer, in general, to reach the topmost peak of erotic delight and so he measured his pace by hers. Her broad belly was a soft mattress under him, her breasts cushions under his chest, her warm depths receptive to his thrusting. As the sexual act continued, Eila was no longer apart from him; he felt her mounting excitement within himself.

That she had a great capacity for sensuality he had no doubt, otherwise she would not have been invited to join the Order. But she was still only a Neophyte and unawakened to the uses to which sexuality could be put. She had to be aroused from the purely carnal sensations that were overwhelming her so that the physical experience could be raised to a higher level. If a ceremony were performed without any awareness of its meaning, then its metaphysical quality would not be activated.

He took her head between his hands and made her look into his face as he spoke to her. Her mouth was wide open, her sighs were loud and continuous.

'Praise to the god in his temple,' he gasped out, thrusting harder into her.

'Praise him in his power,
Praise him for his mighty acts,
Praise him for his excellent greatness . . .'

Eila's eyes opened wide in amazement and she shrieked loudly as the orgasm took her. At once Jonathan relaxed his will and poured out his offering in the temple of her big body. Through his spasms he heard the altar bell chime seven times again and, as he and she grew calmer, he heard Tuomo reciting the words of benediction.

CHAPTER 8
TIME BOMB TICKING

ON THE Monday after his weekend return from Finland, Jonathan was early into the office to get the report of his sales trip onto tape from his notes. His intention was to have the report typed as soon as his secretary arrived at nine. From past experience he was sure that Derek Braithwaite would be shouting for the report the moment he reached the office. So Jonathan put a message on the still unoccupied desk of Braithwaite's secretary to the effect that the report was being prepared and would be available by ten o'clock. What he expected to happen was that Braithwaite would try to get at him before the report was ready. By keeping it short, he was pretty certain of having it on paper long before ten, so that he would be able to take it with him when he was sent for.

To his surprise, no message came from Braithwaite's office. When the report was ready, Jonathan read through the top copy meticulously for possible mistakes, found none, and walked down the corridor with it. Nancy Tait was on the telephone in Braithwaite's outer office. She glanced at him for a moment and went on talking quickly while he waited.

It was in Jonathan's mind, watching her, that no one could accuse Braithwaite of hiring an attractive secretary. Like everything else about him, she was more functional than decorative, though she could hardly be out of her twenties yet. She was a small woman, not much over five feet tall, slender to the point of being skinny. Whatever bosom she may have had was lost under a loose fitting, mud coloured dress. Her hair was middle brown, parted centrally, coiled tightly round her head and held in place with pins. Physically she presented a mousy impression, though seen in profile there was a set to her mouth and jaw that hinted at determination.

When she put the telephone down, Jonathan gave her a copy of his report and asked her to let Braithwaite know that he was ready to discuss it with him whenever it was convenient.

'I'll have to let you know,' she said bleakly. 'He's far too busy now to even look at it.'

'Something up? I'm a week out of touch.'

'There's a problem come up over his American trip. The Chicago distributor has let us down badly.'

'Chicago – I've met him. Dave Arnison, the fat man with the Mexican bandit moustache.'

'That's him. He was over here about six months ago.'

'What's he done – sent a consignment back? We can always re-route it to the Middle East. The expatriates out there will eat anything with a British label on it.'

'It's no joking matter, Mr Rawlings. There was a letter in this morning from Chicago saying that the Arnison business has gone bankrupt. We've lost a big distributor and there's a lot of money owing to us that we may never get now. Mr Braithwaite is furious about it. He can't talk to anyone in Chicago yet because of the time difference, but he's been busy ever since he came in this morning talking to our lawyers and having figures worked out.'

'Then he won't have time for me. Well, I've got plenty to do. I'll be around when he wants to talk about Scandinavia.'

Nancy looked at him doubtfully.

'You'll be in the building, will you?' she asked. 'You know what he's like if people aren't available when he wants to see them.'

'I'll be in the building all day, except at lunch time. Tomorrow's another story. I'm going to the Swindon factory to talk about a possible new style of Christmas packaging for Sweden.'

'I'll let him know that you'll be out of London tomorrow.'

Jonathan went back to his own office. One of the difficulties of working with Braithwaite was that he tended to overreact. For him, every problem became a crisis. In Jonathan's opinion, that was a sign that Braithwaite was played out. Apart from that, if it was true that Arnison owed Dovedays a lot of money, then Braithwaite hadn't been making sure that the account was kept right up to date. That seemed out of character – Braithwaite's attention to detail was notorious. He must be slipping. His health had not been good over the past year or two – during his climb up through the company he had given himself a stomach ulcer which might be getting worse.

Jonathan shrugged the thought away and telephoned the company's factory at Swindon to arrange a meeting there the next day with the local manager. Before getting too far involved with the suggested Christmas special for Bohman in Sweden, he wanted some hard figures to work with. The factory costing was one item in the equation. Then there was the profit the company expected to make, which depended on the bulk price to Bohman after discount, and that related to Bohman's judgment on what the retail price in the Stockholm shops should be. It might turn into an interesting project. If the figures looked right and Bohman went ahead with the order, Jonathan would be able to offer the same basic package to Christensen in Copenhagen, which would extend the production run and improve the profit margin. On the other hand, when the figures were worked out, there might not be enough in it to justify going ahead at all.

The day passed quickly and productively for Jonathan, broken only by a quick lunch with a friend in the shipping business in a nearby restaurant. Five o'clock came and went, the building started to empty out and Jonathan carried on at his desk, jotting down possible quantities to discuss the next day at Swindon. Sometime after five-thirty Nancy Tait put her head round his door. She looked harassed.

'You're still here? I thought you'd be gone by now,' she said.

Jonathan gave her a meaningless smile.

'He's waiting to see you now,' said Nancy. 'Don't keep him too long – he's had a bad day.'

She had her coat over her arm. Jonathan watched her walk jerkily along the corridor towards the lifts and felt mildly sorry for her. If Braithwaite's day had been bad, hers would have been worse.

He found Braithwaite with his jacket off and shirt sleeves rolled up, lying back in his swivel chair with his feet up on his desk. He gave the appearance of reading the Scandinavian report and ignored Jonathan's entrance. Well used to these tactics, Jonathan sat down and waited calmly. After some minutes Braithwaite grunted and threw the stapled pages casually on to his desk so that they slid across the polished top and fluttered to the floor. Jonathan let them lie for a few seconds, then picked the document up and put it back on the desk.

'That's all you've got to report, is it?' Braithwaite began.

'That's the essence of it, boiled down for you.'

'You spend a week of the firm's time and God knows how much of its money flitting round Scandinavia and I get three pages to cover it. Is that right?'

Braithwaite's hostility was so predictable and so inappropriate that Jonathan almost laughed.

'The figures in those three pages add up to an extra hundred thousand pounds of business this year on top of what we expected to do in Scandinavia,' he said in a matter-of-fact tone. 'I could have given you the figures on half a page or I could have written a detailed account of my movements in ten pages. Three pages seemed to cover it adequately.'

Braithwaite looked at him stonily over the top of his heavy, black framed spectacles.

'Don't talk to me about a hundred thousand pounds of business. Figures on paper aren't sales, not by a long chalk. We haven't made a sale until the goods are shipped and paid for. I thought even you knew that much.'

'We have firm commitments from our distributors to meet the targets we set for them. That may not be the same as actual sales, but it's as much as we ever get from anyone at this stage.'

'They can commit themselves to hell and back, for all I care,' said Braithwaite. 'The only piece of paper worth a light is an order with a signature on it.'

As Jonathan had expected, the meeting with Braithwaite was not going to be a discussion between business colleagues but a pointless wrangle between incompatible personalities. He composed himself for it, as he had many times before.

Over the years, Braithwaite's bully boy approach to his work had built up the company's overseas sales from very little to about a quarter of its total business. With a record like that, his position was virtually unassailable and he was highly rewarded by the company. He produced results and profits and the only problem from the board room viewpoint was the question of who would eventually succeed him. In a few years' time when he reached the company's mandatory retirement age for directors, a thoroughly experienced successor would be needed. Even earlier, if his health deteriorated. That was the role for which Jonathan had been tacitly cast when he joined Dovedays. The difference in operating style between Braithwaite and himself indicated that Braithwaite's fellow directors were aware of their colleague's limitations and wanted a change in due course. But five years with Braithwaite had brought Jonathan to the point where he was almost ready to throw in his hand and go elsewhere. The prize might be a big one, but the course was destructive.

As Jonathan saw it, the unflagging drive in Braithwaite which had been the basis of his success was very largely disguised resentment. In his heart Braithwaite hated the world. That meant that he secretly hated himself. Why that should be so was beyond Jonathan's insight, but the outcome was something he was trying to cope with daily. Years of seething resentment had not merely ulcerated Braithwaite's stomach, it had destroyed him as a human being. His entire personality was as corroded as his stomach and he was incapable of any sort of constructive relationship with another human being – friendship, respect, affection, regard.

Jonathan looked at him closely. Braithwaite was obviously not well. His face was pale and his forehead was beaded with sweat.

'The Scandinavian trip is all wrapped up,' Jonathan said reasonably. 'The signed orders will arrive in the mail after we confirm prices in writing. You've had a hard day and you look tired. Why don't we call it a day and go home?'

Braithwaite's feet came off the desk and thumped down on the floor.

'I'll go when it suits me. And you'll go when I tell you to,' he snapped. 'What's your hurry – is tonight your Lodge night?'

'What do you mean?' Jonathan asked in surprise.

'You needn't try to fool me. I've seen you more than once slipping out of the building with your little black attaché case.'

The implications of what Braithwaite was saying sent Jonathan's thoughts racing. What could such a man possibly know about the Noble Order?

'It's all a lot of damned nonsense,' Braithwaite went on. 'You're like a gang of schoolboys playing at secret societies with your trouser legs rolled up. You needn't look surprised – I've read about what Freemasons get up to in their little aprons. It's rubbish for weak minds.'

Inwardly Jonathan sighed in relief. It would suit him well enough to have Braithwaite believe that he was a Freemason.

'You've read a journalist's account of what he thinks Masons believe and do,' he said mildly, 'but I'm certain that you've never heard the truth from a Mason himself.'

'All right then, you tell me what antics you get up to!'

'If you've read about Masonry, you must know that no Mason ever talks about it to outsiders. There's no point in asking.'

Braithwaite leaned forward, arms on his desk, glowering, thick bodied, heavy, bad tempered, an old bull about to charge.

'Do you really suppose that I can be bothered with your stupid little secrets? I just wanted to hear from you that you're one of them, that's all. You've told me what I was waiting for.'

'I can't see what difference it makes to you whether I am or not.'

'I'll tell you what difference it makes. I never wanted you here in the first place. You're a bloody know-it-all. You weren't my choice for the job and I don't mind telling you that straight to your face. When I interviewed applicants for the job you got, I put you at the bottom of the list. Got me? Right at the bloody bottom, with *useless* written by your name.'

'I fail to see why you offered me the job if you felt like that.'

'You fail to see, do you? That's the right word for you – *fail*. You're a born failure.'

'If that were even part way true, you'd have fired me years ago. The fact is that I've succeeded with every assignment you've ever allowed me to handle – and succeeded far above expectation.'

'You needn't play games with me. You know why you got the job and I know. It was fixed in advance. Somebody pulled strings and I was landed with you. What interests me is finding out who's your Mason pal among the directors. Is it the managing director? No, he wouldn't be such a fool. Is it Maclaren? Come on, tell me.'

Jonathan sat in thought, hardly listening. He knew that the Order had used its influence to help him into his present job, but how it had been done was as unknown to him as to Braithwaite. No director of Dovedays and no other employee besides himself was a member of the Order. Yet somewhere there was a link. And there must also be a reason.

'It doesn't matter a damn,' Braithwaite went on when he saw that Jonathan was not going to answer his question, 'and I'll tell you why. I'm going to have you out of here. You can make it easy on yourself by resigning. Or you can do it the hard way. It makes no difference to me. Only bear in mind that when I say the hard way I don't just mean sacking you. That would give you a chance to go snivelling to your Masonic brother on the board, wouldn't it? No, it won't be like that. You're going to come such a cropper that nobody will be able to save your neck. You'll be kicked out of here in disgrace and nobody's going to want you after that. You'll end up sweeping the streets for a living.'

To Jonathan's perceptive eye the aura about Braithwaite had become almost visible. The energy emanation emitted by his nervous system under strong emotion had intensified to the point where it could have been photographed by the Kirlian method. It pulsed dully about the man like a personal atmosphere, brownish in colour, shot through with sooty black whorls and jags of dark red. Hastily Jonathan recited words under his breath to protect himself against the almost visible hatred.

'Then shall the righteous man stand in great boldness before the face of such as have afflicted him and make no account of his labours . . . the hope of the unrighteous man is like dust that is blown away with the wind, like a thin froth that is driven away with the storm, like as the smoke which is dispersed with a tempest and passeth away . . . but the righteous man shall live for evermore; his reward also is with God and the care of him is with the highest. Therefore shall he be made Master of the Kingdom, and the Crown shall be his.'

Fortified, he looked calmly at Braithwaite.

'Are you presenting me with an ultimatum?'

'By God, I am! And don't imagine that I don't mean it. I've got my finger on everything that goes on in this department and I know how to make things happen. Something very special is being set up for you. You're going to be caught out red handed in something so bad that you'll be lucky to escape going to prison, that I promise you.'

Jonathan stood up.

'I'll leave you to your plans,' he said. 'I've no intention of resigning.'

'You'll regret it!' Braithwaite bawled after him as he left the office.

If only I'd had a tape recorder with me, Jonathan thought as he made his way out of the empty building.

Driving home through the evening rush hour traffic he gave some serious thought to his position. Braithwaite had made it finally clear that there was no room for both of them – not that he had been in much doubt before. On Jonathan's side there was more involved than personal pride. Whatever subtle pressure had been exerted to put him into his job, he was good at it. And more than that, he had been put there by the Order for reasons of its own. That made the decision to stay or to leave a matter of more importance than the mere earning of a good living.

Jonathan was utterly certain that his assessment of the present and future development of Dovedays' overseas sales were both more ambitious and more realistic than Braithwaite's. He was convinced that he could without too much difficulty restructure the department and its operating methods so as to double sales in less than five years. For some considerable time he had been privately working on a plan to do just that. It was in his briefcase wherever he went, bound in a neat grey folder, his sales projections, rationalisation plans of systems, costings, promotional budgets, factory production, warehousing and shipping schedules – all pointing to a satisfactorily rising profit curve. He knew better than to offer his plan to Braithwaite, who would throw it unread into the nearest waste bin and tell him to stop misusing his time.

Although Jonathan had told Braithwaite that he had no intention of resigning, the issue was by no means as clear cut in his heart. In the last few years he had come close to walking out more than once. To find another job would remove a great deal of sheer stupid unpleasantness from his working life. He remembered Thornton, who had tipped a glass of wine down Braithwaite's trousers to make a point as he left the company. That was a childish way of scoring, but to Thornton there were few alternatives.

It was not enough to make Braithwaite look ridiculous. If Jonathan went, he wanted his leave taking to be accompanied by a loud enough bang to rattle Braithwaite in his seat. Though at bottom he did not want to leave. The prize was there for the taking – Braithwaite's job and a directorship of the company. But now it was no longer a matter of doing his job well and sitting Braithwaite out. The threat to discredit him had sounded all too real. What had been a war of attrition looked like turning into a blitzkrieg. With complete access to all the records and documentation of the department, it should not be beyond Braithwaite to falsify figures to make it look as if Jonathan had been on the make.

Once again Jonathan's thoughts came back to the point that the Order must have had good reason to help him into Dovedays in the first place. The reason might be no more than part of a long term plan to get members into positions of influence and power in business and the professions – that was an accepted part of its earthly considerations. There might be more to it than that. But there was no way of finding out. Such things were privy to the Elders of a Lodge and never discussed or divulged.

There was only one answer Jonathan could see. Braithwaite must be dealt with quickly.

CHAPTER 9
THE BOTTOMLESS PIT

IN CHISWICK, on the western outskirts of London, Jonathan parked his car in the driveway of his house and went in. It was a detached house in its own gardens, much too big for a man living alone, by ordinary standards. He had bought it ten years before when it was relatively cheap, partly as an investment and partly because it gave him the privacy he wanted to pursue his interests and to entertain as he wished. As an investment, its market value had quadrupled; as a base for his private interests it had proved ideal.

He dumped his briefcase in the hallway and went straight upstairs to shower away the distracting feelings of hostility clinging about him after his confrontation with Braithwaite. The house was neat and clean. The woman who came in daily to tidy it had washed the dishes, made the bed, plumped up cushions, dusted and vacuumed. All that he knew without checking. It was part of his routine of bachelor domesticity.

When he felt purified in mind as well as clean of body, he

turned off the hot water and dried himself. Instead of dressing again, he went to his private chapel wrapped in a bath towel. Members of the Order established in their homes suitable places for personal spiritual exercises and for ceremonial workings. Jonathan had devoted one of his upstairs rooms to this purpose. The door was kept securely locked and he cleaned the chapel himself. He was sure that the daily woman wondered what he kept hidden in there and tried to look through the keyhole whenever her curiosity got the better of her. But the keyhole was covered on the inside and the windows were permanently and heavily curtained.

The room was pitch dark as he unlocked and opened the door. The touch of a switch turned on small concealed spotlights and transformed the room into a place of glowing colour. From floor to ceiling the walls were covered by murals, the uncovered wooden floor was painted grass green and the ceiling was of midnight blue, spangled with small gold stars.

From a wardrobe just inside the door Jonathan took a loose robe of sky blue silk and put it on, tying it around his waist with a golden cord. He sat cross legged on the floor, hands resting lightly on his knees, and composed himself for meditation. On the wall he was facing there was painted a life size picture of a naked man, viewed frontally. His feet were wide apart and his arms reached out sideways so that he fitted into the silver outline of a five-pointed star. The points of the star touched the sides of a green square enclosing it and, around the square, touching its four corners, there was a circle in celestial blue, its circumference brushing the ceiling and the floor.

To anyone with a passing acquaintance with the art of Renaissance Italy and, through that, of classical Greek thinking, the painting on the wall pronounced silently the assertion that man is the measure of all things. To an adept, it carried an even mightier significance than that. Jonathan sat comfortably relaxed, letting the meaning of the image fill his conscious mind and slowly permeate through to his unconscious, where it would bring about the desired effect.

The star encompassing the man on the wall symbolised the five elements of which he was made and of which he claimed command; earth, water, air, fire and spirit. The green square about the star represented the world and all material creation. The blue circle around the square was an emblem of perfection and infinity and therefore of God.

At the exact centre of the circle, square and star lay the carefully delineated genitals of the man, his penis erect and ready. The whole picture identified man with the universe and its source and established the dynamism of sexuality as the centre of all, the unity of the generative force in man, nature and God.

The painting was the work of a very skilled artist, a Fifth Degree member of the Order who understood its symbolism. The well muscled body depicted was solid and lucent, the calmly triumphant face staring down from the wall was Jonathan's own. By putting this sacred glyph on one wall of his private chapel, Jonathan was stating his own mastery of the elements and of nature and his unity with their originator. Only an adept as advanced as he would dare make this claim.

When the picture had done its work and his mind was clear, he got up and went to the altar in the centre of the room. It was in the shape of a cube upon a cube, its top level with his navel. It was built of wood and brightly painted on the top and all sides. On the top was shown the Macrocosm of Vitruvius, the naked man in the star, with concentric circles in the colours of the four primary elements – yellow for earth, grey for water, blue for air and red for fire. On each of the sides of the altar were painted one of the four Tablets of the Watchtowers of the Universe in Dr John Dee's system. That of the east was a square subdivided into 156 smaller squares, each containing its appropriate hieroglyph. The other Tablets were equally complex, each in its appropriate colour.

Above each Tablet was drawn the sigil of the elemental King it represented and, in the Enochian language, these were TAHAOELOJ, THAHEBYOBEETAN, THAHAOTAHE and OHOOHAATAN. As is customary in Dr Dee's system, the words are reversed so that the adept does not accidentally summon the elemental force they name by pronouncing them or even forming them in his mind when he looks at his altar. When they are really required, the adept reads them off backwards and pronounces them.

The magnificent altar stood in the centre of a six-pointed star painted on the floor in gold, for Jonathan had passed beyond the use of the five-pointed star he had seen in use in Tuomo's own chapel in Helsinki. The star was contained within a silver circle, which its points touched.

Jonathan knew himself to be at a turning point in his life. He wanted to know what influences were at work on him and about him. To this end he took from within the hollow altar the Book of Changes and a bundle of yarrow stalks. This system of divination had been used by the Chinese for four thousand years and Jonathan had found on many occasions that it gave him a valuable insight into himself. He lit charcoal in a small censer standing on the altar and sprinkled sweet smelling incense onto it, then took the yarrow stalks and went slowly through the lengthy and complicated procedure that led him at last to the sign *Wei Chi*. He knew it at once – its components were fire above and water below, not the best of all combinations. He leafed through the Book of Changes until he found the sign and the commentary on it – a young fox crossing a stream gets its tail wet.

The application to himself was obvious. He was the young fox. Braithwaite's menacing attitude was the stream. He could only get across at some cost to himself. As always, the Book was gently suggesting caution. It might be better not to attempt the crossing. He could pull back, resign his job, get away from Braithwaite forever. Yet the suggestion was also there that he could cross the dark stream if he were prepared to pay the price – get his tail wet.

He put away the I Ching and brought out his Tarot cards. Divination by these has always been misunderstood by the uninitiated, who believe that the chance arrangement of cards can reveal the future. Reading the future is manifestly impossible, the future not yet being determined. The Tarot cards are a method by which the intuition of the adept can be aroused and brought into action, to see into the roots of things and to better understand his own secret motives, fears and hopes. This insight can be used as the basis for future action which will not be self defeating by opposing conscious wish to unconscious resistance.

There are many ways of using the Tarot cards. One method uses the entire pack of seventy-eight cards, another reduces it to fifty-six cards arranged on the table in three crescents. Another makes use of fifty-four cards, spread in a crossed arrow pattern. Yet another discards all but twenty-one cards, and another uses only ten cards in a spiral pattern. All methods were taught to members of the Order and were used in accordance with whatever degree of detail was required in the reading.

The method which was particularly the Order's own had as its objective the clearing away of all ambiguity and all danger of misreadings through overstraining the intuitive faculty to comprehend the relationships between too many cards. This was the method Jonathan chose.

Keeping clear images of Braithwaite and himself in his mind, he shuffled the pack three separate times and followed the prescribed procedure of dealing the pack into three stacks and then dealing the stack on the left into new stacks until he had reduced the pack to seven cards. According to the Order's tradition, the seven cards in his hand portrayed the distilled essence of the influences at work on him at that time. If he could understand their message properly, his right course of action would be apparent to him. In this, he was using the Tarot in the same way that he had consulted the Book of Changes. He fully expected the message to be the same, though the Tarot would be less condensed than the Chinese.

He put the top card on his altar and dealt the others round it in the form of a six-pointed star, all face down. He paused for a moment or two to clear his mind before turning up the central card. And as he saw it he smiled in satisfaction, for it was the King of Pentacles. Most evidently it represented himself and was a sign that the reading would be a true one. The card showed a seated king wearing a crown, in his left hand a gold disc inscribed with the five-pointed star and in his right hand a golden sceptre.

He turned up the first star point card; the Queen of Cups, a most unlooked for sign. It showed a young woman crowned and seated on a great throne by a sea shore, holding out a covered golden chalice. Its significance was that a woman's devotion would be of great service to him in his present state. He puzzled over it for some time, running through in his mind the many women he knew to see if he could divine which one was indicated. Eventually he left the mystery unresolved for the time being and turned up the next card, working clockwise. The Three of Wands – a red-robed man looking out to sea at three ships sailing past in the distance. Its meaning was success in business and prosperity. The man was obviously Jonathan himself again, watching his plans come to fruition.

The next card reversed the mood abruptly. The King of Swords stared up at him, stern faced, holding a long bladed sword upright against his shoulder, ready to strike. A man of authority and, since the card was upside down, it added the information that the power was being used in a cruel manner and with evil intent. There could be no doubt as to who that was; only Derek Braithwaite fitted the description. The next card took the matter further. It was the Ten of Swords, showing a man lying dead, face down on the earth, ten long swords stuck into his back. It meant what it depicted, affliction and defeat, and Jonathan knew that he was the man lying face down and vanquished. He flipped over the next card and the story was confirmed by the Lightning-struck Tower. The card showed a jagged bolt of lightning flashing out of the sky to destroy the top of a tall tower, from which two men were falling headlong to death on the sharp rocks below. It was not merely a reinforcement of the Ten of Swords, it added something else – that the catastrophe would be unforeseen and sudden when it came. In the falling figures Jonathan saw himself again.

Only one card was still face down. He left it untouched for a while, absorbing the message of the six cards he had turned up. The reading had promised well at the beginning, suggesting success and plans accomplished, but it had turned threatening when Braithwaite appeared. Jonathan felt that he was poised on a knife edge.

He reached out to rest his fingers lightly on the back of the last card. It would be the decider, according to which side of the scale it came down on, fortune or calamity. When he felt ready, he turned it over quickly.

It depicted a white-robed woman decked with flowers who calmly and without effort was closing the jaws of an angry lion with her bare hands. The name of the card was Strength and it meant that action and fortitude were required. Of that he had no doubt. But to complicate matters, the card was upside down, which was an indication of strength being used wrongly.

Jonathan stood in thought for a long time, combining in his mind the total meaning of the seven cards. Until he had turned up the final one, the reading had been clear to him. Now it had become ambiguous and could be misleading unless he was cautious. If he took the Strength card to be part of the Derek Braithwaite sequence, the meaning was that Braithwaite was abusing his authority to bring about Jonathan's downfall and it negated the bright promise of the first three cards. If the last card had been the right way up, the reading would have been that by strength and fortitude Jonathan was able to overcome the threat posed by Braithwaite and so achieve his goal of success in his work. Perhaps both meanings of the last card should be taken together, he thought, turning the card sideways while he pondered.

When he related the reading back to the I Ching image of the fox crossing a stream and getting its tail wet, he finally concluded that what was indicated was that Braithwaite's abuse of power could be countered by a greater show of power, amounting also to an abuse of it, by himself. In that way he could perhaps switch the import of the Lightning-struck Tower so that one of the figures falling from it to destruction was Braithwaite.

He put the cards away and resumed his cross legged pose on the floor, staring at the mural of the naked man-god while he thought about the implications of the two oracles. There was a price to be paid for the dangerous course of action that had been formulating somewhere deep in his mind ever since he had left Braithwaite's office that evening. That was to be expected. When you fight, you run the risk of being hurt. The aim was to win and then nurse the wounds. In practical terms, Braithwaite must be neutralised now. A particular woman could be of great assistance, but there was no time to wait to identify her. The matter was too pressing – the Lightning-struck Tower indicated that.

The Noble Order of the Masters of the Temple was founded in order to guide its members along the paths of light towards the ultimate Light. But where there is light there is also dark. The Order's teaching brought self awareness, not only of the light and dark elements in the human psyche but of the corresponding creative and destructive forces at work in nature and the universe. Jonathan had learned how to call up the creative forces within himself and the external forces of which they were part. He knew that by analogous means he could call up the destructive forces if he chose. He knew too that the right and left hand paths eventually converge on the same point like the two halves of a circle. The right hand path seeks liberation by detachment from the world; the left hand path seeks the same end by total acceptance of the world.

Where there are two paths, to choose one is to deny the other. But as he thought about what he was going to do, into Jonathan's mind came a fragment of one of the liturgies of the Order:

> 'For such as understand the planes of God
>   for them shall be two gardens –
> Which of these will you deny?
> Therein are two fountains of running water –
>   which of these bounties will you deny?'

The words ran through his head unbidden like a mute warning, until at last he recited the end of it aloud:

> 'And therein two fountains of gushing water –
>   which of these bounties will you deny?
> And therein fruit
>   the date palm and the pomegranate –
> Which of God's bounties
>   will you and you deny?'

The spoken verses seemed to hang in the air about him until he waved them away with his hand, as if they had been a trail of bitter-sweet incense. His choice was made. The time for doubt was past; only courage would serve his turn.

He hung his blue silk robe in the cupboard and went downstairs in an ordinary bath robe to make his preparations. The outline of what he intended was clear in his head and he needed to work out the details. Ignoring food, he opened a bottle of claret and sat in his living room making notes and sustaining himself with the clear red wine. A picture of Braithwaite was needed. There had been one in a recent issue of the company journal, he recalled. He found it – a photograph of Braithwaite shaking hands with a department store buyer visiting from Australia. He cut out the Braithwaite part of the picture and set it aside. There was a passage in the New Testament he would require. He took the Bible from his bookshelves and leafed through the pages until he found his reference. He marked the verses he wanted and put Braithwaite's picture in as a bookmark.

He needed a suitable incense. Not the aromatic mixtures normally used but something to bring the appropriate taste and odour to his ceremony. He made a compound in his kitchen – pepper, powdered aloes, benjamin, flowers of sulphur, all bound together with a little malt vinegar into a thick paste. He left it to dry out while he checked his notes again and drank another glass of wine. There would be no possibility of using notes when he started and so he needed to be sure in his mind that he knew what he was aiming at. It was towards eleven o'clock before he felt ready to start.

Upstairs in his chapel he put on not the blue robe he had worn earlier but one of scarlet hessian, tied round his waist with a heavy black cord. These things had no power in themselves. Their virtue was in assisting to set the mood he wanted, to establish the frame of mind, to match his acts, to be reminders of his single purpose, as the incense would be. Then, at the supreme moment, every fibre of his body and every channel of his mind would strain outwards in a massive rush of will in the direction he intended. The blue silk was unsuitable because it had the feel of tranquillity about it; the touch of the hessian on his body and its scarlet colour would arouse, however subliminally, connotations of fire and blood.

There were precautions to be taken for his own safety, mental and physical. Outside his circle he drew on the floor with red chalk a triangle – to the north. Inside it he lettered in the same colour the name ABADDON and on it he set an iron pot in which he kindled charcoal. Over the charcoal he put a thin wire mesh and on that the major portion of the pungent incense he had made. Its sharp and oppressive odour was already drifting up in a thin column of smoke as he took his steel sword from the altar and traced round the triangle with its point. As he did so he visualised a stream of golden fire gushing from the sword point as an affirmation that whatever should come within the triangle would be held there by the power of his will until he chose to let it depart.

Back inside his circle, he traced it round with the sword point, energising it as a barrier between the seen and the unseen worlds. This has always been the way of those who wish to call up great forces to do their will. He did not draw a second circle inside the first, nor write the holy names of God on the floor, as Aleister Crowley had done in the Algerian desert, for in drawing the one circle Jonathan had established and affirmed his own identity with the Infinite. For so advanced an adept, that knowledge was sufficient to protect him from possession and destruction so long as he remained inside his perimeter.

On his elaborate altar he had set a five branched iron candelabrum with red candles before turning off the electric lights at the beginning of his preparations. The candles were spluttering and wavering, though the room was closed and sealed. Moving round inside the circle, Jonathan performed the banishing rituals of the pentagram, forcing himself to see the five-pointed stars drawn on the air with the sword point, as if in tracery of fire. Then moving again around the circle, he performed the summoning rituals and called upon the Lords of the Watchtowers to be present and witness. After that he stood still for a time, the sword point down on the floor between his bare feet, his hands crossed on the hilt, his mind exploring and analysing the effect of his preparations. Within him all was strength and determination; outside all was hushed and waiting. And the distinction between inside and outside was dissolving, so that there was no arbitrary division between himself and the rest of the universe. When we are born, the ego includes everything. Later on it begins to detach itself from the external world, so that the normal ego consciousness in adults is merely a shrunken vestige of a feeling which once embraced the universe. In Jonathan, the uninitiated man's fear of being an isolated spark of consciousness in a vast and hostile cosmos was gone. He knew himself at that moment to be a nodal point in the web of force and being which is the cosmos.

Satisfied that all distracting and irrelevant forms had been banished and that he had correctly aroused the guardian powers that were within himself and outside himself and were one, he laid the sword on the altar with its point aimed at the triangle, while he faced east. On the wall in front of him, dimly illuminated by the flickering candle light, there was painted from floor to ceiling a representation of the Tree of Life of the Cabala, with the serpent of wisdom twining up its trunk. The tree had six branches, three to the left and three to the right, opposite each other in regular fashion, each with a shining fruit at its tip. There were four more fruits on the trunk, one at the very crown and the lowest one at root level.

The Tree is represented in many ways, according to the interpretation of the artist. Jonathan had instructed the man who painted his chapel to copy from an illustration he had found in a five-hundred-year-old book by Ramon Lull, a

Spanish adept. But however it is drawn, to initiates the Tree and its ten shining fruit reveal ten facets of God, the structure of the universe, material and non-material, humanity's path back to God the source of all things, and much else besides. A version of this glyph appeared in the private chapel of every member of the Order, to remind the adept of these things, in much the same way that Christian churches are adorned with stained glass windows depicting saints, or paintings and statues of them, according to the denomination of the worshippers.

The Sufi mystics taught that God planted this Tree with his own hand and breathed his spirit into it. In this sense, the whole of the cosmos is seen as a tree which has grown from the seed of the divine command: Be! It has sent down its roots, sent up its trunk and spread out its branches so that the material world and the world of symbols and the world of archetypes are all contained by it.

Facing this picture, Jonathan visualised a great cloud of light above his head and raised his right hand to draw some of this light into himself, his fingertips tingling as they touched first the light, then his own forehead. He completed the Cabalistic cross, touching his navel, his right nipple, his left nipple and folded his hands before his face, saying aloud in a commanding tone: *Malkuth ... Din ... Hod*, which in English means *The kingdom, the power, the glory*, the Hebrew names of three of the shining lights on the Tree. As he spoke the words and felt the power inside himself Jonathan imagined himself growing to tremendous size, until at last he stood upon the earth as on a foot stool and his head was among the stars.

In centuries past, adepts who wished to call up and make use of the forces inherent in nature and themselves, whether they thought of them as gods or demons, protected themselves by writing the holy names of the Old Testament God around their circle and then called upon the forces to appear in the name of the New Testament gods – the Father, the Son, the Holy Spirit. The founder of the Noble Order had wanted nothing to do with this second-hand self inflation. He had gone for much of his ritual to the Hermetica, texts written in Egypt in the Greek language.

'If you do not make yourself equal to God, you cannot comprehend God, for like is comprehended by like. Outleap the body and expand yourself to unmeasured greatness; outstrip all time and become eternity; so shall you apprehend God.'

The ceremony Jonathan was performing was very different from the one he had followed in Copenhagen with Annemarie or in Stockholm with Britt, and from the one in Helsinki with Eila. They were of lesser Degrees and he had remained within the bounds of what they could understand. It was only in his own Degree, the Seventh, that an adept could attempt what he was doing now – standing above the universe, eye to eye with the gods, not as a worshipper or as a supplicant but as an equal. Not that he was equating himself with God, for that path leads directly to insanity, but with the god-forms through which men and women try to approach God.

Ablaze with inner power, he returned to his own size, took up the sword again and saluted the Watchers of the Universe at the four points of the compass. And since there was no one of a less Degree present, he called the Watchers by the names they were given in times past and so saw them in their splendour just beyond the limits of his circle. With the sense of their presence strongly upon him, he took from his altar a golden six-pointed star, a small replica of the large star painted on the floor within his circle. He held it high above himself with both hands, then solemnly lowered it until it fitted around his head like a crown. It seemed to him at that moment that the shining Watchers beyond his circle bowed to him as they beheld him crowned and full of power.

Jonathan performed this ceremonial with the exactness and joy of long familiarity. He had stood in many such circles and reached out to touch the forces which are at the same time manifestations of God and manifestations of himself. He had come to know the trodden paths towards the Infinite and in his explorations he had discovered how to exorcise the negative and destructive forces which are the natural twins of the creative forces. Part of his training in the Noble Order had been to separate out the destructive forces of his unconscious and externalise them, project them outwards from himself, so that he could visualise them beyond his circle of protection and contemplate them without fear or horror and by this means conquer them. But this ability to master them could also be used to unleash them to wreak havoc. Jonathan saw emotions not as fixed states, even though descriptions such as anger, fear, grief, anxiety, guilt, suggest fixed and uniform states which persist if no action is taken to release them. To Jonathan emotions, whether negative or positive, were not static but in motion. Anger, he knew, tends to adjust itself naturally, unless it is compressed, like the explosive in a hand grenade, until it bursts out in violence. From different points of view, anger can be seen either as a demon rushing up out of its prison in the human psyche, or as a particular channelling of psychic action. By acting angrily, he could call up anger – channel his psychic energy along a chosen path.

He moved round his altar until he was facing to the north, looking along the blade of the sword on the altar top towards the triangle he had chalked on the floor outside his circle. Into the small censer on the altar he put the remainder of the unpleasant mixture he had put together in the kitchen. The chapel was already filling with the reek of the smouldering pot in the triangle; the smaller censer near him filled his nostrils with its sharp smell in seconds. He switched on the cassette player inside the hollow altar and turned it to full volume. The tape was already wound to the section he wanted to play. Like a blow in the face, a raucous music filled the room, rattling kettle drums and blaring trumpets, interspersed with chords of grinding dissonance.

As the music hit him, Jonathan breathed in deeply and concentrated on the force of destruction inside himself, the blind, raw, venomous aggression that lies beneath the surface of even the most civilised of men. As it stirred within him, he snatched up a dagger with a thin sharp blade from the altar and slashed at the air about him as he thought of Derek

Braithwaite, letting his hatred boil up unchecked until it filled him like a cauldron of boiling tar. His legs and body trembled as the adrenalin surged through him, his heart raced and his breathing became forced and ragged. He began to stamp his feet rhythmically and to chant a wordless song of hatred, as if he were a primitive tribesman of long ago, working himself up in a war dance for a berserk charge at an enemy, to smash and spear and trample him underfoot.

In the heart of the red rage that seethed through him, there was one tiny and silent point of control. Before that was blotted out, he seized in claw-like fingers the Bible, where he had marked a passage, and screamed out the words from the page at the top of his voice:

'And he opened the bottomless pit and there arose a smoke out of it, as the smoke of a great furnace, and the sun and the air were darkened by the smoke of the pit. And there came out of the smoke locusts upon the earth, and unto them was given power, as the scorpions of the earth have power. And it was commanded that they should not hurt the grass of the earth, neither any green thing, neither any tree, but only those men which have not the seal of God on their foreheads.'

Jonathan paused for a second to draw in great shuddering breaths, clinging to his almost vanished point of control as he roared out again:

'And to them it was given that they should not kill them, but that they should be tormented five months, and their torment as the torment of a scorpion when he striketh a man. And in those days shall men seek death and not find it, and they shall desire to die and death shall flee from them.

'And the shape of the locusts were like unto horses prepared unto battle, and on their heads were crowns of gold, and their faces were as the faces of men. And they had hair as the hair of women, and their teeth were as the teeth of lions. And they had breastplates of iron, and the sound of their wings was as the sound of many horses and chariots running to battle. And they had tails like unto scorpions, and there were stings in their tails, and their power was to hurt men five months.

'And they had a king over them, which is the angel of the

bottomless pit, whose name is ABADDON.'

Had any uninitiated person witnessed the scene in Jonathan's chapel, he would have unhesitatingly concluded that here was a raging madman. Jonathan's body in the scarlet robe shook and twisted with passion, his face was purple-red, his eyes bulged from their sockets, his mouth strained open to release a howl of mindless rage. His red hair hung tousled about the star crown as he stamped and jerked, his bare feet drumming on the wooden floor.

At the very peak of his paroxysm, before his mind collapsed, Jonathan projected from himself the tearing fury he had induced, aiming it at the triangle outside his silver circle. The thick column of bitter incense rising up from the iron pot there swayed and bellied out as Jonathan screamed:

'Abaddon, Abaddon, Abaddon, Abaddon, Abaddon – appear! I command you!'

To his straining eyes it seemed that he discerned in the smoke of the censer a tall leathery form with dark, furled wings. Lank black hair hung to its bony shoulders; its face was almost human, until the mouth opened to reveal pointed animal fangs. At once Jonathan pulled up the loose left sleeve of his red robe and sliced the sharp dagger across the soft inside of his left arm five times. As the blood ran, he held his arm over the altar to let the drops fall into the censer. They hissed and went up in the threads of smoke rising to the ceiling. While he bled, Jonathan stared at the thing he had commanded to show itself to him in the Triangle of Exorcism and howled dog-like in his triumph.

The evil to which he had given the biblical name Abaddon was the same force that Aleister Crowley had summoned in the desert when he attempted to penetrate the Tenth Aethyr. Unlike Crowley, Jonathan had no intention of becoming possessed by it. He had summoned the evil from inside himself and projected it outwards as a separate entity. He had not let it take control of him totally.

In the shifting candle light, Jonathan could see the furious lust to destroy half materialised outside his circle, waiting for his charge, as it must.

On the altar lay the torn out picture of Braithwaite.

Jonathan focused his attention on it, the tip of his dagger hovering over it, his bared left arm still dripping into the hissing charcoal, filling his throat with the reek of burning blood. He spoke in a voice filled with harsh authority to the thing in the triangle.

'Abaddon, angel of the bottomless pit, king over the tormentors of men, hear my will and obey it. Tear away from this man Derek Braithwaite his health and his faculties and consign him to the living dead. Torment him with the fever that consumes by day and by night, until his strength is burnt away. I give to you his head, his eyes, his tongue, his teeth, his mouth . . .

As he mentioned each part of Braithwaite's body, he stabbed the point of his dagger into the corresponding part of the picture.

' . . . So that he may not be able to utter what it is that gives him pain. I give to you his neck and shoulders, arms and hands, that he may not be able to help himself in any way. I give you his chest, liver, heart and lungs, so that he may not be able to sleep, his shoulder blades and back, so that he may not be able to escape pain as he lies in his bed . . .'

The dagger point stabbed through the flimsy paper again and again.

'I give to you his man's parts, so that he may no longer be a man. I give to you his thighs, knees and feet, so that he may not be able to stand. I give him to you utterly, so that he may be tormented.'

The printed picture had been reduced to tattered rags of paper. Jonathan stabbed through it once more, very hard, and left the dagger standing upright in the wooden altar top.

Sweat was pouring down his face and body. The scarlet robe was plastered clammily to his chest, belly and buttocks. He summoned up his remaining strength and roared out his dismissal.

'Abaddon, you have heard my will. Do my bidding or I will consign you back to the bottomless pit, there to be bound forever in chains. Be gone!'

To his fevered mind, the tall column of incense puffed out and the messenger of evil vanished and there was only the foul smelling smoke.

There was a numbing weariness of body and mind in Jonathan after the expulsion of so much rage, even though he had only half glimpsed Abaddon. To compel a natural force to materialise wholly drains an adept beyond his power of recovery in many instances. The most celebrated French initiate of the nineteenth century, Eliphas Levi, half materialised a benign force in Bulwer-Lytton's London house and fell unconscious from the effort. In the 1920s, Aleister Crowley and a disciple invoked one in the attic of a Paris boarding house. Instead of the expected force, Set showed himself again. The disciple died of a heart attack when he realised what was happening. Crowley's body was strong enough to survive, but his friends found him gibbering in a corner of the attic the next day and it required a stay in a Paris mental hospital to bring him back to what passed with him for sanity.

For all practical purposes, Jonathan knew, it is not necessary to completely materialise a natural force. So great an undertaking was performed only very rarely in the Order, as a test of the strength of an adept's will. What he had accomplished was sufficient for his purpose – his ill-wishing had unleashed a current of hostile psychic energy at Braithwaite which would damage him very severely.

Trembling with fatigue now that the act was done, Jonathan extinguished the bad smelling censer on his altar. He took the long sword, now almost beyond his strength to lift, and moved round his circle slowly, halting at east, south, west and north to thank the Watchers for guarding him. This was more than mere form, for there is always risk when a destructive force is unleashed. When the Watchers had withdrawn, Jonathan made the sign of the Cabalistic cross again, calling on the Kingdom, the Power and the Glory to banish any minor unseen forces he may have accidentally attracted to him, for such things hover around ceremonies of destruction where blood is spilled, like flies over bad meat.

Unless they were chased away, they might follow him when he stepped out of the circle and cause disturbance in his everyday life.

At last all was finished, the candles blown out, the iron pot in the triangle extinguished, the hidden extractor fan switched on to clear the fumes from the closed chapel. Jonathan dropped his sweat soaked scarlet robe on the floor and went naked to the bathroom to shower and attend to his gashed arm. And that done, he crawled exhausted into bed and fell into a deep sleep.

CHAPTER 10
TOWER STRUCK BY LIGHTNING

JONATHAN'S ARM was very sore when he woke up the next morning. He shaved and showered, dressed the angry red cuts and put his clothes on. Before going downstairs he made sure that his chapel was securely locked. A cup of coffee and a slice of toast in the kitchen and he was on his way by eight-thirty. From where he lived it was easy to get to the motorway and soon he was driving out past Heathrow Airport, heading west towards Swindon.

In the opposite direction was the commuter traffic into London, a solid three lane column crawling along. By the time they reached the London exit, the drivers would be lucky to be moving at more than walking speed. In the direction Jonathan was going, thirty-ton trucks with British, German, Belgian and French number plates were hammering along towards Bristol and South Wales with their cargoes.

Jonathan enjoyed driving fast. On this particular morning he had a special feeling of release which he indulged to the full. He ignored the maximum speed limit, put his foot down hard and skimmed along the outside lane of the motorway, flicking past the thundering trucks. In his ears the muted howl of his engine and the dull roar of the airstream around him blended with the music from the radio into a symphony of physical power and spiritual elation.

The question tugging at his mind was what had befallen Derek Braithwaite as a result of last night's ceremony of cursing. He had not the least doubt that Braithwaite had been struck down. The only way to find out was to contact the office, but that might be to attract unwelcome attention to himself. There was no way of guessing in advance what course the ill wishing had taken, but there was sure to be office gossip after the event. Sometimes, as he had observed, even the most imperceptive of people enjoy a gleam of insight that defies logic. He wanted no connection in anyone's mind between Braithwaite's destruction and himself. So, hurtling along with the speedometer needle rock steady on a hundred and ten miles an hour, he took a firm decision not to telephone London before noon that day, and even then not to enquire directly about Braithwaite. That settled, he gave himself up entirely to the enjoyment of speed, the miles racing back under his wheels. Sooner than he had expected, the Swindon turn off sign rushed towards him.

The Doveday factory there was one of the two which had been totally modernised and re-equipped in the past year. Its increased capacity reduced production costs considerably, so long as its greater output could be sold. This was the simple equation that had sent Braithwaite and Jonathan flying round Europe and Scandinavia. The biggest sales push of all would be in the United States that summer.

Jonathan parked outside the administration block in one of the spaces marked *Visitors* and looked at the long, single storey building that housed several million pounds' worth of machinery. Up at one end was the tall tower housing the flour silos, with a road tanker parked at its base. The boiler suited driver was connecting a thick hose from his vehicle to an inlet built into the tower wall before switching on his pumps to blow another twenty tons of flour into one of the silos. Down at the other end of the factory a line of trucks with Dovedays' name on their sides were backed up to a loading bay, where fork lift trucks bustled about as they packed pallet loads of big cartons into the vehicles for despatch.

What takes place inside this building, thought Jonathan, between silo and loading bay, can make the difference between a working profit and a crippling loss. If those of us who sit in offices in London, assessing markets and issuing instructions which determine what happens inside this factory, get it wrong, a lot of people down here can lose their jobs.

Briefcase in hand, he walked briskly into the administration block and a few minutes later was sitting in the general manager's office, a cup of instant coffee in his hand.

Tom Bridges was one of Dovedays' younger factory managers. He had been transferred to Swindon as a promotion from the York factory. At York he had been assistant to the general manager and, like Jonathan, had been given a hard ride by a boss not overly impressed by new ways. A man with an engineering degree did not fit well into the York general manager's scheme of things. To him an engineer was a man in oil stained overalls who kept machines running. Bridges had soldiered on cheerfully, moving by steps from the technical side into the general management side of the business. His worth had been recognised eventually in the consistently above average results of the York factory. Still only in his mid-thirties, he was not in complete command of the new Swindon factory. His goal, as Jonathan saw it, was a transfer to the London office in due course, with a seat on the board as production director.

Bridges had blossomed since his transfer and promotion. He was a short, very dark haired man; thick necked and broad of shoulder. His appearance inspired a sense of physical confidence that had served him well. He and Jonathan got on well together, not being in competition with each other.

'Coffee to your liking?' Bridges asked.

'It's dreadful, and you know it, Tom. You'll do yourself untold harm if you drink this stuff every day. Why don't you buy a percolater out of the petty cash and teach your secretary how to make real coffee?'

Bridges affected a country cousin style when he was relaxed.

'That's all very well for you city folks in your glass palace up in London,' he said, 'but down here in the wilds we have to work hard to support you. Somebody's got to earn the money so you can get blind drunk at lunch every day and go out on the town with loose women of an evening. We don't have time for frills like real coffee, even if we had the cash.'

'My God – that sounds like a build up to asking me to eat lunch in your factory canteen. I should have brought my own sandwiches.'

'I checked the canteen menu specially for you, Jonathan. It's shepherd's pie, baked beans and chips. And then rhubarb pie with custard. You can't get a meal like that in London, not even at the Savoy Hotel.'

'Damned right you can't! So I've got the message – you expect me to take *you* out to lunch, even though I'm the visitor. All right, tell your girl to book a table somewhere and we'll get down to business.'

'It's already booked. Thank you for the invitation.'

'You are evil, there's no doubt of it.'

'I'm only a poor factory manager. They don't let me spend the firm's money on high living. That's for you big shots.'

Jonathan opened his black briefcase and took out a sheaf of papers.

'I've come slumming in this wasteland of yours to talk about Christmas in Scandinavia. More specifically, boxes of goodies for the tiny tots. These are last year's sales figures by country.'

'Christmas? We've only just got over Easter and I haven't even planned my summer vacation. What's the rush?'

'I'm just back from a week round the Scandinavian countries, talking to our distributors about targets. I thought I'd go through it with you while it's still fresh in my mind. One of the things that came up was what went wrong last year.'

'Nothing went wrong last year,' said Bridges sharply, his joking style forgotten. 'You told us what to make and what packs you wanted. We made and delivered on schedule. No problems.'

'Bullshit. Our distributors off-loaded all the special presentation packs onto the retail outlets, but a post Christmas check showed that across the four Scandinavian countries about twenty per cent of the packs were left on the retailers' shelves and had to be disposed of at cut price rates. That's not very good news. It probably means that the retailers will cut their orders by half this year so as not to have product left on their hands in January with bloody jingle bells printed all over the pack.'

Bridges nodded.

'Not only that,' Jonathan went on, 'my personal estimate, based on talks with our Scandinavian distributors, is that we only met about two thirds of our potential Christmas market out there anyway, in terms of loading up the retailers.'

Bridges still said nothing.

'The question I have to ask myself is,' said Jonathan, 'who screwed it up? We make good products. We've got good distributors. We've built a good reputation in the frozen north. So I'm looking for answers.'

Bridges thought for a moment before asking:

'Are you minuting this meeting? Copies to all the top brass in London office, including the cleaning ladies?'

'Does it make any difference?'

'It's an irritating mannerism to answer a question with another question.'

'You write the meeting report yourself then,' Jonathan offered, 'and I'll sign it as if it were mine. Does that ease the situation?'

'So long as you don't change a single word of what I write, it's a deal.'

'Good, we're agreed then – no report of this meeting. Everything off the record.'

'I knew you'd come round to see it my way, Jonathan.'

'So unwrap the dirty washing.'

'In my very humble and entirely inexpert opinion,' said Bridges, dropping back into his relaxed style, 'one of the reasons why our Christmas presentation packs might not have rung the bell very loudly in some overseas markets is that your esteemed employer, Mr Derek Braithwaite, cut a few corners in his totally understandable and praiseworthy desire to maximise profits.'

'And Scandinavian sales may have been affected by this, you think?'

'I'm sure that's what they told you out there, when you weren't either falling about drunk or bedding tall blondes, as is your executive privilege, of course.'

'The distributors' opinion was that we didn't take local taste preferences into account properly,' Jonathan agreed. 'What we seem to have shipped was good of its kind, but more suited to the British market taste. Too many of the milk chocolate coated biscuits in the selection and not nearly enough of the ginger and spice varieties. Would you go along with that?'

'How would I know what they like in foreign parts? I make what I'm told to make. What I do know is that when we sent up first cost estimates to your respected boss, he shouted at me down the telephone and then came roaring down here like a rhinoceros with an attack of piles. So we made the pack cheaper by using varieties straight off the production line, some from here, some from York and some from the Scottish plant. Our overseas Christmas pack was very nearly the same as the ones we make for Christmas here, good quality but very sweet tooth. The only real difference was the foreign words on the outside. From memory we brought down the cost per pack by about fifty per cent, as instructed. I can have the exact figures looked out for you, if you want them.'

'I'd like a note of them before I leave. Let's talk about next Christmas and what we're going to do. I want to sell fifty per cent more of a suitable pack through the retailers at a higher price.'

'For you, anything. But let me point out ever so gently that your revered master will kick the roller skates from under both of us when he hears what you have in mind.'

'Let me worry about that. For practical purposes Scandinavia is my personal territory now. There's no time for another tour this year, for him or for me. So as I'm the last man back from there, I've got the edge on him.'

'I like to see a man who believes in the power of reason, even when the facts all point otherwise,' said Bridges. 'I'll have some advance costings done for you, based on what we used to sell out there before we lurched off sideways last year.'

'And based on a fifty per cent bigger off-take.'

'Did you ever sell encyclopaedias for a living? You've got the real foot-in-the-door, sign-here-please approach. Bear in mind that my figures will be based on today's raw material prices plus something for the expected cost inflation. Is that good enough?'

'For now. But to get the distributors behind us solidly again I want to send them sample packs by the beginning of September, with a firm price.'

'That's no great problem, so long as you allow a margin to cover unforeseens.'

'I'll remember that.'

They talked on until about midday, when Bridges remembered that Jonathan had not toured the factory since it was re-equipped. He sent for white overalls for both of them and while these were being fetched, Jonathan took the opportunity to telephone the London office.

'Any messages?' he asked his secretary.

'Nothing that can't wait until you're back tomorrow. The letter you were expecting from Mr Egeland in Oslo came in this morning's mail.'

'What does it say?'

'There's two pages of figures. It looks like an arithmetic lesson.'

'That's his wily Norwegian way of baffling us. Just look at the last paragraph and give me the gist.'

'It says that bearing in mind the foregoing – that means his sums, I suppose – he thinks it will be possible, subject to the conditions mentioned earlier, whatever they were – to accede to your request and increase sales in Norway by the end of the current calendar year by a factor of seventeen and a half per cent.'

152

'Does he really use words like that?'

'You don't think I made them up, do you?'

'That's all right then. Scandinavia is buttoned up for this year.'

She had said nothing about Braithwaite, the one person he wanted to hear about.

'Anyone want me in the office?' he asked casually.

'No.'

'Fine. I'll be here until about four if anything comes up and after that I'll be on my way back to London.'

'Nothing urgent's going to come up,' she said. 'Mr Braithwaite's not in today.'

With that he had to be content. He put on the white coat and white hat Bridges offered and they went on a tour of the factory. They walked the length of the production lines, from automatic dough mixers like giant spin dryers, to the six feet wide endless strip of dough, passing between rollers that cut out biscuit shapes like big confetti and fed the holed web back to the beginning of the process to be rolled through again. They watched symmetrical rows of biscuit shapes, like soldiers in columns, marching into the long tunnel oven on a wire mesh conveyor belt. The air was sweet with the smell of sugar, chocolate, dried currants and baking. All along the line Tom Bridges stopped for an encouraging word with the white clad men and women operating it, seemingly knowing all their names without effort. Beyond the oven, the conveyor carried the now golden-brown biscuits into a waterfall of liquid chocolate, then through an air drying tunnel and on to where deft fingered women worked the packaging machines.

'A production line like this is like a church organ,' said Bridges. 'You can play tunes on it. You can change from one product to another with no fuss at all. You can run the line for maximum output or you can run it for least cost. And I've got six of these organs right here under this roof.'

When he had duly admired the factory, Jonathan took Bridges out to lunch to talk in an informal way about possible plans for the future of overseas sales. The two of them understood each other well. Both were on the way up and there was an unspoken pact to assist each other's climb as the older men above them faded away into retirement.

The visit confirmed what Jonathan knew already. Braithwaite had been slipping for some time and was better out of the way. He had no qualms about what he had done to remove him.

In the London office the next day he was still unable to satisfy his curiosity about Braithwaite. He made an elaborately casual visit to Nancy Tait and found her withdrawn and uncommunicative. All he got from her was that Braithwaite was ill and she did not know when he would be back. Jonathan was compelled to suppress his curiosity as best he could and get on with his work. Finally he rang up a friend and arranged to play squash with him that evening to relieve the tension by physical effort.

The next day brought the news he was waiting for. Halfway through the morning he was asked to see the managing director. He made his way three floors up the building and presented himself to the secretary in the outer office.

'Go right in, Mr Rawlings,' she said. 'Mr Bennett is waiting for you.'

Bennett's office was large and handsomely furnished. As Jonathan went in, Bennett got up from behind his vast desk.

'Come and sit over here,' he said. 'There are things I want to talk to you about.'

At the far end of the room from the desk were four black leather armchairs grouped around a coffee table. As he sat down, Jonathan guessed how important this meeting was. If it had been ordinary business, they would have talked across Bennett's desk. To be invited into the studiously casual club chairs meant that Bennett was going to be very far from casual.

'I've ordered some tea,' he said, and exactly on cue his secretary came in with a tray and busied herself serving them. Bone china cups, Jonathan noted; milk in a silver jug, a selection of the company's more expensive biscuits on a plate.

Peter Bennett was in his late fifties; tall, thin, with well cut hair greying over his ears, an expensive dark suit and a carefully chosen tie, the very picture of a successful British businessman, all courtesy and affability. But look closer, Jonathan thought, and there is a coldness in the pale blue eyes and a sharpness of the nose to indicate that the courtesy is a way of concealing the toughness of his character until he decides to reveal it. He had joined Dovedays about ten years earlier from one of its major competitors, where he had been finance director, to understudy the last Doveday in the business. Jonathan's guess was that Bennett had been brought into the company by the chairman of the board and was his man. Henry Doveday, the last of the dynasty that founded the business, had retired and taken his wealth to Ireland, away from the Inland Revenue. More than once Jonathan had surmised that his own appointment had been engineered by Bennett against Braithwaite's wishes, though there was no connection he could trace between Bennett and the Order.

'You know that Derek Braithwaite is away from the office ill,' he began when his secretary had left the room.

'Yes, I checked with his secretary this morning whether there was anything urgent I could take care of.'

'Quite so. Was there?'

'She said not. But I am not overly happy about Australia.'

'You must tell me about that later. The thing is, Derek's had a good deal of ill health of late. It's his wretched ulcer, of course. He worries too much.'

'He's a very diligent man,' said Jonathan, playing the loyal subordinate until he knew more of what was in Bennett's mind.

'A very apt description. His present illness is more serious than his usual few days off. He collapsed completely the other evening and he's in hospital. His ulcer perforated and they're having a devil of a job to save him from dying of peritonitis.'

A devil named Abaddon, thought Jonathan, a man-faced locust with a scorpion's tail. He stung Braithwaite as I commanded him. Braithwaite will be at death's door for five months, though he will not die. I forbade that.

'It sounds extremely serious,' he said, for Bennett.

'Yes. I've been talking to the surgeon. I went to visit Derek but he was still in intensive care. The surgeon told me that there's an awful lot wrong with his innards, apart from the ulcer. He's going to be away from the office for a long time.'

'I see.'

'This has come at an awkward time for us. I don't have to tell you how important it is to get our overseas sales into top gear in the shortest possible time. Home sales are spending a fortune on advertising, but a lot of that is just running harder to stand still. The board was looking to overseas sales to keep the new plants at capacity output.'

'And we've made a start,' said Jonathan.

'What makes you say that? Europe does not look like coming up to scratch so far, from what I understand.'

'France and Germany are always doubtful for us, but Scandinavia as a whole will be over the target figures this year and will do even better next year.'

'You've just been out there, of course. I had the impression that you were running into problems.'

'By no means. I've got a copy of my report on Scandinavia here if you'd like to see it. It's only three pages.'

While Bennett was reading the report which Braithwaite had contemptuously flicked across his desk to the floor, Jonathan studied the paintings hanging round the office. Bennett's taste ran to abstracts, large and regular shapes in pale colours, carefully balanced visually. The pictures spoke in a whisper of a wish to impose a pattern of order and harmony on the potentially discordant. Not for the first time, Jonathan reflected that while adepts and artists had known for many centuries the effects of colours on states of mind, scientists had only recently stumbled on the correspondences and were still trying to explain them in their own terms. Green is the colour of harmony, red of energy, yellow the colour of cheerfulness, and so on, in the scientific account of Dr Max Luscher. But Luscher's investigations were little more than exposing people to different colours and checking their blood pressure. The Noble Order had been using subtle blends of colour to induce specific states of mind since its foundation. The secret system of colour correspondences could be traced back from the Order for at least two and a half thousand years and perhaps even went back to the time when the earlier life forms from which humanity evolved first acquired the ability to distinguish colours in their natural surroundings.

'First rate,' said Bennett, putting the report down. 'Did Derek read this before he was taken ill?'

'He read it on Monday morning and we had a brief talk about it later that day.'

'You did very well in Scandinavia. Apart from the figures, on which you are to be congratulated, your assessments of the strengths and weaknesses of our distributors' organisations are particularly valuable. Did you write the same sort of report after your earlier tour of Western Europe?'

'I was with Mr Braithwaite on that trip. He wrote the report.'

'Have you seen it?'

'No, he didn't give me a copy. I made some notes of my own impressions of the distributors we visited, but that was for my own record only.'

'I'd be interested in seeing a copy of those notes if they are as useful as these.'

'I'll have a copy sent up to you.'

'The thing is,' said Bennett, 'Braithwaite is going to be away for some considerable time, as I said before. In the ordinary course of events I would naturally expect you to take over the department in his absence and keep it running properly and profitably while the board had time to consider the long term prospects. But these are not ordinary times – we are passing through a crucial period. A failure now in overseas sales would materially affect the overall company profit this year and next year. That would put me on the hot seat at the shareholders' meeting. The question I have to ask myself and answer quickly is whether you are ready to take over now and put some momentum into our overseas sales drive.'

Jonathan leaned forward to tap the Scandinavian report on the low table between the tea cups.

'I know that I can do it,' he said simply.

'I'm inclined to agree. Your report suggests so.'

'In the final analysis,' said Jonathan, 'is there any other choice? To find a replacement for Derek Braithwaite from outside would take months. For a newcomer to find out how the business operates would take more months. That writes off the rest of this year. I'm here now and I know the business.'

'I can't argue with that. As of now you are acting head of overseas sales, until the situation clarifies. I shall want you to keep me fully informed at all times.'

'Naturally.'

'How do you see your first move?'

'The strategy we worked out last year is still sound, though it's been delayed. I don't want to change it. I can do nothing to improve the position in Western Europe immediately, though towards the end of this year that may be a different story. The next step is the American tour planned for the week after next. I shall have the tickets and reservations changed to my name, inform our contacts over there and then go out and do the job.'

'Have you been there before? I can't remember.'

'Only to New York, briefly. The trip planned covers the whole country, except for Chicago now.'

'Yes, there seemed to be some confusion about whether we are going to get our money or not. Braithwaite promised to let me have details. Perhaps you will look into it and let me know how we stand, as a matter or priority. You feel there is no point in going there?'

'The purpose of the trip is to get our sales moving upwards fast, not to pick up the pieces of a past event. The lawyers can do that better than I can. With no functioning distributor in the Mid West, there's nothing I can achieve there in a few days. Replacing Arnison will take some time and will have to be deferred. I can easily go over for that purpose later in the year after I've had time to look into the possibilities.'

'You seem to have your eye on the ball already. Is there anything you want to raise with me just now?'

'Only the question of salary.'

'Leave that with me for now. Your new responsibilities call for an increase in salary, of course. I'll have a word with one or two of my colleagues and we'll arrange something.'

Back in his own office, Jonathan told his secretary that he was taking over the department until further notice.

'Does that mean that you're moving into Mr Braithwaite's office?' she asked.

He'd given that some thought. To stay where he was might be to signal that he was only standing in temporarily for an absent boss. To move his base of operations would indicate that he was in full charge.

'Yes, I'm moving in right away. I intend to bring Aymes in here from the general office to look after the work I've been doing. I want you to stay with him and give him a hand. Is that all right?'

'Can't I move up with you?'

'Not for now. Aymes will need your knowledge and experience. I'll see how I get on with Nancy. Will you tell the switchboard to put my calls through to the other office?'

'Right. I nearly forgot – there was a call for you while you were with Mr Bennett.'

She gave him the slip of paper. It said that Miss Karin Wikstrom was in London overnight and it gave a number at which she could be reached. Jonathan's mind was so full of his immediate plans that he had to make an effort of memory to place the name. She was the SAS stewardess he had talked to on the flight between Oslo and Stockholm.

'Do you want me to get the number for you?'

'Not now. I've far too much to do. It will have to wait.'

He put the message slip into his pocket and went down the passage into Braithwaite's outer office. Nancy Tait was on the telephone.

'Come in as soon as you are free,' he said to her briskly as he went through into Braithwaite's office, seated himself at the big desk and looked casually through the clutter in the drawers. It was a minute or two before Nancy came in.

'What are you doing?' she asked shrilly. 'You've no right to pry into Mr Braithwaite's desk!'

'Sit down, Nancy. I want to talk to you. I've just been with the managing director and he's put me in charge of the department. I shall be working from this desk from now on.'

'Why bother to move?' she asked shrewishly. 'You won't be in here for long.'

'I shall be here for longer than you imagine. Mr Braithwaite is much worse than anyone realised. It's going to be months before he's up and about again, and a long time after that before he'll be ready to work, if ever.'

He paused to let the significance of his words sink in. He was containing his temper in the face of her evident hostility. Loyalty in subordinates was a quality he appreciated, even to so improbable a person as Braithwaite. If it could be transferred to himself, well and good. If not, she would have to go.

'Is he really that ill?' she asked in a small voice. 'Is he going to die?'

'All I know is what the managing director told me after he had seen the surgeon. He's very ill indeed, Nancy. Now as you know, things have to go on here in the meantime. I'm here to make sure the department keeps running and I want you to help me. How long have you been working here?'

'I've been with Mr Braithwaite nearly seven years. Before that I was in the general office. I came to Dovedays straight from school.'

'That's a fine record with the company; one to be proud of.'

'I'm sorry if I spoke out of turn just now. It was the shock of seeing somebody else sitting at his desk.'

'That's all right,' said Jonathan, his eyes suddenly opened. 'I'm sure that you and I will get along well together. Only what has to be understood between us is that while I sit at this desk I really am head of the department. You have to work for me one hundred per cent, not half for me and half for someone who is not here. Do you see what I mean?'

She's been Braithwaite's girl friend for years and I never spotted it, he was thinking. I'm not usually that imperceptive. That wily old fox covered his tracks so well that he fooled us all. If I'd got onto that trail earlier I could have neutralised him through her. If the need ever arises, I still can. I'm not having him back here after the five months.

'I understand,' said Nancy.

'Good. There are one or two things I think I ought to know more about. The position in Australia is one of them and you'll know better than I do what the other problem areas are. We've got to get them all cleaned up fast. So get the appropriate files out and we'll make a start first thing tomorrow on cleaning up any dark corners. What I want to do today is to draft a letter to the American distributors telling them that I shall be visiting them instead of Mr Braithwaite and that all appointments still stand. That's one thing. The other is to talk to Mr Aymes and brief him to take over my job while I do this one.'

'Telex is better than writing letters,' she suggested. 'The American postal service isn't much better than ours, even using airmail.'

'Right. Ask Aymes to come and see me and while he's here, you start drafting a suitable message for telexing and let me see it before it goes. We'll leave Chicago out, of course.'

'The flight connections and hotel reservations haven't been cancelled for Chicago yet. Mr Braithwaite planned to go and use the time there to talk to Arnison's lawyers about the bankruptcy.'

'Change it for me, then. I don't want to talk to American lawyers for two days. And get our own lawyers to come here for a meeting sometime tomorrow afternoon. I'll want someone from Accounts to brief me fully before then and to sit in on the meeting. Got all that?'

'Yes, Mr Rawlings.'

While he was waiting for Aymes to arrive, Jonathan found the message slip in his pocket. He was about to screw it up and flick it into the waste bin when something about the configuration of the name on it caught his eye. Idly at first, and then with increasing interest, he jotted down on a notepad the numerical value of the letters. The number of Karin was eleven; the number of Wikstrom was also eleven. In the Order's system of numerology, eleven is a particularly significant number. It can be seen as the sum of one, the number of God, and of ten, the number of the world. To find the number twice in one name was more rare. Two elevens gave twenty-two, the number of a master. Each eleven could be reduced to two by adding the digits and two is the number of woman. The twenty-two could be reduced to four by addition and that is the number of steady, practical, industrious people. There was no problem of interpretation here. Karin Wikstrom would lead a routine life until someone awakened her inner nature and she realised her unusually great potential for spiritual development.

The intercom on his desk interrupted his thoughts.

'Mr Aymes is here,' said Nancy.

'Hold him out there for just a minute while I make a call.'

He dialled the number on the message slip, was answered by a hotel switchboard and was put through to her room.

'Karin, this is Jonathan Rawlings. Shall I pick you up about eight for dinner?'

'That would be very nice,' she said in her slightly accented English. 'How shall I dress?'

'As fancy as you like and we'll go dancing afterwards. Do you have an early flight tomorrow?'

'No, I have a day off. I can go back on the last flight tomorrow.'

'Tell me something – when is your birthday?'

'That was last month, the seventh of April.'

Seven and four is eleven, he thought.

'Fine, we'll celebrate it a bit late. Which year were you born?'

'In 1957. Why do you ask?'

He jotted the numbers on his pad and totalised them to twenty-two.

'So I know how many candles to ask for on the cake,' he joked. 'Until eight, then.'

'Until then.'

He hung up and flipped the switch that put him through to Nancy Tait.

'Send Mr Aymes in, Nancy. And rustle up some coffee, please – we're going to be here for hours yet.'

Karin Wikstrom is the Queen of Cups in my Tarot reading last night, Jonathan was thinking. So many elevens and twenty-twos puts it beyond any possible doubt. She is bringing me a priceless gift without knowing it. And the gift is the means of neutralising Braithwaite's malice forever. And it's too late now – I've already done it a different way. I moved against him one day too soon. All I can do now is to entertain her tonight and then contact Turesson in Stockholm so that he can select someone to start to recruit her into his Lodge, where she will be a Queen in no time – perhaps even Master of the Lodge after him!

'Come in, Ronny,' he said to Aymes. 'You've been promoted. Sit down.'

CHAPTER 11
SEVEN MILES HIGH

AT HEATHROW Airport, Jonathan made a sustained effort of will to save himself from being drawn into the free floating anxiety that exuded in an almost visible mist from the crowds of people moving at cross purposes, checking in, showing passports to officials, shunting through the hand baggage search, waiting for flights to be called, striding down seemingly endless corridors to where the aircraft were waiting. It was with a sigh of relief that he sank back into his seat as the TWA jet to New York at last went rumbling down the runway and lifted off like an ungainly bird.

The past week had been a busy one, long hours at the office going over files and reports with Nancy Tait, back tracking on Braithwaite's decisions and dispositions of the previous months. There had been three meetings with Bennett to keep him informed of what Jonathan proposed and how he intended to tackle various long standing problems. There had been his encounter with Karin Wikstrom, a success from the start. Together they swept along on a wave of enthusiasm through dinner and the dancing and the drinking until by the time they reached her hotel room, their expectations were at a peak. He had discovered that within her strong and well shaped body there was a fragility that touched him. As Queen of Cups she brought him the priceless gift of herself. The next day he had personally telephoned Turesson to give him Karin's Stockholm address, so that events could be set in motion.

Two days before he left London, Jonathan had attended a meeting of the London Lodge and was moved by the ceremonial proceedings. A magnificent array of well over two hundred Knights and Ladies, surcoated, booted and with swords at their belts sat under a forest of banners – blue, white, red, green – bearing every heraldic animal and device. Above them was the star-spangled midnight-blue ceiling of the Temple. Before them the six-pointed star of Solomon the King blazed in gold from the floor. When the veil of the sanctum slid back to the sound of trumpets, the members rose as one in respect for the Grandmaster on his golden throne between the pillars of the Temple.

The twin columns that stood before the entrance to the Temple that King Solomon built in Jerusalem were named Boaz and Jachin. They represented the two forces on which the universe rested, the male principle and the female principle, yang and yin, phallos and kteis. Since no description of them is given in the Book of Kings, the Noble Order had followed a design dating from the rebuilding of the Temple by Zerubbabel, after its first destruction. The Boaz pillar on the right was painted white and fluted spirally; the Jachin pillar on the left was black and fluted vertically. Between them, crowned in glory, sat Miles Brentwood, Master of the London Lodge and Grandmaster of all the Lodges of the Noble Order throughout the world.

On the wall behind him, from floor to ceiling, was the *Phi* symbol of the Order, the circle bisected by an upright straight line, and round it were lettered the Latin words that meant 'From God are we born.'

On the right of the sanctum, beyond the pillar, stood the Grandmarshal of the Lodge holding his ivory baton of office. To the left of the sanctum stood the Guardian of the Grail, Rowena Davids, holding before her with both hands her lidded golden chalice. She was a friend of Jonathan's from years back. Together they had enjoyed many memorable times, when they had gone to the very limit of the Order's teaching on the spiritualism of sexual union. On one especial occasion he and she had performed together the marriage of Shiva and Shakti to such effect that they slept for a night and a day afterwards and awoke filled with elation and insight.

The Lodge meeting was a regular one, not a special one to upgrade a member. In consequence it was part ceremony and part business. As the opening fanfare died away, the Grandmaster led the standing Knights in the opening prayer:

> 'Powers of the Kingdom,
> Be beneath my left foot
> And within my right hand . . . '

The recitation was not, as is often the case in ordinary churches, the mechanical repetition of a formula of which the meaning has been all but forgotten. So sharp was the concentration of the men and women about him, so strong willed their call to the Shining Ones, that Jonathan could sense the walls and roof of the Temple falling away, until the Knights and Ladies stood in a compact body, face to face with the manifest universe in all its immensity. At the words:

> 'Conduct me between the two columns
> On which the whole Temple stands . . . '

even the universe faded away and they knew themselves to be in the presence of the Unmanifest.

The Grandmaster held his office for life. Masters of Lodges held office for as long as their bodily powers enabled them to conduct the quarterly rites of obligation. The two other major offices in each Lodge, that of Guardian of the Grail and that of Marshal, rotated every six months among Seventh Degree members. By tradition, the changeovers were at the spring and autumn equinoxes, the two days in the year when day and night are of exactly equal length, but they were announced well in advance to give the chosen enough time to prepare themselves in the details of the ceremonies.

Towards the end of the meeting the Marshal called out *Sister Candour* and she made her way from the rows of heavy wooden chairs to stand in the centre of the golden star on the floor. Candour was the Lodge name for a university teacher of mathematics, a tall and thin woman of fifty named Alice Jameson. She was required to recite the Profession of Righteousness, and when she had done so without challenge, the Marshal said:

'Sister Candour, it is the will of the Elder Councillors that you accept the high office of Guardian of the Holy Grail in this Lodge at the autumn equinox. Is it your will also?'

Alice had been a member of the Order for nearly thirty years, Jonathan knew. She had become a member right at the end of Hans-Martin Frick's life and term of office and the only time she had ever seen him was at the taking of her first oath as a Neophyte. Later on, when she married a publisher, she persuaded him to join the Order. He too, with her aid, had eventually reached the Seventh. Jonathan could see him across on the other side of the Temple, looking mighty proud of his wife. Looking at Alice, Jonathan wondered briefly whether, apart from the greying of her hair, she was much different in appearance from when she had stood in the same star to take her Neophyte oath so many years before.

As the unenlightened rate such things, Alice was not

sexually attractive and probably never had been. In the Order that meant nothing at all. Pleasure of all kinds was highly regarded as a way of exploring body and mind and developing both to their fullest capacity. But in the great ceremonies conducted in private in members' own chapels, the danger of coupling with a conventionally attractive partner was that personal aesthetic considerations could distract the attention. If that were allowed to happen, then the union was no more than the everyday friction of skins, an uninitiated surface action that aroused no deep reverberations within the partners and sent no vibrations out into the cosmos to stir the great powers. From this point of view, the Hollywood version of sexuality and the Order's concept of it were wholly opposed. If personal aesthetic values were the sole value of the act, the result was a short lived gratification of the senses. For ceremonies where personal values meant nothing, women like Alice, past their youth, plain but libidinously learned, were greatly prized. In mating with her, ordinary sexual attraction had no hold; she and her partner were more easily able to become unindividualised Female and Male, joined together in an act of reverence and worship.

It was very fitting, Jonathan reflected, that Alice should be honoured by the Order in this way. What happened next took him by surprise. As Alice returned, straight shouldered and smiling, to her seat, the Marshal said:

'Brother Illumine, stand forth now before this company of the Knights and Ladies of the Noble Order of the Masters of the Temple.'

Obediently, though his mind was racing, Jonathan got up and made his way through the rows of chairs with their banners until he stood in the open space in the golden star, facing the Grandmaster on his throne. The Marshal spoke again:

'Before this company, will you recite the Profession of Righteousness?'

Jonathan took a deep breath and let his voice ring out clearly.

> 'I have done no wrong;
> I have not been covetous,
> I have not stolen,
> I have killed no man...'

In speaking the familiar words, Jonathan was testing them in his mind, as he had been taught to do. Was he stretching the truth, he asked himself, was he open to challenge?

> 'I have done what is pleasing to the gods'

But had he? He had fulfilled all the obligations required of him, but in striking down Braithwaite he had performed an action which ran counter to a basic tenet of the Order: *Give only good, expect only good.* But since that form of words was not a part of the Profession, he was able to continue to the end without feeling that he was telling any deliberate untruths. He completed the words and waited. No voice challenged him. The Grandmaster took up the liturgy:

> 'Blessed is the man
> That walks not in the counsel of the unrighteous,
> Nor stands in the way of sinners,
> Nor sits in the seat of the scornful...'

When he had finished the blessing, the Marshal put to Jonathan the question he had put to Alice – the invitation of office in the Lodge.

'Brother Illumine, it is the will of the Elder Councillors that you accept the high office of Marshal of this Lodge at the autumn equinox. Is it your will also?'

In his many years in the Order, Jonathan could not remember a time when a Knight under the age of forty had been offered the office of Marshal. At the very least it meant that the Elders had their eyes on him and were pleased with what they saw, to so honour him.

'It is my will,' he said, head up and shoulders back.

'Then it shall be so.'

All this he savoured in memory as the TWA 747 climbed up to its cruising altitude and the busy stewardesses served pre-lunch drinks. He felt that he had established two secure bases, one in Dovedays by taking over Braithwaite's job and the other in the Order by his unexpected elevation to high office. And only a few hours ahead of him lay America, where by his own intelligence and energy he intended to consolidate his new status by doing the sort of job Braithwaite could never have hoped to achieve. And by contact with the American Lodges of the Order, he would see to it that word would get back to London that he was not only worthy of the honour to be bestowed in the autumn but, in due time, ready for more. In some years, who knew, perhaps even the mighty office of Grandmaster might be his. To Jonathan that thought brought the same breathless and hushed expectation that a Catholic cardinal might feel when he contemplates his chance of being elected to the Papal throne.

The airline lunch was much better than he expected and he drank half a bottle of red Californian wine with it. That too exceeded his expectations. By mid-afternoon the meal was cleared away and the screens set up for the in-flight movie. He watched the first ten minutes, found it boring and switched his earphones to music. He lay back in his comfortable seat, eyes closed, listening to the Brahms symphony that was playing. After a while he dozed off.

He dreamed of his undergraduate days at Cambridge in the early 1960s. It was a happy dream, a dream of good omen, in that his university years had been a time when he was wholly engrossed, mind and body, in pleasurable activity. He had read for an Honours degree in Classics. He enjoyed the work, the texts, the critical analyses, the lectures and the tutorials, stretching his mind to grasp the thoughts set down by men long dead about their world, its politics, its wars, pleasures and disasters. At school he had been compelled to row and had never found it interesting. At Cambridge he took it up in earnest because it was no longer obligatory, and he put in four afternoons a week on the river. Even on overcast and drizzling days, there was a keen sense of physical anticipation in being one of an eight, drifting on the slow current, waiting for the sharp cry of the cox: 'Are you ready? Row!' Then the smooth swing of backs, the thrust of thighs and legs, the pull along the arms, as the boat cut through the water. Practising fast starts, long steady hauls for mid-race, then the excitement of the cox pounding his fists on the sides of the boat and screaming out, 'Give her ten . . . one, out . . . two, out . . . three, out . . .' and the huge spurt of power to heave the boat forward at top speed, until arms, legs and back were protesting at the strain, but still keeping going, sweat pouring down the chest and face.

Study and sport, and his other great interest, sex. He had indulged them all to the full in those years. Though there was a great preponderance then at Cambridge of men over women, he had always been able to find a girl to share in his interest. Whether his sexual activites detracted from his performance on the river was of no importance to him – he enjoyed both. It may have kept him out of his college's first boat, but he was happy enough to row stroke in the third boat in the May Bumps in his second year.

That had been a great day for him. The river at Cambridge is too narrow for side by side racing and so the event of the year is the Bumps. Each college enters its boats and all start at the same gun shot, in a long line astern, the order of starting being determined by the results of the previous year. The object of the race is to catch up with and bump the boat ahead, while avoiding being bumped by the boat astern, by out-rowing both. A boat that is bumped pulls over to the bank and is out of the race. The next day, the race is run again, bumped and bumpers changing places. The year that Jonathan stroked his college's third boat it had started eighteenth in line and in three days of racing it moved up three places, an heroic effort. In his last year he had been too close to his Finals to devote so much time to the river and that year, though his boat was not bumped, it moved up only one place.

High over the Atlantic on his way to New York Jonathan woke up, his dream fresh in his mind, the towpath crowded with cheering undergraduates as he inspired his crew to their victory. He smiled as he woke. Good days, they were, days with no complications. It was at Cambridge also that he had taken his first blind step towards membership of the Noble Order of the Masters of the Temple. He recalled that event vividly. It was an evening in summer, not long after his twentieth birthday. He was with his Latin tutor, Dr Challey, for his weekly six to seven hour. They reviewed his reading programme since their last meeting and the work to be done before their next, then Challey had passed on to his comments on Jonathan's weekly essay.

'Quite good,' said Challey, slumped in an armchair and sending up clouds of blue smoke from his pipe. Jonathan had a certain regard for him. Challey at that time was nearly sixty, a tall beak nosed man who always wore dark suits and a spotted bow tie. He was the author of several books in the college library, mainly on the economics of the Roman conquest of Gaul.

'Thank you,' said Jonathan. *Quite good* from a man as hard to please as Challey was equal to unqualified praise from any other teacher.

'What about this bit, though?' Challey asked, taking his pipe from his mouth and stabbing at the pages in his hand with the stem. '*Quod superius est sicut quod inferius*. What's that got to do with Seneca?'

'I was trying to make a point about his philosophical debt to the Stoics. Seneca says in one of his treatises that we each have a god within us, for good or evil, who treats us as we treat him. The quotation seemed apt.'

'How do you reconcile a pious sentiment like good and evil within us with what we know of Seneca's life – first tutor and then top civil servant to the Emperor Nero? If the college chaplain took bribes and debauched young women, you wouldn't pay much attention to his preaching in chapel, would you?'

'I don't anyway, though I'm sure he leads a blameless and saintly life.'

'You haven't answered my question. You've only told me that you don't attend chapel.'

171

'You're asking me whether we should judge a man's worth by his words or his deeds.'

'Since you've turned it into a question of moral edification, we'll leave it. Do you know the rest of your quotation, or is it just a tag you picked up somewhere?'

'*Quod superius est sicut quod inferius, et quod inferius est sicut quod superius ad perpetranda miracula rei unius.*'

'Good. What does it mean?'

'As above, so below; as below, so above, to achieve the wonder of unity.'

'To achieve the unity of what?' Challey asked.

'Of God and man, I suppose is meant.'

'Do you know where your quotation comes from?'

'It was written on the Emerald Tablet of Hermes Trismegistus.'

'And who was he when he was out and about?'

Challey was obviously amusing himself at Jonathan's expense.

'He was the legendary founder of Hermetic philosophy and belief.'

'You certainly have been doing some extra-curricular reading, Rawlings. I wonder you have time to get through the work I give you if you are pursuing interests like that.'

'I've given you no cause for complaint, Dr Challey.'

'I didn't mean that. To be candid, you're one of my best pupils. I fully expect you to get a First in your Finals. That being so, I am not anxious for you to stray too far from the required reading, except in so far as your own special interests open up new perspectives of understanding for you.'

'I believe they do. For instance, it seems to me that the Emerald Tablet is getting at the same thing as Plato when he said that the physical world we know is only a reflection of a deeper reality, the World of Forms.'

'Or the World of Formation,' said Challey, as if to himself, but Jonathan picked up his words at once.

'The World of Formation is a term from the Cabala,' he said. 'It means much the same as Plato's term – another plane of reality of which our world is a reflection or emanation.'

'You know about the Cabala too?' Challey asked, raising his thick eyebrows. 'How very interesting. Can you expound the Tree of Life to me?'

'If you wish.'

Challey put his pipe away and sat upright in his chair.

'Go on, then,' he said, very alert.

'In Cabalistic belief,' Jonathan began, picking his words, 'all things that exist, men and women, animals and plants, the earth, the sun, the universe, are aspects of God, who in his totality is unknowable to us. He is described as the Limitless Light. This concentrates into a point of focus called Kether, which means the Crown, and is the first aspect of God which is even partly comprehensible to the human mind. From this point of focus come two further emanations; Hokmah, meaning male wisdom, and Binah, meaning female understanding. The basic assumption of the Cabala is that there are three successive spiritual worlds underlying and sustaining physical reality.'

'You described these worlds as emanations,' said Challey. 'That's a vague word. How do you define it?'

'I define it to myself as unfoldings. The flower is not inside the tiny bud, except potentially, and yet the bud unfolds into a flower. The bud is not physically in the stem, yet its possibility is there, since the bud appears out of the stem. And all of the plant – stem, leaves, buds, flowers – are present as potentials within the bulb, though you cannot find them by cutting the bulb open.'

'Have you ever cut a bulb open to look?'

'Why, yes, in biology class at school.'

Dr Challey sat in thought for a while, filling his pipe again.

'Not too bad an exposition,' he said at last. 'Fairly lucid, though not inspired. Do you know what is said to happen when a master expounds the inner meaning of the Tree to his disciples?'

'No, what?'

'A golden light begins to glow about him. It grows brighter as he continues, until it fills the place where he is and his listeners are forced to shield their eyes from the glory about him. There are some who think that the convention of painting Christian saints with a halo around their heads was borrowed by artists from this tradition. Others maintain that it was copied by early Christian artists from the Roman convention of depicting the sun as a god in human form with rays of light shining round his head. You can take your choice.'

'The two versions may be the same,' said Jonathan. 'The symbol of the plane of the resurrected gods is the sun, the god-form which dies every evening and is resurrected every dawn. Perhaps only a master who had reached that level and was filled with light could expound the meaning of the Tree in so profound a way.'

Challey looked over his spectacles at his pupil.

'You've clearly thought about this more than once,' he said. 'What turned your interest in this direction?'

'Curiosity.'

'I don't believe that. I've been teaching bright young men like you for more years than you've lived and I think I've got some glimmering of insight into how their minds work. Wasn't there someone older than yourself who guided your interest this way?'

'I can't tell you that,' said Jonathan.

'Does that mean you are unable to tell me or unwilling to tell me?'

'Both.'

'I see. Would I be far wrong in saying that you had given that someone binding promises?'

'Not far wrong.'

'In a circle, was it?' Challey asked casually.

'You can't know that,' said Jonathan in surprise.

'I can guess. Well, Mr Rawlings, your hour is nearly up. Perhaps we can arrange to talk about this interest of yours on another occasion, not in a tutorial hour.'

'Why, certainly, if you wish to.'

'Good, we'll arrange something. Meanwhile, until the dinner bell rings to summon us to hall for whatever the kitchens may be pleased to serve us this evening, here is another question for you. Do you see any similarity between what you have outlined and the current astronomical theory of an exploding universe?'

'I haven't read much about astronomy or cosmology. As I understand it, the theory is that at some stage in the remote past, all the energy that has ever existed was concentrated into a mass of infinite density and then exploded outwards in the form of pure radiation. After a time, the temperature of the explosion dropped enough to allow the radiation to form into particles, and later still these particles aggregated into atoms, so that eventually matter was created out of energy. Still later the atoms accumulated into pieces of matter of all sizes, some of which is still inter-stellar dust and some of which clumped together to form stars and planets. Is that how the theory goes?'

'Good enough for someone who hasn't read much about the subject,' said Challey drily. 'Do you see that as a scientist's version of your Limitless Light concentrating into a point of focus and then by stages emanating the universe?'

'It differs in one important respect. It suggests that the big bang took place at some definable point in time and that we are being carried along willy nilly on the debris of the explosion. All very mechanical. The system represented by the Tree of Life is one of continuous emanation. All things are sustained in being because the Limitless Light continues to pour itself out at every moment.'

'So you are prepared to challenge the astronomers, are you?'

Off in the distance the dinner bell began to chime.

'I ploughed through a book by Professor Wittgenstein last year,' said Jonathan, 'merely from curiosity, as he was a Cambridge celebrity. I didn't expect to get much out of it, because modern philosophy is not my subject. But he wrote one thing which stuck in my mind – that the meaning of the universe lies outside the universe, not inside it.'

'And so?'

'By definition, scientists can only seek meaning inside the universe because their methods are to count, measure and dissect.'

Challey got up and put his pipe into his jacket pocket. Jonathan rose with him.

'I knew Wittgenstein tolerably well when he had the chair of philosophy here. Walk across to hall with me while we talk. Do you know that Wittgenstein's undergraduate studies at Vienna before the First War were in engineering, not philosophy?'

They left Challey's book lined rooms and made their way side by side across the quadrangle towards where the hall bell was still chiming.

'Only one of his books was published in his lifetime, you know,' said Challey. 'Two or three others have appeared since, but there's still a lot of his work unpublished.'

'Why didn't he publish more in his lifetime – wasn't he pleased with his work?'

'I don't know. He was a strangely shy man in many ways.'

Dr Challey was as good as his word. He made a point of inviting Jonathan to visit him when time permitted and they talked further about the Cabala and other related matters, on which he proved to be extremely well informed. By stages the relationship between them developed from tutor and pupil into friendship. It was not until his last term at Cambridge that Jonathan found out why Challey had encouraged this development.

During the Second War, twenty years earlier, Challey had been put to work by the Government, like many other academics. What sort of work it was, Jonathan never discovered, as Challey would never be more specific than 'my time at the Ministry'. From this reticence Jonathan concluded that it had been highly secret work and that Challey was still bound by the Official Secrets Act, though it was not easy to imagine what use any secret department of government might have had for a university teacher of the language, literature and history of the ancient Romans. Years later, with the benefit of hindsight, Jonathan thought that it might have been in some aspect of economic warfare, as it was during this period that Challey became acquainted with Hans-Martin Frick, who was also putting his talents to work on behalf of his newly adopted country.

Frick had just established his Noble Order of the Masters of the Temple in London and was looking about with great care for potential members. Challey was nearly forty at the time, unmarried and agnostic, and had lived for much of his adult life with the mystery religions of the ancient world as a reality that had shaped the literature and history he taught. One of his most interesting books was an illustrated exposition of the initiation ceremonies painted on the walls of the Villa of the Mysteries which archaeologists had unearthed at Pompeii. Frick's cautious probing of Challey revealed a spirit in harmony with his own, but foiled of a means of self realisation in action. It didn't require much persuasion to induce Challey to accept initiation into the Order, once he had been told enough to convince him that its liturgy and ceremonials were a valid expression of age-old beliefs.

By the time Jonathan became his pupil at Cambridge at the beginning of the 1960s, Challey had progressed to the Seventh Degree and was a fulfilled man. When he trusted Jonathan's understanding and discretion, he began to hint at the existence of an organisation of men and women who shared a body of belief and knowledge and met to actualise their beliefs. Jonathan could still recall exactly how he first heard of the secret organisation. As an exercise he set out to reconstruct in Latin the original pagan initiation ritual on which the biblical Book of Revelations was based. First he eliminated the Christian interpolations and references to Jesus and then he constructed connecting links, in the style of the original. Challey was quite impressed by the results and gave him the benefit of his views on Christianity.

'It is necessary to distinguish between historical fact and later interpretation,' he said. 'That is, we must distinguish between Yeshu, a wandering Jewish preacher and Jesus Christ, one of the three aspects of the Christian deity. We can more or less establish that Yeshu was born in rural Galilee during the reign of King Herod the Great, and we know that Herod died in the year 4 BC from non-biblical sources. He grew up to be a pious Jew and followed his father's trade until he had a vision of union with God which changed the course of his life. He gave up work and took to itinerant preaching in the small towns and villages around Lake Galilee. When he eventually took his message to the wider audience of Jerusalem, the people mistook him for the leader they were expecting to appear and drive the Roman army of occupation into the sea. Before things got out of hand, the local Roman governor had him arrested and executed for political agitation. We date that event to the procuratorship of Pontius Pilate, who held office in Palestine for ten years until he was dismissed in the year 36 AD. So there is our historical framework.'

'Can so personal a vision be shared with others?' Jonathan asked. 'Are there words in any language to explain what it is like to catch a glimpse of God?'

'No, that has always been the problem. To continue, after the execution of Yeshu, his followers began the long process of creating Jesus Christ from what they could remember of what he had said and done. Those things which they felt he ought to have said but didn't, they freely borrowed from the Jewish scriptures we now call the Old Testament. And as the real Yeshu receded further and further into the dim past, a new power structure emerged – the Christian Church – capable of any and every atrocity as it connived at political control and a universal totalitarian state firmly based on the model of the defunct Roman Empire.'

'I remember reading somewhere,' said Jonathan, 'that the success of the Christian Church proves the truth of its message.'

'A highly bogus argument. In its early days, the Church recruited by offering a guarantee of life after death to anyone who would agree that Jesus Christ was a god. Then when it became stronger, it extracted money and obedience by threatening torture after death to anyone who denied its basic proposition. And when it had real power, it inflicted real torture and painful death on anyone who queried even the most absurd of its invented beliefs.'

'It sounds as if you see religion in Europe as more or less an extension of politics.'

'Of course,' said Challey, 'in much the same way that war is an extension of diplomacy. In England we have been mercifully free of the power of the Christian church for some time, though others are not. In Ireland and in Poland, to give you only two examples, religion is still an extension of the political struggle. Nor is the United States free of this ancient calamity.'

'Why do you say that?'

'A presidential candidate in America has to come to terms with strong religious leaders because he needs to try to secure the Baptist vote, the Methodist vote, the Catholic vote, and so on. He is not wholly free to act in the light of reason or conscience – he must make at least token obeisance to the various spokesmen of Jesus Christ if he wants the support of their flocks at the poll.'

'Obeisance to the spokesmen or to their view of God?'

'It comes to the same thing. The significance of Jesus Christ in Christian mythology is simply stated. They have made him a judge. He hands out sentences of eternal bliss or eternal damnation according to whether you have conformed to the requirements of his spokesmen on earth.'

'The requirements vary from sect to sect.'

'Not in the three main tenets. One, you must believe that Jesus Christ is the only god-form there is. Two, you must give part of your earnings towards the upkeep of his spokesmen. Three, you must accept that sexual relationships are inherently unchristian.'

'What would your strolling preacher have made of that?'

'We know precisely what he would have made of it,' said Challey. 'He quoted from Isaiah to make his point: "*These people honour me with their lips, but their heart is far from me; in vain do they worship me, teaching for doctrine the commandments of men.*" Could anything be more apt?'

'What do you suppose was the message of Yeshu, then?'

'That is also simply stated: *The kingdom of God is within you.* The Noble Order teaches exactly the same message.'

'Which Noble Order?' Jonathan asked immediately.

'Its name is known only to its members.'

On another occasion Challey lent Jonathan a book on Tantric belief, published in English in Bombay. The text was not very explicit, but from the many illustrations of couples united in involved sexual embraces Jonathan was able to glean something of the central importance of bodily coupling as an expression of spiritual truths. He certainly wanted to know more about any group of people who could synthesise in one intellectual system the mystical teachings of the Cabala and the ecstatic rites of Tantra, the mysterious Noble Order which Challey had referred to in passing.

Jonathan graduated in 1963 and surprised both Dr Challey and his own father by opting for a career in business instead of either teaching or government service. His decision was influenced to some extent by his private assessment of the course of his father's life as a school teacher and his observation of the narrowness of academic life as instanced by the university teachers he had come into contact with. But beyond that, he wanted to get into a system which presented opportunities to make more money than either teaching or the higher reaches of the civil service could offer. He made a start as a management trainee in the marketing department of Proctor and Gamble and, as soon as he could afford it, he asked Challey to recommend him for membership of the Noble Order.

After that, Challey had to stand aside and let two Inquisitors determine whether he should be accepted. They interviewed him at length over a period of months before they were satisfied that he was a suitable person. Even after he had been accepted as a Neophyte, Challey was not permitted to be his guide, though they remained good friends and met fairly often in London. The Order's method was that each member was assigned as a pupil to a member of the opposite sex who was one Degree higher, so that there would be a sexual bond between teacher and pupil. The Elder Councillors who arranged these things generally coupled together in the learning process men and women of divergent personalities and backgrounds, so that each would shape the other. Jonathan's first *guru* was a woman in her middle thirties, a widow.

She was a thin, fair haired, active and practical woman. After the accidental death of her husband she had taken control of his successful office cleaning business and ran it as well as he ever did. She had a twelve year old son away at boarding school and to Jonathan she was unlike anyone he had met before. At Cambridge his sexual activities were conducted with young women of his own age. Dorothy Mawson was a good ten years older and vastly more experienced carnally than even the randiest of women undergraduates. Jonathan was used to learning from books; Dorothy was uninterested in books. If he said to her 'I've been reading Regardie's book about the Golden Dawn teachings . . . ' she would interrupt with, 'You can tell me about that later. Let's get on with turning ourselves into god-forms – why have you still got your clothes on?'

Their meetings took place in her West Kensington apartment, a large and comfortable place, except that one room was kept locked and had no furniture other than a square wooden altar and its walls were hung with pictures of the gods of ancient Egypt. It was his first encounter with a private chapel.

After a year with her, Dorothy proposed him for advancement to the Second Degree. By then he had come to know her mind and body well and to like her greatly. When a man and a woman, robed and crowned, face each other across an altar on which sweet-smelling incense is burning and, reciting the prayers and responses together, extend their will and imagination to take on the forms of Osiris and Isis, a deep bond is formed between them. And when, in the god-forms they have assumed, they unite sexually in the mode prescribed by the ancient books, the bond is made well nigh indestructible.

Fifteen years on, when Jonathan had reached the Seventh and Dorothy the Fifth, the bond was still intact.

By that time Jonathan had formed similar bonds with other women. The pairings were changed for each Degree and his next teacher was Susan Heaslop, a senior official in the Ministry of Defence. By the time he was a Third he had not only a teacher but a pupil of his own assigned to him, for that was the way the Order worked to instruct its members how to climb the ladder of Degrees, which was its way of showing them how to discover and climb the ladder of selves towards the ultimate self.

CHAPTER 12
THE SACRED MOUNTAIN

THE LONG descent to Kennedy Airport was bumpy. The big jet heaved and swayed as it sank down towards the runway, its passengers strapped into their seats and silent. Somewhere behind Jonathan a small child was crying on its mother's lap, upset by the unnatural motion and sensitive to her suppressed fear. The lurching continued until the concrete came up in one final rush to meet the plane, the wheels smacked it with a sticky sound and the engines roared to decelerate the run. New York lay under a heat haze, the temperature up in the eighties and the humidity uncomfortably high. Jonathan took his briefcase and went with the crowd from the plane towards Immigration, sweating in the change of atmosphere.

Heathrow had been permeated by a feeling of anxiety, Kennedy was enswathed in hysteria. The queues at passport control pushed, fretted and fumed. In the big hall, the build up of violent auras was so overpowering that Jonathan muttered a calming mantra to protect himself from it. Once past the passport desk, the tension grew worse as men and women hustled to and fro trying to identify their luggage in the chaos and lug it towards the customs men, jostling each other with heavy bags and emanating great waves of angry frustration. Though air travel had been a routine part of his business life for years, Jonathan never failed to be amazed at how easily airports reduced sensible people to the level of snarling beasts.

In his mind he drew a circle of cold fire about himself as he formulated silently the words that would guard him and activated them:

'Greatest of all, basis of all, power behind all, lord of the universe, initiator of all life; you have instructed me, you have commanded me to rise and make my way in this my everyday life. Let there be turned aside from me whatever evil may come to threaten my well-being.'

Much reinforced and free of jostling and the high pitched tension about him, he edged his way forward to the long table where uniformed customs officials were slowly examining every item of clothing in every single suitcase presented for their inspection. Or so it seemed, until Jonathan's turn came. The official looked at him thoughtfully, marked his luggage and waved him on without a word.

The long taxi ride to Manhattan was as potentially nerve shredding as the passage through the TWA terminal. Oppressive heat bore down harder as the tall buildings closed in around him and impatient traffic filled the air with exhaust fumes. Jonathan rode calmly through it, secure inside his protective aura. When he checked in at the hotel and the bellman carried his baggage up for him, he was delighted to see that the booking he had taken over from Braithwaite was a whole suite, not just a room. Evidently Braithwaite was accustomed to travelling in comfort. There was a large and brightly furnished sitting room, two double bedrooms with beds that looked eight feet wide, a bathroom with a bath big enough to take two or three people at once. The scale of it caused him to speculate on Braithwaite's activities on sales trips.

He showered to get rid of the sticky feeling he had picked up at the airport and considered what to do next. It was too late by London time to call his office for any messages; it was too late by New York time to make any worthwhile contact with Dovedays' people there. It was too early to go for dinner and far too hot and crowded outside to take a stroll. He was, he realised, slightly off balance from the long flight to be thinking like that. He decided to orient himself spiritually.

He hung the Do Not Disturb sign outside his door and drew the curtains to dim the bedroom he had chosen. In only his bathrobe he sat cross legged on the bed, his hands resting lightly on his knees. The Order's ceremonies were normally performed facing to the east, but that would be to put the whole of the United States at his back and three thousand miles of ocean before him. Therefore he sat facing west, slowed his breathing and gathered his forces together within himself.

Twenty floors above street level, he visualised himself sitting on the peak of Mount Meru, the sacred mountain and the navel of the world. His eyes focused on infinity, by an act of will and imagination he caused the sacred mountain to assume reality for him. As it solidified beneath him, he no longer saw the walls of the building about him. They dissolved like vapour, so that he could see the city below him, then further out still, until the disc of the world was laid out clearly for him, its great rivers, lakes, forests and mountain ranges, near and far.

Though a man may know intellectually that the earth is a sphere spinning through space, his immediate and personal experience of it is as a flat disc with himself at the centre. This was how mankind saw it at the dawning of human consciousness; this is how each man still secretly knows it. Jonathan was creating subjectively this primal awareness of the world as an extension of himself. Mount Meru was the upright axis of his own spine, the circular world about him was an extension of himself. His vision became all embracing until he could see the ocean at his back as clearly as the land in front of him. By stages he imposed his inner view of the world on the other world he knew intellectually to be there, until he fused subjective and objective realities into one.

Out beyond the rim of the world disc lay the realms of the gods, guarded at the four points of the compass by the Watchtowers of the universe. Jonathan gazed mildly at each in turn without turning his head, calling out softly the name of each, to the south, then to the west where the continent ended at the Pacific, then to the north and the ice of the Arctic, then to the east where the Atlantic Ocean ran to the rim of the world he had created. He spoke the names of the Watchers aloud so that they would recognise him and be witnesses to his ceremony.

Before him the whole of the United States was stretched out in his view. At his feet lay New York and beyond its suburbs he gazed across the farmlands, the industrial cities, the small towns, and further yet, to the plains of the Mid West and on to the long ridge of the Rocky Mountains and over that to the deserts of Nevada and to the Californian coast. He saw San Francisco on its finger of land and Los Angeles sprawled over miles of hot, dry earth. From his vantage point he saw, half to his left, past Washington with its domed Capitol building, down the length of the Allegheny Mountains to the flat-lands of Alabama and on to where the Mississippi ran to New Orleans. His gaze followed the coastline around the Gulf, past Galveston and Corpus Christi, until the land changed into Mexico.

Slowly he integrated all he saw into his own being. When he had absorbed it, he turned his gaze outwards further still into the realms of the gods. But his mind was dazzled and he was forced to withdraw into the world disc again. Then that too faded, the sacred mountain dissolved beneath him, and he was back in his own body, sitting cross legged and upright on a hotel bed.

He sat in thought for a while, questioning how successful his orientation had been. The vision had been true, the feeling of unbounded power had been present in him. But something of importance had been lacking, for he had been earth bound.

The Noble Order's mysteries were based on the psychic

energy aroused by the physical union of male and female. Working alone, he had not been able to go beyond the world vision. The final shift of consciousness to the highest level had not take place in him. He could not move unaided out beyond the world rim past the Watchers, who had turned him gently back. If a woman of the Order had been present, there would have been no barrier, the way would have been opened for them both. The ceremony, he concluded, had been useful only as an exercise; it had not been effective as an act of possession of what he had seen.

The conclusion was displeasing to him. To attain his present worldly status he had dared to evoke from the depths of the cosmos within himself the destructive force he had turned against Derek Braithwaite. The demonologies of the Middle Ages are filled with tales of adepts summoning up darkling powers to destroy their enemies, tales now totally discredited by scientists, teachers, psychiatrists, ministers of religion and all men and women of average common sense. But Jonathan knew that no one with a regard for his own mental and physical survival would venture lightly on such an undertaking. Holy names of gods or archangels inscribed around a circle are no sure protection against energies of that magnitude, as Aleister Crowley and many others since him have found to their cost. It was unacceptable to Jonathan to have risked calling up so monstrous a force and then have his subsequent endeavours end in failure. Whatever it involved, he had to return to London crowned with success.

His ceremony of orientation must be repeated, in company with a woman. There were Lodges of the Noble Order in many parts of the United States, but not in New York, a city the Order regarded as too profane to concern itself with. No Lady of the Order was within immediate reach and in Jonathan's mind the matter was too urgent to postpone. He would have to make do with what he could find. Fortunately, the means were to hand – amongst the personal papers and belongings in Braithwaite's desk he had come across a thin black notebook listing telephone numbers in major cities all round the world. There was no indication of who the subscribers were, but that was hardly necessary. Jonathan dialled one of the three numbers listed for New York and got a middle aged woman's voice. He explained that he was a visitor and was in search of company.

'No problem, honey. You want black, white, Chinese or Chicano company?'

'White, please.'

'Be about thirty minutes – OK?'

He had not chosen white out of preference or prejudice. For sexual purposes the colour of a partner's skin is wholly irrelevant. But Jonathan's purpose was not primarily sexual; that aspect of it was incidental. For his proposed ceremony of orientation he felt that a white woman would be more effective, in that her people would have been identified for a much longer time with the ordering and establishing of the United States. The other ethnic groups had only very recently elbowed their way into positions of economic and political opportunity. Their role was still insecure and their personalities would bear the traces of insecurity.

While he was waiting he drew the curtains completely and turned off all the lights except one bedside lamp. He poured himself a drink from the bar he found in the sitting room and sat down to think through how he intended to direct the ceremony. Necessarily, the woman must remain unaware of it, otherwise she might take fright. That posed certain problems of procedure, but he had it clear in his mind by the time the discreet tap came at the door. He opened it and stood aside to let his visitor in. She was about nineteen, he guessed; small and slender, with long dark hair and more make-up than she needed. She looked quickly around her with the knowing glance of one who had seen a great many hotel rooms and could evaluate the occupant's financial worth to herself exactly. That done, she gave him a quick, tight smile and said *Hi!*

'Hello. My name's Jonathan. What's yours?'

'Tracey. You sound British – are you?'

'Right. I'm a visiting fireman, as they say. Would you like a drink?'

'Scotch on the rocks. You've got a nice layout here.'

As he poured the drink for her and another for himself, Jonathan reflected that her name was no more Tracey than his own. From the look of her, she had started life as Bridie Murphy or Anna Kowalski. Girls like her never used their own names in hustling, and rarely used the same name for more than a week or two at a time. It made it harder for the police to identify them if they were arrested. Not that it mattered in the least. She was a woman and therefore she could be a sacred vessel. He handed her the drink and sat down.

'That's a pretty dress, Tracey. The colour suits you.'

'Thanks. As I've never met you before, how about getting the business side over so that we can get friendly?'

'That's fine with me. How much?'

'Two hundred. OK?'

He had guessed the amount long before she had set foot inside his room and had four fifty dollar bills ready in the pocket of his dressing gown. Tracey took the money without a word and tucked it into her shoulder bag.

'Let me show you the bedroom,' said Jonathan, and she followed him in.

'You wanna take my clothes off?' she asked, giving him her meaningless little smile again.

'You do it,' he said, 'while I sit over here and watch.'

She reached behind her back to unzip her peach-coloured dress, short enough to expose a good half of her thighs, and pulled it over her head. Her half cup brassiere was mostly black lace and did nothing to conceal her well-shaped breasts. She turned her back to him while she rolled down her tights, bending over to wiggle her bare buttocks at him invitingly. When she turned to face him again, her shiny black briefs were the smallest he could recall seeing on a woman, being no more than a hand-sized triangle of material held with strings over her hips. She lay on the bed, knees up, her head hanging over the edge, to look at him.

'Like me?'

'You're very attractive,' he said.

At another time and in another place Jonathan would have accepted her as a person, a woman made of flesh, bones, blood and nerves, with a brain and a mind of her own, someone to treat with human consideration. But just then he saw her not as a living woman with whom to establish any relationship at all, however fleeting, but as a warm slit to be used in his ceremony. Though he was as yet unaware of it, this change in his sensitivity to others had come about since his psychic assault on Braithwaite. No adept, however advanced, can summon up such forces of destruction from within himself and direct them at another without himself being affected. Jonathan was not the man he had been before the orgy of hatred in his private chapel.

'So come over here and do something about it,' Tracey suggested.

He threw his robe over the chair he had been sitting on and joined her on the broad bed. She wriggled round to put her head on the pillows, one arm bent, the hand behind her neck, exposing a smooth armpit, the other hand resting lightly on her thigh, near her groin. Her well-rehearsed whore's gestures amused Jonathan, particularly the way she arched her back to let him undo her brassiere, and the way her eyes closed, as if in passion, as he ran his hands over her breasts and shoulders, belly and thighs. He was not exciting himself by touching her, as she thought, but accustoming her to his touch. He was careful not to touch her nipples, guessing that any attempt to excite her would arouse inner resistence. He was banking on the fact that most whores despise their customers and take pride in feeling nothing while they are being used, so maintaining their integrity. As long as he was cautious, she would be off guard and he would be able to establish a rapport between them.

'You wanna take my pants off, Jonny?'

Her hips lifted off the bed as he slid the stretch string over her buttocks and down her legs, the removal of the wisp of black material exposing a patch of dark brown hair clipped short and small. She parted her thighs as he stroked up the insides of them, not touching her slit.

'How you want to do it?' she asked. 'Me on my back, me on top of you, blow job or what? Just name it.'

'I'm in an old-fashioned mood,' he answered, smiling at her. 'You on your back and me on top.'

'For this town that's pretty straight, but it's your party.'

Her tone was more relaxed. The money was in her purse, the mark wanted a simple screw on top of her. All she had to do was lie with her legs apart and in five minutes it would be over and she would be in the bathroom. And five minutes after that she'd be out of the hotel with two hundred dollars and ready for the next man. She was unaware of the effect on her of Jonathan's hands, stroking her shoulders, her upper arms, her sides, her thighs, staying clear of her breasts and genitals.

In the section of the Temple library in London accessible only to those of Jonathan's Degree, were unpublished works by several members based on the findings of Franz Anton Mesmer and their own experience of the application of his findings. Though the German doctor had been denounced in his own time and afterwards as a fraud, he had stumbled on the power of suggestion to influence the human mind, though at first he had not himself understood what he had found. Sigmund Freud, a hundred years later, used hypnosis to reach the hidden depths of the mind without acknowledging that Mesmer had pioneered the way. Jonathan knew, from trying out what he had read in the Order's guarded archives, that most people can be put into a pleasant trance if a rapport is established between the operator and the subject. Modern hypnotists require the paraphernalia of lights, swinging medallions and words, but Mesmer's original way was simpler, depending on no more than a soothing touch of hands in the early stages.

Very gently he moved Tracey away from the pillows so that she lay across the bed, her head to the direction he had established as west and her legs to the east. He handled her with great delicacy as he eased her towards the edge of the bed until she lay with her legs over the side and her feet touching the floor. He parted her legs and went on stroking her thighs and belly, as if he were gentling a nervous horse, speaking quietly and soothingly, words of no particular meaning: *'there ... there ... easy ... easy ... that's fine ...'*

Tracey's eyes were closed and she was half asleep and completely off guard, the hard barriers around her ego dissolving in pleasant non-sexual sensation.

'That's good,' said Jonathan slowly, 'Just relax for a minute ... you're a lovely girl, Tracey ... just relax.'

What actually takes place when a person is hypnotised, or as Jonathan preferred to call it, mesmerised, after the good doctor, is not understood by doctors or psychologists after two hundred years of medical experience of it. The reason why one person should submit control to another is inexplicable. The reasons suggested range from physical – a suspension of communication along the nerves or within the brain – to psychological – a yearning masochism, or even a form of mild sexual gratification. Whatever the reason, the process works and Jonathan knew how to make it work for him.

'You are asleep, Tracey,' he said, 'but you can hear my voice.'

He climbed off the bed slowly and stood between her parted legs, looking down the length of her naked and vulnerable body.

'You are deep asleep,' he said, his voice full of confidence and quiet authority. 'You hear nothing but my voice, nothing at all. You will do whatever I say. Do you understand me?'

Her voice was utterly toneless as she said *yes*, hardly moving her lips.

'Listen to me carefully, Tracey. I am going to lie over you and put it up you. You will feel very good. You will lie still and enjoy the feeling.'

Standing on the floor, he leaned forward over the girl, opened her expertly with his fingers and slid his erection into her. He braced his arms on either side of her to take the weight of his body, so that only their genital areas were in contact. Now, after the preparations, there approached the moment he had been waiting for. He closed his eyes and began to recreate in his mind the world disc he had created earlier when he was alone. It formed in his mental vision with the ease of long practice. He was on the peak of the sacred mountain, contemplating the lands, rivers, forests and seas of the world below him.

The woman he was using as a sacred vessel was not of the Order and could contribute her body but not her mind to the working. Simplicity was therefore of maximum importance. Aloud, but softly, Jonathan spoke in salutation to the Guardians of the Watchtowers, using gentle names for them so as not to cause any disturbance in the sleeping girl's mind, whatever her religious upbringing might have been.

> 'Behind me, Raphael,
> Before me, Gabriel,
> On my right hand, Auriel,
> On my left hand, Michael;
> Air, water, earth and fire,
> Here in this woman.'

The order was reversed from the usual one in that he was facing west and not east, where Raphael would have been before him. But they were there, witnessing his ceremony, as they were always there when an adept called to them. Jonathan brought clearly into his inner vision a part of the world disc he had created, the United States. He saw it laid out before him from east coast to west coast and when he had it fast in his mind's eye, he recited:

> 'I who am a perfect king
> To the people entrusted to me by God,
> I who am by God's command their shepherd,
> Have never tarried, never rested . . . '

As he spoke, he opened his eyes slowly, imposing his inner vision on the naked girl who lay under him, until he saw her body as an incarnation of the whole of America. Her up-rearing breasts were the distant range of the Rocky Mountains, her belly the wheat plains of the Mid West. Her mound, into which he was plunged, was the city of New York, the base from which he was extending his control outwards to all those he would meet and have dealings with in this land.

> 'I was called by the great gods,
> Wherefore I became the good shepherd
> Whose staff is straight and strong;
> My shadow has stretched out across this city...'

While the words were still sounding in his mind and about him like the after-vibrations of a struck gong, he said to the mesmerised girl,

'Tracey – you are sexually excited by the feel of me inside you.'

He watched her face become flushed, her head roll slowly from side to side on the bed cover. She began to sigh, then her breathing became short and ragged. Her breasts rose and fell beneath his gaze, her nipples hard; her thighs trembled against his legs.

'Tracey – come!' he commanded. As her body went into spasm, he continued in a strong voice,

> 'I have gathered my people into my arms,
> That they may thrive under my protection;
> I shield them in my peace
> And protect them in my wisdom...'

Tracey's orgasm was brief. Jonathan commanded her to come again, holding his mind steady and intent upon the words of his prayer as her wet slit clenched and unclenched on his shaft. She almost took him with her, but he held on, determined to extract the greatest possible effect from what he was doing. This was no shared experienced of diversity out of unity and the solace of unity out of diversity as he and Britt had enjoyed in Stockholm as Shiva and Shakti. The girl who called herself Tracey was here to be used in his power play, body and mind. The rape was not physical, since she had consented to copulation and accepted money for the use of her body. The violation was psychic. At the extreme moment he would fuse the release of sexual power in her body and mind into his own and turn it to his own end. And the girl would never know what he had done.

He let her rest for a minute or two while mentally he crowned himself with the golden six-pointed star of power, the Seal of Solomon the King. Then he started his incantation again from the beginning: *I who am a perfect king* . . . and as he did so, he began to move inside her for the first time, short, hard thrusts. As he approached the end of the incantation he commanded Tracey to come again and this time her orgasm was long and tumultuous, arms thrashing, legs kicking. Jonathan went with her and as he ejaculated mightily into her heaving belly, he gasped out the final phrases,

> 'Here in this city I have spoken my word
> Into this woman's body
> And have erected my image as king.'

Spent by his efforts, he lowered himself forward to lie gratefully on the girl's hot and sweating body. He was satisfied that the ceremony had been effective. He had set up through the joint orgasm a powerful and lasting vibration that would affect all that he would do in America. It was time to send the girl away now that she had served her purpose.

'Tracey, listen to me. Do you hear my voice?'

'Yes.'

'When I tell you to wake up, you will wake up. You will not remember anything of what has happened in this room except that I had you once and that it was short and quick. Now . . . wake up.'

Her eyes opened as he pushed his body up from her, found his footing on the floor and withdrew from her very wet slit.

He turned away to pick up his bathrobe and put it on as she automatically closed her legs and sat up.

'Enjoy your party, Jonny?' she asked, her voice back to its normal tone of faint cynicism.

'Great,' he said, turning to smile at her. 'The bathroom's through there if you want to shower.'

Without a word she picked up her clothes and made for the bathroom. Jonathan sat on the bed cross legged and thanked the Watchers at the compass points, using the names by which he had summoned them, then gratefully dismissed them. He felt very good indeed, filled with power.

He had it in mind to write an account of what had happened and how he had achieved it for inclusion in the library of the Order in London. He had many times before mesmerised women of the Order, willing partners in what he was doing, but this was the first time he had ever done it without the subject's knowledge and consent. As far as he knew, nowhere in the Temple library was there a first hand account of anyone achieving this to so great a purpose. He felt that he had advanced the stock of knowledge of the Order and opened up a new line of investigation and experiment for others. That pleased him.

Tracey came out of the bathroom, fully dressed, and made for the door.

'So long,' she called over her shoulder. 'Call me again if you get lonely.'

Poor silly girl, he thought. She thinks that she has somehow got the better of me because she has some of my money. If she could even begin to understand what she has given to me, she would come back and ask for a hundred times that amount. Or maybe she would run screaming out of the hotel and be taken to a mental ward. As it is, she has what she wants and I have what I want, so we are both satisfied.

He made for the bathroom to shower before going out for dinner. He was hungry and eager.

CHAPTER 13
A DEAL

SHARP AT nine the next morning Jonathan presented himself, briefcase in hand, at the offices of European Food Imports Incorporated, his company's East Coast distributors. They were housed in a suite of offices in the Chrysler Building. His first encounter was with the receptionist-switchboard operator, a serious looking black girl wearing huge spectacles.

'Hi,' she said, 'can I help you?'

'Mr Bachrach is expecting me. My name is Rawlings.'

'Oh, sure. Hold on while I get Lois to take you in to Mr Bachrach.'

As she half turned to flip a switch on her board, the way her breasts rolled under her white shirt stirred in Jonathan's memory a forgotten dream from the night before.

He was in a room full of people standing about chatting, like a big cocktail party, except that no one had a glass. Tracey tugged at his arm to get his attention and he saw the top curve of her breasts over the low cut and ridiculously short dress she wore. He looked up to her face and saw that her cheeks were wet with tears and her heavy eye makeup was smeared.

'You stole it from me,' she sobbed. 'Give it back.'

He tried to hush her up, but she went on with her wailing complaint until everyone in the room fell silent and stared at him. In his embarrassment he smacked her across the face to shut her up.

Karin Wikstrom in her airline uniform was there. She put her arm round Tracey's shoulders.

'It is wrong to take without giving,' she said.

'But she's a whore. I paid her. She doesn't know anything.'

'Not with her mind, but she knows. Give it back to her.'

'There's no way now,' he protested. 'It's done.'

'You will never use another woman like that,' Karin said as

she led the sobbing girl away from him.

'That's what you think!' he called after her. 'I'm a Seven – I can do what I like.'

'I am an Eleven,' she answered over her shoulder from across the big room.

Jonathan suppressed a shiver at the memory of the dream. Had a voice spoken from his inner self to warn him of something important in this garbled way? Had he stolen rather than bought? He put the thought away for later consideration. There was too great a need to keep his wits about him now to allow himself to be distracted by a fragment of a dream.

Lois, the secretary, led him past the receptionist and through a long room where seven or eight men and women were at work at their desks. Jonathan took note of everything he saw and kept his mind open to every fleeting impression. Bachrach's enterprise figured largely in his plans for the future, if the reality matched the expectation. He liked the look of the general office; the employees appeared to be working well and interested in what they were doing. Beyond the main office there were two doors, labelled respectively *Howard F. Bachrach* and *Stanley P. Bachrach*.

Howard Bachrach's office was a good sized room, well decorated and furnished in a strictly businesslike way. There were no pictures on the walls, no potted plants in corners. On Bachrach's desk stood a framed colour photograph of his wife and two children. To Jonathan these were all pointers to the person he had to deal with.

Bachrach stood up and reached over his smoked glass topped desk to take Jonathan's hand and shake it heartily. He was a tall man, inches over six feet, broad shouldered and strongly built. Jonathan put him in his mid-forties, though his curly dark hair was already streaked with silver. He was in shirtsleeves and his tie, though loosened, was reasonably formal in design.

'Glad to meet you again,' he said. 'Call me Howard. How was the flight? Take a seat. Like some coffee? Lois – bring two cups of coffee, black for me. Cigarette? Cigar? How's everything at Dovedays? All the labour union troubles settled up?'

Jonathan seated himself and grinned.

'Fine,' he said, disposing of all the questions at once. 'How's business?'

'Pretty damn good. Sales up nearly twenty per cent over this month last year. One or two snarl-ups to iron out, but nothing we can't handle.'

'No problems with our products, I hope.'

'No, our business with you is going great. It's an outfit in France I'm having a little trouble with, Bosquet Frères in Rouen – you ever heard of them?'

'No, what do they make?'

'Forget it – they're out as of now. What's the news on my good friend Derek Braithwaite?'

'He's still in hospital and will be for some time yet.'

'Too bad. We've had some pretty wild nights on the town together when he's been Stateside. I guess his ulcer perforated.'

'That's how it started. He was rushed to hospital for emergency surgery, but while they had him opened up they found quite a few other problems.'

'That's too bad,' Bachrach repeated. 'Is he going to be OK?'

Dark angel of the bottomless pit, Jonathan thought, your torment is as the torment of a scorpion when it strikes a man and your power is to hurt men for five months.

He put a note of warm sympathy into his voice for Bachrach.

'I don't know. He's a very sick man. Even if the doctors get him back on his feet, I don't think he'll ever work again.'

'That's terrible – he's not even sixty yet. That's a bad break for Dovedays.'

Bachrach's natural ebullience had evaporated. Jonathan spoke briskly to dispel the feeling of oppression, deliberately choosing phrases which he judged would strike the right note for Bachrach's life view.

'That's the way it goes, Howard. What we have to do is

forge ahead and achieve as much as we can, because none of us knows how long we've got. Somebody always has to pick up the ball and run with it. You know that better than most because you took over this fine organisation from your father when he was ill.'

'I wasn't even forty when the old man keeled over with a heart attack and the doctor said he couldn't work any more,' Bachrach agreed. 'That was a tough day for me, but I can truthfully say that I've done right by him over the past ten years. We weren't in this building then – the old man started the business down near where the boats come in from Europe. What he had was mostly a big warehouse and a piece partitioned off to make offices. Yes, I think I've got reason to be proud of what I've made of the business he started. It's gotten bigger than he ever expected. When I drive out to see him weekends he can't believe the success we're having. There's a dozen employees right here in this office and in the old man's day there were never more than two. I've got twenty salesmen out covering the major chains in three states. Everything's on computer now; stock levels, shipping, billing. And the new warehouse – you should see it – a manager, a supervisor and twelve men handling the merchandise as it comes in from Europe and breaking the shipments down for trucking out.'

'That's something to be proud of in ten years,' said Jonathan. 'Now I'm trying to achieve in my way just what you did – pick up the ball and run with it.'

'You'll do fine. You're working for a big corporation and a good one. You're about the same age I was when I took over here. And from where I sit, you look smarter than Derek Braithwaite.'

'Good of you to say that. There's a lot I want to talk to you about, besides the routine business I'm here for. Have we got plenty of time today?'

'You've got my whole day if you need it, including lunch. You'll have a chance to meet my brother Stanley when we go out to eat.'

'I'd like that. I want to meet as many people as I can while

I'm here. I have to learn a lot very fast. My beat has been around Europe until now, and over there I know what I'm doing. Here in your country I don't. I'm trying to do Braithwaite's job without his experience of business in the United States. As you said, Dovedays is a good company to work for, as long as you produce results.'

'It's tough everywhere,' said Bachrach. 'Is this the start of your sales pitch?'

Jonathan laughed.

'I haven't got one, Howard. When we get round to that part it's only a question of quantities and prices. You know what we make and how it sells – I don't have to tell you that. No, what I've been turning over in my mind is the question of the whole Doveday arrangements in the USA. What I mean is this – the way Braithwaite set it up, we deal with you on the East Coast, another distributor in the Mid West, another in the South West and no less than two on the West Coast. It's good to know your distributors personally and do the rounds to keep in close contact with them. I'm sure you do that yourself.'

'Right,' said Bachrach, his face sharp as his mind raced ahead to see to the end of the train of thought Jonathan had started. 'I take a trip with each of my salesmen once a year to personally meet the most important buyers. That's twenty weeks a year I'm out of this office and on the road. But it pays off, believe me.'

'I believe you. But in my case, as you see, Braithwaite has bequeathed to me a system which makes it impossible to see the people I should be seeing. As things stand, the best I can do is to visit each distributor in America and Europe once a year for a day at the most. As for getting out to the Far East and Australia – I'll have to hire someone like me to get out there.'

'So hire a couple.'

'It doesn't answer the real question. There's no time for me to meet any of the really big buyers the distributors deal with, to get the feel of the market and to plan forward on product range and pricing policy. All that has to be left to the distributors, who hopefully pass on the information.'

'I think we do a pretty good job for you,' said Bachrach.

'You do, Howard. Your sales far outstrip the other US distributors because you're on top of your job all the time. If the others were as good as you, I'd be a happy man.'

'I appreciate that.'

'You see my problem with the system – it's old-fashioned and it doesn't work too well any more. Braithwaite was an old-style travelling salesman at heart. Don't misunderstand me, I'm not knocking him. The way he set things up was right twenty years ago. But times have changed and business is very much more sophisticated now. Suppose you pick up your telephone to call me in London to say that, for example, a big supermarket chain is interested in taking fifty thousand cases of our product. They'd want fast delivery and a special price. Right?'

Howard Bachrach's eyes gleamed at the thought of such an order.

'Now if we had things organised differently,' said Jonathan, 'I could be on a jet two hours after your call and the very next day you and I could walk into the buyer's office side by side to clinch the order. That's the way to do business here, isn't it?'

'Damn right!'

'But the way things are, when you made that call I'd be in Oslo or Munich and you wouldn't be able to reach me for hours and I'd be too far from my office to take fast action. The big order could go cold on us.'

'I don't want to talk out of turn,' said Bachrach softly, 'but something like that happened three or four years back. I had an important special deal lined up and Braithwaite couldn't break loose from his desk long enough to get over here.'

'How did you handle it?'

'Only one way – I took a night flight to London, worked out the details with him and flew back the same afternoon. I made him agree to pay the air fare.'

'Good for you. What I'm coming to is this – later this year I'm going to recommend that we change the entire Dovedays overseas sales set-up. I want one main dealer here in the US to cover the entire country and take care of the other distributors, agree prices with them and show them how to build up their own business in our product. For Europe I shall suggest one main dealer for the whole of Scandinavia and another for the whole of Western Europe. Once I can free myself from the everyday operation, I can give my time to working on the really big deals.'

'You had me fooled for a while,' said Bachrach. 'I thought you were one of those polite and modest Brits struggling to get by. Now you're beginning to sound like a tiger.'

'With the kind of competition there is in the US from American biscuit makers and subsidiaries of British makers operating here, unless we upgrade our selling and marketing operation we'll be run off the market.'

'Cookies, Jonathan, not biscuits. You have to learn the language. Who are you putting up for this top spot in the US?'

'You, of course. You know that damned well.'

'I guessed you might be getting round to it. But I'd have to give it a lot of thought. I've got this business right here to run. What you're talking about is a wholetime job.'

'That's no problem for you, Howard. You've brought this business to where you can make your brother President or what you call him and he can keep it moving forward. He'd still be working for you.'

'I'd have to think hard about that.'

'Two other factors to throw into your thinking. The first is that there's a limit to how far you can go as a European food importer for the Eastern States. My way, you'd keep that and have the chance to build up another coast to coast business as well. Second point, there's a business recession on the way. The more interests you have a slice of when they all slow down, the better off you'll be.'

'Recession? You're crazy. Business has never been better.'

'In the last four years the price of oil has been multiplied by four. The price of all energy will climb with oil. The Arabs will not stop at four times. Now they have seen that they've got the world by the balls they'll keep on twisting hard. As energy costs keep spiralling up, the cost of all manufactured products will go up in line. Here in the States you're still cushioned against world oil prices, but it will get to you. Back home and in Europe we can see the signs of the approaching recession already. So you'll have it here too, though later than we do.'

'I don't buy that.'

'You don't have to. Just ask around the banks and check what their business projections look like for the next five years.'

'Recession or not, I like the idea of building a second business. Let's get Stan in and talk some more about it.'

Stanley Bachrach was a younger version of his brother. Lois brought in more coffee and the three men sat around Howard's desk and talked for the rest of the morning and right through lunch at a nearby restaurant. Almost as an afterthought, Howard and Jonathan settled the business that was the ostensible reason for the visit. Bachrach guaranteed a twenty-five per cent increase in his current Dovedays sales and, in an expansive gesture, had Lois type a letter to that effect, signed it and handed it to Jonathan.

'Got anything scheduled for this evening?' Howard asked casually.

'No. My next stop is San Francisco, but I haven't called the airport to make a reservation yet.'

'Chicago used to be the next whistle stop on Braithwaite's itinerary.'

'Arnison has gone broke on us,' Jonathan explained. 'The lawyers are sorting out the position. Why don't you check the possible replacements there and suggest someone. A recommendation from you would help my proposition back in London. You need someone there you can work with and trust.'

'I'll do that. How come you didn't mention Arnison before?'

'Because I want you to look at my plan on its long term merits, not have you grab at a quick opportunity.'

'I was right about you – you've got what it takes to make this plan stick. Well, now, if you're hanging loose this evening, how about you and me hitting the town together?'

Naturally, thought Jonathan, a business associate in town is the perfect excuse for Howard Bachrach to have an evening away from wife and family.

'I'd like that, Howard. Why don't you meet me at the hotel when you're ready.'

'I'll call my wife and tell her I'm staying in town. She's expecting that, anyway, knowing that you're here. What kind of place has the hotel given you?'

'Very adequate,' said Jonathan, grinning broadly. 'I've taken over the suite booked for Derek. Big sitting room, two bedrooms, bathroom big enough for a water polo match.'

'Great. You won't mind if I bring along a couple of ladies to liven up our evening? We've talked enough business for one day.'

'I expected nothing less of you, Howard.'

Jonathan made his way back to his hotel to write and mail a short report to London, enclosing Bachrach's letter of intent. That should get him a cheer from Bennett, he thought. While he was waiting for his host of the evening, he reflected that it was a pity that he had no stop-over in Chicago this trip. America's second most important city had a flourishing Lodge of the Noble Order and it would have pleased him to have made the acquaintance of its Master, whose writings in the Temple library he had found illuminating.

The Chicago Lodge was less than twenty years old and had been built on foundations laid by others; in particular, Arthur Edward Waite. Waite was New York born but lived most of his life in London. He became head of the Order of the Golden Dawn after its founder, Macgregor Mathers, moved to Paris and after the Irish poet William Butler Yeats had tried and failed to run the Order. Being Catholic educated, Waite set about changing the Golden Dawn to make membership of it compatible with Christian belief. He altered its rites and banished the old gods of Egypt, insisting that only the Trinity should be invoked. As a result, the Golden Dawn withered and died. That may have been Waite's secret intention, since after its demise he established another group; not an Order, but a Fellowship of the True Rosy Cross.

In distant Chicago, Paul Case, a high ranking Golden Dawn member there, saw which way things were going and with a number of other members founded a movement he named the School of Ageless Wisdom. This turned itself into the Builders of the Adytum as it gained strength and after Case's death in 1954 its headquarters were moved from Chicago to Los Angeles. Soon after that the Masters of the Temple moved in to establish a Chicago Lodge of their own. The ground had been broken for them, the time was right to plant.

A large part of the population of Chicago descends from Scandinavian, German and Polish immigrants of a century before. The grip of the Christianity of their grandfathers' homelands, whether Catholic or Lutheran, had been relaxed in the city of boundless opportunity they had helped to build. The ambitions and optimism of post-war Americans made them want to reach out further on the spiritual plane as well as the material one. Christianity traditionally offered little beyond the promise of eventual forgiveness of sins in return for obeisance to a confusing god. Those who had made good in Chicago were attracted in droves to the prospect offered by the Noble Order – a path to the infinite through equality with the gods.

The Order's approach to worldly wealth was also appreciated, namely, that eventually to become leaders of the civilised world and to liberate the human spirit, the Order needed to command wealth. Though Jesus may have been a penniless preacher, the church founded on the memory of him acquired money and land until it was powerful enough to impose its beliefs on millions of people by force. The Noble Order had no intention of trying to impose salvation by force, that being a patent absurdity. Each man and each woman must achieve personal liberation, said the Order, and the ownership of wealth aided the process by making it possible to set up Lodges and to have time to work together towards the personal vision.

That notwithstanding, Jonathan's planned trip to Chicago had been cancelled by Arnison's bankruptcy, an event which Braithwaite ought to have foreseen if he had been on top of his job. Under Jonathan's regime, Dovedays' overseas business was going to be conducted very differently.

Howard Bachrach arrived at about seven with two women in tow, both in their late twenties and with a facial resemblance that suggested that they were related to each other. They were both dark haired and dressed as if for a party.

'Jonathan, I want you to meet Barbie and her sister Julie,' said Bachrach, beaming.

They were in the sitting room of Jonathan's suite. He smiled and shook hands and popped a bottle of champagne he had ready on ice, to exclamations of delight from the women.

'Here's to a wonderful evening,' he said.

He soon came to understand that Barbie was a fairly long term interest of Howard Bachrach's. Sister Julie was along for the ride. After the champagne was finished they went out to dinner and then on to what Bachrach insisted was the latest fashionable disco in New York. Jonathan worked hard to ensure that everyone had a good time – for him the point of the evening was that Bachrach should thoroughly enjoy his extra-marital interlude. His continuing goodwill was part of Jonathan's future business plans. None of it was difficult to accomplish; Bachrach wanted Barbie to enjoy her evening so that she would be appropriately compliant, Julie and Barbie simply wanted to have fun. Jonathan answered questions about London, kept the glasses filled and made the women laugh as much as possible.

Some time after midnight they made their way to Jonathan's hotel suite. He gave them brandy in balloon glasses and then, so as not to embarrass Howard Bachrach, who was nuzzling Barbie's neck on the sofa, he took Julie by the hand and led her quietly away into the bedroom he was using. The other couple would find their own way into the other one when they were ready.

He did not greatly wish to sleep with Julie, but it was part of the package. Once the bedroom door was closed, he picked her up and carried her to the wide bed.

'Lover . . . ' she whispered as he expertly stripped her. She had a well proportioned body, suntanned even so early in the year, except for white strips across her breasts and loins. Jonathan treated her with regard, arousing her with his hands and lips and then letting her achieve orgasm at her own pace after he mounted her.

He timed his own release to hers. The act was pleasurable, though without any significance. Julie fell asleep quite quickly once she was satisfied, her arms about his neck and her warm belly pressed to his hip.

Composing himself for sleep, Jonathan speculated whether she might have been produced on some earlier occasion for Braithwaite's delectation. It seemed more than possible. How had she coped with that thick bodied and clumsy man's lust, he wondered. Then another thought made him grin in the dark – if Julie had any inkling of how he had used another woman's body on this bed the evening before, she would not be clinging to him with such affection.

CHAPTER 14
A MEMORIAL ON THE MOON

JONATHAN WOKE up in the beautiful city of San Francisco to see a pale blue sky through his hotel windows. He got out of bed and stood by the glass to admire the view across the waters of San Francisco Bay, clear over to the distant shore. Then, after he had showered and dressed, he called the contact number he had been given in London. A man's brisk voice answered.

'Who is this?'

'Jonathan Rawlings. I'm visiting from England.'

'That's great. I was expecting to hear from you today. Where are you?'

'I'm staying at the Hyatt Regency. Can we meet this evening?'

'Come round about six and we'll have dinner later. Do you know the address?'

'No, but it will be in the directory.'

'Got a piece of paper?'

Jonathan wrote down the address he was given and went down to the hotel coffee shop for breakfast. What was called the lobby in most American hotels was here styled the 'atrium' and from his table he could look up seventeen stories into the hollow centre of the building. Balconies above each other in diminishing perspective ran round the walls and were the way into the rooms. From them looped growing greenery that made the inside of the hotel look like the hanging gardens of Babylon. On the side that had no balconies, cylindrical glass lifts were gliding smoothly up and down the wall without visible means of support. Jonathan enjoyed his surroundings so much that he ordered more coffee and sat for a while just watching people come and go.

When he was ready, he asked for directions to the nearby financial district, refused the doorman's offer of a taxi and walked. It was a warm, bright day and only a few blocks to the office of Dovedays' local man, Warren Copp.

Copp was younger than Bachrach, younger even than Jonathan. From a pre-trip check of the files, Jonathan knew that Copp did not own the company, but he was a major stockholder in it. He sat behind the standard large-sized executive desk, wore a casual suit and a knitted tie and looked keenly relaxed. At least, that was the description that came into Jonathan's mind as they shook hands. They went through the usual pleasantries and preliminaries and then got down to talking business. And after a while, Jonathan began to think that he was walking on quaking ground. Copp was polite, helpful and not very interested in Dovedays' products or anything that Jonathan said.

They had been talking inconclusively for nearly an hour

before he found the cause of Copp's coolness.

'Your Mr Braithwaite said much the same thing last time he was here,' said Copp in reply to a statement about the growth of American sales of Dovedays' products. 'By the way, how is he? Your telex said he was sick.'

Underlying Copp's words was an antagonism that told Jonathan what he wanted to know.

'He's very sick indeed. So sick that he's out for good.'

'That's too bad,' said Copp casually.

'I'm the new man,' said Jonathan firmly. 'I'm not just filling in for somebody else. I'm here to stay. And I'm not Braithwaite or anything like him. Right?'

Copp looked at him more closely, getting the drift.

'I guess you're not. To tell you the truth, I never got on with that man. Something about him bothered me. Was he good at his job?'

'What do you think?'

'That's what I thought.'

'Let's forget past problems,' said Jonathan. 'Let's look at your dealings with Dovedays as a straight business proposition. We've got a good product range, we're reliable and trustworthy to do business with, we sell right across the States. How can I help you to make your business with us more profitable to you than it has been?'

'That's a fair question.'

They talked on better terms for some time after that. Copp's main point was that the West Coast was not the East Coast and tastes and lifestyles differed, making it hard for his sales team to achieve worthwhile sales of a British product. Jonathan quoted the sales figures of the Los Angeles distributor in refutation. Copp shrugged.

'The fact is,' Jonathan suggested, 'you're running a pretty big operation of your own here and our product range is just one of the many that you handle. Your salesmen probably go for the easy sell first – the products they know they can move in quantity. That's just good sense. Our products are right down at the bottom end of their list. They try, but not too hard.'

'You sound as if you've been a salesman yourself,' said Copp. 'That's how I started too, but not for long. We both know the score – salesmen have to make a living and they can't do that by pushing small-selling lines.'

'Let me outline to you a possible plan to help your sales team and to help you.'

He dangled before Warren Copp the prospect of having the free services of the top man to be in the Doveday US network, Howard Bachrach, to motivate his team, reorganise his sales and help sell more product. That interested Copp and they talked until after midday.

'Look at the time. Come and eat with me while we talk some more, Jonathan.'

'Fine. Thank you.'

'I'm parked about a block away. I'll take you to one of my favourite fish restaurants. How's that?'

By the end of the afternoon he had Warren Copp listening with great interest to his proposition, but without commitment. At that he had to leave it for the moment.

Just before six that evening he got into a yellow taxi and was driven to meet the man he had spoken to on the telephone that morning, Brent Fesler. The driver took him west along California Street, past China Town and turned north on Powell towards Russian Hill. For the first time, Jonathan appreciated how steep the hills are on which the city is built, with their cable cars clanking up and down them. Fesler's apartment was on the second floor of a new building. He proved to be a big, wide shouldered and balding man in his late forties, dressed in the casual West Coast style – in his case, an open necked shirt and tight leather trousers.

'Glad to meet you,' he said. 'Come on in and meet the gang.'

In his large and expensively furnished sitting room, a group of men and women were talking and drinking. As he was introduced, Jonathan imprinted their names on his memory by relating them to physical characteristics. There were three women; Debbie Munroe, late thirties, plumpish of figure, slow spoken; Billie Ryan, a few years younger, Chinese or

Filipino instead of Irish as her name suggested, with a great mane of black hair like a lion; Ginny Shafer, middle thirties, long legged, narrow hipped, short smooth black hair and an alert expression. There were two other men besides Brent; Steve Parker, fortyish, black skinned and handsome, and Matt Ryan, the only one wearing a tie, mid-thirties, athletic of build, rimless spectacles and obviously the donor of his surname to exotic Billie.

'Take a seat,' Brent urged. 'What will you drink? There's everything, but most of us seem to be guzzling chilled white wine. Ginny started us on that – it's part of her diet.'

'That will suit me fine. Is it Californian grown?'

'You bet. Straight from the Napa Valley. Tell me if it matches up to the French wine you drink over in Europe.'

'Very pleasant,' said Jonathan, sipping. 'As good as an average French white.'

'Well, now you're here, let me explain. Like I said this morning – or did I – we've got a big occasion coming up at the Temple on Saturday if you're still around then. Ted asked me to extend his hearty welcome if you can make it.'

'Ted?'

'Our Lodge Master. He was planning to meet you here, but he's all tied up with something. He's hoping to join us later on. He wants to see you.'

'And I'd like to meet him, of course. But till then, I'm here with you friendly people.'

'That's right. What do you think – will you still be around on Saturday?'

'I have to go to Los Angeles before the weekend. But if I'm finished down there by Saturday, I could always fly back.'

'We'd be glad to have you with us. Anyway, this little bunch of friends is a working group, as you've guessed for sure. We get together between Temple meetings to work together.'

'Brent's our sort of unofficial head in the group,' said plump Debbie. 'He's a Seventh, which gives him an edge over the rest of us. He's my teacher and Matt is my pupil.'

'And Steve's my pupil,' said Ginny, crossing her long legs

and leaning back in her chair. 'Billie and Matt are married to each other. Brent and I used to be married. So we're like one big family.'

'I'd have to draw a diagram to follow all that,' said Jonathan, grinning at her.

'Let me fill your glass up,' said Brent, bottle in hand. 'Before you arrived we were talking things over and we came to a decision. On the principle of *Give only good and expect only good*, we decided to arrange something special for you at Ginny's place after dinner.'

'I'm delighted. What good do you expect from me in return?'

'We'd like you to give us the history lecture. It's not often we get a visitor from the Mother Lodge. OK by you?'

'By all means.'

The 'history lecture' was a formal recital of the foundation and pedigree of the Noble Order, from the time of the Knights Templar in Jerusalem through the successor organisations to the new foundation by Hans-Martin Frick. Members learned it by heart. On the face of it, the request for him to deliver it was so simple that Jonathan cast around in his mind for the reason. The men and women entertaining him were Fifths, Sixths and Sevenths and had no need of the formal recital. He concluded that what they were asking was for his own interpretation – the request was a gentle way of putting him through a test to ascertain whether he was worthy to join them in anything of importance later on.

'One more drink and I'll oblige,' he said, holding out his glass. 'What time is dinner?'

'I've got a table reservation for seven-thirty, so there's plenty of time,' Brent answered, pouring out the pale gold wine.

Jonathan sipped it slowly and talked to bushy haired Billie sitting next to him while he searched his mind for a presentation that would capture the interest and imagination. When it came to him, he put his glass down and stood up, as was the tradition on such an occasion.

'If you are ready, ladies and gentlemen,' he said.

They were silent at once, waiting for his words. When he started, Jonathan threw off the social manner and spoke with the authority of a Seventh Degree Knight of the Order, one already designated Marshal of his Lodge from the next equinox.

'You have heard and read more than once,' he began, 'how Hans-Martin Frick, of blessed memory, was inspired to establish the Order of which we are members. You know how the Order took root and flourished until it had Lodges and Temples in all European countries on this side of the Iron Curtain, and in the lands that were once part of the British Commonwealth, Australia, New Zealand and South Africa, and also here in the United States. Your mentors have told you that Hans-Martin Frick, first Grandmaster of the Noble Order, was before that an honoured member of an earlier organisation, the Order of the Temple of the Orient, and Master of its Swedish Lodge. You have heard how he took his Lodge out of the sovereignty of its newly elected Grandmaster in the 1920s. To repeat the history of our own Order would not enlighten you further, since you know it as well as I do. Instead, I shall relate to you the story of one member of the Order of the Temple of the Orient, Jack Parsons, since there is much that we can learn from what occurred in his life if we are to avoid his ending.'

He heard a small murmur of surprise at the mention of Parsons' name. He continued boldly.

'John Whiteside Parsons was born in Los Angeles in the year 1914. He became a scientist and was sufficiently highly regarded in his profession to be one of the founders of CalTech's rocket propulsion laboratories. By that time he had come into contact with an Englishman named Wilfred Smith, who had lived for some years in Canada before moving south to Pasadena, just outside Los Angeles. Smith was a member of the Order of the Temple of the Orient and in Pasadena he set up a Lodge, under the authority of its then Grandmaster, Aleister Crowley, from whom Hans-Martin Frick had broken away. The main precept of that Order, then and now, is *Do what thou wilt shall be the whole of the Law*.

Wilfred Smith's will was to fornicate in secret with the young wife of his new and enthusiastic member, Parsons, and he made her pregnant. This course of action by a Lodge Master we may contrast with our own discipline, where fornication in private for pleasure is discouraged between members.'

'But we do it for pleasure besides in ceremonies,' said Brent Fesler.

'We do it openly and with the knowledge and consent of all those touched by it, whether in a ceremony or for personal reasons,' said Jonathan. 'Does anyone suggest otherwise?'

'No,' a chorus of voices assured him.

'By his act, Smith demonstrated that he was unfit to be Lodge Master, as evidently he held the sexual act to be a furtive private matter and not a sacrament. His partner, Helen Parsons, also demonstrated that she was unworthy of membership of the Order of the Temple of the Orient, however debased it had become under the leadership of Crowley. When the matter was brought to his attention, he instructed the couple to go into retreat together and in due course he expelled them from the Lodge.'

'Crowley kicked them out?' Matt said in surprise. 'I thought he allowed everything.'

'You misunderstand him. He would not let the Lodges of his decadent Order become private pick-up bars or suburban wife swapping clubs. He was possessed by an evil force, which is why his Order fell into ruin. But his frantic couplings with woman after woman were acts of destruction rather than of lust. Samael, as I need hardly remind you, is very different from Namah, and therefore despised by Set.'

There was silence in the room for a few moments while they pondered the implications of what he had said and the powerful names he had spoken.

'After the expulsion of Smith and Helen Parsons, Jack Parsons was appointed Master of the Pasadena Lodge, for by then he had attained the Seventh, as his Order understood it, though our own Order would not have accorded him that status. As his new partner he took his wife's younger sister Betty, then in her twenties and also an initiate. Again he had made an unfortunate choice – only a year or two later she ran away with another member of the Lodge, Ron Hubbard the writer.'

'He may have been great as a rocket scientist,' said Brent, 'but he didn't get on too well with women, that's for sure.'

'He was misled by the corrupt teachings of his Order,' said Jonathan. 'He was never able to develop a proper attitude towards women. He was careless with them.'

'Hold on,' Ginny interrupted sharply. 'Just what do you mean by careless?'

'Take it easy, Ginny,' said Brent, mildly. 'Jonathan is a Seventh. There is no way a person can attain that and be a sexist or a racist.'

'Let him speak for himself,' she insisted. 'He said careless. Like careless with an automobile.'

Brent looked at Jonathan enquiringly.

'Both of the women had been brought up to regard themselves as adjuncts to men,' said Jonathan. 'That was inevitable at the time. Parsons was careless in not understanding this and helping them to cast off the role playing into which they had been conditioned and become free-standing persons. You may argue that they should have been able to do this for themselves without the help of a man, but you must remember that we are talking about the attitudes of thirty years or so ago. The status assigned to women then was much the same in the United States as in Europe. I cannot apologise for history, I can only tell you what happened.'

'Go right ahead,' Brent urged him.

'We must also bear in mind that part of Crowley's teaching was that women exist for the use of men.'

'Can you prove that?' Ginny challenged him.

'There is a passage in one of his books, *De Arte Magica*, in which he advises his male initiates on their choice of partners for sexual rites. I can't quote it from memory but it is to the effect that it is better for the women to be in ignorance of the sacred nature of the work to be performed. He also describes the ideal female and I can quote his words because they stick in the mind – *robust, vigorous, eager, sensible, hot and healthy*. That is to say, his interest was in the woman's body and he wanted no spiritual or intellectual participation from her.'

Though he was not at the moment aware of the hypocrisy of what he was saying, Jonathan had in effect given his listeners a description of his own attitude towards the hooker whose body he had hired and used in New York.

'No wonder Parsons got himself deserted twice if that was the way he saw women,' said Ginny.

'Worse was to come. Bereft of the two sisters in succession, Parsons decided to have no more truck with human women, but to summon an elemental in female form to serve his sexual and ritual purposes.'

His statement produced a hush. After a while, Ginny asked,

'Did he succeed?'

'He used the method taught by Crowley to higher Degree members of the Order of the Temple of the Orient, a variant of the Enochian Calls for the powers of the elemental tables which Dr John Dee worked out in England during the reign of Queen Elizabeth the First. Such evocations lead to self destruction in the long run and are no part of the teaching of our Order.'

'Give us just a hint,' Brent suggested.

'At your own peril. The name of the elemental to be summoned is written in the pyramid and the correct Enochian Call is sounded. The elemental responds at once, since its whole desire is to incarnate in human form. At this stage it is present but invisible and insubstantial, and dangerous. If the summoner is a man, he performs a further evocation using his erect penis as a source of power and his semen as the substance from which the elemental can form a visible body for itself.'

'Parsons did this and it worked?' Matt asked.

'He performed this evocation for eleven consecutive nights in 1946 and there arrived at his home a female being with red hair and slanted green eyes. She called herself Marjorie

Cameron and said that she was visiting from New York. She proved to be as docile and obedient as elementals are said to be, her wish being to please Parsons in every way so that he would not dismiss her back to the place she came from. After some time, he became so pleased with her that he married her.'

'Legally married, you mean?' Brent asked.

'Yes, he had divorced the sister who ran away with Wilfred Smith and he had never married the other. When Crowley in London heard of the new marriage, he warned Parsons that he was running a terrible risk. His method of summoning an elemental to carry out your secret wishes carries an express warning; that the adept must not let himself be seduced from the love of the Infinite into the love of the inferior that he has evoked. Parsons was too far gone in self delusion to heed him. He was in his thirties and for the first time ever he had found a perfect sexual partner. Perfect in every way, of course, since she was his own incarnated wish fulfilment. Though he could not see it, to us it is obvious that his sexual ceremonies with her were meaningless as sacraments. They were, as we say, rites of vain observance. He might just as well have used a blow-up plastic dolly.'

'He was moving away from the light, not towards it,' said Ginny.

'So much so that after three years of this delusion he came to believe that he was ready to cross the Abyss with the aid of his red haired, green eyed wish fulfilment and so become a Master of the Temple.'

'The poor guy was crazy,' said Brent.

'He failed, naturally, and the shock left him in a dangerously unbalanced state of mind. By then Crowley had died and the new Grandmaster, Karl Germer, was occupied with other matters and unable or unwilling to help him. He was compelled to follow his path through uncharted and menacing territory, dragging the members of his Lodge after him. He survived the unsuccessful attempt to cross the Abyss for about three years, which tells us something of his inner strength. His life ended in 1952 in the laboratories of CalTech, when he dropped a bottle of fulminate of mercury and was killed by the explosion.'

'He surely brought that terrible ending on himself,' said Steve Parker, his shiny black face solemn.

'His own defects of character were the immediate cause,' said Jonathan, 'but those defects were left uncorrected and made worse, by the teachings of Crowley's Order. Does anyone here think that Parsons would have attained the Seventh in our Order?'

'No way,' Steve answered. 'His hang-ups would have been identified before he got to the Second and remedial action taken to straighten him out.'

'A person who calls up an elemental to screw is past straightening out,' said Ginny tartly.

'No argument there,' Jonathan agreed. 'By then it was too late. But as Steve said, his Order failed him. It failed him and all its other members because it had been corrupted by its Grandmaster. From this circumstance we perceive again the wisdom of Hans-Martin Frick, who foresaw the pit into which Crowley would plunge the Order of the Temple of the Orient and who, by his own will and work, preserved for us the knowledge of the way to the Infinite Light by refounding the Order in its original purity as the Noble Order of the Masters of the Temple.'

There were murmurs of approval from all present.

'One more word about Jack Parsons,' said Jonathan. 'It would be wrong to dismiss his memory by saying *The wicked fall into the pit that they have digged*. In other circumstances I think he would have become a great adept. Let me quote from memory some words he wrote:

"The impact of virulent patriarchy as expressed in the Christian religion has impinged on Western culture in a wave of triple destruction. First, by expanding the father image into a god monster, it has denied each son the possibility of his manhood. Second, by debasing the mother image into a demon virgin angel, it has denied each daughter the possibility of her fulfilment. Third, by imputing the concepts of nastiness, shamefulness, guilt, indecency and obscenity to the sexual process, it has poisoned the life force at its source."

'There is one more thing to tell you about Jack Parsons, initiate of a debased Order. He has a memorial which few can ever have. For his work on rocket fuels, his scientific successors named one of the craters of the moon after him, John Whiteside Parsons.'

As Jonathan sat down, the eight men and women applauded him briskly. Brent stood up to thank him.

'Well, friends, that was quite a history lecture. We're very grateful to you, Jonathan. I'd heard the name Parsons before, but that was about all. You've given us plenty to think about. Anybody want to ask a question?'

'What happened to the Lodge after Parsons blew himself up?' Steve asked.

'It collapsed. There was no one suitable to become Master. When our own Order established a Lodge in Los Angeles in the late fifties, several of the former Order members tried to join, I have been told. They were screened very carefully, I imagine, in case they were still tainted.'

'Are any of them still members, do you know?' Ginny asked.

'I don't know. That was twenty-five years ago. Why do you ask?'

'I'd be interested to meet and talk to someone who knew Parsons personally and find out what sort of man he was.'

'So would I, Ginny, but I think it's too late now to start enquiring into the antecedents of members.'

'One thing I'd like to know,' said Brent. 'What happened to the elemental? Did it vanish when its evoker died, or is it still around getting laid?'

'I can't tell you what happened. Just be careful if a red haired woman with slanted green eyes takes her pants off for you next time you're in Los Angeles.'

They all laughed at that.

'If there's any more questions,' said Brent, 'you can ask them over dinner. Let's get across to Ghirardelli's and eat, and then we'll go to Ginny's place for the big event. OK?'

CHAPTER 15
UNVEILING

IN THE restaurant Jonathan found himself seated between Ginny and Debbie. The food was good, the wine plentiful, the talk wide ranging.

'Do you like San Francisco?' Debbie asked him.

'I haven't had time to see much of it. I took a stroll around Union Square yesterday after I arrived here, and then up Grant Avenue through China Town. I saw some of the waterfront at Pier 39 at lunch today. What I've seen I like.'

'Have you heard of our San Francisco Satanists?' Ginny asked.

'The famous Church of Satan? I've heard it mentioned, but I'm not well informed. I remember reading that it claims a membership of thousands. Can that be true?'

'Depends on what you mean by member. Their place is down on California Street. As far as I know the members are scattered round the US and don't have to visit their Church.'

'Was it founded by a local?'

'I think he's from across the Bay in Oakland. His name's Anton LaVey and he used to be a police department photographer.'

'A job almost guaranteed to turn anyone off humanity,' said Jonathan.

'I guess so,' Ginny agreed. 'Shooting pictures of murder and accident victims is not a career I'd go for. Whatever the reason, he got a little group together years back and set up his Church of Satan. He's a great press agent – he got himself so much coverage in the tabloids that all kinds of folk just flocked in to join up.'

'Do they believe in anything coherent, or is Satan worship just an ego trip for frustrated office workers and bored housewives?'

'As far as I know, they meet to work out their emotions. They have Friday meetings when they argue out their hostilities. It's a kind of mix of est and AA, if you get me.'

'A catharsis of the emotions I can understand. But do they believe in an objective Satan as well? For that matter, do they believe in any sort of god?'

'I don't know too much about them,' said Ginny, 'but a woman I know who's been there told me that it's a sort of diluted Crowley system. The inner group mess with the Enochian Calls, which sounds like lighting a fire in a dynamite factory. I got the impression from my friend that LaVey is really an atheist laying on psychodrama for his people. The Satan bit is only advertising to bring in the crowd.'

'The headline grabber is that they have a woman lie naked on a kind of altar right through the meeting,' said Debbie, 'but she's only for looking at, like a strip show.'

'It's pretty sexist,' said Ginny, 'otherwise they'd have a naked man lying alternate Fridays.'

'In my experience there are not many atheists about anywhere,' said Jonathan. 'Most people who call themselves atheists are only in revolt from the church imposed morality of their childhood. Teenage rebels without a cause at forty.'

'How's that again?' Ginny asked.

'Atheism, to use the word meaningfully, is a philosophy based on the belief that there are no gods, good or evil, and nothing in the human psyche that survives the death of the body. An atheist has to believe that the universe, its galaxies, the earth and all living things are the accidental by-products of random atomic and chemical combinations.'

'That sounds kind of hard to maintain,' said Brent, his interest caught across the table.

'As a belief system it is impossible to validate and difficult to defend,' said Jonathan. 'Physical science has accidentally led us into accepting a kind of mechanical evolution and a view of ourselves as conscious robots programmed by our chromosomes and glandular secretions. And yet a text book used by medical students in your country and mine runs to well over one thousand pages to catalogue the parts of the human body, bones, organs, nerves, muscles. Grey's *Anatomy*,

I mean. And it is only a catalogue. It doesn't attempt to describe the functions of the parts or how they can go wrong. To get into that needs whole libraries of medical books.'

'Is that right?' Brent asked. 'A thousand page parts catalogue? You surely have to narrow your vision down to the limit to make yourself believe that a contraption as complicated as that has no purpose beyond reproducing itself.'

'This is a very old way of trying to prove the existence of God,' said Jonathan. 'I first came across it at school in the writings of a Roman lawyer who lived in the time of Julius Caesar. Thomas Aquinas, the Catholic theologian of the thirteenth century made a big play with it. In the Order we need no such intellectual proof, of course. We know that the universe is sustained in being by God.'

'You said there aren't many real atheists about,' Debbie said, 'but how about the Soviets?'

'State imposed atheism is a political means of breaking the hold which the Russian church used to have. Lenin destroyed the Orthodox Church for the same reason he destroyed the Czar – both were parts of the same power structure. As you know, the irony of history caught up with Lenin after his death. His own atheist government deified him and put his mummified body on show, just as Christian leaders were made saints and their relics displayed in churches to encourage the faithful.'

'You've been around Europe,' said Debbie, 'you know more about that than we do.'

'I've travelled a lot on business and for pleasure. In various parts of Europe I've seen parts of saints preserved from past centuries; whole hands, dried heads, thigh bones, fingers, toes, skulls, complete skeletons. It's all there for anyone who wants to see.'

'Getting back to LaVey,' said Debbie, 'underneath all the trash he may just be saying something which needs saying.'

'Like what?' Ginny asked.

'He may be saying that people put themselves in chains by not understanding their own nature.'

'I'll buy that,' said Ginny. 'We've been shown how to break the chains and run free.'

'People do not examine their own nature because they are afraid to,' said Jonathan. 'From childhood onwards they acquire a burden of guilt that becomes back breaking by the time they are adults. A sense of their own inadequacy eats away at the roots of their being. That's why shrinks, as you call them, get so rich in America.'

'Is it any better in England?' Ginny challenged him.

'Not a bit. But continuous psychotherapy is too expensive for us.'

'So what happens?'

'The usual things. Men retreat into mindless evasions of reality like golf, or watching football games, or gardening, or getting drunk. Women become depressed wives and numb themselves with child care and daily doses of Valium. What else could happen?'

'Other people besides shrinks get rich,' said Brent. 'An hour's drive round the Bay here there's our own bunch of Rosicrucians at San Jose. They've got a whole park, with Egyptian temples and statues of gods and offices and a computer and their own mail order university. I've been out to see it and believe me, it's big business. For fifty dollars a year all the wisdom of the ages will be delivered right to your door in neat monthly packages by your friendly neighbourhood mailman.'

'It's near San Francisco, is it?' Jonathan asked. 'I didn't know that, though I know its activities are worldwide. I've seen some of its literature. The Ancient and Mystical Order Rosae Crucis – that's the outfit you mean.'

'AMORC for short,' Brent agreed, 'founded by Dr Harvey Spencer Lewis some time in the 1920s and still going strong.'

'I can tell you something about him you may not know,' said Jonathan. 'He was a member of the Order of the Temple of the Orient, through which we trace the descent of our own Order.'

'You're putting mé on,' said Brent. 'He was a New York

advertising man who came out here and got rich by selling his own brand of uplift.'

'Maybe he was, but I can assure you that Lewis was authorised by the Mother Lodge in Germany to establish in America a Lodge of the Order of the Temple of the Orient. That was before Crowley became Grandmaster. As I understand it, Lewis became frightened by the sexual teachings and turned his Lodge into what it is now, a mail order business selling self awareness.'

'You should write a book on some of the things you know,' Ginny suggested.

'I'm working on a historical outline of failed Orders,' said Jonathan, grinning at her. 'I think I shall call it Dead Branches on the Tree of Life. Not for publication, of course, only for Temple libraries.'

'Why not publish it?' she asked. 'It could be a big hit.'

'How would the vice president in charge of finance at AMORC react if I described in detail a tantric sex rite as performed in Crowley's time, along with the information that this is where Lewis started? There's another strange Order of the Temple of the Orient offshoot in Chicago, founded by a man named Lucien François Jean Maine, who was born in Haiti and became an initiate in Europe. He combined the tantric teaching with his own home brand of voodoo. I was hoping to get more information about them from our own people in Chicago, but my visit there was cancelled this trip. As I understand it, the Ordo Templi Orientis Antiqua, as they name themselves, worship Choronzon, that is, the god Set, who possessed and eventually destroyed Crowley.'

'I've just remembered something,' said Steve. 'There's an outfit in Pasadena right now which calls itself the OTA. Maybe its granddaddy was Parsons' Lodge that you told us about.'

'What do the letters stand for,' Jonathan asked, his curiosity aroused.

'Stands for the Order of the Temple of Ashtart. They've got a regular bulletin called the Seventh Ray. I saw a copy –

that's how I heard about them. It had some stuff about the Cabala, but mostly they're interested in sex ceremonies – King Baal and Queen Ashtart – that sort of thing.'

'They're probably just a revival,' said Jonathan. 'They can't be very advanced on the path if they content themselves with summoning Queen Esther, beautiful though the ceremony is. There's always the danger that they may inadvertantly summon her in her dark aspect.'

'Brent, we're running out of wine over here,' said Ginny. 'How about ordering some more to keep Jonathan talking?'

'I seem to be hogging the conversation, Ginny. Let me tell you one last joke about AMORC and then I'll shut up.'

'We don't want you to shut up, we want you to talk. You know so damned much that you've got us hooked. What's the joke?'

'Dr Harvey Spencer Lewis was given his charter to set up a Lodge by Theodor Reuss, Grandmaster of the Order of the Temple of the Orient. About twenty years later, when Lewis was making big money out of AMORC, Crowley, who followed Reuss as Grandmaster, as we all know, found himself very short of money. And as he regarded all the property of his Order, wherever it might be, as his to dispose of, he wrote to Lewis and demanded a quarter of a million dollars, that being the valuation he put on Lewis's business.'

'Think big,' said Brent, grinning. 'What did he get?'

'Not one dollar.'

Ginny lived in the grandeur of Nob Hill in San Francisco, not far from the Masonic Auditorium. During the meal, Jonathan had learned that she was a vice president of an advertising agency and her ex-husband, Brent, was in the same line of business. He filed the information in his memory for possible future use in Dovedays' business.

Once inside her apartment, Ginny took the two other women to her bedroom to undress and put on robes, leaving the men to use her guest room for the same purpose. Five minutes later, all in long blue robes, they assembled outside the closed door of Ginny's private chapel.

'Ginny always lets newcomers go in first,' Brent explained. 'That way they get used to it without distraction. It's quite something.'

Ginny unlocked the door and pushed it open.

'Go ahead, Jonathan,' she said. 'The light switch is to the right of the door. We'll give you a minute or two.'

Jonathan crossed the threshold into the dark room, felt for the switch and pressed it. The impact of bright colours that sprang into being was almost like a physical blow. He swayed involuntarily and let his eyes slowly take in the decorations of Ginny's chapel.

To his left, on the wall which he at once knew was north, there was a design not unlike his own design at home of a man in a five-pointed star, a usual theme for high degree adepts with money to spend. But while Jonathan's design was a life size and realistic portrait of himself apotheosised, Ginny's was an eight feet tall naked woman, legs akimbo, arms upraised, enclosed in a pentagram of glittering silver, and that in turn enclosed by the circle of infinity in luminescent blue. The figure of the woman was idealised, painted in greens, blue, silver and gold, not flesh tints, the style almost cubistic in its abstraction.

On the east wall, from floor to ceiling, glowed a representation of the Tree of Life, the ten vividly coloured fruits filling almost the entire wall and dwarfing the trunk and branches on which they were set. He stared in amazement at the contiguous whorls of brilliant colour – indigo, scarlet, green, orange, violet, white, yellow. The unusual structure of the picture gave him a new gleam of understanding. He decided to ask Ginny if she would let him have a colour photograph of the design to take away with him.

He turned to the west wall, wondering what he would find. It was a wild seascape, a tumultuous dark green sea by night, the rearing waves tipped with white. Above the grey cloud banks shone a crescent silver moon. The symbolism was not lost on Jonathan. The moon was Ginny herself as Isis, brooding over the mighty forces of the unconscious mind. He welcomed this affirmation of her personal pride and confidence.

The door to the chapel was in the centre of the south wall. He advanced towards the double cube altar and turned to see the fourth design. The wall was painted a grey so dark as to be almost black. Two standing stones were shown on it, one either side the door, nine-foot rough-hewn menhirs of the sort he had seen many times at prehistoric sites in Britain.

Ginny came into the chapel, followed by the others.

'The pillars of the Temple,' he said, gesturing towards the menhirs, 'what an original interpretation.'

'I got the idea from seeing the Rollright Stones in Oxfordshire on a trip to England a couple of years back. I guess you've seen them.'

'I was brought up only about forty miles away. An aunt took me there more than once. Something you must have considered – everyone entering your chapel must pass between the pillars.'

'No one ever comes in here in ordinary clothes or without a mind clear of worldly considerations.'

'I congratulate you on the splendour of your chapel, Ginny. Who was the artist?'

'Debbie. She teaches art at Berkeley. Didn't she tell you?'

The style of private chapels afforded a glimpse into the inner heart of the adept, Jonathan thought, not for the first time. In Helsinki, Tuomo Rantala had created a chapel of nature with his forest scenes. In his own house, Jonathan had set out to create a chapel of the powers. In the home of other members he had seen a chapel of the sun, a chapel of the galaxies, a chapel of the Limitless Light. On one occasion, never to be forgotten, he had been invited into the chapel of the Order's Grandmaster and found it to be an awe inspiring creation of the sacred alignments, where all perspective was confounded. Only an adept could survive in it without becoming spatially disoriented and collapsing in giddiness.

While these thoughts were flitting through his mind, Steve and Matt covered the top of the altar with a velvet cloth to protect its pictures and fitted to it a black padded board, six feet long by three feet wide. They aligned the board east and west and secured it with metal fastenings. Meanwhile, Billie and Debbie placed and lit tall candles in heavy silver holders at the four points of the compass, just outside the drawn circle on the floor. Brent touched his arm.

'I guess you know what we plan for tonight, Jonathan.'

'The unveiling of the goddess. I feel privileged to be here.'

'We call it *The gate of vision*, but I guess the old name is best.'

'In New York I sat upon the peak of Mount Meru,' said Jonathan. 'The power is strong in me still. Which of the women is offering herself?'

Before Brent could answer, they heard the door bell ring. The thick door of the chapel still stood open during their preparations, or they would have heard nothing from outside.

'That must be Ted,' said Ginny. 'You get it, Brent, while I finish up here.'

Brent nodded and left. It occurred to Jonathan that if in London he opened his front door to anyone while dressed in a loose blue robe, he'd get a reaction of astonishment. Here in San Francisco, the life style was so casual that no one would raise an eyebrow. They would probably assume that it was some sort of ethnic costume, 'ethnic' being the polite word for foreign.

Brent came back and gestured to Jonathan to come outside the chapel. There he was confronted by a giant of a man, six and a half feet tall, broad as a door, suntanned and sandy haired, built of solid muscle, though he looked to be nearly sixty.

'Jonathan, I want you to meet Ted Werner, Master of the San Francisco Lodge.'

The hand that enfolded Jonathan's hand looked big enough to grasp and pulp a water melon. Werner had a slow and measured way of speaking, much like a banker or a judge.

'Jonathan, I'm very pleased to have this opportunity of getting to know you. Please excuse me for not joining you before dinner, but I got held up over some urgent business. Brent tells me that you gave his group a very thought provoking history lecture. I'm sorry I missed that.'

'I hope you can stay now that you're here,' said Jonathan. 'I've read your monograph on Tarot meditation and I've been looking forward to meeting you.'

'I'm pleased to think that London Lodge thinks my little effort worth keeping in its library. Certainly I'm here to stay. Brent, tell Ginny to hold on while I change.'

He chuckled and patted the flat leather briefcase under his arm.

'Have to take my own robes everywhere, Jonathan. Nothing else will ever fit me. Be right with you.'

Jonathan went back into the chapel, leaving the door open and stood with the others in the circle. The electric light had been turned off and the murals were darkly magnificent in the soft candle light. While they waited for the Lodge Master to join them, they gazed at the pictures in meditation, readying themselves spiritually for the ceremony. Jonathan saw without surprise that Ginny was facing the seascape, her lips moving silently. Brent, Steve and Matt were looking at the Tree of Life wall, their expressions tranquil as they rehearsed its mysteries in their minds. Bushy haired and Chinese-looking Billie looking sixteen years old in the candle light, was staring at the mural of the deified naked woman, her slender arms held out towards it.

Debbie had sunk to her knees, her attention fixed on the representation of the standing stones. And Jonathan too found himself drawn to this rather than to any of the more vivid and complex images. He stood beside Debbie and rested one hand on her shoulder, feeling the warmth of her skin through the thin robe.

'The pillars of the universe,' she said quietly.

'Male and female created he them,' Jonathan replied.

It was as if the pillars drew his spirit out of his body to rest between them. Debbie felt the same pull, he knew, for by placing his hand on her shoulder he had established a bond of empathy more real than the exchange of words. In silent awe he and she meditated on the pillars as symbols of the two manifestations of God in nature, the yin and the yang, the lotus and the jewel, dark and light, female and male.

All nature is a vast reflection of that which is within us or else we could not know it – the traditional words formed themselves in Jonathan's mind, but whether he spoke them aloud he did not know. They were all so rapt in silent contemplation of the mysteries symbolised by the murals that no one observed the Master come into the chapel and close the door to shut out the city. He stood among them, his arms upraised, and in his deep, slow voice, said,

'From God are we born.'

His words pulled them gently away from their thoughts and all turned to face him. Ginny spoke formally,

'I thank you for honouring my chapel, Master.'

That done, she became her usual brisk self.

'Jonathan, you stand right there while we see to the circle. We do this as a team. Right, let's go.'

Jonathan and the Master stood side by side near the altar while the group went into action. The circle around them on the floor was traced over with a sword point, traced again with burning incense, and a third time with consecrated water, the banishing and invoking pentagrams were drawn in the air, the Watchtowers summoned – all this with efficient and graceful movements and with commanding confidence – so that Jonathan could hardly tell which of the group was performing which part of the preparations, so like a well rehearsed ballet was it. Then it was complete and the robed group of men and women stood within their circle, their boundary between the world of men and the realms of the great ones, the outward and visible sign of their own integrity, their inner security, their unity with the infinite.

All movement and voices ceased as the group spaced themselves around the rim of the circle, facing in to the Master at the altar with Jonathan at his right hand. Werner was magnificent in a long robe of gold brocade which denoted his office as Lodge Master. Facing east across the altar towards the great mural, he intoned the formula of the Cabalistic Cross, touching his forehead, his navel, then his nipples in turn, before joining his palms before his face. In

English, as it is most usually said, the words are *To thee the kingdom, the power and the glory forever*. In his own ceremonies Jonathan used the Latin version, preferring the more sonorous ring of the language. It was in these words he had blessed Eila in Helsinki before entering her as a god entering his temple. The Master of the San Francisco Lodge surprised him by using the Hebrew version of the words,

'Ateh malkuth ve geburah ve gedulah leolahm.'

He turned to face west and round the circle all turned with him to look at the picture of the raging sea and the serene moon above it.

'This holy chapel is open in the mysteries of Isis,' the Master intoned. 'Our work this day is to tread the path towards the gate of vision.'

He moved away from the altar with slow steps and placed himself in the eastern part of the circle and stood still as a stone pillar. His part was complete and from then on he became a silent watcher.

Brent, as leader of the group, took over. He stretched his arms out sideways as if to embrace all present and asked formally,

'Who will offer herself as the path to the gate of vision?'

'I will,' Debbie answered.

'Then be our path.'

The exchange had been rhetorical, Jonathan knew; a set form of words, the decision having been made before any of them came into the chapel. He might have guessed that Debbie had been chosen when he saw her meditating before the standing stones. At some level of himself, he had known, and had been drawn to stand alongside her.

So far the only music had been that of human voices raised in the ceremonial phrases of charging the circle and summoning the Watchers from beyond time and space. Brent touched a hidden control set into the alter and fast, racy music crashed through the chapel. It was nothing Jonathan had heard before and he took it to be by a contemporary American composer. Debbie stripped off her blue robe and stood naked, the candle glow making her suntanned body shine golden. She stood in contemplation for a moment or two and then whirled into a vigorous, twisting dance in time to the music, moving clockwise in the space between the central altar and the ring of men and women just inside the circle drawn on the floor.

Earlier on, Jonathan had described her to himself as plumpish, in comparison with Ginny and Billie. He revised his opinion as he watched her dance. Her figure was not fashionably spare, but full and soft. Her shoulders were straight and comfortably padded with flesh, her breasts round and well formed. She was high waisted and her hips and belly long and handsomely curved. Her large triangle of pubic hair was as dark brown as the hair on her head, her thighs were rounded, her calves sturdy, her feet high arched. Unbidden, the words of Solomon rose up in Jonathan's mind:

> 'How beautiful are thy feet, O prince's daughter,
> The joints of thy thighs are like jewels,
> The work of the hands of a cunning workman...'

Debbie's bare feet made a slithering sound on the floor as she twisted and turned, her arms rising and falling with the music.

> 'Thy navel is like a round goblet,
> Wherein no mingled liquor is wanting;
> Thy belly is like an heap of wheat,
> Set about with lilies...'

A woman with a body made for the sexual act, Jonathan thought, her soft roundness a perfect contrast to the hard angularity of a man. Her breasts jumped and rolled with her movements, as if they had a life of their own.

> 'Thy breasts are like two fawns
> That are twins of a roe;
> Thy neck is like a tower of ivory...'

Faster and faster Debbie whirled as the music wound itself up with drums and saxophones and wailing electric guitars towards some not far off climax. She was dancing herself into a trance like state, side tracking her conscious mind with the intoxication of movement and sound. Droplets of sweat trickled down between her breasts and the length of her back, her breath rasped as she pushed herself towards the point of physical collapse. Still the music went faster and louder, whipping her into exertions beyond what she could endure, until, at the very height of the dance, the music cut off sharply in mid note, unfinished and unresolved. With a cry that was only barely human, Debbie swayed on legs that were folding beneath her and sagged forwards. The nearest man, Steve, caught her under the arms before she fell to the floor. Her head hung sideways against her shoulder, her legs were bent and rubbery. Steve picked her up, his black face emotionless, and passed her to Brent.

'Jonathan,' said Brent, turning to the altar with his burden.

Jonathan went to help him arrange Debbie on the black velvet surface over the altar. She was limp and unmoving, her eyes open but not seeing. They laid her on her back, arms by her sides, palms turned upwards, her legs parted to expose her genital lips, her feet turned outwards. Under his hands, Jonathan felt her skin clammy and unresponsive. For the first time he noticed that she had short fingers and broad hands.

They had placed her with her head to the east, so that Brent could stand at her head and face the sea and moon picture behind Jonathan. Brent raised his arms towards the picture and invoked the shining powers, from earth up towards the infinite.

> 'Powers of Malkuth,
> Be beneath my left foot and within my right hand;
> Hod and Netsah touch my shoulders...'

As he recited the familiar words, his well projected voice grew stronger and more imposing, until he addressed the goddess-form symbolised by the seascape:

> 'Binah, be my love!'

Then he addressed her in the words written by Lucius Apuleius, a long dead priest of Isis.

'Blessed Queen of Heaven, whose ebbs and flows control the rhythm of our bodies, whether you are pleased to be known as Ceres, the original harvest mother, or as Artemis the healer, or as celestial Venus, who couples the sexes in mutual love, or whether as dread Proserpine, to whom the owl cries at night – Blessed Queen, you who wander through many sacred groves and are venerated with many different rites – I beseech you, by whatever name, in whatever aspect, with whatever ceremonies you deign to be invoked – hear me now!'

In his hand Brent held the Egyptian looped cross, the sign of life itself. Small bells were attached to it and as he shook it over Debbie they chimed melodiously. His voice grew more impassioned as he continued the prayer,

'Universal mother, mistress of the elements, primordial child of time, sovereign of all things spiritual, queen of the dead, queen of the immortals, sole manifestation of all gods and goddesses that are, Queen Isis, favour me now!'

He touched the sound control on the altar and gestured with both hands to Steve and Matt to approach. From the tape he had set going there came a woman's clear voice, marvellous in its purity of tone, singing a slow and reverent song. It puzzled Jonathan for a moment, then he placed it as a hymn to the Virgin by a modern Spanish composer, though the man's name escaped him. He shrugged the distraction aside to concentrate on assisting to build up the atmosphere Brent required. Though the hymn was addressed to the Virgin of the Christian church, it was appropriate enough to the goddess on whom they were calling. Styled as the crescent moon she was a virgin, her potentiality unawakened, like Debbie in her present state of entrancement. When the crescent became a full moon, her powers were full and she could be the mother of a god and the mate of a god.

Jonathan stood at the foot of the long topped altar, holding Debbie by the ankles in the manner prescribed for this ceremony. Steve and Matt stood on either side of her, deftly stroking her shoulders and breasts, rolling her dark red nipples. Brent stood with his back to the north, half way along her unresisting body, stroking her belly with one palm and the insides of her thighs with the other. Debbie was trembling as she became sexually aroused; the feel of her skin under Jonathan's restraining hands lost its clamminess and became vibrantly alive. He saw a flush spread over her neck and face, her breasts rise and fall as her breathing quickened, her belly and thighs quiver. Her ankles tried to move further apart to expose her slit to Brent's touch, but Jonathan held her tightly, imposing restraint on her. The whole sexual energy building up within her was to be accumulated in her loins, as if she were a human battery being charged. The ceremony would fail if she were allowed to discharge the energy in orgasm.

When the hymn ended, Brent took his hands from Debbie's body and Steve and Matt at once did the same. Only Jonathan kept a grip on her ankles to remind her of the restraint she must herself apply. She was gasping loudly in her high state of arousal, her mouth wide open. After a pause long enough for the tape to rewind at fast speed and to allow Debbie to achieve a plateau of sensation, Brent, Steve and Matt recommenced their ministrations to her body, slowly now, aware of the need for delicacy of touch to keep her at a high peak of excitement without allowing her to go over the edge. Her plump buttocks were lifting off the black velvet as she tried to thrust her open slit onto Brent's fingers.

The hymn ended for the second time. Debbie's limbs and body were shaking so violently that Matt and Steve held her by the wrists while the tape rewound, to prevent any attempt on her part to touch herself and precipitate the orgasm that she was squirming for. The music began again, a clear voice soaring in a calm flight of adoration. The men's hands moved ever more slowly and carefully on Debbie, inching her towards the physical release she craved but not letting her achieve it. She was crying out in her arousal, little mindless cries of near ecstasy, while long, rhythmic convulsions ran through her body from neck to knees. For the third time the hymn ended; Brent stood away from her, Steve and Matt held her by the wrists.

The Master's deep voice sounded triumphantly through the chapel:

'She shall appear in heaven; she shall traverse the sky; she shall be side by side with the gods of the stars; she shall have a place in the boat of the sun; it is so written.'

While Jonathan and the other two men held Debbie to prevent her from thrashing about, Brent began to stroke lightly upwards with his fingertips from her curly pubic bush towards her navel.

The Order taught that there are six important centres of life energy within the human body, discoverable by anyone making even the most cursory attempt to focus attention inward, though their existence was meaningful only to adepts knowing how to make use of them. The Order named these centres 'lotuses', following the Eastern tradition and instructed its members to visualise them as buds that could be made to blossom and so bring about a change of consciousness. The root centre was at the base of the spine, at the perineum, and was visualised as a lotus flower with four red petals. The one at the level of the genitals was a vermilion lotus with six petals. In Debbie these centres were fully charged and the buds opened out into blossoms by the sexual energy that had been induced in her by physical manipulation. Brent's purpose now was to direct the stream of life force upwards, with Debbie's co-operation. When, under the impulse of his fingertips it struck the bud behind her navel, she would feel it as the opening out of a blue lotus with ten petals. And as he urged the fire serpent force higher still, at the level of her heart she would feel blossom inside her a twelve-petalled golden lotus.

Her body was no longer shaking in pre-orgasmic thrills. It looked strong and alive, her skin glowing and her muscles taut. At the level of her throat she would sense the sudden unfurling of a bud into a purple lotus of sixteen petals. In her mind she would hear the sound of gongs being struck. And as

Brent urged the energy up to the sixth centre, between her eyebrows, there would be the unfurling of a pure white lotus with two petals and within the vibrations of the gong she would find a single point of stillness and hold on to it, sensing it grow larger and larger.

There is an inner door in the mind, unsuspected by most, but well known to adepts, which is the entrance into a higher reality. The door is also a secure barrier to prevent that other reality from flooding through to overwhelm the everyday reality which is a lesser form of it. Adepts who learn to pass through that door and explore beyond, come back with a new vision of themselves, the world and the universe. Non-adepts try to achieve this by the use of such drugs as LSD, but their pilgrimage is short lived and separate from the rest of their experience and therefore without much significance. Adepts need no chemical means to reach the hidden world, for they know how to use sexual energy from male and female coupling to open the door for them whenever they wish.

Debbie had not been allowed to attain orgasm because the aroused life energy was required to open the door in her mind so that all present could share her journey through it, not just one man. Brent took his fingers away from her forehead and stood back. She had passed through the inner door but was not trapped in a closed sphere of drug induced hallucination. She could hold the door open and so become the gate of vision for others.

The men released their hold on her as Brent stood away. Debbie sat up gracefully on the velvet padded board, crossed her legs in the basic yoga posture and rested her short-fingered hands on her knees. Her eyes were open and bright, her body calm. From where he stood before her, Jonathan looked up into her composed face and thought: *how beautiful she is*. We say that a goddess has manifested in her, or that she has assumed a goddess-form, or that the goddess-force inside her has unveiled itself . . . yet none of these phrases we use to describe this moment ever seems adequate to engross the transformation that has taken place. Minutes ago she was a frenzied creature thrashing on the brink of orgasm. Every man here, including me, wanted with all his being to leap on top of her and explode with her into the mother of all orgasms. Now she is supremely in control of her own being, physical and non-physical; she has become oracular, a door to wisdom, a gate of vision. There is not a man here who dare touch her even with his hand at this moment.

Debbie's dark brown eyes were on his face, seeing him and seeing beyond him into the hidden world. Jonathan knew that world well, for he had been there; many a time he had lain naked on a similar altar while three or four women adepts had excited him to the point of no return and then directed the fiery energies upwards through his lotus centres.

'Debbie, what do you see?' he asked.

'A rose garden with a wooden fence around it.'

'Who is there?'

'A girl in a long white satin dress and a young man. They are both very beautiful.'

The image tugged at Jonathan's memory but he was unable to place it.

'Debbie, how did they get into the garden?'

'The girl says that they helped each other over the fence. It is not a high fence.'

That was not difficult to interpret in terms of sexual imagery, but it lacked any personal implication for Jonathan. He tried again:

'Does she say anything else to you?'

'She says that they will enjoy together the fruits of their friendship.'

'Then let them do so undisturbed. Tell me about Warren Copp, Debbie.'

She was silent for some time, her unblinking eyes gazing mildly at Jonathan and through him.

'A spirit in the wrong body,' she said at last.

'A homosexual?'

'A woman's soul in a man's body. He came to this city from Ohio because he thought he would be free here.'

'And has he found his freedom?'

'In this life he cannot.'

'Where is he at this moment?'

'In a bar with others like himself.'

Jonathan knew from past experience that questions about future events would get no answers. He asked,

'Has he yet made a decision about the matters I discussed with him?'

'He decided to do all that you suggested before you left him.'

'He said nothing.'

'He is wary. It is decided. He will help you in what you want.'

Greatly relieved by what he had heard, Jonathan asked the traditional last question before stepping aside to let another take his place before the oracle.

'Debbie, my heart is open before you. Tell me what you see.'

'For those who know the alignments there are two gardens. Which of them have you denied?'

Without knowing it, Jonathan clenched his fists. Debbie's words had brought back vividly the memory of the night he had summoned boiling black hatred from his own depths to hurl at Derek Braithwaite. He had recited that passage to himself in his turmoil of mind before going into his chapel:

> 'For such as understand the planes of God,
> For them shall be two gardens –
> Which of these will you deny?'

She hadn't quoted the words correctly, so she did not know them by heart. But she had picked them out of his mind and she was applying them to him. She understood their meaning – and probably all that he had done was open now before her. He shuddered at the thought.

'Debbie, give me a name.'

'Where everything is one, there can be no separate names. I will give you a number and the number is five.'

That was Braithwaite's number. Debbie could see everything.

'What shall I do?' Jonathan asked, fearing the answer.

His question was not answered directly, but the meaning was plain.

'Since God is the totality of all things,' said Debbie, 'he can have no name.'

Jonathan bowed to her, as required, and moved away to the rim of the circle. Ginny took his place before the oracle, but Jonathan's mind was so full of what had been said to him that he neither listened nor cared about her questions and answers. The message which Debbie had given him, or rather the reminder that she had given him, was that in damaging Braithwaite he had committed an act of violence against himself.

CHAPTER 16
A VIEW OF HOLLYWOOD

IT WAS about nine the next morning when Jonathan got back to his hotel. He had spent the night with Ginny, after the others had left, and over a breakfast of honey toast and coffee she had given him a set of colour photographs of her chapel. She had also offered a tape of all that Debbie had said during the ceremony of unveiling. He took the pictures with gratitude but refused the tape. He had no need of it to remind him of the words etched onto his memory: there can be no particular names where all is one.

At the hotel there was a message waiting for him, asking him to call Warren Copp. He rang from his room.

'Man, you either go out early or come in late,' said Copp's voice in the ear piece. 'I tried to contact you when I got to the office at eight this morning.'

'I stayed out late,' said Jonathan. 'I've just got in.'

He was in no hurry to ask Copp what he wanted – he was sure he knew.

'Everybody finds their own fun in this town, I guess,' said Copp. 'Your Mr Braithwaite used to do just the same when he visited here.'

'I promise you he didn't do what I did, Warren. My adventures last night would have blown Braithwaite's tiny mind.'

'Must have been quite a ball. Well, I called you because I did some more thinking about the business we were talking yesterday. Is there time to get together before you take off for L.A.?'

'All the time you want. I was planning to take a cab out to the airport in a while, but it can wait.'

'I feel bad about throwing your schedule out. Tell you what, I'll come over to the hotel right away and we can talk. OK?'

'I'll be waiting for you in the coffee shop.'

Jonathan packed his belongings, phoned down to have his bag collected and rode in one of the sliding glass lifts to the coffee shop. He was just ordering coffee and danish pastries when Copp slid into the seat opposite him.

'Sounds good,' said Copp. 'Make that double.'

Jonathan shook hands with him across the table. Copp was wearing dark sunglasses and looked tired under his Californian tan. His night out had not been as satisfactory as Jonathan's, it seemed.

'Were you born in San Francisco, Warren?' Jonathan asked casually.

'No, I'm from Cleveland, Ohio. I moved out to the Coast right after leaving college.'

'I can see the attractions – equable climate, cosmopolitan city, all that and more.'

'Beats Cleveland any time,' Copp agreed.

The waitress served their order, complete with glasses of iced water.

'You feel more at home in San Francisco?' Jonathan prodded gently.

'More than anywhere else I've been. I've got a good thing going here – the business, my own home, a lot of friends. All that makes a man feel pretty settled.'

'You and I are in much the same position. I've got a good job and better prospects, a home of my own in West London, friends chosen for their special qualities.'

'Are you married?' Copp asked.

'No. I like women but so far I haven't met one I want to tie up with. I sleep around, as the saying goes.'

'Don't we all,' said Copp.

Jonathan ate in silence for a while, leaving it to the other man to open the subject that had brought him to the hotel. He had done what he could to make it easier for Copp, by changing the seller-buyer stance into the more equal position of two men of about the same age and background making their way in the world in roughly comparable directions.

'I got to thinking after you left the office yesterday,' said Copp, 'and it seemed like a good proposition you outlined. My outfit doesn't rate very high on Dovedays' list of US outlets, I guess, but you put your finger on the reasons. The business is here to be got, but it doesn't come easy, not like some other imported products do. What I need is a guy like Bachrach to fly out here regularly and help me get some push into the sales team. If you can guarantee that, I'll go along with you.'

'Guarantee is a big word, Warren. At this moment I can't guarantee anything. But I'm sitting in the driving seat and, as I see it, Dovedays will go along with my plans to reorganise overseas sales. Braithwaite's gone for good. They've got me instead, and they'll do things my way for as long as it makes sense.'

'So what do you need to get your plans approved up top?'

'All I need is the co-operation and goodwill of all the company's distributors.'

'You think you can get it?'

'Look at it from your own viewpoint. What have you got to lose by going along with me? Nothing. If it doesn't work out, you'll be just where you are now. But it will work out, and that will increase your business considerably.'

'I'm sold,' said Copp, reaching across the table to shake Jonathan's hand again. 'How soon can you get things started your end?'

'This is the strategy – I fly back to London next week, talk to my managing director about this trip and hand him the plan all neatly typed out in a coloured folder. He thinks about it for a few days, then calls me in to go through it with him and answer any questions he has. He tries the plan on a couple of other directors of the company. They think about it and look for hidden problems. There aren't any. So then the whole thing goes up to the next meeting of the whole board of directors. They kick it around for a while, invite me in to answer any more questions and then tell me to go ahead.'

'Simple as that?'

'One thing I've got going for me is that not one of the directors of Dovedays understands anything about overseas sales. They know all about home sales, production, finance, planning and everything else it takes to run a big company. But not about overseas sales. Braithwaite created that singlehanded and it has always been left to him. Now he's gone. Twenty per cent or more of the company's business was in his hands. Because of replanting, output is running a third over last year and the home market can't absorb half of that, not even with an advertising campaign costing the equivalent of two million dollars over the next three months.'

'Sounds tough.'

'Then just before they hit the panic button in the board room, up jumps this bright young man who has understudied Braithwaite and he says: Gentlemen, I've toured our outlets in Europe and the USA and I am convinced from what I have seen that we can sell much more product than we have in the past. It's all typed up in the folder in front of you, current sales, trends, future estimates, all in tidy little percentages.

And just to show you that it's real, those percentages are also translated into pounds sterling for you.'

'So how do they react?'

'They shake my hand and say: My boy, you're a credit to the organisation. Have a cigar.'

'Man, you really should have been a salesman,' said Copp, smiling.

'I am.'

'How long will it take you to put together this gold plated report when you get back to London?'

'I wrote it a long time ago. All I need to do is update the figures.'

'You don't waste time.'

'At heart I'm just a hustler,' said Jonathan, making Copp's smile grow broader.

'I thought maybe you'd like to take this back with you,' he said, handing Jonathan an envelope.

'What is it?'

'If you don't open it, you'll never know.'

It was the confirmed order Jonathan had been expecting, the official reason for his visit.

'Thanks, Warren, I give you my word that when the new set-up is rolling, I'll be right here with Howard Bachrach to make sure that you get all the help you need.'

When they parted, Jonathan took a taxi to the airport and from there telephoned the Dovedays man in Los Angeles to tell him that he was on the way.

'What time do you set down here?' a meaty voice at the other end asked.

'Noon.'

'I'll ride out to the airport and pick you up. We can eat lunch together.'

'Fine. How shall I recognise you at the terminal?'

'I'll wait by the Hertz desk with a cookie box under my arm. How about you?'

'That's easy enough. I've got red hair.'

In the event, they spotted each other simultaneously. Vern

Willis was a short, burly man nearing sixty, bald on top, grizzled over the ears and deep tanned. He wore no jacket and his magnolia shirt was short sleeved to expose brawny arms and open necked to show a mat of greying hair. Maroon slacks and two-tone loafers completed his casual outfit. They shook hands and Willis said,

'I'd have spotted you even without the red hair. In a suit like that you just have to be British. Call me Vern.'

'It's nice to meet you, Vern. Thank you for driving out to the airport. Don't you like the suit?'

'Sure. It looks as if it was made to fit you, so it has to be foreign.'

They went out to the car park, Jonathan carrying his lightweight case and briefcase. In San Francisco an hour ago the temperature had been in the comfortable sixties; here it was up in the eighties and the sky was hazed over. He was pleased to get into the air conditioned coolness of Willis's oversized car.

'Do people really call you Jonathan?' Willis asked, 'not Jonny?'

'People call me Jonathan.'

'OK. This your first trip out to the Coast?'

'Yes, and I'm loving it.'

Willis manoeuvred his long vehicle out of the car park and headed for the airport exit.

'Got a call from Howie Bachrach yesterday,' he said, surprising Jonathan.

'Do you know him well?'

'Well enough. We do a little business together. He buys some of the stuff I bring in from Japan and Hawaii and I buy some European specials from him. He told me about your plans.'

'Good,' said Jonathan, wondering if he were losing the initiative. 'Then all the cards are face up on the table. What's your reaction, Vern?'

'Should have been done years ago. I tried to get your boss to see it the last couple of times he was here.'

'He's not my boss anymore. It's my deal, not his.'

'OK, count me in. If Howie's agreed to mastermind the US operation for you, you've got a good man on your team.'

'I'll be alongside him. I'm not planning to hand over and opt out.'

'Sure, I understan˙ Now you've got that old bastard Braithwaite off your back you want to start scoring points with the top brass back home. I'll go along with that.'

'My thinking is that Bachrach would carry a big permanent stock of product in New York, which we keep topped up. You would draw on his stock – you'd be buying from him, not from Dovedays. And he would be personally available to help with your sales strategy and development.'

'He told me that. I'd like to have him come out to the Coast two, three times a year.'

'How's business right now?'

'Pretty good, Jonathan, and getting better. I'm expecting to push sales of Doveday products up by around twenty-five per cent in the second half of this year. You won't have any problems in delivering, will you?'

'None at all. We're geared up for bigger output.'

'How about your famous British labour troubles?'

'We're through those and out the other side. We're in business now to make and deliver all you can sell.'

For all practical purposes Jonathan had the two assurances he wanted from Willis and could have taken the next flight out of Los Angeles. Other considerations dictated against that. He wanted to gain the personal goodwill and trust of Dovedays' key people and that meant spending time with them.

'Time to eat,' said Willis as the car rolled along a concrete freeway at the regulation fifty-five miles an hour. 'You want the full works like Braithwaite – cocktails, three courses, wine and all that stuff?'

Jonathan looked at him sharply, but Willis was grinning.

'You pick the place, Vern, and I'll eat what you eat. And pay the bill.'

'You're getting away cheap. There's a drive-in along here that serves the best hamburger this side of Santa Monica.'

In the restaurant they sat on stools at a long counter while a sleek haired Mexican girl of no more than sixteen served them hamburgers and coffee. Jonathan asked Willis where he came from.

'Right here. I'm a born Angelino and that's something most of the people living here can't truthfully claim. The city was a lot smaller when I was a kid. It didn't have all these freeways and automobiles. After I got married I moved out of town and bought a home in the San Fernando Valley – that was a pretty good place to live then, all orange groves and horse ranches. Now the Valley's pretty well covered in streets and houses, like everywhere else. You wouldn't believe how big L.A. has grown in the last twenty-five years. It's swallowed up all the towns that used to be separate – San Fernando, Santa Monica, Burbank, Pasadena, Anaheim, Santa Ana, clear down past Newport Beach, and that's forty miles south of where we're at now, and we're just riding into town from the airport.'

'You're a family man, then?'

'Been married to the same woman for nearly thirty years. That's kind of a record around here. We've raised two sons and two daughters, all married now except the youngest girl and she's still in college. Got two grandchildren.'

'You sound like a solid rock in shifting sands. How do you do it?'

'You really want to know?'

'That's why I asked.'

Willis chuckled right down to his paunchy belly under the magnolia shirt.

'It's not too hard. You do what you know is right and you don't let people stampede you into foolishness.'

'I go along with that, though it's not as easy as you say.'

'Never given me any problems.'

'I believe you, but other people find it hard to hold on to a life plan like that.'

'You know why?'

'Tell me,' said Jonathan, smiling. 'This should be good.'

'Too many people are instant nothings, that's why. They let themselves be talked into thinking they can be instant somethings. They think all it takes is a bundle of dollars. Or better yet, a handful of credit cards. Be Rock Hudson now and pay next month, OK? So the men get their hair done in little cutie curls and hang gold chains round their necks, and the women get their titties blown up by a cosmetic surgeon and wear clothes that show their belly buttons. So they think they're instant somethings, but you know what they really are?'

'What?'

'Same old instant nothings – in debt.'

Jonathan laughed.

'Who talks them into trying to be something they're not?' he asked. 'Commercial interests, television, films, what?'

'Commercial interests, hell! That's just a name for other instant nothings who've found a way of getting to be instant somethings by selling junk ideas to the other poor slobs.'

'Are you a religious man, Vern?'

'Never been inside a church in my life. If Jesus loves me, that's OK by me. And if he doesn't, that's too bad.'

'You're a rare kind of creature – you accept complete responsibility for your own life. I'm impressed.'

'You eaten enough, or do you want a portion of cheesecake?'

'I'll have the cheesecake.'

'They do it good here. I'll take a piece myself.'

'After what you've said, I don't know whether you like living here or not.'

'Sure I like it. Maybe some of it's tacky, but that's the way it is. I wouldn't want to live anywhere else.'

'You reminded me of some words I haven't thought about for a long time. Try this for size: Our own people for greed's sake threaten to make a ruin of this great city by their folly. So comes the common evil into every man's house and the street doors will no longer keep it out. It leaps over the high hedge and surely finds a man, for all he may go to hide himself in his inner room.'

'That out of the Bible?'

'No, it's something I remembered from my college days. It was said by a man called Solon who drew up a code of law for the city of Athens about two and a half thousand years ago.'

'Still makes sense,' said Willis. 'The chance to make a fast dollar leads people into a lot of foolishness.'

'That and sex,' said Jonathan.

'You said it. I like this town because I was born here and I've always lived here. But if I was coming in from the outside, I'd have to ask if it was a good place to live and put down roots and raise a family. As of now it's the dream palace – instant glamour, instant sex, instant good life, everybody got three automobiles and a jacuzzi in the back yard – all that foolishness. There's nothing instant to be had that's worth the having.'

Jonathan reached for the bill, but Willis put his beefy hand on his arm and stopped him.

'I'll pick up the tab,' he said. 'You're a visitor.'

Outside in the car he looked hard at Jonathan and asked, 'You want to go back to my office and play games with paper like we're working, or shall I show you something to remember when you get home?'

'We can do the office bit tomorrow, Vern. I'd like to see the sights with you. Where to?'

'We'll ride up to Hollywood and you can see Sunset Boulevard and the Strip and the rest of it. I'll drop you off at your hotel when we're through.'

'Let's go,' said Jonathan, wondering why Willis had suggested the tour.

In Hollywood their first stop was outside Graumann's Chinese Theatre, a cinema in garish mock oriental style. The tour buses were there in strength, and crowds of sightseers were jostling each other to catch a glimpse of the hand prints and foot prints of past movie stars in the concrete forecourt.

'Relics of mortality,' said Jonathan, still not sure why he was there.

'Now take a look across the street,' said Willis.

Not far down was another cinema with a huge illuminated advertisement outside announcing that *Deep Throat* was in its sixth continuous year of showing there. As they got back into the car, Willis asked,

'See what I mean?'

'Public taste has changed.'

'Taste, hell! There's always been plenty of sex around. We used to call it romance. I'm twenty years older than you and I haven't forgotten the big stars like Claudette Colbert, Irene Dunn, Anne Heywood – them names mean anything to you?'

'Only in so far as I've seen them in old movies on TV.'

'They had class. Now you can go into that movie house across the street for a dollar or two and watch a woman suck a man off, giant size. You telling me that's no more than a change in public taste?'

'Would you ban it?' Jonathan asked as they drove away.

'No, I'd try to teach people to rate themselves higher than to pay to see stuff like that, if I had the chance.'

'So would I. Second hand sex can be demeaning.'

'That's a fancy word, *demeaning*, but I guess it covers it.'

'But you know, Vern, those screen ladies you admired in the thirties and the forties were not invariably virtuous. I recall reading in a history of Hollywood's great days that Joan Bennett had a lover who was shot in the balls by her husband. I could think of other instances if I tried hard enough, but what I am saying is that there was a discrepancy between the public image of some of those ladies and the manner in which they amused themselves off screen.'

'Sure, everybody knows that. But private and public is what I'm getting at.'

'You've got me puzzled, then. What do you want, public morality and private permissiveness?'

'I'm not explaining myself right. Leave aside the movies.

Do you know how many pornomotels are operating in the L.A. are right now?'

'I don't even know what a pornomotel is, Vern.'

'Like a regular motel, only the rooms got waterbeds and non-stop porno movies right there on the TV screen at the foot of the bed. You take your girl there for the afternoon, or the whole night if you've got the stamina, and get turned on by what you see.'

'I'd have thought that most women would resent the implication that their lovers need that sort of stimulus.'

'The women like them. Then there's the clubs couples can join together. Everybody drifts around naked, in and out of the pools and bedrooms and everybody screws whoever they like.'

'Not your taste, not my taste, but we are not guardians of public morals.'

'I'm not getting through to you. Back in the drive-in where we ate lunch you said that greed and sex lead people into trouble. I'm just showing you how wrong people can get sex. The romance bit twenty or thirty years back was foolishness, maybe, because it wasn't too real. But real or not, we set a value on sex. Nowadays people screw each other as casual as saying *hello*. It's got no value at all when you can join a club and get it off with strangers twice a night. You follow me?'

'You've led me a roundabout way, but you appear to be saying that people are devaluing their own sexuality to the point of triviality. Right?'

'Now you're with me. Seems to me that if you trivialise something as important as sex, you're a sick person and you're going to be sicker. Sick in the head, I mean.'

Jonathan chuckled. Vern Willis's hickory philosophy was not a long way removed from the sacramental view of sex taught by the Noble Order.

'Sick in the sense that they undermine the basis of their own self esteem,' he said. 'I agree with you there, Vern.'

'I see you like fancy words. Now you take your ex-boss. He'd have a hooker up to his hotel room every night he was here. What the hell's the point of that? Two minutes getting her clothes off, two minutes feeling her up, two minutes humping; goodnight, honey, I'll call you when I'm in town again. I asked him about it one time and he told me I must be past it if I didn't know why. That make sense to you?'

'Nothing Braithwaite ever did made sense to me.'

'He spent a lot of time in the topless bars. Dragged me with him once or twice to watch the dancers' titties bounce up and down. He took hookers to pornomotels sometimes and he wanted for me to arrange for him to join one of the screwing clubs.'

'I never suspected that he enjoyed so vivid a sex life,' said Jonathan.

'Monkey tricks.'

'I must thank you for showing me Los Angeles as Sin City.'

Willis turned his head to grin at him.

'It's no more that than any other place. They just make more noise about screwing here than in Iowa City. You hiring yourself a woman tonight?'

'No,' said Jonathan, laughing. 'I'm having dinner with some people here.'

'You got friends here in L.A.? Anybody I know?'

'Maybe, the name is Herron.'

'No, don't know any folks called that. What business they in?'

'I don't know. I've never met them before – they're friends of people I know back home and I'm looking them up to say hello.'

CHAPTER 17
EARTH AND SKY

THE HOME of the Master of the Los Angeles Lodge, to which Jonathan had been invited for the evening, was well outside the central city, at Marina del Rey, on the coast. It was a big house of white-painted boards, set back from the pavement behind a well tended lawn. Jonathan paid off his taxi and walked along a flagged path to the nail studded door and rang the bell. It was a warm evening, the sky had cleared and the temperature was down to the upper sixties.

A good looking woman answered the door. At a glance Jonathan took in her sharp chinned, intelligent face, thick arched eyebrows over very dark brown eyes, sleek black hair piled high on top of her head – all this as she smiled and held out her hand and said,

'Hi, I'm Angie Herron. You must be Jonathan Rawlings. Come on in.'

It was impossible not to look at her breasts, huge, round and obviously unconfined, under her knee length tunic of gold lame, so closely fitting as to make her nipple prominent through the material. Following her into the house, Jonathan noted that her buttocks, though well shaped and fleshy, were not of the same Peter Paul Rubens proportions as her bosom.

'We're having a cook-out in the back yard,' said Angie. 'It's family night tonight. Tomorrow's our big Lodge night – Friday. Hope you can be with us.'

'Why, yes. I've a business meeting tomorrow morning and then my time's my own until Monday.'

'Are you planning to go home then?'

'No, I'm due in Dallas on Monday.'

The back yard proved to be half an acre of patio, swimming pool and lawn, enclosed by a six foot hedge of close cropped dark green shrubbery. A man in white cord trousers and a gold embroidered shirt was tending a barbecue. Another woman was swimming in the oval pool. She turned over to wave at them and Jonathan saw that she was swimming naked.

'Meet my husband, Greg,' said Angie.

Greg Herron was a slender man approaching fifty, his yellow hair set in a mass of small curls. His handshake was firm and direct.

'Glad you could come, Jonathan,' he said. 'How do you like your steak?'

'Medium rare, thank you. I bring you greetings from the Grandmaster in London.'

Herron looked at his wife and smiled.

'You tell him, Angie. Have a drink, Jonathan.'

Angie led him to a glass-topped table set with bottles and an ice bucket.

'Scotch on the rocks?'

'Yes, that's fine. What should you tell me?'

'Greg's not the Master of the Lodge. I am.'

'Since when, if I may ask.'

'I was elected just two weeks ago. The notifications have gone out but maybe the details didn't reach you before you left London.'

'Congratulations, Master,' said Jonathan, raising his glass to her. 'What was the reason for the election?'

'Our last Lodge Master found himself unable to perform the rites of obligation at the spring equinox. Well, he *is* nearly seventy, so I guess it was no great surprise. It took quite a while to organise the election, what with people being away and others wanting time to think it over. But here I am.'

'The first woman Lodge Master,' said Jonathan. 'It had to happen, of course. But you don't look old enough to be a Seventh.'

'Is that a compliment?'

'I'm not sure,' he said, grinning at her.

'I'm as old as you – maybe a year or two older, I guess. You're a Seventh, so why shouldn't I be? You want to sit with me while Greg gets on with the cooking?'

They sat side by side on a multicoloured garden swing big enough to seat three or four people.

'That's Greg's sister, Orline, in the pool. She spends a lot of time with us when we're home. You'll like her. We always skinny dip when we go in swimming here – there are no neighbours to bother us.'

'How do you know that I am a Seventh?' Jonathan asked.

'I talked to Ted Werner in San Francisco on the telephone. You made quite a hit there, you know that? Ted wants me to put you on a flight back there for their Lodge meeting, but I told him we were going to keep you right here for ours – if that's OK with you?'

'I'd like to be at your meeting, Angie.'

In truth, he was unwilling to return to San Francisco since Debbie had become the gate of vision. All those present in Ginny's chapel had heard the questions he had put to her and the answers she had given him. If they got to speculating, the secret he wanted forgotten might come out into the open and their attitude to him would change drastically.

'What brings you to the Coast, Jonathan. Business?'

He told her something of his business trip and asked what she did.

'I'm in TV. Greg's in real estate. You must like my figure, the way you keep looking.'

'What man could resist?'

'Would you believe that when I first came to L.A. I had little breasts no bigger than oranges? Having them fixed gave me drive and self confidence.'

'How long ago was that?'

'About ten years back. When I was only thirty-two round the bosom I felt timid and that held me back. Since I've been forty inches round, there's been no stopping me.'

'Hey, Orline, come out of the pool and dry off,' Greg called to his sister. 'We're nearly ready to eat.'

Orline swam lazily to the edge of the pool and hauled herself out. Her long hair was plastered to her neck and back and her entire body was the golden tan colour Jonathan had come to accept as the norm for California. As she stood naked at the pool's edge, squeezing water out of her hair, she saw that she was longer in the thigh than her sister-in-law, but she had the same round, over-size breasts.

'The same surgeon did Orline's bosom,' said Angie. 'She had it done first and when I saw the result I wanted the same.'

'Attractive though your breasts are,' said Jonathan, 'they would not have got you elected Lodge Master.'

'They didn't hold me back either.'

All that Jonathan knew of the Los Angeles Lodge was that it was a large one by European standards. By definition it must have roughly equal numbers of male and female members in order to function properly. And if the election had been a contested one among its Sevenths, which was likely, then at least two thirds of the members must have voted for Angie Herron in the first ballot, or she would have been eliminated. And eventually, every member must have voted for her election, since final unanimity was required. In truth, he was still trying to adjust to the fact of a woman Lodge Master. For all his years in the Order he had been accustomed to accepting women as equals in status and more advanced in Degrees, until he became a Seventh. The adjustment he was now making was to Angie as his superior.

'Om . . . klim . . . srim . . .' he said slowly, to resolve the matter within himself.

Om is the sound which encompasses all the knowledge of the different planes of the universe; *klim* represents in sound the sexual desire of a god; *srim* is the tonal figuration of the female energy of abundance, the source of cosmic fulfilment. These are not real words, but sounds which produce their effect on the mind by the vibrations they set up, when pronounced properly and activated.

Angie understood him perfectly.

'Yes, that surely was part of the motivation for my election,' she said. 'A marriage of sun and moon. I am working hard to be worthy of the trust placed in me.'

'Come and get it,' Greg sang out, putting steaks onto plates.

They sat at a long white garden table on the patio to eat. The steaks were large, juicy and perfectly cooked; the cole slaw and salad were crisp, the red Californian wine as good as an average claret. Greg and Angie in their leisure clothes were in striking contrast to Jonathan in a lightweight grey suit, and Orline, at the other end of the couture spectrum, was wrapped in a striped towelling robe, her long, damp hair tied back with a green ribbon. Jonathan was enjoying the setting, the food and the drink. What was required to complete the pleasure was some good table talk. He set out to achieve it by asking Angie how she had come to join the Noble Order.

'I've been a member for about ten years,' she answered obliquely, 'but I guess you could say that my quest began some time before that. Have you ever heard of Mike Warnke?'

'No, is he one of us?'

'When I first met him he was a Satanist in San Bernadino. That's about eight miles east of here. He was recruited into the coven by his pusher when he dropped out from college. He'd be eighteen then, going on nineteen. He'd got all mixed up about God early on in life. He was reared in Tennessee in a hell-fire preaching Baptist way and then after his folks died when he was just a kid he was sent to live with his married sister and her husband in San Bernadino. They put him in a Catholic school and for a while there was some pressure on him to study to be a priest. But when he got to college he had all the time he wanted to drink and take dope and screw around and he turned into just another freaky dropout.'

'Evidently with a difference,' said Jonathan, 'otherwise his name would be forgotten along with the thousands of others who dropped out in the sixties.'

'That's right. Mike had a real deep down gut feeling about God, even though he couldn't take what had been handed out to him by the Baptists and the Catholics. When he was initiated into the coven, he was like a missile lifting off the launch pad. The other members maybe half believed, or maybe were just along for the kicks, the sex and the dope. But not Mike. Before anybody knew what was going on, he'd made personal contact with the devil of the coven.'

'By that I take it you mean the Christian image of evil?'

'Sure, that's all we knew. Well, the coven was mostly a protest against everything. But Mike did more than protest. He opened himself up as a channel for the force of destruction to pour through.'

'You were a member of this Satanist coven?' Jonathan said, his interest caught.

'I was a member before Mike joined.'

'What sort of people were they – mostly students?'

'All kinds. There were some students, and there were some teachers too. Businessmen, housewives, clerks, salesmen, even a few preachers and at least one priest I knew. There was nobody over thirty that I recall.'

'How did you come to join, Angie?'

'I was one of the bored wives. The man I was married to then had a pretty good job and I didn't work. If you can think of anything more soul destroying for a woman than cleaning house and cooking dinner, day after day, I'd like to hear about it. I wanted excitement and escape. I was thirty years old and childless and going nowhere. When my neighbour started hinting about a coven, I was ready for it.'

'Did you find what you wanted?'

'First off, there was the excitement of being part of something secret. And there was the sex. My marriage had gone flat on me. Suddenly I had all the sex I could handle. It really was a liberating experience for me at first. But I guess you know the problems that come after a while.'

Greg entered the conversation.

'The unwelcome lesson most of us have to learn the hard way,' he said, 'is that unlimited promiscuity devalues human sexuality to worthlessness. Angie was far more spiritually aware, even then, than the others, and she reached that conclusion after only a few months of unlimited screwing.'

'Strangely enough,' said Jonathan, 'the business associate I was with this afternoon said much the same thing, not from experience but from observation, I think. *Monkey tricks* was his description.'

'Like Greg says, that's where I'd got to when Mike was made coven master,' Angie continued. 'He changed it all. He brought the dark force right into the circle with us and scared hell out of me.'

'Into the circle with you?' said Jonathan. 'He risked that?'

'He knew no better,' said Greg. 'From what Angie has told me about him he was like a child that's got hold of a loaded gun. You can guess what happened.'

'He became possessed,' said Jonathan.

'He surely did,' Angie agreed. 'He became so possessed that the guys who ran the dope in across the Mexican border decided that Mike was bad for business. He was out of their control. So they got a girl to O.D. him between screws and they dumped him.'

'Did he die from the overdose?'

'No, he fetched up in a padded cell in the county hospital.'

'The similarities with Aleister Crowley are strikingly obvious,' Jonathan said. 'Same repressive childhood, same break-out into drugs and sex, then total possession by the dark force.'

'There's a similarity with Charles Manson too,' said Greg. 'He had a miserable childhood to rebel against. And he got going in a group which based itself on Crowley's writings. By the time he formed his own group, the force of destruction poured through him in such a torrent that all separate identities were lost in it. His followers were automata, waiting to be told what to do, when to eat, when to sleep, when to copulate. One day he told them to kill and they went to Sharon Tate's house and murdered her and four other people there. And the next day they went to Leno LaBianca's house and murdered him and his wife.'

'Mike Warnke could have gone the same route as Manson,'

said Angie, 'especially after he'd been dumped. He had the power to form his own group right away and really blast off. But he didn't. When he got out of the hospital he joined the Marines and was shipped out to Vietnam. And would you believe it, he was converted back to Christianity by two evangelist buddies. How's that for a twist?'

'Surely he had no choice at that point,' said Greg. 'He'd opened himself up as a channel. Then he got frightened by what he'd done. He wanted to block off the channel and the only way he could think of was to turn to the Bible god of his Baptist childhood.'

'Yes, that would be the logic of an untrained mind,' Jonathan agreed.

'Right,' said Greg. 'Limits had been set on his understanding by his upbringing. He never met anyone who could show him a wider horizon. Angie was caught in the same trap herself.'

'How did you break out, Angie?' Jonathan asked.

'After Mike had been dumped, things went back to where they were before he took over. The new coven master didn't have the same power in him. One night there was a big meeting where I got myself laid by five or six men in the circle, one after the other, and it was a real downer. The coven devil wasn't visiting us anymore. I lay there on my back and the thought that came into my head was that these guys were just using my body as a convenience to relieve themselves. Nothing real was happening at all. So I got up and went home to think about it.'

'A moment of bleak realisation,' said Jonathan. 'Many a woman would have O.D.'d herself then.'

'That never entered my head. I took a close look at my life and I didn't like what I saw. So I packed my things, said goodbye to my husband and took the next bus to L.A.'

'And your first step, though you could not have known it, to becoming Master of the Lodge of Los Angeles,' said Jonathan thoughtfully. 'The bus ride was your road to Damascus.'

'I don't see it that way. I truly think that my first step was when I joined the coven. So it was a blind alley – and a dirty one at that. But it made me aware of the hidden world inside all of us.'

'What happened to Warnke, do you know? Did he manage to exorcise himself by means of Christianity?'

'He was shipped back to the Navy base at San Diego after his tour of duty – that's down the coast a way from here. The channels he'd opened up can't be blocked off easily – we know that well enough. He fought his possession for a long time. After he got his discharge from the Navy he set up as a full time preacher. He was on TV more than once and got himself a lot of publicity trying to rescue kids from other Satanist groups.'

'Your own life underwent a change no less dramatic.'

'Right. I'd finished with all that Satanist stuff. Either the pushers manipulated you or the coven devil manipulated you or you were just a hole to screw. Who needs it? I got a job right off in L.A. as a secretary. One of the first friends I made here was Orline, and through her I met Greg. We got married just as soon as I could divorce my first husband.'

'What Angie hasn't told you,' said Greg, 'is that when we met I was already a Second in the Order. It was because of me she joined. She turned out to have such understanding and potential that she soon caught me up. We both of us became Fifths in the same month. Now we're both Sevenths and she's the Master of the Lodge.'

'Naturally, the Order helped my career as I climbed the Degrees with Greg,' Angie added. 'These days I run the TV station.'

'And what about you, Orline?' Jonathan asked, turning to the other woman.

'I'm a Fifth,' she said. 'Greg persuaded me to join the Order about the same time Angie did. I guess I'm slower than she is in reaching understanding.'

'Don't put yourself down,' said Jonathan. 'To become a Fifth you have stood bound and naked in the dark to be mocked and humiliated and scourged. You have won through that ordeal and have been dubbed a Sovereign Princess of the Rose Cross. You have been accepted by the members of your own Lodge and therefore by the Noble Order worldwide as a Lord of the Threshold between the two worlds. That's a great thing to have achieved.'

'The Order has changed my life,' said Orline, smiling at him. 'I guess it changes everybody's or there would be no point. I left my husband some years back because I knew that never in a million years could he ever begin to understand what the Order was about, even if I'd laid it out for him in diagrams. He had all the spiritual awareness of a roast turkey. The world is full of people like him – good, solid citizens, hard working and forward looking, sensible, generous and so lost in the appearances of this world that they are totally blind to what is inside themselves and their own potential.'

'And yet,' said Jonathan, 'I never cease to marvel at the American spirit of quest. Our own Noble Order has established Lodges and Temples in a dozen cities from Boston clear across to the West Coast. Even Crowley's debased version of Templarism has groups in such unlikely places as Pittsburgh and Cincinnati besides its major presence here in California. In addition to the mail order Rosicrucian society operating at San Jose, there are at least two other Rosicrucian groups operating in the US with pedigrees going back to pre-Crowley beginnings.'

'Here's one for you,' said Greg. 'Did you know that in Salt Lake City, the centre of Mormonism, there is a branch of the Paracelsus Research Society?'

'That I like,' said Jonathan, laughing at the incongruity. 'It's as if the Sufis opened a mosque in the Vatican City.'

'Different strokes for different folks,' said Angie. 'Why don't we clear these dirty dishes away into the kitchen and then we can go into the chapel, if you'd like that, Jonathan.'

'I'd like to see your chapel. Do you have any particular ceremony in mind?'

'If you'll go along with us, we'd like to try the separation of earth and sky.'

'It's a long time since I've taken part in that,' said Jonathan hesitantly.

'Same with us. We were talking about it a couple of days ago and we realised that none of us has ever done it more than the one time we were taught it. But now that I am Lodge Master, I have to make myself skilled in all the ceremonies. So how about helping us out?'

'The marriage of Shiva and Shakti has the same basis and is generally preferred,' Jonathan reminded her.

'Sure it's preferred, because it's more pleasurable. Isn't that reason enough to go the harder route? When things get preferred because they're enjoyable, we run the risk of turning into a bunch of suburban swingers.'

'I accept the reproof,' said Jonathan formally, knowing that he was in the wrong. 'Assign me the hardest role to remind me that there is no one easy way to truth.'

'You asked for it, so you'll get it. You will be Earth, I'll be Sky.'

The private chapel was upstairs in the house, a large square room with shutters closed over the windows. Angie led them in, wearing the golden robe of a Lodge Master. The rest of them were robed in white. It was a chapel of the Egyptian god-forms, colourful and overwhelming. In the centre of the eastern wall was painted a golden sun disc at least a yard across, the image of the originator and sustainer of life on earth. On the west wall was the goddess Isis, eight feet tall, her face calm and beautiful, a circlet of gold around her head supporting the disc of the full moon on her forehead. Her long black hair fell to her bare shoulders, her round breasts were uncovered. A blue belt around her waist supported an ankle length skirt striped in white, yellow and red. Her arms were outstretched in a gesture of protection and in her right hand she held the looped cross that was the Egyptian sign for life.

Her husband and brother Osiris was on the north wall. He was depicted as a man of about thirty, with a smooth and impassive face above a chin-beard that was bound tightly with crossed gold thread. On his head was the tall double crown of the Pharaohs and from neck to feet he was swathed in a tight fitting robe of white linen. His arms were crossed on his chest and he held the crook and flail which symbolised supreme power.

Jonathan turned to look at the south wall, through which they had entered the chapel. There loomed the image of the god Set, murderer of Osiris. His body was that of a powerful man and wore only a twisted loin cloth. His head was that of a predatory animal, long jawed and fanged, low browed and with upright, square topped ears. In one hand he held a curved sword and in the other a long bladed spear and with both he menaced whoever looked at him.

Where is the Tree of Life, Jonathan asked himself. He turned back to the east wall, where it should be, and found it. Ra, the sun disc, was its central fruit, dwarfing the other nine almost into insignificance, so that he had not fully taken the picture in at first sight.

Orline lit the tall candles on the floor and the incense burner. The electric light was switched off and the door closed.

'What do you think of it?' Angie asked Jonathan.

'Very powerful. Why did you put Set on the wall?'

'To remind us of the power for destruction we have to contend with in ourselves. There's no point in trying to ignore it. We have to face it head on and overcome it. Are you ready to start?'

'I'm ready.'

The three of them ranged themselves behind Angie as she faced to the east across the central altar and intoned her opening prayer,

'Powers of the Kingdom,
Be beneath my left foot and within my right hand . . . '

She completed the prayer and continued with the tracing of the circle on the floor and the summoning of the Guardians. Jonathan saw why she had been elected Master of the Los Angeles Lodge. She could project her voice in solemn command, half an octave lower than her normal speaking voice. Her movements were hierarchic in their authority. In the soft candle light she seemed to be a head taller than any of them.

Her gestures were imperious as she made the sign of the Cabalistic Cross, touching her forehead, navel and nipples, and then a fanfare of trumpets sounded joyfully through the chapel as she touched the altar briefly, uplifting their spirits.

'This holy chapel is open in the name of Ra. We come here tonight to celebrate the mysteries of the separation of earth and sky. First we will meditate on the greatness of our creator and sustainer in his name of Atum-Ra.'

As Jonathan gazed in silence at the sun disc on the wall before him, he saw that it was glowing. He concluded that the paint had been treated to make it luminescent, and then put aside the thought to let himself be drawn into the meaning of the golden symbol. For a little while he reflected on the sun as a huge fire ball, pouring out its substance in heat, light and radiation, showering its energies onto the earth to warm it and make it fruitful, so that the seed would germinate in the soil and the plant push up into the light and be food for animals and for men, Atum-Ra, who sustained all life on earth.

The power of the symbol drew him deep into its core, where the unimaginable process of nuclear fusion transmuted atoms. Here was the very crucible of creation, in which matter was changed into energy. At last he reached the point where he saw the sun as a god-form thundering through space, all flame and spirit, Atum-Ra, whose untold millions of years of pouring out of his own divine substance had brought about the emergence and development of life on earth, until intelligent organisms had been evolved to contemplate the glory of Ra.

Jonathan's hands were raised in adoration, palms towards

the sun disc, when a touch on his shoulder brought him gently back to awareness of his surroundings. Greg indicated the altar and Jonathan helped him to move the double cube from the centre to the northern quadrant of the circle, to make space for what was to be done. Orline unrolled a prayer mat, about four feet long by two feet wide, and spread it on the floor, east to west. Even in the dim candle light, Jonathan could make out that it was a magnificent oriental carpet, its woven design that of a stylised tree with whorls as branches and birds sitting within them.

The music began again, a solemn processional orchestral piece that Jonathan could not place. Angie stood on the prayer mat, facing the sun, and recited the words which began the mysteries of the separation of earth and sky.

'The god Atum-Ra, who bore within him the sum of all existence, rose by an effort of his will from the abyss of chaos. Out of his own substance he created his children, Shu and Tefnut, twin brother and sister.'

In time with the words, Greg and Orline, who had been seated cross-legged on the floor in the eastern quadrant of the circle, rose gracefully and stood facing each other, their hands joined, so that their robed figures were silhouetted against the glowing sun disc.

For a moment, Jonathan's mind tracked back to the sauna in Finland where he had unwarily triggered off overwhelming lust in himself. No woman adept would have received him, because of the devouring nature of what he had aroused. But at Tuomo's suggestion, Lilsa had rescued him and he had consecrated the outpouring by assuming the form of Atum and speaking the god's words: *I took my member in my hand, I ejaculated into my shadow, I sent forth issue as Shu, I poured myself out as Tefnut* . . .

The god had spoken his words of creation and there before him stood Shu and Tefnut, brother and sister, clad in white, strong and beautiful. Greg, in the person of Shu, led Orline by the hand to the centre of the circle and gently pulled her down onto the prayer mat, as their enactment of the Egyptian creation story continued. Orline lay on her back, her loose white robe pulled up to her waist and her legs wide apart. Greg lay on her in simulated copulation for a few seconds, then stood up and helped her to her feet. He spoke in the person of the god Shu:

'I lay with my sister. I knew her as a wife. And Tefnut brought forth issue, twins at a birth, Geb my son and Nuat my daughter.'

Hand in hand, Jonathan and Angie took their places as Geb and Nuat and bowed low in honour before their divine parents. Greg continued, speaking as Shu, his voice strong and tranquil,

'And Geb also lay with his sister and knew her.'

At this point in the ceremony, simulation ceased and the words were made flesh. Jonathan stripped off his white robe and lay naked on the prayer mat. Angie stood at his feet for a moment, looking down at his body, then pulled her golden robe over her head and dropped it on the floor. Her hands went to the back of her head and her dark hair cascaded down below her shoulders. She knelt between Jonathan's thighs and then lay forward on him, her breasts and belly pressed close. Jonathan put his arms round her and held her to him as she squirmed and rubbed her body against his, until his member rose hard between them.

Her face was expressionless, though her eyes were closed. From its solemn beginning, the music had swollen up into a pounding rhythm. Angie sat up across Jonathan's loins, giving him the sight of her big, round breasts, while she took hold of his erect part and inserted it into herself. She pushed down to drive it in deep and lay forward on him again, her arms about his neck, and began to move on him rapidly.

Jonathan let the sexual pleasure flood through his whole being, his mind intent on being the god Geb, locked in union with his sister. Under her urgent thrusting, his excitement mounted quickly. He saw only her impassive face within a curtain of long hair that enclosed them both. But Greg, playing the part of Shu, was beside them on one knee, his arms outstretched over Angie's moving back. Fast approaching orgasm as Angie pounded at him, Jonathan heard the words of Shu as at a distance:

'They lay together closely, their union denying the words of Atum-Ra. He commanded me to separate them, and I obeyed the word of Ra.'

Greg's hands and forearms slid between Jonathan and Angie's bodies. He jerked her violently upwards in coitus interruptus. She arched over Jonathan, balanced on her hands and feet, her heavy breasts hanging above him, wailing in frustration as his essence streamed out between them. Orline, in the form of Tefnut, knelt behind Greg, her hands under his arms to help support the weight of Angie's body as he held her away from Jonathan.

'And the word of Atum-Ra was fulfilled, so that the two were parted from each other. And Geb was the earth beneath and Nuat was the sky above the earth.'

With their own bodies, the four of them had acted out the creation of polarity in the universe, the establishment of the dynamic tension between positive and negative. Atum-Ra had risen by his own act of will from the abyss of nothingness, just as in Cabalistic teaching the Limitless Light had concentrated itself into a single point, which had then unfolded as Binah and Hokmah, the female and male principles, as Atum-Ra had from his own substance brought forth Shu and Tefnut, male and female twins. But in the Egyptian account, the children of Shu and Tefnut had attempted to withdraw into primal self sufficiency by their sexual union and were parted violently so that the process of creation could continue. The same experience was at the heart of the marriage of Shiva and Shakti which Jonathan had enacted with Britt in Stockholm – the separation into male and female in order to bring about the flow of the universe. In Chinese thought the same poles of cosmic energy are called yang and yin, positive and negative, male and female, light and dark, earth and sky. The adept seeks to hold the two in balance.

All this was implicit in the celebration of the mysteries of Geb and Nuat, vigorously expressed in bodily action to impress it on the adept's mind as personal experience instead of theorising. When Angie and Jonathan were robed again and standing to face the sun disc, Angie solemnly closed the proceedings. As they left the chapel, Jonathan was reflecting upon a saying he had learned from Dr Challey, even before he had been invited into the Noble Order:

> 'God is not comfortable,
> He is not a kind uncle,
> He is an earthquake.'

CHAPTER 18
AN ARMY WITH BANNERS

THE MEETING of the Los Angeles Lodge was the largest gathering of the Order Jonathan had ever attended. In his borrowed uniform he sat in one of ten chairs with white banners over them reserved for visitors from other Lodges. There were two other visitors to his left and four to his right. In all, the Temple had seats for over five hundred people, set in rising tiers on opposite sides of the room.

The occasion to which he had been invited was the reception into the Order of a new member. All Lodge members were eligible to be present as witnesses, and the attendance was impressive, the large oblong Temple filled with the contrasting colours of personal banners above the chairs – greens, reds, blues, golds – against the white and windowless walls. The door from the robing room was closed and the Knight Sentinel stood with his back against it, drawn

269

sword in his hand. Under the star strewn black ceiling, the assembly sat in silence, listening to the calm and elegant statement of inner assurance of a Handel violin sonata.

An army with banners, marching towards God, Jonathan thought.

As the music ended, Angie Herron's voice spoke commandingly from behind the veil of the sanctum at the eastern end of the Temple:

'Knight Sentinel, is the Temple secure?'

From the far end came the traditional response,

'The Temple gate is locked and I stand here to guard it with my life.'

'Are all those within the Temple true members of our Noble Order?'

'Every Knight and Lady within the Temple has given me the true word before entering here, three hundred and eighty-seven members of this Lodge and seven members of sister Lodges.'

'It is well. By the power vested in me as Master of the Los Angeles Lodge of the Noble Order of the Masters of the Temple, I solemnly declare this sacred Chapter of the mysteries open.'

The veil slid open between the two pillars to reveal Angie, crowned and seated on a great ornate throne. To her right was the Marshal with his ivory baton and to her left the Guardian of the Grail, holding with both her hands the lidded chalice. The assembly rose in respect, to a soaring fanfare of trumpets and organ. On the plain white wall behind the sanctum there slowly blossomed in scarlet the *phi* symbol, a circle bisected by an upright line, and around it the words: *From God we are born*.

In English, Jonathan noted, not the Latin *Ex deo nascimur* as used in London and in all the European Temples he had visited over the years.

They sat again, to the rattle of scabbards on chairs, and waited expectantly. From the door there came a heavy knocking. The Marshal looked at Angie for permission before calling down the length of the Temple to the Sentinel.

'Who seeks admittance to the Temple?'

The Sentinel slid back the deliberately large bolts top and bottom of the heavy door and opened it just enough to hold an exchange of set questions and answers with someone outside. He turned back to the Marshal to report that a stranger was seeking admittance.

'Is the stranger alone?'

'No, Brother Discernment stands as the stranger's sponsor.'

'Then let them enter.'

If the sponsor is a Brother, Jonathan thought as the Knight Sentinel swung the door wide, then the postulant must be a woman. And in she came, took one step past the door and stopped, looking about her in amazement. Naturally, the first time any postulant sets foot in the Temple was when, after months of teaching, enquiries and examination by the Inquisitors, the day of admittance came.

From the threshold, the woman looked down the length of the Temple between the tiered rows of Knights and Ladies in their uniforms under their coloured banners, past the great golden interlaced star on the floor, to the sanctum where the Master sat enthroned and crowned, flanked by her two officers. At this moment, every postulant was overwhelmed by the scene, whatever the Lodge, dumbfounded by the richness and strangeness of the assembly and the building.

As the heavy door was closed and bolted behind her, the woman's sponsor put a hand under her elbow and led her forward slowly between the rows, letting her gather her wits and become accustomed to her surroundings. She was a woman of about thirty, Jonathan noted, of middle height, her light brown hair cut short in a sort of petal cut around her head. Postulants were told to dress well for their reception and this being Southern California, she wore a broad-sleeved white Mexican blouse tucked into tight fitting scarlet satin trousers. Nearly half her face was covered by huge circular sunglasses.

The sponsor halted halfway along the Temple, so that both

he and she were standing in the centre of the six-pointed star. For a full minute no one moved or spoke. The postulant was staring at Angie on her golden throne, and Angie, looking unbelievably imperial, was staring back. Finally Angie nodded to her Marshal, who took one step forward and asked,

'What is your name?'

'Loretta Van Wissink Fox,' she answered, sounding nervous.

'Is that your own name or that of a man you have married?'

'My own name is Loretta. Van Wissink is my father's surname. Fox is my husband's surname,' she said, showing that she had her wits about her, nervous or not.

'Why do you come here, Loretta?'

There was a painful pause, during which all feared that she had forgotten the proper form of words. Her sponsor touched her elbow warningly and she blurted out,

'I am here to seek admittance to your Order.'

Angie as Master took no part in these preliminaries. As the postulant was a woman, the Marshal put the questions. For a man, the Guardian of the Grail would have officiated.

'Are you of full age and free?'

'I am twenty-eight years old and a citizen of this country by birth.'

'Does anyone vouch for you?'

'I vouch for her,' said her sponsor, Brother Discernment.

'By what right?'

'As a Knight of this Order. The Inquisitors have assured me of her worthiness.'

'What is your rank, Knight?'

'I am a Fifth.'

The Marshal faced Angie and announced that all was in order and that Loretta could be received, if the Master so willed. Angie was sitting very upright in her high backed throne, her forearms along its wooden arms. She addressed the postulant for the first time.

'Loretta, so far nothing has been said or done which would make it impossible for you to withdraw. If it is your will, the

Temple door is behind you and the Knight Sentinel will unbolt it and let you pass freely. But if you continue now in the desire to become a member of this Order, the name of which is still unknown to you, then you must persist to the end. Nothing then will permit you to break the ties which bind you to us. Do you understand this?'

'Yes.'

'Listen well, Loretta, for these words are never spoken twice – is it your will to withdraw now or to remain with us forever?'

In the silence that followed, the sponsor neither touched nor prompted her. The decision was hers alone to make. Before speaking, she looked to her left and to her right at the rows of Knights and Ladies, then at the golden chalice in the hands of the Guardian and at the baton held by the Marshal. At last she looked Angie squarely in the face and said that it was her will to become a member of the Order.

A single trumpet sounded an upward soaring call as Angie, unobserved, touched the concealed controls in the arm of her throne. As the last note died away, she said,

'You have been guided and supported to this moment by your sponsor, a worthy Knight of this Order . . .'

As she was speaking, the lights in the Temple faded, until only the sanctum was lit and Loretta standing in the golden star.

'But now you must go on alone, guided and supported only by your own courage and determination. Are you prepared for this?'

'I am ready.'

'Then read aloud the words written on the eastern wall of the Temple.'

'From God we are born.'

'What do you understand by those words?'

The ceremony of receiving a new member into the Order was an ordeal for the postulant, not as severe physically and psychologically as the upgrading ceremony to the Fifth, which Jonathan had last witnessed in Stockholm. The ceremony of reception was adjusted to the level of understanding of those seeking admittance but, as it was the first of seven ceremonial initiations which the Order utilised to mark the successive Degrees, necessarily it involved an ordeal of testing.

When the Master was satisfied that Loretta had absorbed and understood the preliminary teaching well enough to respond to her questions, she handed over to her officers for the next part of the ceremony. The music changed to a darkly disturbing mutter as the Marshal raised his voice threateningly,

'The world of the Everlasting came through me, saying:
Is it time for you to dwell in your house
while this Temple lies waste?'

There was a pause, then the Guardian of the Grail took up the theme, her voice hard and urgent,

'Consider your ways:
You have sown much and reaped little;
You eat, but you have not enough;
You drink, but are not filled by drink.'

The Marshal took over again,

'Consider your ways –
Go up to the mountain and bring wood
and build the Temple,
And I will take pleasure in it and I will be glorified.'

The Guardian spoke, her voice bitter,

'You looked for much and it came to little,
And when you brought it home, I did blow upon it,
Because my Temple is waste,
And you run every one to his own house.'

The menacing words and music combined to produce a sense of desolation in the listeners, in particular, in Loretta. The imposing figures in the sanctum beyond the pillars were telling her what she already felt, that her worldly life was void, a meaningless scramble for fleeting gratifications and vain observances. The muted music ran on alone, underscoring the message, until at the very depth of its pessimism, it was cut off sharply and a worse silence followed.

Alone in the small spotlight centred on the six-pointed star, Loretta looked forlorn, her shoulders slumped forward. Angie spoke from her throne,

'Have you understood what Temple lies waste and waiting for you to build so that the Everlasting may be glorified in it?'

'The temple of my body and spirit.'

'You have said well. Cast off all worldly finery so that you may be clothed anew in the uniform of this Order and be received among us.'

With slow fingers Loretta unbuttoned the cuffs of her blouse, pulled it over her head and let it flutter to the floor. She reached behind her back to unfasten her brassiere and that too fell. Her time of testing had come in the silent and darkened Temple in a form that she had not expected. Only her own courage and determination would carry her through it, as she had been warned. She was neither shy nor squeamish, or the Inquisitors would not have let her reach this moment. To strip her body for a lover was a familiar act to her, and a source of pleasure, but like most others asked to stand naked before a clothed audience, she was beset with feelings of vulnerability and inadequacy.

She undid her tight trousers and slid them down her tanned legs, kicked off her shoes and discarded the trousers. Inside the Seal of Solomon the King, she straightened her back again, with only small white briefs and sunglasses as protection from hundreds of inquisitive eyes. For the onlookers, the ceremony was not a strip show; it had no sexual content. Like all postulants, Loretta was being asked to demonstrate in the most unmistakable manner that she brought nothing to the Order but herself, that she came to it naked as a new-born child to seek its protection, that she held nothing of herself back.

Seeing the hesitation, Angie spoke warningly,

'Those who are unable to cut the three knots of shame, hate and fear are not worthy of being initiated into this path.'

In a burst of resolve, Loretta peeled her briefs down her legs, stepped free and threw them away from her into the surrounding darkness. And finally she removed her oversized sunglasses and dropped them onto her blouse on the floor. She clasped her hands behind her back and stood boldly naked before them all. Her figure was average good, Jonathan thought; breasts a little spikey, belly broad and smooth, legs rounded. From the memory of his own acceptance into the Order many years before he knew the determination it took to undress and stand totally exposed before the members.

The Guardian advanced from the sanctum and offered her chalice to Loretta to drink from. The wine of initiation was only very slightly laced, Jonathan knew, to give the postulant a feeling of mild exhilaration as the ceremony continued. Thornapple juice was used in Europe; he remembered that the Americans called it Jimson weed.

When the Guardian was back in her place, Angie spoke to the naked woman in the star.

'Loretta, since you have come before us submissively to ask for the protection of the Order, it shall be granted to you. First you must be dressed as we are.'

From beside the throne the Marshal went forward to the star, carrying over his outspread arms the uniform of the Order. The lyrical serenity of a Mozart flute concerto sang through the Temple as he helped her to dress. First she put on the short tunic of dark grey which symbolised the chain mail of the first Knights of the Temple.

'This symbolic coat of chain mail is the armour of knowledge,' said Angie. 'What you learn with us will be your protection against those who may try to harm you.'

Over the tunic went the sleeveless surcoat of white linen

with its scarlet sign above the heart.

'The surcoat which covers your armour is the secrecy you will maintain in all things to do with the Order. Your knowledge of hidden things will be safe from the eyes of strangers.'

The Marshal knelt before Loretta to help her on with the knee-length boots.

'Your boots symbolise your energy to go forward, your daring. In this Order there is nothing you may not dare.'

Lastly, the Marshal buckled round Loretta's waist a broad leather belt with a sheathed sword attached.

'Your sword represents your will,' said Angie. 'When you have learned how to wield it properly, all ignorance, prejudice and hostility can be cut down.'

The Marshal walked slowly round Loretta, checking that everything was correct, much like an army sergeant checking before a general's inspection. Then he stood beside her and waited.

'Remember these things,' said Angie. 'Think of them each time you are dressed for the Temple. Boots, armour, sword, surcoat. That is to say – *dare, know, will, be silent*. Have you understood this?'

'I understand.'

The Marshal led her forward and stationed her before the throne.

'Loretta,' said Angie, 'you have passed through the ordeal and have conducted yourself with courage. In the presence of these Knights and Ladies of the Noble Order of the Masters of the Temple, repeat after me the oath of a Neophyte. Draw your sword and hold it upright in front of you.'

There was no tremor in Loretta's voice as she swore obedience to the rule of the Order and silence on its mysteries.

'And may I be scourged with whips, my life ended by the axe and my flesh consumed by fire if I break this oath,' she concluded.

An organ salute heralded the oath taking. At this stage, thought Jonathan, the oath sounds merely theatrical to the

Neophyte, a dramatic form of words with little personal relevance. But as the Neophyte advances deeper into the Order's work, he eventually comes to realise that the penalties are real punishments which guilt visits on him if ever he breaks the oath of obedience and silence. The whips and fire in the mind can be as painful and deadly as those applied to the flesh.

Angie stood up as the organ music roared to its triumphant close and slipped over Loretta's head a striped ribbon on which hung the insignia of the First, a simple interlaced six-pointed star in gold with a red stone like an eye set in the centre.

'By my authority as Master of this Lodge, I create you now and forever a Lady of the Noble Order of the Masters of the Temple.'

She took Loretta's hands and kissed her on both cheeks as the organ music sounded once more in triumph. When she resumed her throne, the Marshal turned Loretta to face down the Temple. He stood beside her, holding her by the hand, his ivory baton raised for silence, and in a loud voice he proclaimed the new member. As he spoke, the light grew, revealing to her the packed rows of Knights and Ladies, all their eyes on her. They rose to their feet and applauded her as the Marshal led her to her appointed seat on the top row behind Jonathan. When she was seated, he took from where it had been lying hidden behind the chairs her personal banner and affixed it above her, eliciting more applause from the onlookers.

The banner was a design of broad silver diagonal bands on a dark blue background, the significance of which was not immediately apparent to Jonathan. But what mattered was that the design had a meaning for Loretta.

Because of the numbers present, the banquet which followed a Temple meeting had been arranged to take place in the ballroom of a good downtown hotel owned by a Lodge member. Since the secrecy of the Order's existence meant that not even its name could be mentioned to outsiders, the staff believed that they were preparing for a convention dinner of sales agents. Jonathan had already arranged to sit beside Angie's sister-in-law, Orline, and to leave with her early. He was taking her away for the weekend and had reservations on a late flight out of Los Angeles Airport.

CHAPTER 19
RED AND BLACK

ON THE short flight from Los Angeles, Orline told Jonathan how Las Vegas achieved its notoriety.

'After the gold and silver mines had been worked out, it was just another Western ghost town for a long time – a few saloons with poker games, the kind of thing you see in John Wayne movies. Then a New York racketeer called Bugsy Siegel came out to the West Coast to escape various raps hanging over him. He discovered Las Vegas around 1945 and saw its potential. It's within easy reach of L.A. but it's over the State line in Nevada, where gambling is legal.'

'A gangster with vision?'

'Sure. He borrowed millions of dollars from his mob friends back East and built the Flamingo, the biggest hotel and casino anyone had ever seen then. There was plenty of money in California to attract to his tables; not just movie money but the big wages ordinary people were making in war industry factories. But it went wrong for him. Maybe he was slow in paying off his backers, or maybe they wanted all the action themselves, but whatever it was, a hit man shot the top of his head off one night. By then everybody with the right kind of money to invest was out here building hotels and casinos. Vegas took off like a moon rocket.'

'I hope that Mr Siegel has a fitting memorial in the local cemetery to his enterprise.'

'No, they buried him in the Jewish cemetery in Hollywood. He liked to screw around with movie stars, and that's where the hit man caught up with him.'

The Delta Airlines jet smacked down on the runway and the gaudiness of Las Vegas closed in around them as soon as they left the plane. The long moving floor from plane to terminal passed between endless signs advertising hotels, stars appearing in shows, car rentals, bars and casinos. At intervals, disembodied voices enthusiastically extolled various delights of the town.

'Besides gambling,' said Orline, 'another thing that's legal in Vegas is prostitution. You look up an escort number in the directory, call them and they send a girl right over. Or you can stop by their offices and shop around.'

The terminal building was decorated much like Santa Claus's grotto in any large department store, though every available corner held a bank of slot machines, with people busily feeding coins in and pulling handles to set the coloured wheels whirling.

'Do you suppose they're arriving or departing?' Jonathan asked.

'Leaving, I guess, and trying to salvage a few dollars before flight time.'

From the airport it was only a short taxi ride into Las Vegas. Jonathan had seen pictures of it, but the reality was astounding. Coloured neon displays reached up into the night sky, whorls of red and gold, cascades of light in yellow and green, fountains and animated illuminations soaring upwards like a silent firework display.

'How do you like it?' Orline asked, her hand resting on his thigh as they sat close in the back of the taxi.

'It's garish and tasteless and exuberant and I love it at first sight. What very exhilarating people you Americans are.'

The taxi rolled down the Strip between vast hotels and dropped them at Caesar's Palace. Jonathan checked in with his credit card, a custom he had learned in the past week travelling in the United States, and they were shown up to a room with a bed eight feet wide.

'I need a shower,' said Orline.

The time was nearly one in the morning.

'Don't be long,' said Jonathan, 'I simply have to go and see this place for myself.'

'Where's the rush – everything in this town stays open twenty-four hours a day, casinos, whorehouses and wedding chapels.'

Jonathan busied himself hanging his clothes in the closet while Orline undressed. She was a good choice, he thought, looking at her big breasts and golden tanned body. After the Earth and Sky ceremony he had spent the night with her and found her to be lascivious and enthusiastic; so much so that he wanted more time with her and had invited her away for the weekend. The disparity in colour between her long, straw coloured hair and her much darker pubic bush caught his attention as she went naked into the bathroom. He made a mental note to ask her why she didn't match the lower to the upper.

He sat down to flick through the magazines and publicity publications provided by the hotel to advertise the hotel's own facilities and other outside attractions. When Orline came back, wrapped in a bath towel, he was engrossed in an advertisement for the Silver Bell Wedding Chapel, where, at any hour of the day or night, eager couples could be legally married for twenty-five dollars, inclusive of a bouquet for the bride, a bottle of champagne after the ceremony and a colour photograph of the happy newly-weds. For a few dollars more then Chapel would lend the bride a wedding dress and provide a tape recording of the ceremony.

At the dressing table Orline combed out her long hair and made up her face. She stood up and unwound the towel to display her body.

'Are you sure you want to go down to the lobby, Jonathan?'

He dumped his magazine and patted her well fleshed bottom.

'Put some clothes on,' he said, grinning. 'How can I do you justice when my mind is filled with curiosity about what is happening in the casino downstairs? I give you my word we won't stay long.'

'Well, OK. Hey – you're not a big gambling man, are you?'

'No, that's not why we came here.'

She rummaged through her bag and pulled out a shiny white dress to slip over her head. It came to halfway down her thighs and was low cut enough in front to expose her bulging breasts almost down to her brown nipples.

'How's that?' she asked.

'Fine, but is that all?'

'You're right. I forgot to put panties on. Hold everything.'

Eventually he got her down into the hotel lobby. It was bigger than the biggest hotel ballroom he had ever seen and it was crowded with people pressed close round the gaming tables that seemed to stretch on into the far distance under a row of gigantic chandeliers. They found seats in one of the bar areas and an attractive waitress bustled up at once. In keeping with the pseudo classical theme, she wore a short white Hollywood Grecian style tunic that ended where her legs forked. Her breasts were pushed up by a platform brassiere and were as exposed as Orline's. Hair was piled high on her head and hung down her back in ringlets. Jonathan glanced round and saw at least half a dozen other waitresses exactly like her.

'I'm sure that only a very few really decadent Caesars went in for this sort of thing,' he said, 'and they must have been the ones who enjoyed life to the full. What shall we drink?'

'A dry martini, please.'

'That's one American drink I can't come to terms with. I'll have bourbon on the rocks. How often have you been here before, Orline?'

'Twice, both times with my husband. He liked to gamble. I was left alone for hours while he sweated himself to death at the crap tables. Both times he dropped more than we could afford. The last time we were here he lost about ten thousand dollars and I didn't speak to him for a week.'

'This unreal town with its air conditioning and illuminations out in a desert was built with money lost on the tables, of course.'

'That's a good thought to hold on to, Jonathan. I don't see you as a loser, but you can get carried away here by the excitement around you.'

The waitress brought their drinks, served them very deftly and gave Jonathan her big smile as he paid and tipped her well.

'I never gamble,' he said. 'I only bet when I know that I'm going to win.'

'Every bust-out gambler here knew he was going to win.'

'No, I don't mean when I think I'm going to win, or believe that I'm going to win. Only when I know. There's a difference.'

They talked a while over the drinks, but Jonathan was eager to see more of what was going on and soon they were drifting round the vast casino, pausing here and there to watch. At one of the crap tables a woman of sixty with orange dyed hair was rolling the dice and shrieking at them to get hot. Round the table a throng of people were talking, laughing, egging her on, betting against her or for her.

'Too fast and too easy to make mistakes,' said Jonathan. 'Do you feel the vibrations the people there are setting up by their anxiety? Once you get drawn into that vortex you'd go round and round with it until you were sucked through the hole at the bottom and came to your senses broke.'

'You can feel the vibrations, sure, and so can I, because we know about such things. My ex-husband never did and he ended up broke twice.'

They moved on to a bank of roulette tables and stood by the busiest of them to observe. About twenty people were playing the table, some with large stacks of chips in front of them. The game went much faster than in European casinos and there was much more talk between the players. After eight or nine spins of the wheel, Jonathan closed his eyes for a moment and said quietly to Orline that red would come up next time. The bets went down, the croupier spun the wheel and flicked the ball. It rattled round and settled in red eighteen.

'How did you guess that? You could have made money on that.'

'I don't know how I know, but sometimes I just do. There's even a word for it – cryptesthesia – which doesn't explain anything at all.'

'Is it like a premonition?'

'What I think happens is that I unconsciously analyse a pattern and predict what should come next if the pattern continues. It doesn't always work out right, but often enough.'

'It sounds useful. Is that why we came to Vegas?'

'We came to enjoy ourselves.'

They halted at one of the black jack games. A pretty girl behind a kidney shaped table slid cards out so fast to the half dozen players that she could have been a Mississippi river boat gambler from the old days.

'Now this is one of the few games I understand,' said Orline.

'In theory it's about the only game where the player has a long term chance of beating the house. But it's a slow and tedious way to win money.'

'Look at that – if that woman had stood on sixteen she would have won when the dealer's hand bust.'

'Come away, Orline, or you'll be pulled into the whirlpool.'

'Right. You know what, I'm hungry, even though we ate dinner before we left L.A.'

'So am I. Let's find somewhere where'll they give us a fine meal and a bottle of good wine and then go to bed.'

'That I like the sound of,' she said, taking his arm.

In Las Vegas there is no time, no day, no night, it is never late and never early. There are no public clocks, one consults a watch. It is lotus land, where people eat when they are hungry and sleep when they are tired, without reference to the hours of the day or night. Dinner for two in the middle of the night is no more outlandish than eggs, bacon and coffee in mid-afternoon or getting falling-down drunk at seven in the morning. Because the casinos stay permanently open, for some people the day is always just beginning, for some it is just ending, and others are midway through their day.

By the time they got back to their room it was nearly sunrise. Jonathan drew back the heavy curtains from the windows and took his bearings. The window faced more or less east and they were high up in the building. He and Orline stripped naked and stood hand-in-hand by the floor-to-ceiling plate glass and waited. At first he was very conscious of Orline's body so close beside him, her long yellow hair and oversize breasts, the smooth curve of her belly and her well shaped legs. And he guessed that she was equally conscious of him. But she was a Fifth in the Order, Sovereign Princess, and so able to control and direct her sexuality into whatever channel she chose. Gradually the stirrings of carnality in both of them faded out as they stood in silent meditation.

The sky over the sickly glare of the coloured neon was changing and paling. Out over the desert, though they could not see it, the horizon was turning pink, until when the red gold tip of the sun appeared, they both sensed it at once. They raised their hands towards the rising sun in devotion, palms upwards and there, in the unlikely setting of a town built on naked greed, Jonathan began the hymn to the rising sun and Orline spoke the responses:

> 'We salute you at the beginning of the day,
>   *Father of all living.*
> The heavens declare your glory,
>   *And the earth your strength.*
> Your going forth is from the end of the sky,
>   *And your circuit is unto the ends of it.*
> We are your children,
>   *Engendered of your seed.*
> We praise you in your glory,
>   *And salute you in your might.*'

They bowed towards the east and Jonathan took Orline's hand again to lead her to the broad bed. The first light of day was creeping into the dark room.

'It's a long time since I was up early enough to say those words,' said Orline, running her hands over Jonathan's bare chest.

'That's true for most of us.'

'Angie has this special cult of Ra, so she's usually up for sunrise. Well, you've seen her chapel, so you must have guessed that. Me, I prefer another way.'

'Which way is that?' he asked.

In answer, Orline assumed one of the attitudes of the goddess Shakti, exposing her slit, inviting worship.

'Then I will be Shiva,' said Jonathan, understanding immediately.

This was not the dance of creation he had taught to Britt in Stockholm, but the enactment of another variant of union through god-forms. Orline was sitting upright on the bed, her back to the headboard. Her knees were splayed wide apart and the soles of her feet pressed together. Jonathan lay face down on the bed and kissed the soft lips of her genitals. Orline put her palms on the insides of her thighs and pulled the outer lips apart so that his tongue could enter her. In tantric worship, as taught by the Noble Order, the vagina has a special significance in this ceremony, representing the ultimate reality manifesting itself through its female principle in visible and tangible flesh.

As her sexual arousal mounted, the human personality of Orline was submerged by the tide of divinity rising inside her, until she became Shakti, as Britt had. In such intimate proximity to the manifestation, Jonathan was swept along with it, his ego sense extinguished. He was an instrument of worship, no longer in control of his actions.

There came a moment when he was impelled to raise his head to kiss her belly and then higher on up her magnificent body, to suck at her taut nipples. It seemed to him that rays of red light emanated from the whole of Orline's body, surrounding her in a fiery aura of divinity. The decision came from elsewhere, not from his own desire, as he took her by the hips and pulled her slowly down from her sitting position until she was underneath him. Strong legs clamped round his waist and he moved to the slow boom of a brass gong sounding inside his head to time his thrusts.

The psychic energy released by their ceremonial orgasm flickered about them like fire before expanding into a vast transparent bubble that contained them. The bubble was balanced, rising and falling slowly, on a fountain of crystal water springing up from the middle of a sunlit lake. Beyond the lake were lawns of smooth, emerald green grass, where brilliant peacocks trailed their long tail feathers and then stood still to raise them into multicoloured fans. Beds of red roses and thickets of fruit trees with golden apples on their boughs contrasted with the green of the grass in a landscape to delight the senses. A snow white doe was drinking from the lake, poised on delicate legs, and when a great tawny lion came out of a rose thicket to lap at the water, the doe stood and watched it mildly.

Locked in their union, Shakti and Shiva floated in their bubble of ecstasy in the midst of the garden of earthly delights. Only very gradually did the fountain that held them aloft sink down until the bubble rested on the surface of the lake, then it faded into nothingness.

The garden was gone and Jonathan and Orline were lying together on the wide bed. They were silent for a while, rapt by the vision. Orline spoke first.

'We made it there together – and it was like forever.'

'It was forever,' said Jonathan. 'There is no time there. We were gods outside of time.'

He knelt upright on the bed between her legs to recite the prescribed form of thanksgiving to the god who had admitted them to a state of grace:

> *'Non nobis, domine, non nobis,*
> *Sed nomini tuo da honorem,*
> *Propter benignitatem tuam,*
> *Propter fide tuam.'*

Orline repeated it after him, using the English form of words:

> 'Not unto us, lord, not unto us,
> But to you be the glory
> For your mercy and faith.'

After that they went to sleep in each other's arms. It was well after noon when they woke up and ordered a hearty breakfast to be sent up. For the rest of the afternoon they lazed beside the hotel swimming pool in the hard and clear Nevada sun, diving into the water to cool off from time to time. They talked of their common interest in the Order and many other things. Orline told him something about the riding school she owned and operated outside Los Angeles and he told her something of his lifestyle and work. Jonathan found Orline to be an agreeable companion. She evidently found him to be so too and eventually she sounded him out on a possible visit to England.

'That would be very nice,' he said, slightly surprised by the pleasure he discovered in himself at the idea. 'We could have an enjoyable time together. I'm due for some time off before long and we could do the sights. I know – if you come over in September you can see me installed as Marshal of the Lodge at the equinox. You must stay with me as my guest, of course. I'll show you London and some of the countryside. The weather is often good in September.'

'I'd really like that, Jonathan. Can I fly direct to London from L.A.?'

'Yes, it's about eleven hours. There's an evening flight from L.A. that arrives the next morning. From where I live it's less than half an hour to Heathrow Airport. I could pick you up and have you home in time for breakfast.'

'It's a date! As soon as I'm home I'll start planning the trip and write you with the details.'

In the romantic sense, Jonathan was incapable of being in love with anyone. He had a capacity for deep and lasting affection based on respect and liking, and the usefulness of marriage as a social arrangement had been apparent to him for years. Almost without exception, his business colleagues were married, so that at dinner parties and other functions he was generally odd man out. Necessarily, his business entertaining was mostly in restaurants, there being no one to organise his household. The right wife would be a help to his career now that he was on the threshold of Dovedays' boardroom. It went without saying that he would only marry a member of the Order. Privately he had appraised several women of the London Lodge as possible partners, but so far none had seemed quite right.

As he and Orline baked under the desert sun, it was in his mind that she might well be a possible wife for him. She was intelligent, attractive, capable, responsive. She was already a Fifth, which he regarded as a minimum. She had money of her own from her divorce settlement. She was related by marriage to the Master of the Los Angeles Lodge. He visualised her in various settings, to see if the picture was credible. Orline at a London Lodge meeting, Orline taking part in a ceremony in his private chapel with two or three close friends, Orline as hostess at dinner for business contacts, Orline at a country weekend shoot . . . it all had the right sort of feel about it. She could be what he was looking for. And, in turn, he might be what she was looking for in a life partner. It was well worth inviting her to England and getting to know her much better.

For the evening he had reservations for a dinner show at the MGM Grand, not far from Caesar's Palace. They showered and dressed and had a drink before strolling hand in hand along the Strip. Since sunset the temperature had fallen into the high seventies and was bearable. The MGM Grand proved to be even bigger than the hotel they were staying in and its lobby casino was enormous. The show room was as large as most theatres Jonathan could remember, and with a much larger stage. The dinner was edible, though undistinguished; an adjunct to the spectacular performance on stage –

a fast-moving, bright, brassy, colourful kaleidoscope of singers and dancers, liberally interspersed with tall, bare-breasted showgirls with gold-sequinned strings about their loins and feather plumes on their heads.

Jonathan ordered champagne with the meal, being in a festive mood, and brandy afterwards.

'They can't be making any money out of this show,' he said. 'If you multiply the charge per head by the number of people in the audience and then divide by the wages bill for performers and back-stage workers, the answer comes out at zero.'

'Sure. They don't even try. The point is that to get out of here we have to go through the casino, and most of these people will drop money at the tables. That's what Vegas is all about.'

'Then in due course we will move slowly but deliberately through the gaming room, not pausing to be tempted by dice or cards, and back to our hotel, where I have something important to do which will require your co-operation.'

'Like what?' Orline asked, smiling affectionately at him.

'I'll demonstrate when we get there.'

'Let's go, then.'

Back in their hotel room, he asked her to undress.

'We're going out again in a while,' he explained, 'but I want to make sure of something first.'

'Must be pretty important,' she said, shrugging her golden shoulders out of the white dress. 'What are you planning, Jonathan?'

'You are of high enough Degree to have mastered the method of meditating on top of the sacred mountain and orienting yourself. What I want to do now is an advanced form of that. It will be new to you, but I'll lead you through it step by step.'

'But why do you want to do it right now?'

'Before this night is over I intend to collect a reasonable sum of money from the tables down in the casino.'

'You think that you can win at gambling by sitting on

Mount Meru? I never heard that before and it sounds all wrong.'

'If you put it like that, I would agree with you. But that's not how it goes.'

'How does it go, then? I want to know what I'm getting into.'

Jonathan sat down beside her on the edge of the bed, thinking fast. He wanted Orline's wholehearted co-operation, body and mind, and she was either too intelligent or too scrupulous to give it unquestioningly. In New York he had simply rented a woman's body and taken what he wanted. With Orline, the relationship was much more complex.

'Have you ever heard of an English adept named Sepharial?' he asked.

'No. Should I?'

'He wrote a number of books. I thought that you might have come across one of them in your Lodge library.'

'Tell me about him.'

She was sitting naked and cross legged on the bed within arm's reach, her long fair hair cascading over her shoulders and her prominent breasts.

'His name was Walter Richard Old,' said Jonathan, 'and he was born in the English Midlands, in Birmingham, about a hundred years ago. He became interested very early in the Cabala, so much so that when he moved to London in his mid-twenties, he very quickly became a member of Helena Blavatsky's inner circle of initiates. There were about a dozen of them who lived with her in her house in St John's Wood. After her death he branched out on his own. You remember that down in the casino I correctly forecast that red would win? Well, like me, Sepharial was interested in cryptesthesia, though that word had not been invented in his day. He could from time to time invest money in the stock market or the commodity market in the sure knowledge that he would be right. Not just have a hunch, or believe that he was right, but absolutely *know*. When I came across his work on the subject, years ago, I was fascinated to discover that someone else had followed this same path.'

'He must have been a rich man.'

'No, no more than I am. There's an inner warning that goes along with the ability – you mustn't overdo it or it will vanish. So you space it out, make enough for a comfortable life, no more than that.'

'Did he know what made it work?'

'He had no more idea than I have. He gave his ability a sort of astrological basis, to try to explain it to himself. But I've investigated his systems and methods and it's no more astrology than random chance.'

'But he needed some sort of explanation?'

'Maybe not for himself, but he needed some acceptable explanation when he found a way round over taxing his ability by selling his knowledge. In the 1920s he made a good living out of selling a so called astrological horse betting system at £50 a time. In today's money that's at least ten times as much – over a thousand dollars a time.'

'He sounds like an interesting man. I'll check the library when I get home to see if any of his books are there.'

'Now, what I have in mind is to use this ability in the casino. But first I want to sharpen my sensitivity and open my unconscious wide, and for that I want to perform a little ceremony with you. There is nothing in it which goes against the Order's teaching, I promise you. Will you trust me?'

'Sure. I can always pull out if I don't like it.'

Jonathan took his clothes off and started his preparations. Between the big bed and the floor to ceiling windows there was plenty of space for what he intended. He switched off the electric lights and experimented with the thick curtains until he found that the seven-eighths drawn position gave him the dimness he wanted and left just enough light from the neons outside to permit him to operate. He stood Orline in the middle of the clear space and asked her to concentrate on assisting him in what he was doing.

He had kept back a table knife from the breakfast tray delivered by room service hours before and long since cleared away. Washed and consecrated to his purpose, it was the best substitute for a ceremonial sword that he could lay hands on. He used it to trace on the carpet a circle around Orline and himself, nine feet across.

'I charge you, circle of power,' he said as he drew it, 'that you shall be a boundary between the world of men and the realms of the gods.'

The words themselves had no power, but they served to focus his mind and Orline's on the true defence, a raising of their own psychic barriers against outside disturbance. He used the knife again to draw in the air the banishing pentagrams, east, south, west and north. Then, not knowing what unfamiliar forces of malignity might be lurking in so curious a place in Las Vegas, where the human passions of violent greed, agonising frustration and bitter disappointment seethed throughout the day and the night, he took the unusual extra precaution of going once more round the circle, tracing to the four quarters the six-pointed star which contained within its sacred geometry the essence of the Order's knowledge and power.

He paused to listen with his inner senses.

'Does the room feel clear to you, Orline?'

'Clear and calm.'

'Good. Help me with the summons.'

Together they called upon the Lords of the Watchtowers, facing each direction in turn.

'They are here,' said Orline. 'I feel them watching us. Are you sure you know what you're doing?'

'Yes. Their gaze is mild and unperturbed. They have watched me do this before. Are you ready?'

'What do you want me to do?'

'Lie on your back with your head to the east and your knees up and apart.'

'But to orient myself I need to sit upright, you know that.'

'I'm showing you a different way.'

She lay on her back on the carpet as he had directed. Jonathan stood between her parted legs and made the sign of the Cabalistic cross. He felt himself drawing down strength for what was to come and when he was filled with it, he knelt between Orline's drawn up legs and started a rhythmic stroking with his fingers between her thighs, his aim being to excite her slowly.

'The world disc, Orline – create it in your mind. First see the crossed circle, and when that is fixed in your sight, expand it outwards and give it substance.'

The crossed circle, a circle with two diameters drawn at right angles to each other, is one of the oldest of human symbols and signifies the world.

'The disc of the world, Orline. You are at its centre. The lines of direction run out from your slit to the four quarters. Seek them. To the east the line runs up the length of your spine and out through your head. To the west it runs out between your legs and on to the horizon. To south and north the lines from your open slit pass through your hips and extend to the rim of the world. The centre of the entire world is here, where my fingers touch you. The world disc is an extension of you, of this soft slit that is suddenly alive and aware because I am touching it.'

'I see the world about me,' Orline whispered. 'I see it all, mountains, rivers, forests, oceans. Round its edge is the realm of the gods and they are watching us.'

'With my right hand I touch the sacred mount,' said Jonathan in a strong voice. 'I lay my hand on the centre of the world.'

He too was creating in his mind's eye the same vision as Orline. By using the lines that quartered the circle he could coincide his vision with hers. He held the two in harmony for some time, to make sure that the overlapping would not slip later on.

'We see it together, Orline. Keep it clear in your mind and at the same time listen to my words.'

He was ready at last for the ceremony he had been only partly able to perform in New York. Tracey the hooker could contribute only her body then, but Orline was a Fifth in the

Order and could contribute body, mind, training and experience. He continued his slow stroking of her genitals as he recited in a commanding tone,

> 'I who am a perfect king,
> To the people entrusted to me by God,
> I who am by God's command their shepherd,
> Have never tarried, never rested...'

Orline's body, pale against the carpet in the dimness of the room, quivered in sensual delight as she used the sexual energy his fingers were arousing in her to give solidity to the image of the world about her. She was well trained, one tiny part of Jonathan's mind said.

> 'I was called by the great gods,
> Wherefore I became the good shepherd,
> Whose staff is straight and strong...'

Orline's head was pressed back, her big breasts pushing upwards as her back arched up off the carpet. Still she held fast to the image of the world disc she had created and did not let it be dissipated by orgasm.

'Orline, listen well. Let the world disc be America and no more. Change the image to yourself as this land. It will be easy for you, for you are of this land. Here is the centre, where my fingers touch you, and from this centre the life energy flows out to give substance to the image. You are America. Your knees are the Rocky Mountains, your belly is the wheat plains of the Mid West, your breasts are the range of the Appalachians. See this.'

While he instructed her, with his own vision he imposed the same image on the woman's body lying before him.

'Yes,' she gasped, 'I see it clear. I feel it. Yes.'

Jonathan lay forward on her and slid his sacred part deep into her, the way well prepared. He thrust hard and fast to bring them both to orgasm quickly while the vision of the continent was real about them. In time with his movements he cried out the concluding lines:

'My righteous shadow has stretched out across this city,
I have gathered all its people in my arms...'

The city, the centre of Orline's body, the sacred mount on which he was enthroned, the slit he had impaled and possessed, was Las Vegas. Then for a second he thought he had mistimed the ceremony as Orline's gasps turned into a climactic wail, but he ejaculated strongly as he forced out the final words:

'Here in this city I have spoken my precious words,
And erected my statue as king!'

So powerful was the image they had established between them that it seemed to him that he was a god pouring out his substance on to the earth beneath and taking it into his dominion. Orline felt it too, and when at length he withdrew from her and sat back on his heels, she turned over and round so that she was lying face down at his feet, her hands between his knees, as if she were a suppliant. She was almost stammering with awe as she said,

'Lord, who shall abide in thy tabernacle,
Who shall abide in thy holy mountain?'

Jonathan stroked her hair to calm her while he gathered into himself the virtue that seemed to flicker about his body like neon lighting. Eventually Orline came to herself and knelt upright so that he could kiss her mouth.

'I thought I was being torn apart,' she said. 'There was a god in you taking possession of my body and soul. Is that a ceremony of the Seventh?'

'No, it is my own. Stand up now.'

Together they stood to thank the four Guardians and to dismiss any harmful forces that might have been attracted.

They dispersed the circle, showered quickly and dressed.

Down in the casino on the ground floor the Saturday night gambling was at fever pitch. This suited Jonathan, people pushing each other to get to the tables, much money being passed over, a great deal of chatter. A quick strike would receive little attention.

They made for the line of roulette tables, found seats by one of them and Jonathan bought a thousand dollars worth of chips. At each spin of the wheel he put a ten dollar chip on Odd. The wheel spun again and again and he was neither winning nor losing much, just establishing himself as a player in the croupier's awareness. He was watching the numbers all the while, not thinking about them, simply letting them register on his mind. Orline watched the wheel at first, then turned her attention to Jonathan when she understood what he was doing.

After twenty-seven spins of the wheel he was sixty dollars down from his constant bet on Odd. Orline saw his eyes close for an instant before he reached out across the table to put five hundred dollars worth of chips on seventeen black. Almost all the other players betting on numbers were hedging their bets by covering four numbers with their chips, quartering the odds if they won. Jonathan put his bet firmly in the middle of the seventeen square and waited. The wheel spun, the ball rattled round it, clicked into a slot and the coupier in a white shirt and thin black tie called seventeen black and effortlessly raked in all the losing bets on the table. He pushed a hefty stack of chips towards Jonathan and gave him a quick appraising stare.

'Wow, you did it!' Orline breathed in his ear. 'That's fifteen thousand dollars you won there. Now what?'

'I don't know yet. Wait a while.'

He went back to his ten dollar bets on every spin, this time backing Even instead of Odd. In a minute or two there was a waitress at his elbow with complimentary drinks on the house for him and Orline, flashing him a broad smile and a glimpse of her scarcely covered breasts as he dropped a ten dollar chip on her tray as a tip. And though the game had proceeded without a pause after his win, without a word being uttered by the croupier other than his working patter, behind him stood a pit boss from nowhere, a chunky young man in a dark suit and a striped tie, his casual glance at table and players hardly masking his inherent hardness.

After another thirty spins, Jonathan was two hundred dollars down on his ten dollar bets before he knew what to do. He suddenly drained his glass and put five hundred on twenty-three red. Orline's fingers dug into his arm nervously as the ball rattled round the wheel, clicked, jumped and came to rest in red twenty-three. Jonathan filled his pockets with chips as the game rolled on and led Orline away from the table under the cold stare of the pit boss.

'How do you do it?' she asked, her voice fast and exultant. 'Can you control the ball someway to make it stop where you want?'

'No. I don't think so. My theory has always been that I unconsciously analyse a pattern. Very little in life is random, even gambling sequences. There's a very complex pattern there somewhere.'

At the cashier's cage he exchanged his chips for a packet of high denomination currency notes. They went to the bar and he ordered a bottle of champagne.

'You could make enough that way to live without working,' said Orline, 'like the man you told me about – Sepharial.'

'I like my work. Besides, it's neither good to be greedy nor wise to be a constant winner. Some casino or other would take it amiss if I won too often. They'd think I was cheating and I'd wind up in an alley with my head kicked in.'

'How often do you do it?'

'A couple of times a year – usually when I'm on a business trip or on holiday. Occasionally in London, but they really hate big winners there, so I am careful. There are more gangsters in London casinos than there are in the whole of Las Vegas.'

'Do you spend the money?'

'Some of it, if there's anything I really want, such as a

picture or a carving or a really expensive holiday. But my job pays well enough for me to do about everything I want to do. So a good half of all I win this way gets invested.'

'You're a surprise package, Jonathan Rawlings. I thought I had you pegged when we met at Angie's, then you surprised me by asking me away for the weekend, especially when you suggested Vegas instead of one of the Mexican resorts. Today you surprised me again. I know that you're a Seventh but that ceremony of yours an hour ago really rolled me out flat. Now I've learned something else about you in the last few minutes. What's coming next?'

'You'll have to make that trip to England in September and find out.'

'That I'm really looking forward to.'

'And so am I, Orline.'

They got up very early the next morning and took a taxi out to a ranch not far from the town where they could hire horses. They rode out across the desert in the cool morning air, and though Jonathan was not an expert rider, he managed to stay on the big western saddle even at a light gallop. Orline's style was professional and with her long yellow hair streaming out behind her she looked magnificent. All too soon the sun was high enough to make them turn back through the sage brush. They showered together in their hotel and the showering turned into a sexual encounter standing up, which left them gasping and giggling.

After breakfast they took another cab to downtown Las Vegas so that Orline could show him the Horseshoe Casino, the only place in the world which has one million dollars in currency on permanent display – ten thousand dollar bills, a hundred of them side by side between two sheets of plate glass hanging inside a six foot high horseshoe shaped frame.

'Not exactly subtle,' Orline said

'But effective,' he answered, grinning. 'It gives the visitors something to aim for.'

Even at eleven on a Sunday morning the Horseshoe was half full of busy gamblers and the tables were all in use.

'You don't want to try again?' Orline asked, gesturing towards the green baize.

'No, I've done enough. Let's go shopping.'

They browsed around the gift shops and in true traditional Las Vegas winner style, he bought Orline a greatly over priced gold necklace out of his winnings. They lazed the afternoon away beside the hotel swimming pool and early evening found them at the airport. He kissed her warmly as they parted.

'I'll phone you as soon as I check into the Fairmont in Dallas,' he promised.

'I've really enjoyed myself with you,' she said. 'Watch out for yourself, Jonathan. I'll be with you in September. That's a promise.'

After her flight had been called, he bought a news magazine and sat in the bar to wait for his own plane. But he did little reading. Orline had made a deeper emotional impression on him than any other woman in his life.

CHAPTER 20
GOOD OLD BOYS

'YOU MEAN you want me to let some New York hot-shot tell me how to run my business?' Darrel Luddy asked incredulously, 'Now hold on there, boy.'

It was the worst moment of Jonathan's American tour. They had met in the plush lobby bar of the Fairmont and sized each other up over a drink or two. Luddy looked Texan in a stereotyped way; tall, craggy jawed, wearing a silver-grey lightweight suit and a shoestring tie. He had hand tooled cowboy boots that disappeared up his trouser legs. The business talk had gone well at first and Jonathan had invited Luddy to have lunch with him in the hotel restaurant. Halfway through the meal he began to outline his future plans for the Dovedays distributor network in the United States.

Luddy sat with his fists on the table, knife and fork bolt upright in his hands on either side of his vast steak, his face a turmoil of outrage.

'No,' Jonathan spoke quickly, 'what I'm trying to do for you, Darrel, is to speed up our deliveries to you, that's all. As things stand now, we ship to you through New York. If we can have permanent stock warehoused there for you to call on, it would take weeks off the present delivery time. That's what I'm trying to achieve.'

'No New York yankee hot-shot can tell me how to run my business in Texas,' Luddy grumbled. 'Maybe you don't know this, being from Europe yourself, but they're all crooks and gangsters, near as damn it, in New York.'

'I give you my solemn word that Dovedays will never have dealings with crooks or gangsters, in New York or anywhere else.'

'A lot of them are perverts up there, you know that?'

'Good God forbid,' Jonathan exclaimed, trying hard not to laugh, 'what makes you say that?'

'I've heard things and I've read things,' said Luddy, his jaw tightening. 'Now, here in Texas we don't go along with ways like that.'

'That's good to hear,' said Jonathan firmly, 'but let me tell you something.'

'What's that?'

'For all the unwholesome ways they may have in New York, they can't outsmart an honest businessman like you. I can prove that.'

It sounded ridiculous as he said it, but the whole exchange between them had degenerated into near farce and needed to be played that way. He wondered briefly whether Luddy was being serious or role playing for reasons of his own. Not that it mattered much either way. If Luddy's objections were real, he could be talked out of them; if they were an act, then he was waiting to be bought off. The point at issue was to get him to accept the new plan so that it could be presented back home as unanimously agreeable to the American distributors.

'Howard Bachrach is a good businessman,' he told Luddy. 'I've got some figures in my briefcase I'll show you after lunch. He works hard and he's got the north-eastern states well covered. But for all that, when you look at the population in his territory and the population in yours – Texas, Arkansas, Alabama, Louisiana, then you are beating him in sales per head, year by year. That says to me that you're a better businessman than he is.'

'Mighty nice of you to say so, though my volume's not as good as his, for sure.'

'That's only a matter of time. Your progress in the last couple of years has been outstanding. If we had a Better Business Award, you'd be the one to get it. And when I bring my boss out here to make your personal acquaintance, he'll shake your hand and say *Mr Luddy, sir, you're a man I respect.*'

Pure unsliced ham, thought Jonathan, watching to see how Luddy took it.

'That would be Bennett, I guess. I never met him, only Derek Braithwaite, and now you.'

'Braithwaite played his cards close to his chest. That's not my style – I like the cards face up on the table.'

'That must make you a damn poor poker player.'

'I meant in business. Poker's a different thing entirely.'

Luddy started to eat again, which Jonathan took as a sign of easing tension – or a preliminary to stating his terms.

'Derek plays a pretty good game of poker,' Luddy said ruminatively. 'I was real sorry to hear about him being so sick. Is it sure he's never going to get back to work again?'

'Look at it this way, Darrel, he's been a sick man for years and kept on going. It had to catch up with him sometime.'

'Never thought he was that sick. His ulcer played up sometimes. But he liked to live it up. You know that?'

'Yes, I've been on trips round Europe with him.'

'He always was a pretty horny man. Last time he was here in Dallas I took him to a select sporting house outside of town and damn me if he didn't take two girls upstairs with him at the same time. What do you think of that?'

'For a man of his age that commands respect.'

'It surely does. Day after that he put in eight hours with me in my office and that night he sat six hours straight in a poker game and then caught an early flight to Chicago. I just can't believe that a man like that could collapse so fast.'

Maybe you can't, Jonathan thought, but when a man feels the sting of the angel of the bottomless pit, his strength is as nothing. The poison of Abaddon is festering in Braithwaite's guts. He has played his last game of cards and fornicated with his last whore.

'Still,' Luddy went on, 'here you sit instead of him and that makes things look different from where I sit. And sure as hell it looks different from where you sit, with this newfangled idea of yours to put gangsters in charge of your business in the USA.'

Got you, thought Jonathan, you've been stringing me along with your good old country boy act. What it comes down to is arranging satisfactory terms and you'll go along with me – as long as your terms are acceptable to me.

'Maybe even perverts,' he said, straight faced.

'You and me have got to sit down together and work this thing out,' said Luddy, giving no hint that he knew his bluff had been called. 'Might take some time. You got itchy feet to get back to England?'

'I'm here for as long as it takes. What do you have in mind?'

'I like to know who I'm doing business with. In Texas we don't buy a horse off the first stranger that rides into town and says he owns it. We'll take some time together, you and me. Tomorrow we'll ride out and let you see how the product is merchandised by my boys. Maybe even talk to a buyer or two in the food markets. That'll give you some idea about how

Doveday products shape up on the shelves here and the mean kind of competition we're up against.'

'Sounds like an interesting programme. Do you have anything in mind for today?'

'We'll go on over to my office and take a look at some of my figures. You can see over my computing system, and I'll bet you it's as good as anything them mobsters got up in New York. Don't think I've told you, but we're pushing out through Atlanta into South Carolina, kind of expanding the territory. Maybe they've got more people in the North East, but we sell harder. If New York wants to move in down here, we'll take Washington into our territory first.'

'Great,' said Jonathan, making a mental note that he must take steps before long to prevent any demarcation disputes arising over distributors' areas. That was a problem Braithwaite had never had to face, since he'd never motivated any of them to sell more than their natural inclination suggested.

After lunch they climbed into Luddy's bright red Cadillac.

'You want to take a swing through the downtown section before we head out to my place?' Luddy offered.

'Fine. I don't suppose I'll see much of it otherwise.'

The heart of Dallas proved to be surprisingly small, about eight blocks from north to south and the same from east to west. In the main it was composed of office buildings and business premises. Luddy named them as they passed.

'That's the Republic National Bank Tower and right over there's the Dallas Federal Savings Bank . . .'

They rolled past the Hilton Hotel, the Hyatt Regency Hotel, the Court House, the Nieman Marcus department store, Luddy in fine guide-book style, until he announced as they went south.

'That's the First Presbyterian Church of Dallas and right across the intersection is the Masonic Temple, and next to that across the street is the Scottish Rite Temple.'

'Very impressive,' said Jonathan, glancing at the two multi-storey buildings. 'Back home the Scottish Rite is known as the Ancient and Accepted Rite.'

'That so?'

'From memory I think its first Lodge in the USA was at Charleston.'

He knew he had made a mistake as soon as he had said it. The two buildings had not been pointed out to him without reason.

'You know a lot about it, Jonathan. I guess you must be on the square.'

Dare, know, will, be silent, Jonathan reminded himself, too late.

'No, I'm not a Mason.'

'Then how come you know about it?'

'I don't. I remember things that I've read, that's all.'

Luddy chewed that over for a while.

Once outside the heart of Dallas, freeways ran off in all directions. Luddy eased his huge vehicle along at a steady forty-five miles an hour.

'Where do the people live?' Jonathan asked.

'What people?'

'The people of Dallas. Back there was tiny and I saw no homes.'

'Everybody lives way out. There's a ring of communities right round the city. You do a lot of book reading?'

Obviously he was not to be diverted so easily.

'Not much nowadays. There isn't time enough.'

'What kind of book would it be that you read that in about Charleston?'

'A history of the settlement of the eastern States, I imagine,' said Jonathan as vaguely as he could.

'For a man who claims to remember things, you're not exactly remembering very well.'

'Of the making of many books there is no end, and much study is a weariness of the flesh,' Jonathan quoted lightly, trying to lose the subject.

'But God shall bring every work into judgment, with every secret thing, whether it be good or whether it be evil,' Luddy capped his quotation and thereby astonished him. 'Ecclesiastes, chapter twelve.'

'I see that you're a religious man, Darrel.'

'Lifelong member of the Baptist church. That surprise you?'

'A little, after your account of outings with Braithwaite.'

'Hell, messing with women is just ordinary human nature. I reckon that God don't get too fussed over that, just over real wickedness. Not that I'd come right out and say that in front of my minister on Sunday, in case he misunderstood me. You a church going man yourself, or one of these godless atheists like they have in New York?'

'The fool hath said in his heart: there is no God,' Jonathan quoted.

'Psalm fourteen,' said Luddy. 'Leastways you remember the Bible.'

'They can't all be atheists in New York,' Jonathan teased him.

'Maybe, maybe not. But with all them gangsters and perverts running loose in the streets, you'd have to look mighty hard to find a decent god fearing Christian soul.'

'You forgot to show me where President Kennedy was murdered in Dallas.'

'We passed right by.'

'Where?'

'The Hyatt Regency. They built that on the spot.'

They spent the afternoon at Luddy's office talking discounts and sales projections. Then, after an early dinner in a French-style restaurant at Turtle Creek, Luddy took him to a friend's home where a poker game was in progress. Jonathan joined the circle of stolid men in shirt sleeves round the table and lost consistently for the first hour while he came to grips with their individual methods of play. After that he soon caught up. Luddy was a sound player, though predictable, and Jonathan was careful not to out-do him. At the same time, he had to win enough to let Luddy see that he was no soft touch. When the game broke up soon after midnight, Jonathan was about a hundred dollars up and Luddy had won nearly twice that.

A useful evening, thought Jonathan, though a dull one. I would have been better occupied with the members of the

Dallas Lodge of the Noble Order.

Luddy kept him busy all the next day, driving round to visit big food stores where Doveday products were selling, talking to store managers and to one or two more senior executives. They went west as far as Fort Worth, thirty miles away, stayed there for dinner and got back late to Dallas. The next day was even harder. They took an early commuter flight to Austin, two hundred miles south, to the round of Luddy's best wholesalers and outlets there, and flew back to Dallas for dinner.

'Pity you can't stay on any longer,' said Luddy, over dinner. 'I could take you to Houston tomorrow.'

'I'd like to, Darrel, but I have to get back to London.'

'You going through New York?'

'No, I'm taking a direct flight from here about six tomorrow evening.'

'Too bad. You'd like Houston.'

'I'm sure that I would, but you've proved your point already.'

'What point would that be?'

'You know your business and you don't want any help from outside Texas.'

'Now did I say that?'

'You didn't have to. So all right, I promise that no one from New York will try to interfere with the way you operate. But I still want you to order from New York instead of from London when my reorganisation plan comes into effect.'

'You're pretty sure it will?'

'It's plain horse-sense. It will cut down shipping costs and speed up delivery. With the output we've got from the new plants, we can keep the warehouse in New York full and you can sell quantity and know that it's right there at the end of your telephone line. Right?'

'I knew that all along,' said Luddy, grinning at him. 'Your plan makes a lot of sense.'

'Then why the run around?'

'I told you, I like to know who I'm doing business with.

Guess I'll have to fly up to New York and take a look at Bachrach's spread.'

'Are you sure you'll be safe?' Jonathan mocked him.

'You know something, before the airlines got so almighty fussy about security I never went anywhere outside the State of Texas without a hand gun. Then all this hijacking foolishness started and now it's got so that a man can't protect himself anymore.'

Jonathan smiled at Luddy lapsing back into his country boy routine.

'You'll be safe with Bachrach.'

'Well, I respect your judgment, so I'll allow that he's not a gangster. The rest I'll take on trust till I meet up with him.'

'He's not even a pervert. We had an outing together last week and he provided a pair of very attractive women.'

'New York women, that would be.'

'What else?'

'From what I've seen, they're skinny and pale faced, their women. They don't eat right and they breathe gasoline fumes all day. Mighty unhealthy. Now here in Texas we're downright proud of our women. They're big and healthy. You must have noticed that.'

'You've kept me so busy that I've had no time to notice anything at all.'

'We'll put that right after dinner. I'd hate to have any friend of mine leave without the pleasure of enjoying the company of Texan womenfolk. I want you to be my guest at that select sporting house I mentioned to you the other day.'

A casual sex encounter was not in the least appealing to Jonathan, but he intended to stay the course with Luddy, the only distributor who had threatened his plans.

'That's very hospitable of you, Darrel. I can't promise to match Braithwaite and sample two.'

'Hell, he was just showing off. Next time I was back there I slipped them girls a few dollars and they told me that he only managed the one.'

'Tomorrow I must do a little shopping,' said Jonathan.

'Have to take a few presents back with me to prove that I've been away.'

'You want me to ride you around?'

'No, thank you, Darrel. You've given me enough of your time. I'll just stroll around the downtown section and find the shops.'

'You'll get mighty hot and tired if you do. Take a taxi to Northpark – they got a big shopping mall there.'

'I'll do that.'

In truth, he wanted some time away from Luddy to make contact with the Dallas Lodge of his Order. In the three days he had been there, all he had been able to manage was a telephone call to the contact number he had been given in London. It was unthinkable to leave the city without a personal meeting, however short.

After dinner they got back in Luddy's car and headed out of town. The drive was nearly an hour, first on a freeway and then along a country road in the gathering dusk. Luddy turned off through an open farm-style gate and drove slowly along another half mile of track across open grassland. Up ahead Jonathan saw a long building, stone and timber built, with a raised porch running the whole length of the frontage.

'It looks like a ranch house,' he said.

'Should do, it started out that way. Used to belong to an old timer who raised horses here. After he died, five or six years ago now, it got bought for Miss Libby to turn into a sporting house. The range was sold off to a syndicate and a lot of money got spent on making the house bigger and more comfortable.'

'Miss Libby is the owner, is she?'

'That's not a sensible question to ask. Miss Libby runs the place and keeps it nice. But between you and me, the place is owned by a syndicate of local businessmen. Miserable sinners, every one of them.'

'You told me that God doesn't concern himself with visits to establishments like this,' Jonathan reminded him.

'You weren't listening good, Jonathan. I said the Lord

don't take much account of a man messing with women. But making money out of it, that's a different coloured horse.'

It was impossible to tell whether he meant it or not. They parked alongside a dozen other cars in front of the house and Luddy led the way up the steps to the porch and rang the bell. The door was opened by a hefty young man wearing a chequered shirt and blue jeans.

'Evening, Mr Luddy, step right in. And you, sir,' he drawled.

They were in a large sitting room, scattered with arm chairs, sofas and low tables. Eight or nine men and a dozen women were sitting in groups, talking and drinking.

'Evening, Judge,' Luddy greeted an acquaintance across the room. 'Evening, ladies.'

Before Jonathan could more than glimpse the scene, a big blonde woman in her late forties bustled up and threw her arms round Luddy.

'Darrel, you hound dog, where've you been?'

'Working, Libby, you know how it is. I want you to meet a very fine friend of mine from London, England – Jonathan Rawlings. Jonathan, this is Miss Libby.'

Before she had time to seize him in her bear hug, Jonathan put his hands on her meaty shoulders and kissed her cheek.

'I'm very pleased to make your acquaintance,' he said.

'Just listen to that British accent!' she enthused. 'You come right over here and talk to me, Jonathan. What do you care to drink?'

'Bourbon and water, please.'

She plumped down in the middle of a sofa near the big stone fireplace, pulling Jonathan down on one side of her and Luddy on the other. A Mexican woman in a grey dress set an unopened bottle of bourbon and glasses on the table beside them, then went for ice and water. Luddy started to pour drinks.

'You'll take a drink with us?' he asked Libby.

'I surely will. Are you visiting with us in Texas for long?' she asked Jonathan.

'I'm sorry to say that it's only a quick business trip to see Darrel. I have to leave tomorrow.'

'That's too bad. You come back and see us again, you hear me?'

'I intend to be back in Dallas later this year.'

They drank to each other and Miss Libby waved at a girl to join them.

'Lou-Ann, this is Jonathan all the way from England.'

Jonathan stood up. Lou-Ann looked no more than eighteen and was wearing a totally transparent pink blouse tucked into tiny crimson shorts.

'Hello, Lou-Ann. Come and join us for a drink.'

She squeezed in next to him on the sofa, one long bare thigh pressed to his leg. She wiggled a little to make her breasts shake for his benefit through the see-through pink, and as they talked inconsequentially, Jonathan weighed her up in his mind. She was pretty in a stolid sort of way, she looked clean and she behaved naturally. And since it appeared that he was required to prove his manhood to Luddy, she would serve as well as any other he could see in the room.

'See what I mean about Texan women being big and healthy?' Luddy asked. 'Now Lou-Ann is as pretty a girl as you'll find in the whole of Dallas.'

'I'll have to leave you folks for a while,' said Miss Libby as the door opened to admit a tall, white haired man. 'You enjoy yourselves now. Sharon will be right with you in a while, Darrel.'

'I'm in no hurry,' he said as she left them to greet the newcomer. 'How about you, Jonathan, you getting itchy with that fine big woman sitting next to you?'

'Why don't you come to my room, honey?' Lou-Ann asked.

'I was waiting for an invitation,' he said, smiling at her.

As he had guessed, she proved to be well trained and capable in the use of her big body. She was also able to disengage her mind from her body, so that she did not truly participate in the act. Just in case Luddy should decide to

311

check with her later, as he had after Braithwaite's visit, Jonathan performed with her a second time and deliberately over-rode her mental barriers to drive her into a gasping orgasm she had not expected.

'You're a lot of man,' she said, when she could speak again.

CHAPTER 21
GATEWAY IN THE MIND

THEY SAT in the deep leather club chairs in the managing director's office; Jonathan, Bennett, and the company's finance director, Kenneth Trale, a heavy red faced man. Jonathan had been surprised at first to see Trale present at the meeting, but on reflection took it to be a sign of the importance Bennett attached to his report on the American sales tour. Trale rated as deputy to Bennett and doubtless was there as a witness to what was said, should one be needed.

Bennett looked up from Jonathan's typed report and fixed his pale blue eyes on him.

'You've done remarkably well in the United States. Wouldn't you say so, Kenneth?'

Trale grunted his assent.

'The confirmed orders are all that we expected and the projections for next year are most encouraging. Will they hold up?'

'Short of a nuclear holocaust or a world recession, I'm sure they will,' said Jonathan. 'I've looked at the selling organisations of our distributors over there and found them to be sound. You've seen the details in the appendix to my report.'

'You seem to have a knack for collecting information.'

'We need it. Our files on the selling and distribution structures of our distributors are very inadequate. I want to build up files on all of them, including their financial strength or weakness, so that there can be no repetition of the Chicago incident.'

'That incident, as you call it, is probably going to cost us £55,000.'

'Yes, I've seen the accountants' first estimates. Something may be recoverable when we hear from Chicago, but I wouldn't be optimistic. We're only one of many creditors and it's unlikely that anything much will be realised from the sale of Arnison's assets to share out.'

'I found your notes on the personalities of the people you met most enlightening. Did you, Kenneth?'

'I didn't see the relevance. These people handle our products just as long as it's profitable for them to do so. Business is about money, not about personalities.'

Bennett's sharp nose turned to point at Jonathan and he understood the purpose of Trale's presence at the meeting. Trale's role was that of accuser, Jonathan was defendant, Bennett was the judge.

'I disagree,' he said, addressing himself to Trale. 'Of course profit is the motive for handling our products, but we are dealing with people who run their own businesses. Some of them are quite large businesses, handling a considerable range of imported goods and in large quantities. The motivation may be nine tenths profit, but there's a part which is related to personal satisfaction with how they spend their working hours. Maybe that's ten per cent of the motivation, maybe it's only one per cent. But it is important because it can either reinforce or destroy the rest. Arnison is the proof of that.'

'I don't follow you,' said Trale. 'He crashed because he was a poor manager of his business.'

'The question is, why was he a poor manager of his business? We've been dealing with him personally for ten years. For the first seven of those years he did very well with our products and I would guess with everyone else's. I've checked back. He was running his business competently enough. Then it slowed down, which indicates that something had changed. Something had happened to cause the change. I met him only once, when he was over here, so I don't know what brought on the trouble. But if we were able to look into his background, we'd find the reason – a broken marriage, drinking, gambling, an expensive girlfriend, a bereavement, a bad illness – any one of a dozen possible things that took his attention away from his business.'

'We can't go spying into people's private lives,' Trale objected.

'Agreed. What we can do is to get to know our distributors better and visit them often enough to be aware of any signs of impending trouble.'

'But Derek's been making the rounds every year. If there had been anything of what you suggested, he'd have seen it.'

'The figures were signalling trouble on the way a good two years ago. We missed the signal and the outcome is that our profits from overseas sales this year will be reduced by however much we have been caught for in Chicago.'

'You've made your point,' Bennett interposed. 'In your notes there is a hint that the man in San Francisco is under some sort of pressure. Are you able to be more specific?'

'Not yet,' said Jonathan, unwilling to discuss Warren Copp's sexual problems. 'That is my impression from talking to him over a couple of days. I would need to know him better before going further.'

'His business with us is reasonably satisfactory. But as you have put this faint suggestion in your report, I have to take it seriously. Do you see any financial loss to us impending?'

Into Jonathan's mind came unbidden a vision of Warren Copp being kicked to pulp by an adolescent in black leather motorcycling gear.

'I think we should keep a careful watch and make sure that the account is up to date at all times.'

'The thing is,' Trale objected, 'we can't have you flitting six thousand miles to hold his hand and take his temperature every five minutes. That applies to all of them. We have to assume that they're grown men capable of managing their own business. All we can do here is watch the figures and use them as an early warning.'

'That we must certainly do,' said Jonathan, 'but there is another way in which we could extend our control.'

'What's that?' Trale asked.

'I've been giving a lot of thought to our system of overseas sales through the present network and looking for ways to make it operate more profitably. Let's take the United States first. Instead of dealing with five or six separate people, we could deal with one in New York. We could sell only to him and he would guarantee to carry enough stock to service the others. And part of the deal would be that he would oversee the sales operations of the others. With their consent, of course.'

'What would that achieve?' Trale asked.

'First, New York would be pushing the others to sell more volume. Second, he's within a few hours flying time of all of them. Third, he would be checking on them at regular intervals between our visits from London. In effect, we would be extending our control.'

'Wouldn't it cost too much money?' Trale asked. 'We'd have to give New York an overriding discount on everything he sold to the other distributors. That would come straight out of our margin. I wouldn't think it's financially viable.'

'It doesn't have to cost us anything at all,' said Jonathan. 'I've put my thoughts down on paper and it's being typed now. When you start balancing the savings in freight costs through bulk shipments to one point only, as against what we are doing now, and then look at the volume indicated by aggregated sales projections of all our American distributors, the calculations come out right.'

'Interesting,' said Bennett. 'When may we see this plan of yours?'

'It will be ready by tomorrow. I'll have copies for both of you.'

'I'm sure you've thought it through,' said Bennett, 'but certain questions pose themselves. For example, can our New York man finance the operation at his end?'

'I don't think he'd have any great difficulty. His own business is very soundly based and I would think he could get bank backing for the right project. But, of course, there are other ways too. One of them is for Dovedays to set up a jointly owned company with him, separate from his own business. He'd have no problems raising money if we were putting in half. Do it that way and half the profit of the joint venture comes back to us.'

'If we put money into setting up a warehousing and selling organisation in New York,' said Trale, 'why do we need him? What's his name?'

'Howard Bachrach. The answer is that we need his ability, not his money, but the two probably go together. Now, looking in the other direction, much the same considerations apply to Europe. If we take Scandinavia, we could operate more effectively and more profitably through our man in Denmark selling on to the other northern countries and monitoring their performance for us. Then when we start applying this reasoning to the rest of the world . . . '

'Quite so,' Bennett interrupted firmly. 'We won't anticipate your paper on the subject. Obviously it contains detailed figures to answer the questions that arise. You must have been thinking about this for some time. You couldn't possibly have worked it out in the day and a half you've been back from the United States.'

'I've been turning it over in my mind for a long time. What I've done since my return is to update the American section.'

'Did Derek Braithwaite ask you to do this feasibility study?' Trale asked.

'No, he didn't.'

'I see,' said Trale heavily.

'On more than one occasion in the past eighteen months I have discussed this plan in outline with him,' said Jonathan, going for broke, 'but he was not receptive to it and told me to stop wasting my time.'

'And you disobeyed him?'

'I'm not paid to take orders unthinkingly. I'm paid to use my brain to make money for the company. That's what I've done. All I can do now is to give you a copy of my suggestions and ask you to consider it as a way of increasing our overseas sales and profits.'

'I can't argue with that,' said Trale. 'It just seems to me that this plan of yours would be better for vetting by Braithwaite first. But as he's not here, I suppose we'll have to look at it in its raw state.'

'It's not that raw. I've worked on it for some time.'

Shortly after that, Trale left and Jonathan stayed on, at Bennett's request.

'You've done very well in America,' he said. 'I hope that this new scheme of yours won't detract from your achievement.'

He means, thought Jonathan, that he hopes I'm not going to make a fool of myself.

'It's a sound plan,' he said. 'I'm only sorry that it was sprung on you like this, without advance warning and a chance to read it privately. But the discussion forced my hand.'

'It's not clever to get into a position where you are forced to show your hand before you are ready to.'

'We can't always choose our own battle ground.'

'Not always,' Bennett agreed. 'I have great hopes of you, you know, as do most of the board. It would be distressing to see your progress halted by premature action on your part. There is a time for action and there is a time for patience. I wonder if you have quite understood that yet. Well, we shall see.'

The words were friendly enough, but there was no mistaking the meaning concealed behind them. Bennett had the reputation of being very tough under his smoothness.

'By the way, Jonathan, I called in to see Derek Braithwaite

in hospital a couple of days ago and he said that he would like to see you on your return. Perhaps you will look in on him.'

'He's still far from well, I understand?'

'He's very ill. After they repaired his stomach, another operation became necessary to remove his gall bladder. You'll find him a shadow of his former self.'

'I will make a point of going to see him.'

He did so that very evening on his way home.

'Please don't stay too long,' said the nurse who showed him to Braithwaite's room on the third floor. 'He's not very strong and he tires easily.'

Jonathan hardly recognised the man in the bed. Braithwaite had lost a lot of weight, the skin under his chin hung loose and his face was greasy white. There was a drip tube from his arm to a bottle hanging on a stand above him and another tube came out from under the covers and vanished into a jar under the bed.

'I've brought you a book,' said Jonathan, sitting on a chair beside the bed.

Braithwaite's head rolled sideways on the pillow towards him.

'You're back then,' he said slowly.

'Yesterday. Your friends in America asked me to give you their best wishes – Howard Bachrach, Warren Copp, Vern Willis, Darrel Luddy. They're looking forward to your next trip over there.'

'You bastard,' said Braithwaite. 'You know damned well I'll never cross the Atlantic again.'

The visit was going to be even more embarrassing than Jonathan had feared. He ignored what had been said.

'Any news of when they're going to let you go home?' he asked.

'Do you take me for a fool? Do you think I don't know what's going on inside my guts? I'm done for.'

'That's not a good attitude to take. The mind and the body are so closely connected that negative thoughts can hinder your recovery. The will to get well is nine tenths of the battle.'

'I don't need you to fill me up with bullshit. I get enough of that from the nurses.'

'Why did you want to see me? I'd have thought I was the last person you wanted at your bedside.'

'Damned right. First off, I hate your guts. I've hated your guts from the first day you set foot inside Dovedays. And do you now why? Because I had you pegged right away as a bright young bastard after my job. Now tell me I'm wrong.'

'I don't think we should have this sort of conversation. I've been told that you mustn't be tired.'

'Never mind about that. This is the last time we'll ever see each other, so let's have some straight talking from you.'

'If you promise not to get agitated, we'll talk as straight as you like.'

'I'm long past getting agitated; you can see that for yourself if you're not blind. So answer me, was I right about you?'

'I'm sure that I can do the job better than you can. Is that what you want to hear?'

'You listen to me, sonny. When you've spent years clawing your way up from nowhere to a chair at the boardroom table, you don't step aside because one of your assistants thinks he's a better man than you are. You hang on to what you've got. You earned it the hard way and it's yours. Understand me? You chase the young bastard off.'

'You made that clear the last time we talked, in your office.'

'And meant it. If this hadn't happened to me, you'd be out on the streets looking for a job as a bus driver by now.'

'Tell me the point of this,' said Jonathan. 'Is it a hate session to get your adrenalin flowing? Part of the therapy, is it?'

Braithwaite raised himself on one elbow, grimaced with pain and lay back.

'No,' he said quietly, 'just the opposite. I've had a lot of time to think about dying while I've been here, in between carving-up sessions in the operating theatre and being drugged into unconsciousness for days on end. I want you to be clear about the way I feel about you so you won't think I've gone soft in the head when I get to the point.'

'You're not soft in the head and you're not delirious. You're as cantankerous as ever, grudging, ungrateful and graceless. So make your point.'

'The point is that I'm afraid of dying.'

'That's only natural.'

'You're a glib devil. Do you know what it's like to be really afraid, lying in the dark on your own with this thought going round and round in your head that it won't be long now before you're blotted out forever? They give you sleeping pills at night, but you don't sleep with that thought in your head.'

Jonathan looked at Braithwaite closely. It seemed to him that around the head on the pillow there was an almost visible aura of fear, grey and roiling.

'Have you talked to your doctor about this?'

'What's the use? To him I'm so much meat to cut up. He can either mend what's wrong or he can't – either way he gets paid. He's only interested in my guts, not what's going on in my mind.'

'Have you talked to a priest?'

'That's bullshit and you know it. All I'd get would be the old run around about the resurrection and the life. It's just words. There's nobody at all knows about it except you.'

'Why me?' Jonathan asked in surprise.

'I've been asking myself the same question for days – why *you*? I loath you. But the fact is that it came to me one night while I was lying here half out of my mind. You're the one I have to talk to, damn you. There's always been more to you than meets the eye. You do your job and act normally enough, but you keep half of yourself hidden. I used to think that you were a Freemason and all that guff, but now I'm sure it's something bigger than that. Am I right?'

Jonathan could see that the conversation might lead him into deep waters. The very existence of the Noble Order was a secret that he was sworn to preserve. Yet the words of the Profession of Righteousness ran through his mind:

'I have given bread to the hungry,
And water to the thirsty,
And clothes to the naked,
And a passage to those with no boat.'

If ever a man faced the dark river with no boat, it was Braithwaite now.

'What can I tell you that will ease your mind?' he asked.

'Is there a God in heaven?' Braithwaite asked.

'In the heavens, in the earth, in the waters, in the stars, in the spaces between the stars, everywhere and in all things. Everything that you see is part of God.'

'Including you and me and the black nurse outside with the big tits?'

'The nurse with the big tits, the saint, the sinner, the leper colony doctor, the rapist in the dark, the garbage collector, the gibbering idiot in a mental home, the surgeon trying to repair your insides, the child molester, you and me.'

'That's a bloody strange God you believe in!'

'That's the God everyone who has ever given it ten minutes thought believes in. The created universe is God made manifest.'

'Made what?'

'Made visible.'

'That's not the way they told it in church when I was a boy. They said that God's up there watching and we're down here, so look out or you'll wind up in hell if you put your hand up a girl's skirt.'

'Like most people, you've discarded that threatening view.'

'I liked putting my hand up skirts too much! But you haven't made it any better, have you? If everybody's God, then nobody's God, so there isn't a God. You're back to square one. You'll have to do better than that.'

'The existence of God is not your main concern, is it?'

'I don't give a damn one way or the other. Just tell me something that will stop me being afraid of dying.'

Jonathan thought for a moment or two. He disliked Braithwaite heartily, but apart from that, it was unlawful to make known any of the Noble Order's teaching to outsiders. He remembered the Greek woman who had implored Jesus to heal her mentally disturbed daughter and had been rebuffed with the words: *It is not meet to take the children's bread and cast it to the dogs*. She had answered: *Yet the dogs under the table eat of the children's crumbs*, so that Jesus was ashamed of his own words and had healed the girl. Could a Seventh of the Noble Order behave any less benevolently, when he was sworn to give bread to the hungry and water to the thirsty?

'In everyone's mind,' he said, 'there is a secret door, but very few know about it. If you locate it and learn how to pass through it, you experience a different sort of reality.'

'That sounds like the famous bird that flies in ever decreasing circles till it vanishes up its own orifice.'

'In a way,' said Jonathan, laughing, 'but it is more practical than that. When you lie awake at night, look for this door and push against it gently. There is no fear on the other side of it.'

'Is this a trick you know how to do? How long did it take you to learn it?'

'Not very long.'

'How do you do it?'

Jonathan remembered the evening in San Francisco when Debbie lay on the alter and he held her ankles while Brent assisted her to arouse the life energy coiled at the base of her spine and direct it upwards to open the gate of vision in her mind. There was no way of teaching that method to Braithwaite in hospital, even if he had been at liberty and willing to do so. What he could do was to set the man on the path to discovery by a well known mental technique used widely, even outside the Order.

'When everything is quiet, make yourself as comfortable as you can, so that your attention will not be diverted by your body. Then create a symbol in your mind and gradually exclude everything else from your consciousness until you see only the symbol, big and bright. It may take you an hour or more the first time to achieve even that much, because other things will keep intruding into your mind and breaking your concentration.'

'What symbol?'

'I'll come to that in a minute. When you can hold the image clear and unwavering in your mind, see it as a sign painted on a plain wooden door. That will take you a long time at first. If you lose the image, start again. If necessary, keep on starting again until you have the door in sight with the symbol painted on it. Then push the door gently and it will open and you will pass through.'

'If I go through, how do I get back?'

'You will find that you can come back at any time you want to. It's only getting in that's difficult.'

'What's on the other side of the door?'

'I can't tell you in words. You have to experience it.'

'It sounds stupid to me. It's like some ragged arse Indian staring at his own belly button till he goes into a trance. I was out in India during the war. I've seen them do it. It's a lot of rubbish.'

'Are you stating an eternal truth or offering an outside opinion?'

'It stands to reason that it's rubbish.'

'It stands to reason that the earth is flat until you fly round it and find otherwise.'

'That's different.'

'You have a typically nineteenth century view of yourself as a battery powered robot and you're worried because you think that the battery is running down and the machine will stop. You're in a trap of your own making.'

'You expect me to believe what you've been telling me?'

'You don't have to believe me. I've told you a way of coming to grips with what is obsessing you. Whether you choose to try it or not is up to you.'

'But it can't be real.'

'There are different planes of reality. You only know one of them, and it is one which you find disagreeable at the moment.'

'I expected better of you, by God I did!'

'You expected me to give you positive proof that you need not be afraid of dying, is that it? Instead I've told you how to start finding out for yourself. You want a map to prove there's another shore on the far side of the river. I haven't got a map with me, so I've offered you a boat.'

'Jesus – I bet you write poetry in your spare time!'

'No, I've no talent for that. Do you want the oars to row the boat with, or shall we forget the whole thing?'

'No need to be so bloody impatient. Anything's better than lying here at three in the morning going mad, even your rubbish. What's the symbol?'

Jonathan considered for a moment. Of the twenty-five usual *tattwas*, only a simple one would serve for Braithwaite's first attempt.

'Imagine an equal sided triangle standing on its base, point upwards. The whole triangle is coloured red. And in the middle of the triangle there is a yellow square. Square inside a triangle, got it. Yellow square inside red triangle, right? Make sure that you visualise the colours very brightly – bright red, bright yellow. The colours are important.'

'Why?'

'Different colours set up different vibrations in the mind.'

'But these won't be real colours, just imaginary.'

'The same vibrations will be set up by visualising them.'

'Sounds unlikely to me.'

'Belief isn't important, only concentration.'

'That's all there is to it, what you've told me? I'm going to discover all the secrets of the universe lying here thinking about a red triangle with a yellow square in it?'

'There are no secrets except those which lie buried in the shadow of men's souls.'

'According to who – you?'

'It would take too long to explain to you who said that and who recorded it, and it doesn't make any difference, does it?'

'It makes a difference whether it was Mae West or bloody Karl Marx.'

The words were spoken to Dr John Dee, three centuries before, by a non-terrestial being, but there was no way Jonathan could go into that with Braithwaite.

'You're looking for a written guarantee again, witnessed by two lawyers, a doctor and a minister of the church,' he said. 'You'll wait forever if that's what you want. Christopher Columbus sailed without a guarantee or a map – you'll have to do the same as he did, go and see for yourself.'

'You're a glib bastard. Clear off and leave me alone, I'm tired.'

There were two letters waiting for Jonathan when he reached his home. One was in an airmail envelope and had American stamps. That would be from Orline, he thought. The other was addressed in his aunt Judith's round handwriting. He stood with a letter in each hand, deciding which to open first. Orline won. She had written a chatty and affectionate letter, telling him of the arrangements she was making for her visit in September. From the tone of it he judged that she was still drawn to him, as he was to her, and that for her too the visit would be a time of exploration and decision. The depression generated by his visit to Braithwaite lifted as he read her letter a second time and thought about her.

Judith's letter was shorter. She said that she had tried to telephone him several times in the last week or so and that he was obviously away from home. Her health was giving cause for concern and she would like to see him.

He telephoned her at once. Her voice sounded as it always had. He visualised her at the other end of the line as they talked, small and slender, light brown hair turning grey, her long and gentle face.

'It's nothing for you to worry about, dear,' she said in reply to his urgent questions. 'You know that my heart's never been strong. Arnold says that it's running down now.'

Arnold was her long-term lover, the local doctor, a pleasant man who wore hairy tweed jackets and drove around to see his patients in an old shooting brake.

'But have you seen a specialist?' he asked. 'I'm not doubting his competence, but he is a country doctor, after all.'

'There's no need to see anyone else, Jonny. I've known for some time that I'm fading gently away. Arnold only confirmed it.'

'But you're not old,' he protested. 'You won't be sixty till October. I'm saving up for a special birthday present.'

'Age hasn't much to do with it. Now don't worry, just come and see me.'

He promised to drive up and stay with her at the weekend. As soon as they had hung up, he went into his private chapel, his mind burdened. He held an image of Judith firmly in his mind while he spread the Tarot cards and read them.

King of Wands, Page of Swords, Two of Pentacles, Ace of Wands, a skeleton with a scythe.

All the signs of a happy and fulfilled life, expectations met, spiritual development, happiness and the shadow of death already over her. He put the cards away sadly and threw the yarrow sticks to see if the Chinese oracle would add anything. The hexagram was *Chung Fu. Time for the sincere person to cross the great stream with courage.*

Jonathan sat cross legged on the floor in his blue robe and stared at the Tree of Life design painted on the wall. There was not the least doubt in his mind that the person he had loved most for so many years was soon to slip away from earthly life. Gradually the shining fruits on the Tree took on their accustomed meanings for him and his sorrow was gently dispersed in contemplation of the mightiness of God.

CHAPTER 22
CHILDHOOD MEMORIES

JUDITH RAWLINGS was so unlike her brother in temperament and physical type that Jonathan had wondered more than once how his aunt and his father could be children of the same parents. Like Jonathan, his father was big, athletic and energetic, but Judith was small and slim, tranquil and never in a hurry. She radiated content, while all too often her brother did not. She had become a major influence in Jonathan's life after the separation of his parents, when he was a small child.

The marriage had been one of many unsuitable and short lived wartime adventures. Robert Rawlings, on leave from the air base where he flew a fighter plane against the Luftwaffe, had met and fallen in love with a nineteen-year-old girl in London. She became pregnant by him almost immediately and they were married. To remove her from the dangers of the German bombing of London, Robert took his new wife to live with his parents in the Midlands and Jonathan was born in 1942 at Worcester, in his grandparents' house.

By the time the war ended and Robert came back to resume his teaching job at the local grammar school, Maureen was totally sick of country life and desperate to get back to London while she was still a young woman. There were rows, reconciliations, more rows, and one day she simply went away, leaving a disillusioned husband and a four year old son.

When Jonathan was old enough to reflect on these matters, a thing that pleased him greatly was the manner of his conception. It had not been planned in the security of marriage but had been the result of a violent outpouring of passion unloosed by the wartime fear of imminent extinction. He believed that so powerful an urge by his parents ensured that the life force in him was stronger than usual and would carry him to great achievements.

Judith had never married. Even as a girl she had a heart murmur and arranged her life to avoid unnecessary stress. After Maureen took the train to London, Judith moved into Robert's home to take care of the child. A coldness developed between Robert and his parents, for he held them mainly responsible for Maureen's dislike of provincial life and her consequent defection. In this, Jonathan eventually came to understand, he was wrong. The cause lay in the personalities of his father and mother. Robert Rawlings flinging a plane about the sky to shoot down the enemy was an heroic figure. Robert Rawlings the schoolmaster was not. Maureen, seen rarely and in romantically contrived circumstances when leave from the air force allowed, was a woman of mystery and passion. As a housewife with a young child, she was not.

Jonathan's father packed him off to boarding school when he was eleven and Judith moved out. By then she had inherited her parent's house and such money as they had left. She lived in the house in which she had grown up, a pretty cottage with a garden a few miles outside the town. When Jonathan was home from school in the holidays, he spent more time with Judith than with his father, for by then Robert was enjoying a long term friendship with another teacher, a widow in her thirties with three children of her own.

'What do they do together?' Jonathan asked Judith, when he was old enough to be interested in relations between men and women.

'How can anyone know that?' she answered. 'They talk a lot about teaching and books. They go on nature rambles. They listen to music a lot.'

'Do they go to bed together?' he demanded.

'I'm sure they do, when they have time. They're both so *busy*.'

'She's not very attractive.'

'You're wrong about that, Jonny. Gwen has a good figure and she's full of life.'

'Does that mean he'll marry her?'

'I can't say. I don't believe that your father will ever risk committing himself that far again. Once bitten, twice shy, as they say. I'm sure they're as happy now as they'll ever be. They'll probably just go on like now.'

'It's hard to think of him with his clothes off lying on top of Gwen.'

'Your father is a strong and full blooded man. He has a lot of years to make up for. Just mind your own business and leave him alone.'

This conversation took place after one of the turning points of Jonathan's life. That occurred towards the end of the long summer vacation from school, the year he was thirteen. He was at home, supposedly doing the school work required for next term, but it was a hot summer afternoon and he was bored. His father had gone out after lunch, saying that he would be back about seven. Going to see his girlfriend, Jonathan thought, instead of helping me with this stupid essay.

On the spur of the moment he decided to visit Judith. She always had time for him. He got on his bicycle and set off. Judith's house was twenty minutes away on a country road, a whitewashed cottage with a thatched roof. Here was where Jonathan had been born and spent the first four years of his life, learning to walk and to climb the out-of-plumb wooden stairs, learning to talk, to know the names of things, playing in the garden behind the house. He remembered little of his grandparents, because of the rift between them and his father.

The day was sunny and hot, the road was quiet and empty. He propped his bike against the wall and went round to the back of the house, wondering why the curtains were drawn at the front windows downstairs. The back door was always unlocked when Judith was at home, and it was easier to go round than to knock on the front door and wait to be let in.

So in he went, a thirteen year old in shirt and shorts, his red hair tousled and untidy. He found Judith in the sitting room at the front of the house, where the curtains were drawn. She was sitting cross legged in a white circle in the middle of the cleared floor and she was stark naked.

He stood with his hand on the brass door knob, open mouthed. She was sideways on to him, her brown hair unbound and hanging loosely down her narrow back, her eyes closed and her lips moving silently as her hands worked at a knotted cord she held. In disbelief, Jonathan's eyes were drawn to her small breasts and then down to her slender spread thighs.

Her eyes opened and she turned her head to look at him. She gave no sign of anxiety at being found as she was.

'Jonathan, I didn't expect you. Are you alone?'

He nodded, unable to speak.

'Close the door behind you and wait there. Don't cross the circle.'

He trusted her completely, for she had been a substitute mother to him for years. He watched in silence as she finished whatever she was doing with the knotted cord. Then she stood up and faced him full-on, her small-boned naked body offered to his gaze.

'Do you know what I was doing, Jonathan?'

He shook his head, dumb with wonder.

'I was praying. Do you understand?'

'Praying like that?' he asked in astonishment. 'With no clothes on?'

'It's the old way. I was speaking to the gods and they were speaking to me.'

'What gods? There's only one God.'

'They tell you that at school, but it's not true. The real gods have existed forever, but people have turned away from them.'

'Why?'

'That's a long story and I don't know if you'd understand it yet.'

'Why do you pray with no clothes on?'

'To let the gods see me as I am. Do you want to pray with me?'

'What were you praying for?'

'Health, strength, understanding.'

'At school we have to pray to be made good.'

'Yes, I'm sure they worry a lot about sin. Do you feel sinful?'

'Not really.'

'Do you think I am sinful to stand here with no clothes on?'

'No – you look fantastic.'

'Then take your clothes off and come into the circle with me.'

He did so, somewhat awkwardly trying to conceal from her his erect state. Judith appeared not to notice it as she took him by the hand and drew him into the circle and made him sit cross legged.

'You see this circle, Jonny. I drew it round me to shut out the world. Now you've come into it, we'll have to draw it again.'

'What's it for?'

'It's a sign. Suppose you have a page in a book and you draw a ring round one word. What does it mean?'

'It means the word is important and you want to remember it.'

'This circle means something like that. It shows you that this space has been consecrated, cut off from the rest of the world as a special place. It's like being inside a church, only this is a place you make sacred yourself.'

'How do you do that?'

'I'm going to show you. You see the four candles standing on the floor. I lit those first to mark the quarters. Do you know what they are?'

'North, south, east and west.'

'Good. The candles are still burning, so I don't have to do that again. I take this dagger and I walk round the circle, starting at the candle in the east, and I trace the circle with the knife point as I go and I say the words that will make me remember what I am doing and why. Like this.'

Fascinated, Jonathan watched her trace the circuit as she said:

'Circle, circle, be my boundary between the world of men

outside and the world of the gods inside.'

She took a bowl of water, blessed it and sprinkled a little salt into it, then went round the circle again, repeating her words and flicking a few drops of water with her fingers onto the outline. And finally she took her bowl of sweet smelling incense and charged the circle a third time with it.

'Do you feel now that we have consecrated our little space here?' she asked Jonathan. 'Can you feel the difference already?'

He nodded, almost speechless with excitement. Judith took her dagger again and faced east.

'The Watchers are here because I called them before you came,' she said, 'but I'll call to them again now you're here, so that they'll know you. Stand beside me.'

'The gods, you mean?'

'No, that's for later. Just stand by me and listen.'

She pressed her palms together and bowed towards the east, calling out in a firmer tone than Jonathan had ever heard her use in his life.

'Watcher on the eastern threshold, guard this circle!'

Then in turn she addressed the Watchers of the southern, western and northern thresholds. The hair on the back of Jonathan's neck bristled as something stirred deep within his mind at her words. He shivered.

'Don't be afraid, Jonny. The Watchers will protect you while you are in the circle. They are your friends. When you understand more, I'll teach you their names. Give me your hands now.'

She stood in front of him, not much taller than he, for he was a well grown and sturdy boy and she was a small woman. She took both his hands in hers and told him to repeat the words after her.

'I most solemnly swear in the presence of the Watchers on the threshold never to reveal the secrets of this circle. And if I break this sacred vow, may air choke me, water drown me, fire burn my body and earth cover me forever.'

His voice trembled as he said it, but her warm hands gave

him courage. As soon as he had said the words, Judith raised her voice to speak boldly,

'Take heed, Watchers on the threshold, that Jonathan has sworn the oath and will not break it. Remember him well.'

Jonathan was beyond amazement as Judith knelt before him and kissed his right foot and then his left foot and said,

'Blessings on these feet that brought you into the circle.'

She kissed his right knee and his left knee, saying,

'Blessings on the knees that shall kneel before the gods themselves.'

He gasped loudly as he felt her lips touch his erection and hardly heard her words,

'Blessings on this sacred part, giver of life.'

Then his nipples.

'Blessings on this breast, shaped in strength.'

She was standing again and her mouth touched his mouth as she whispered,

'Blessings on the lips that shall speak the sacred names of the gods.'

Her hands were on his shoulders as she looked into his flushed face.

'Now you must kiss me the same way, Jonny. Kneel down and start with my feet. I'll tell you the words.'

He sank to his knees before her, rapt in adoration, then pressed his lips to her feet in turn.

'Blessings on these feet . . . '

And then her small round knees and he knelt up to press his lips to the triangle of wispy brown hair between her thighs, his mind whirling.

'Blessings on this sacred part,' he gasped out.

'Giver of life,' she prompted him.

And so to her breasts, his avid lips at each nipple in turn.

'Formed in beauty,' she led him.

At last he stood upright, put his arms round her, pressed his mouth to hers and ejaculated fiercely on to her belly. She held him tightly as his body shook and his legs trembled. When his climax was over, she took him by the hand and led him round the circle, the traces of his manhood on both their bodies, while she called aloud on the Watchers to witness that the gods had blessed him and had spoken through him.

In retrospect, when he understood more, he knew that he had been initiated into a new life that afternoon, however shortened and incomplete the ceremony because of the circumstances. When Judith was sure of him, she arranged a full ceremony, with a dozen of her friends present. Surrounded by naked men and women he had never met before, Jonathan was sanctified with oil, water and wine. By then Judith had coached him in the responses and actions, so that he gave a good account of himself.

'But I still haven't seen the gods,' he said afterwards.

'You will, but there are things you have to learn first.'

See them he did eventually, but not until the following year, when she took him at Midsummer Eve to the Rollright Stones, forty miles away in Oxfordshire. They left their clothes in the car that had brought them and padded barefoot over the short, rough grass in the warm dark into the ring of standing stones. Jonathan tried to count the number of men and women assembled inside the ring, but had to give up. He stood watching as bonfires were kindled outside the stone circle to mark the four quarters and then a circle was consecrated around the line of the rough stones themselves. He joined hands in the sunwise circular dance Judith had taught him and at last there appeared among the breathless throng a tall and muscular man, his brawny chest a mat of thick black hair, his head totally covered by a bull's head mask in gold. Beside him was a calm faced woman wearing only a necklace of bear's teeth and a silver crescent on her head.

'They're not gods, they're only people,' Jonathan whispered.

'Be quiet, Jonny, and wait.'

In the singing, the dancing and the breathtaking sweep of the large scale ceremony, there came a moment when Jonathan discovered what his aunt meant. The tall couple standing silent in the swirl of movement and clash of cymbals ceased to be just a man and a woman. The gods entered into them and were present with their worshippers. At first the transformation frightened Jonathan, until the joyful way in which the others accepted it turned his fear into wonder and awe. When his turn came, he knelt before them and addressed them by their sacred names. The bull headed god stretched out his mighty hand to raise him to his feet and then rested it on his head in blessing. The goddess pressed him briefly to her and the touch of her skin on his body was like cold fire. He experienced such a surge of power and confidence that he felt that he could do everything, even fly.

In holidays from school, Jonathan was with Judith as much as possible and took part in meetings and ceremonies at her home and in the homes of other members of her coven. To celebrate the great festivals of the year they linked up with groups from further afield, as they had on Midsummer Eve. He was fifteen when Judith cast her circle around them both one evening at her own house and showed him how to call down the goddess into herself. He sank to his knees before her at the change. The small and slender woman seemed to him to become regally tall and her body glowed faintly with a silvery light. She raised him to his feet and solemnly called the god into him, so that he was no longer an awkward adolescent but a being charged with strength and power, taller than any man, all doubt and uncertainty swept from his mind, his consciousness expanding to encompass the whole of life from beginning to end.

Judith lay down and spread her legs for him without a word. Their first coupling was almost passionless, a stately ritual of worship in which time and personalities had no part. It was fulfilled and crowned by a shared orgasm that swept them into the realms of the gods that lie beyond the world of men and women.

So matters stood between Jonathan and his aunt, and between him and the others of her coven, through his school years and his university years, a bond of worship in body and mind. But Jonathan was of an enquiring mind and not readily satisfied with the answers she and her friends gave to his questions. Often the only answer they had for him was *because it has always been like that.*

'Why do we eat almond cakes and drink red wine at our meetings?'

'Because they are representations of the power of the gods.'

'Wine I can understand – it is the colour of blood and of life. But why almonds?'

'Because that is our tradition.'

Jonathan needed to know more than that. At Cambridge he had the facilities to read and delve and research and to try to uncover the roots of the traditions. Judith was doubtful of the wisdom of what he was doing.

'You don't have to understand the ways of the gods, Jonny. You know they are real because you have seen them and felt their presence in yourself, many a time. All they want from you is your love and devotion, then they will love you and look after you.'

'Yes, I understand that. But surely we were given our brains to use, as well as our bodies.'

'You've been blessed more than most in brains and body. Be content.'

When Challey discovered Jonathan's interest in the hidden world and began cautiously to sound him out, Jonathan's attention was instantly engaged. Here was someone, he felt, who could make plain the mysteries Judith and her friends were content to take on trust. Challey's neglected book in the university library on the meaning of the murals at Pompeii as the record of a ceremony of initiation impressed him. More than that, in the light of his own initiation, he felt the truth of Challey's interpretation with his heart, not merely understood it with his mind. The talks between the two of them were constrained at first by Jonathan's inability to speak openly of his own experiences within the circle, because of the vows he had taken. But Challey easily guessed the reason and knew enough to understand what Jonathan had seen and learned and felt, so that the barrier between them was dissolved without the vow being violated.

With Challey as guide, Jonathan read the Book of Revelation as an initiation ceremony which had been tampered with by early Christian writers who substituted their own slain and risen God for the original God and so reduced the magnificent cosmic vision to a courtroom scene.

The breadth of enlightenment Challey spread out before Jonathan was immensely more complex than Judith's. It contained her vision and much more besides. In this way he was led towards membership of the Noble Order of the Masters of the Temple and by stages he left behind the simple religion of Judith and her friends. At no time did he discard it, but he saw it as the foundation on which he could build much more and was forever grateful to her.

So many years had passed, he thought, since that sunny afternoon when as a schoolboy he had accidentally intruded upon Judith in her circle. It was a little after nine on a Friday evening when he parked outside her house, the drive from London being slow in the weekend traffic heading for the country. Judith looked pale and more fragile than he remembered, though she was still a pretty woman. Arnold was with her, comfortably settled with a glass of wine in his hand. He had weathered well, Jonathan thought, embracing him after kissing his aunt. He was still straight backed and burly, though well over sixty, still recognisably the man in the bull mask in whom the god manifested so long ago in a circle of standing stones.

'What's this nonsense about Judith's health?' Jonathan demanded.

'You must try to understand and accept, as she has,' Arnold said gravely.

'Now stop it, Jonny,' said Judith. 'There's no point in being upset with Arnold. We'll talk about it later. You must be hungry after your drive. I've got cold roast beef and salad and a bottle of claret. Sit down and let's eat.'

They did not talk about it again that evening, because over

the meal she wanted to hear about his travels. She had never been beyond the shores of Britain in her life, but she was interested to know about the people and ways of other countries. It was mainly through Jonathan that she formed her views of the world, for the only newspaper she ever looked at was the local weekly and she had no use for television. The telephone had been installed only a few years before at Jonathan's insistence, so that he could talk to her between visits. By ten-thirty she was looking tired and decided to go to bed. Arnold took his leave, indicating privately to Jonathan that he would like a few words with him before he went back to London. After he had gone, Jonathan sat alone over a glass of brandy, reconciling himself to the gentle ebbing away of his aunt's life.

The next day was bright and warm and by mid-morning he and she were sitting out in the sun in the well cared for garden behind the house. The usual flowers bloomed in profusion, and some that were not usual in gardens. A bank of scarlet poppies gleamed along one of the stone walls that enclosed her small plot of land, and beyond the poppies stood a clump of thornapple, the white, funnel shaped flowers already in blossom. The fruit, when it ripened, would be the size of walnuts, set with spines. A juice could be pressed from them which, in tiny doses, caused intense sexual arousal and, in slightly larger doses, madness. From where he sat Jonathan could see a bed of monks-hood, dark blue bell shaped blossoms hanging amid dark green leaves. He guessed that Judith had been using the plant's juice for years for her heart trouble, though too large a dose was fatal. Along the bottom wall of the garden were two or three nightshade bushes, their flowers purplish. When the berries appeared later in the year, they could be pressed to extract a juice which loosened the link between body and soul, so that the taker wandered in an amazing and timeless world of erotic fantasy come true – but a dangerous world that bordered on coma and death.

There was a row of yellow flowered henbane, looking remarkably like potato plants to the unwary. The smoke from its leaves, when burned, induced visions. Its juice freed the seer from the limitations of time and space, to contemplate the world and its myriad activities with god-like detachment. Under the shelter of another wall Jonathan recognised leafy clumps of mandrake, from the bulbous root of which could be squeezed a juice which lit a languid eroticism that hours of sex play could not extinguish.

He quoted aloud the well remembered words from the Song of Solomon;

'Let us go up early to the vineyards, let us see if the vines flourish, whether the tender grapes appear and the pomegranates bud forth; there will I give thee my love. The mandrakes give forth a sweet smell and at our gates are all manner of pleasant fruits which I have laid up for thee, my beloved.'

'You've a fine memory for the Bible,' said Judith, smiling at him. 'I could tell you of whole days and nights of lovemaking under the spell of the mandrake.'

'Tell me then.'

'When I was no more than eighteen, I was in love with Billy Stanton. Billy first took me into the circle and I went because I trusted him, though I was afraid, being brought up as a church-going girl. But there was nothing to be afraid of in the circle. The gods of life were there and Billy taught me how to revere them. Later on, Billy taught me about the plants and their uses. The mandrake was my favourite, for there was one special time when we took it together and lay down on his bed. The touch of his hand on my body was better than the whole act of lovemaking with another man, and the feel of his body under my fingers was like a long dream of paradise itself. There was no time anymore, all the clocks in the world had stopped. We kissed each other and touched each other and it was so slow and important that it was happening in the other world, not this one. When he lay on me I thought I would die with the pleasure of it. I haven't the words to tell you how it was, but when we slept and woke up, a whole day and a night had gone. The mandrake had put its spell on us and we were bound together forever after. Or so I thought then.'

'You've never mentioned him to me before. What happened?'

'Billy went into the army in 1939 when the war started and he was killed in France. That was before you were born, Jonny. Have you ever met anyone you could be bound to like that?'

Jonathan told his aunt about Orline at some length, describing her and her background and the impression she had made on him. He also made Judith understand the link between them through the Noble Order, without mentioning its name.

'She sounds right for you,' said Judith.

'I think so, but I want you to meet her. She'll be here in September and I want to bring her to stay with you for a while.'

'You have to make your own decision. I can only tell you if I like her.'

'I know that, but you're never wrong about people.'

'You must be good lovers together or you wouldn't even be thinking about marrying, whatever other reasons you've got for wanting a wife. What's making you doubt? Is it because you've not known her long?'

'There's no doubt in my mind really, and I'm sure there's none in hers. But marriage is not a step to take lightly, with all its implications. Her visit is probably less an exploration than a confirmation of what we both already feel. But I want your blessing, Judith.'

'You'll always have that, whatever you decide to do. What you mean is that you want me to tell you that she's right for you. Why is that?'

'Because I love you.'

'That shouldn't make you depend on me. It never has before. You grew up to live your own life. That's the way it should be.'

'Not dependent. But you have been so much to me – mother, lover, friend.'

'Now that's not sensible. I was only your substitute mother for a few years until your father sent you away to school. And I was never your lover and you know it. The times we lay down together were acts of worship. I've lain down with more men than I can remember over the years, but I've only ever had two lovers, Billy Stanton when I was young, and then after him Arnold. I've always been your friend, you're right about that part.'

'I accept the reproof,' said Jonathan, unthinkingly using the Order's phrase, though it meant nothing to Judith. 'Let's say that I want the two most important women in my life to meet and become friends.'

'That's better. I'm sure I shall like your young lady. Is she as far advanced along the way as you are?'

'Not yet, as we reckon these things in our organisation, but that's only a matter of time. She has progressed beyond a ceremony which I can't describe to you, but it's the equivalent of the death and rebirth ceremony the one chosen to lead your coven has to endure.'

'In that case she doesn't lack courage if she has been through the flogging and burial in a dark place and has harrowed hell and fought her way back to life and rebirth. Do your people do it the same way we do?'

'The meaning is the same and the effect is the same,' he answered carefully, 'though our ceremony is more elaborate and is carried out in a different sort of place.'

'What do you call a woman who has survived your ceremony, can you tell me that much?'

'She is outwardly a Princess of the Rose Cross. Inwardly she is a Master of the Threshold.'

'I don't know anything about the Rose Cross, but I can understand the other name well enough. The threshold between the world of men and the other world. To be called a Master of that threshold is a bold claim, Jonny. It means that you can move between the two worlds at will, at least, that's how we mean it. Does it mean that for you?'

'Yes, it does.'

'Few of us go that far, only the ones chosen to lead covens. Do many of your friends get past the threshold?'

'Unless they are thought to have the potential to go that far, they are not invited to join. Mainly it's a question of how long it takes them. Some get there in a few years, some need half a lifetime.'

'When they get there, they teach others, I suppose.'

'They instruct, yes, though the system's not quite the same as yours. And at the same time they are instructed by others so that they can advance further.'

'What further is there?'

'Beyond the threshold that we both know about, a long way beyond it, there is another and greater threshold. We call it the Abyss.'

'Does anyone ever cross that?' she asked in surprise.

'I don't know. Tradition says that it can be done and has been done, but I've never met anyone who has succeeded. There is no known way. You have to try it alone, if you try it at all.'

'Is that where you are now, Jonny, at the second threshold?'

'I see it so clearly and yet I cannot find the power in me to go soaring out across the darkness which divides the known place where I stand from the shining realm I can glimpse far off.'

'Then leave it alone. You can't force the gods to your will, only pray to them for their loving guidance. Do you know, I don't believe you've ever talked so openly to me about your organisation before. I've never asked you because I know that you've taken vows of silence, as we all do.'

'Yes, I want you to understand what sort of person Orline is and how far she has travelled along the path.'

'You should marry her.'

'You say that before you've even met her?'

'I've listened to you and I'm sure. I heard the god speaking through you. Turn back from this second threshold and find your life in Orline, that's my advice.'

'I'm not sure that it can be that way, Judith. Once you've glimpsed that impossible horizon, I don't think you can ever turn away from it.'

'You must love this woman and marry her – no god can offer you what she is able to.'

'*You* say that?' he exclaimed.

'From what you have told me, the goddess is in her. In her you will find what you are looking for. You can leave crossing the next threshold until it happens by itself. Then it won't be a jump into the dark but an easy step, believe me.'

After lunch Judith went upstairs to nap for an hour. Jonathan sorted through her bookcase for something to read. Mostly she had books on herbs and their uses and on flowers and their significance. Eventually he found a translation of the Buddhist scriptures and settled in an armchair with it. From the inscription on the title page he saw that it was a present from Arnold several years ago. He wondered what Judith had made of it and leafed through until his eye was caught by a passage she had marked. A king is asking questions and a wise man is answering them for him;

'What is the light of mankind?'
> 'The sun, by which a man lives his life, rests, works and returns.'

'But after sunset, what is the light of man?'
> 'Fire is his light then, and he performs his tasks in its glow.'

'When sun and moon and fire are all asleep, then what is the light of man?'
> 'The voice becomes the light then. Even when he can no longer see, a man can follow the sound and advice of the voice.'

'But when the voice is silent, then what is the light of man?'
> 'The soul becomes his light, and by this light he rests, works and returns.'

Thinking about these words, Jonathan slowly dozed off in his chair. Some time later that afternoon Judith came down again in her dressing gown, looking rested, and asked him to go into the circle with her. He pushed the furniture back to the walls of her sitting room and rolled up the faded Persian carpet, while she drew the curtains. On the floor boards her circle was precisely delineated in white. Jonathan took the heavy candlesticks from the sideboard and together they made the preparations, following her rubric.

At last they stood naked in the circle in the presence of the Guardians and prayed to the gods of life in Judith's time honoured words. She stood with her arms raised, her lips moving in silent concentration so intense that Jonathan was caught up in it, as a feather in a gale. Her greying hair, her small slack breasts, her thin shanks, all that made her body, seemed to him to dissolve in a golden haze as her aura blazed into visibility. She stood before him in the form he had known twenty-five years before, a young, smooth skinned woman, firm of breast and thigh, her hair dark, her eyes shining. Lost in the wonder of her power of exteriorising the eternal spirit within her, Jonathan knelt to kiss her feet, her knees, and so upwards, murmuring the words she had taught him when he was a boy. She lay down and spread her legs for him and as he mounted her he found himself reciting words that belonged to his belief rather than hers, though she understood and accepted them:

'On earth my kingdom is eternity of desire; my wish incarnates in the belief and becomes flesh, for I am the living truth.'

CHAPTER 23
OLD PHOTOGRAPHS

MONDAY MORNING in the office was a busy time for Jonathan. He sat at Braithwaite's desk working his way through file after file with two young accountants, determined to find out whether there were any more problems that Braithwaite had concealed. The Chicago bankruptcy had come out of the blue and though Jonathan was fairly sure that he knew the current position with the other American outlets and the Scandinavian ones, he was not entirely easy about those parts of the world which Braithwaite had kept to himself. Most of the European business looked solidly based, but he had a feeling that the Belgian distributor ought to be checked, based on no more than his impression of the man concerned. It was not so much what the numbers in the files said as any hint of underlying uncertainty he was groping for. About the state of the Australian, New Zealand and South African accounts he knew very little and wanted to dispel his ignorance fast.

He was so engrossed with the accountants that the first he knew that there were other problems, nearer to hand, was when the Personnel Director's secretary entered the room. She looked worried.

'What is it?' he said. 'I told Nancy I wasn't to be disturbed.'

'I'm sorry to interrupt, but it's urgent, Mr Rawlings.'

'What is it?' he repeated.

'Nancy fainted at the news and I've sent her home. I thought you ought to know.'

'Fainted? What news?'

'About Mr Braithwaite. We heard about half an hour ago.'

'Sit down, Kate. You two take these files away and keep on working on them. I'll call you back later.'

He waited for the accountants to leave and close the door.

'I hope I didn't sound abrupt, Kate. My mind was elsewhere. You'd better tell me what's going on.'

'Mr Burney got a call to say that Mr Braithwaite's dead. He's gone round to the hospital to see if there's anything he can do before they tell Mrs Braithwaite. It sounds a bit of a mess.'

'What do you mean?'

'They found him earlier today on the concrete under his window. The hospital people were very cagey on the phone. They don't seem to know whether he fell out accidentally or not.'

'I went to see him a few days ago. He wasn't strong enough to get out of bed.'

'That's what Mr Burney said – he was in to see him last Friday.'

'We mustn't let our imagination run away with us before we know the facts,' Jonathan said slowly. 'You said that Nancy took it badly? That's only to be expected. They'd worked together for a long time. Was she all right when you sent her home?'

'No, she was very distressed. I managed to get the name of her doctor from her and I've phoned him to get round to her flat and do what he can.'

'You've done all the right things. I don't know what to say. It comes as a shock. Does Nancy share a flat with anyone? I mean, is there anyone to look after her?'

'No, she lives alone. I'll go there myself this afternoon to make sure that she's all right.'

'Yes, that's very good. Is there anything I can do?'

'Not that I can think of, Mr Rawlings. Mr Bennett's called the directors up to his room to tell them about it. He'll probably send for you when they've gone.'

'Yes. How did Nancy hear about it so soon?'

'She was with Mr Burney talking to him when he got the message. I suppose he told her without thinking.'

'I see, though I don't understand why she was with him. She had a stack of work to do for me.'

'I shouldn't tell you this, but I think you ought to know in the circumstances, Mr Rawlings. She was asking him about the chance of being assigned to somebody else. I don't think she's been happy working for you.'

'But we've been getting on quite well.'

'It's not your fault. I think she's upset every time she sees you sitting at Mr Braithwaite's desk. I know I shouldn't say it, but in view of that and the way she broke down this morning, it looks as if they might have been on different terms than just boss and secretary.'

'No, you shouldn't say it, even if you think it. How people live their lives outside office hours is their own business.'

'I'd never say it to anyone else. I was just trying to warn

you that things may be a bit more complicated than they look.'

'Understood, and thank you.'

The telephone rang. Bennett's secretary asked him to come to the managing director's office as soon as he was free.

When Kate had gone, he sat in thought for a moment, trying to make sense of what he had been told. He had never intended Braithwaite to die, only to be removed from the office. It was given to Abaddon that he should not kill but that he should torment for five months. And in those days shall men seek death and not find it, and they shall desire to die and death shall flee away from them – those were the words he had used when he sealed the curse against Braithwaite. Five months of torment, that was all. And in only half that time Braithwaite was dead. Grey clouds of premonition of catastrophe were threatening to engulf Jonathan. He closed his eyes and mentally surrounded himself with a ring of cold fire. When it was established, he spoke aloud:

'Power behind all, lord of the universe, initiator of all life, you have instructed me and you have commanded me to rise and make my way in my everyday life. Let there be turned aside whatever evil may come to cut off my life.'

Protected and fortified, he made his way to Bennett's office to be told officially of Braithwaite's death and to say the proper words of surprise and condolence.

But worse was to come the next day. He arrived home in the evening to find among his mail an envelope addressed to him in Braithwaite's handwriting. Inside was a single sheet of paper on which was scrawled in pencil the short message: *Look after Nancy for me.*

Jonathan poured himself a good measure of brandy and sat down to ponder its meaning. The mystery of Braithwaite's death would never be cleared up. The hospital version was that he must have got out of bed in delirium and blundered about the room until he fell out of the window, three floors to the concrete paving. A tragic accident and the night nurse would be disciplined for not keeping a closer watch, very regrettable, and so on. Now he had the letter, Jonathan saw it otherwise. Braithwaite had gone out of the window deliberately.

Had he gone looking for annihilation or to free himself from his sick body? The letter gave no indication, but Jonathan was reasonably sure. Men shall seek death and not find it. But some new factor had allowed Braithwaite to break out of the bonds which held him and to find the death which should have fled away from him. It could only be Jonathan's visit, when he had taught Braithwaite a way to overcome his fear.

Evidently he had found the inner door and freed himself from his paralysing fear. And then not knowing that a term was set for the duration of his bodily suffering, he had used his newfound freedom to separate himself from a carcase he believed to be dying slowly and painfully.

I have compounded my guilt, thought Jonathan. First I bring him down and then, out of compassion, I put into his hands the means of ending his own life. If I'd left things as they were he'd have been another month or two in hospital and then would have gone home for good, no longer a threat to me.

Look after Nancy, the letter said. In Jonathan's state of mind the words took on the authority of a commandment. The Order taught very firmly that repentance for wrongdoing was not enough, restitution was also necessary. Whatever the cost, he must make what restitution he could by carrying out Braithwaite's last wish, since he could not restore his life.

He finished his drink and sighed, then looked up Nancy Tait's address in the telephone directory. She lived in the Brompton Road area of West London and he could be there in about twenty minutes. He decided not to phone first.

For a long time there was no answer to the doorbell, though he could see from the street that the lights were on and so she must be at home. He persisted with his ringing until at last footsteps shuffled up to the other side of the door and a voice he hardly recognised asked *Who is it?*

'Jonathan Rawlings.'

'I don't want to talk to you. Go away.'

'But I have to talk to *you*. It's important.'

'Nothing's important. Just leave me alone.'

'Nancy, listen – I had a letter in the post today from Derek Braithwaite. It's about you.'

'You're a liar.'

'I'm putting it through the letter box so you can see for yourself.'

There was a long pause while she took and read it, perhaps more than once. The door opened slowly and there was Nancy, looking dreadful. Her face was blotched and swollen, her brown hair hung in rats' tails about her neck. She was wearing a man's paisley pattern dressing gown, much too big for her, tied bunchily round her waist.

He followed her into the sitting room without a word being spoken. The room had all the signs of recent neglect; cushions unplumped, half a cup of cold tea on the low table, wilted flowers in a vase. Nancy slumped on to the sofa and read the short letter through again, her forehead wrinkled. Jonathan sat beside her and waited.

'What does he mean *Look after Nancy for me*?' she asked.

'I came to ask you that.'

'I don't need you to look after me. When did he write this? There's no date on it.'

'The envelope was postmarked Monday. My guess is that he wrote it on Sunday and asked a nurse to put it in the hospital mail box. It wouldn't be collected before Monday morning.'

Nancy pressed the sheet of paper to her cheek and burst into painful sobs.

'Why you?' she choked out. 'Why didn't he write to me?'

Without thinking, Jonathan moved closer and put his arms about her to comfort and quieten her grief.

'I don't know why, Nancy. He must have had his reasons.'

'But he hated you and he loved me. So why should he write about me to you?'

'Listen and see if this explains anything. He asked me to visit him last week – did you know that?'

'I went to see him on Saturday. He didn't mention you at all.'

'All the same, I went there and we talked for a long time. His attitude towards me seemed to have changed. He thought that I could help him.'

'How could *you* help him?'

'He told me that he was afraid of dying. He thought that I could help him to overcome his fear.'

Nancy pulled sharply away from him.

'That doesn't make sense. You're the last person he'd ask for help.'

'I have no reason to lie to you, Nancy. I think he felt that I was so far from him that he could talk about things he couldn't talk about to those close to him. He wouldn't burden you with his fear, would he?'

'He could have told me. I'd have understood.'

'Yes, but he didn't see you in that light, did he? Towards you he was the protector, the one who took care of everything. He wouldn't reverse the roles, however much he needed reassurance. Do you see that?'

'I suppose you're right,' she said listlessly. 'He always treated me as if I were a child. That's the way he wanted it.'

'And it must have been the way you wanted it. Both of you chose the attitudes towards each other which suited you best. That's what men and women always do. How long were you and he together?'

'Why do you want to know?'

'I'm trying to understand where you are now.'

'Why should you care?'

'Because that letter lays a duty on me which I cannot just ignore.'

She looked at him for a long time through red rimmed eyes.

'Go and bathe your face in cold water, Nancy, while I make some coffee. Then we can talk. Do you have anything to drink?'

'There's whisky in the sideboard. The kitchen's through there.'

Jonathan busied himself in the kitchen, boiling water to

make instant coffee, the only sort he could find there. He made two mugs, took them into the sitting room and poured a generous measure of Scotch whisky into each. After a while Nancy came back, looking somewhat better, her face washed and less red, her hair combed and neat. It was, he saw, much longer than he had ever suspected from seeing her in the office, where she kept it pinned up unattractively at the back of her neck. Loose, it reached halfway down her back. She had changed the paisley dressing gown, which he guessed had been Braithwaite's, for a rose pink one with silver braiding round the hem and cuffs, and she had put on matching slippers.

'Try that,' he said, offering her one of the mugs. 'It's not exactly Irish coffee, but it's the best we can do right now.'

She took it and sipped the unlikely mixture gratefully. She was more composed when she spoke.

'What you said about men and women choosing attitudes to each other that suit them best – I've never thought about it like that before. But that's exactly what Derek and I did, only neither of us ever realised it. Can you explain that?'

'Does it need explaining?'

'You mean we were too stupid to see what we were doing? But we loved each other.'

'I don't mean you were stupid at all. Love is very often a matter of making things fit properly, like a jigsaw puzzle, until you get a picture that pleases both partners.'

'And if the picture pleases, why bother to go any further – is that what you mean?'

'I'm not being critical. You and Derek Braithwaite had something going between you which was important to you both and pleased you both. So why go looking for explanations? They can only complicate it for you.'

'It started right after I went to work for him and it's lasted all this time. I don't know what I'm going to do without him. I feel empty and useless.'

'How old are you, Nancy?'

'Twenty-seven.'

'There's no point in saying that when you are over this

bereavement you'll find another man to start again with, because you can't take that thought in at present. But that's what will happen.'

'There'll never be anyone like Derek.'

'No one is ever really like anyone else. But there'll be someone.'

'You wouldn't say that if you really knew.'

'Knew what?'

'The way it was between Derek and me – nobody could ever understand that except the two of us.'

'I'm sure that's true of every deep relationship.'

She looked at him for some time, her hands clasped round the empty mug.

'I can't explain it, but I have a feeling that if anybody could understand, it would be you,' she said. 'If Derek asked for you to visit him in hospital, he felt the same thing. Yes, he must have, because he sent that letter to you. Would you really understand, or would it be just a big dirty joke to you? The boss screwing his secretary on the side – that's how it looks round the office, isn't it?'

'To some it will certainly look like that. If you intend to go on working at Dovedays, I suggest you say and do nothing that would give rise to sniggering little rumours of that kind.'

'Have I still got a job?'

'When you want it. I know you don't want to work for me any more, but I'm sure Personnel can sort something else out for you. Come back when you're ready. Till then you're officially on sick leave.'

'You know, I've always seen you through Derek's eyes before. Suddenly you look different.'

'You're still seeing me through his eyes. I'm here because he asked me to look after you.'

'He meant that letter seriously, didn't he?'

'I'm convinced of it.'

'Then you'd better see me the way he saw me.'

She got up abruptly and went out of the room, leaving Jonathan wondering what was in her mind. He had calmed her for the time being. He had conveyed to her that she was not quite alone as a result of Braithwaite's death, but that there was someone to lean on for a time. It would be sensible to take his leave as soon as possible and let events take their natural course.

Nancy came back with a large red photograph album clutched to her chest. She stood in front of him for a moment, her face blushing pink, then pushed the album at him and ran out of the room.

Pictures of what, he asked himself, holding the book on his lap. Happy snapshots of outings with Braithwaite, memories of past times? Without any enthusiasm he opened the album halfway through and was astonished by what he saw. He went back to the beginning and turned through the pages slowly.

Page after page was filled with pictures of fifteen-year-old girls. Barefoot in cut-off jeans and a T-shirt, sprawled on a sofa eating an apple. In school uniform of white shirt, pleated grey skirt and knee socks, reading a book. In pyjamas with a pop star's face on the front, brushing her teeth over a wash basin. The variety of clothes and poses was imaginative and considerable.

The pictures were in short sequences, some of four, some of five or six photographs. The schoolgirl reading her book at a table had, by the second picture, unbuttoned her shirt to allow a view of her adolescent breasts as she continued to read demurely. In the next picture she had turned her chair away from the table and had one black-shoed foot up on the chair so that the camera could look along one slim thigh to the crotch of her white cotton panties. The next picture showed her still reading *Elements of Geometry*, but with one hand down inside her panties. On the page beside the sequence, Jonathan read in Braithwaite's heavy handwriting: 'A naughty schoolgirl doing her homework lets herself be distracted from her studies by a tickling feeling between her legs.'

Jonathan's eyebrows arched in surprise. Braithwaite had been highly sexed, because his number was five, perhaps to the point of perversion and excess. But the photographs hinted at paedophilia and even incest, and yet were arch to the point of ridicule.

In the bedtime sequence the girl brushing her teeth had pulled up her pyjama top in the second picture to examine her small breasts in a full length mirror. In the third she was bent over, pyjama trousers halfway down her legs, peering over her shoulder to see the reflection of her bottom in the mirror. 'An inquisitive little girl wants to know if she is growing up properly,' Jonathan read.

All the sequences in the album, and there were at least thirty of them, ended in the same way. The girl kept her clothes on, but by dint of pulling down, aside or up, bared to the camera her small and hairless slit in the final shot. Every sequence was of the same girl, displaying in simulated innocence her half grown breasts and childish parts. And the girl was Nancy Tait, who was twenty-seven and could make herself look fifteen. Jonathan closed the book without looking at any more of Braithwaite's fantasies. This unexpected glimpse into a secret life had brought with it an uncomfortable sensation of being a Peeping Tom.

That was how Braithwaite had regarded Nancy. He had dressed her as a young girl, posed her in scenes of awakening sensuality and, afterwards, had presumably played out with her fantasies of seduction. She had gone along with it for years, acting out a game of childish sexuality aroused by the persistence of a big wicked man.

He put the album on the coffee table and thought about what he should do next. He had brought about a lull in the storm of grief, but she had pushed things beyond anything he intended by exposing to him the intimacies of her years with Braithwaite. To help her was one thing, to be drawn into someone else's private game was more than he was prepared to go along with. The best course was to leave and wait until she achieved some sort of stability before trying to help. He got up and went to look for her to say goodbye. As he guessed, she was in her bedroom, dimly lit. She lay face down on the bed in her pink gown, face hidden in her folded arms.

'Nancy?'

'Have you seen all that you want to see?' she asked, her voice muffled.

'I've seen more than I ought to have seen. There are things which should remain private.'

'Were you disgusted?'

'The pictures made me understand how close together you and he were.'

'Do you mean that?'

'Nancy, do you suppose that I know nothing about the ways of men and women with each other?'

'I'm sure you know more about it than most. Sit down for a minute, there's something I want to tell you.'

He sat on the edge of the bed, wondering what further revelations were coming. Her words amazed him.

'You've inherited me, haven't you? What are you going to do with me?'

'What on earth do you mean?'

'That letter to you from Derek – I've been thinking about it. It's a sort of will. He's bequeathed me to you. I'm yours to do what you like with.'

'Nonsense! You're a grown woman. Your life is your own. I'll help you as much as I can, but I don't own you and I can't accept responsibility for you.'

'Why not? Derek owned me, body and soul, and he took responsibility for me.'

'That was in his nature. It's not in mine.'

'Don't you find me attractive at all? You've seen enough pictures to know what I look like under my clothes. Don't you want to see the real thing?'

'Nancy, I do not want a sexual relationship with you.'

That made her angry.

'Why not?' she demanded harshly, rolling over onto her back.

Her dressing gown was undone from top to bottom and fell away with her movement to reveal to him the adolescent body he had seen in the photographs. As he got up to leave, Nancy moved with the speed of a cat pouncing. Her arms were tight round his neck, her cheek against his, her exposed body pressed close to him. He raised his arms to take hold of her wrists and unwind her from his neck and at once she burst into despairing sobs.

'Please don't go yet!' she gasped. 'I'm alone and afraid.'

Against his own common sense, he put his arms round her to soothe her. The sobbing continued, her streams of tears wetting his face. Only when her paroxysm slowly eased did he become aware of the fierce heat of her body through his clothes. It dawned on him that she was rubbing her tiny breasts against his chest and her genitals against his thigh. Her sobs had turned to gasps. He tried to pull her away, but the grip of her arms grew stronger and her rubbing faster, until with a long wail she convulsed into sexual release.

Her arms loosened from his neck and she sprawled backwards onto the bed, a sly smile on her face at having got what she wanted. Jonathan stood up in a rage and slapped her face, forehand and backhand, rolling her tousled head on the pillow. She threw her arms over her face to protect it as he shouted '*Bitch*!'

Half crouched over her, his arm still raised to strike, he shouted at her until he heard her giggle beneath her crossed arms. Outraged, he smacked at her childish breasts to hurt her. She squealed and kicked at his groin. He caught her by the ankle and twisted the leg away from his parts, opening her thighs to display the small hairless slit of the photographs. His fury was transformed in an instant to lust. He threw himself between her legs, landing hard enough to knock the breath out of her, ripped open his trousers and stabbed into her. This was not her fantasy of seduction – she screamed in fear as he rode her hard and fast until he clamped a hand over her mouth to silence her and held her pinned and helpless with his weight, until his boiling anger gushed out into her.

He pulled away from her and got off the bed. His hand was bleeding where she had bitten it. There were red marks on her shoulder from his teeth. Her eyes were closed, her face pale. She was breathing shallowly and looked only half conscious.

Rape it may have been, he was thinking, but she provoked it and there's no legal comeback. And if she tries to blackmail me with Dovedays, I'll call up for her such a phantasm of a lover to rend her night and day that she will keep her mouth shut.

'Are you all right?' he asked roughly.

'You hurt me,' she said in a small voice.

'You asked for it and you got it.'

'I thought you were killing me. I felt myself dying when you were on top of me. It was terrifying and wonderful at the same time. Nobody's ever treated me violently like that before. You used me – you ripped me open, destroyed my body – it was out of this world, Jonathan.'

That was the first time she had ever called him that. It did not please him.

'Get it into your head that there can't be anything between us,' he said. 'What happened was a blind accident and that's the end of it.'

'You can't leave me now,' she said calmly, sitting up to take off her crumpled dressing gown. 'Derek left me to you. You accepted the bequest when you did that to me. You took me and so I belong to you now.'

'Nancy, I have no taste for playing games with little girls.'

'That's all finished with. That was Derek's game. I like your game better.'

'I don't have one. You made me angry, but it won't happen again.'

'But I want it to. And you've got to look after me.'

Restitution could be a tortuous path, thought Jonathan. But the debt he had incurred had to be paid off, otherwise it might prove calamitous. A thought stirred in his mind as he looked at her naked and underdeveloped body. There was a way to use her masochism to achieve a great purpose – he saw it quite clearly.

'I'll look after you,' he said, 'but it will be my way, not your way. I'm not big wonderful daddy coming here to put his hand up his little girl's skirt and make her feel naughty. Do you understand that?'

'You're a big wild animal, like a lion with that red hair,' she said, smiling at him. 'I'm your prey and you'll claw me and bite me and rip me apart. I shall try to fight back but you're stronger than I am and you'll hold me down and tear into me and coming will be like dying every time.'

Her hand was at the fork of her legs, gently stroking her bare mound.

'You're wrong about that too,' said Jonathan.

'Then be whatever you want to be and tell me what you want me to be and I'll do everything you want. What do you want? Just tell me.'

'You'll find out eventually. It won't be easy to make you understand, but we'll get there in the end. Whether you like it or not, that's another matter.'

'Anything you want to do to me will be wonderful. I want you to use me.'

'I intend to. Let's hope that you won't regret your words.'

Jonathan started to undress. He needed to bend her to his will quickly, in view of what he had in mind, and the sooner he started, the better.

CHAPTER 24
THE SACRED ALIGNMENTS

SO MUCH was happening and changing that it seemed to Jonathan that he was living in an express lift climbing the shaft so fast that the bell ringing as the floors flashed past was a continuous ding ding ding. By day he worked to acquaint himself with the whole of the Overseas Sales Department's recent arrangements and their commercial soundness. He flew to Brussels for a day-long meeting with the Belgian distributor he was unsure about and satisfied himself that the contact could stand for the time being but would need total rethinking when his new plan went into operation. He flew to Dublin for another meeting and came back pleased with what he had found.

In the evenings and at weekends he attended regular Temple meetings, kept up with his friends socially, and read extensively to make sure that he would be perfect in words and gestures when he was installed as Marshall of the Lodge at the autumn equinox in September. He wrote letters to Orline in answer to hers, conscious of the warmth of their expression growing. He called Judith most evenings, however pressed for time he was. Two or three times a week he spent a night with Nancy Tait, who had returned to work as his secretary after only a few days off, and now sat in his outer office radiating satisfied desire, unaware of what she was being prepared for.

The July board meeting of Dovedays debated his plan for restructuring the company's overseas sales, called him in to assure themselves that he knew what he was talking about and treated him with evident respect. The chairman of the company, whom Jonathan had met only fleetingly a couple of times in his years with Dovedays seemed especially impressed.

Later in the day Bennett sent for him to tell him that his plan had been accepted unanimously and that it had been decided to appoint him to the board to give him the authority to carry the plan through. Bennett offered him his warmest congratulations and repeated that he expected much of him. In great elation Jonathan telephoned Orline to tell her the news and to suggest that she made arrangements for a longer stay with him than she had at first intended. The next day the office manager came to see him to discuss how he would like his office, once Braithwaite's, redecorated and refurnished. The transport manager came to discuss what sort of expensive car he wanted ordering. The company secretary visited him to discuss the matter of acquiring the minimum stock holding he was required to purchase as a director and to tell him about the stock option schemes and other benefits he now qualified for. To Jonathan it seemed that he was standing under a shower of blessings. His future with Dovedays was assured and he intended to marry Orline in September and keep her in England.

Orline was very often in his mind these days. He found much pleasure in going over in his mind their conversation together, in as much detail as he could recall, when they were beside the hotel swimming pool in Las Vegas. Especially vivid in his memory was the physical exhilaration of their horse ride at dawn across the scrubby desert, before the sun's heat sent them heading back to town. After they were married he intended to buy two very good horses and go riding with her often, so that she could teach him her own effortless grace in the saddle. He wondered if she would like his house; if not, he would sell it and they would go house hunting together, until they found something she really wanted. Money was certainly no problem. His salary and benefits as a member of the board of Dovedays was adequate for the lifestyle he proposed for Orline and himself and the investments he had made from his casino winnings over the years produced more income each year than most men earned.

The image of Orline that he saw most frequently in his mind's eye when he thought about her was the moment of his first taking note of her. The swimming pool behind Greg and Angie's house in Los Angeles. At Greg's call she had swum slowly to the side of the pool and pulled herself out, to stand naked at the pool's terrazzo edge. That picture was in his mind forever – Orline, long thighed, golden skinned and big breasted, her long hair down her neck and back. Like the goddess herself rising out of the sea at Paphos in Cyprus, to walk among men for the first time.

Jonathan smiled to himself at the romantic phrase that had formed in his mind, and yet he accepted the truth of it. He recognised that for him love in its real sense had first appeared to him at that moment. He recalled Judith's words when he had talked to her about Orline: *Marry her, no god can offer you what she can.* And Judith was a wise woman.

The ceremonies he had performed with Orline, in Los Angeles and in Las Vegas, had a particular sanctity for him. Their shared vision of the garden of earthly delights had reached an intensity and duration he had never known with another woman. That was something they would repeat many times when she was in England with him. And in the same way that he responded to her inner divinity, so had she responded to his, after the ceremony of the Perfect King, when she had put her hands between his knees and called him *lord*.

At night, when he slept alone, he frequently dreamed about her, nearly always the moment of climbing out of the pool and standing naked in the evening sunlight. Always after such a dream he would telephone her, to hear her voice and so have some contact with her, however electronically remote. On her birthday he arranged to have a hugely expensive flower display delivered to her at Greg's house, with a dozen bottles of the best champagne.

Two nights later, he woke from a sweating nightmare in his own bed muttering *my house is on fire*. The smoke filled rooms were so clear in his mind that he lurched out of bed and switched on the light, expecting to see thick and choking clouds filling his bedroom. There was nothing, but even that could not drive his fear away. He hurried downstairs and went through every room looking for smoke, then back upstairs and through every room there, including his locked and private chapel. Only when he was fully awake and rid of the urgent impression did his heart stop pounding. He went back into his chapel and sat on the floor staring at the mural of himself in the five-pointed star while he thought about the dream.

The meaning was clear enough. Everything he had built up

was threatened with destruction; his secular life, his spiritual life, perhaps even his life itself. That was the message delivered to him in one vivid image by that part of himself which knew the truth and could not be deceived by words, excuses or promises.

From inside the brightly coloured altar he took the Tarot cards, shuffled them for a very long time, giving his inner self ample time to communicate its knowledge to the apparently chance mixing of cards. He dealt five cards face down in a star pattern and flicked the first one over. It showed a man sitting up in bed holding his head in despair, nine huge steel swords hung horizontally on the wall behind him.

That was Jonathan only fifteen minutes before, starting up in bed. He could guess now how the rest of the reading would run. The next card showed a red heart impaled on three swords and the one after that was a man hanging upside down from a gibbet. The fourth card showed a man lying face down on a seashore with ten swords stuck in his back and his blood trickling out from under him. The final card was Justice, a stern faced woman, robed in scarlet, crowned and sitting on a throne, a balance in her left hand and an upraised sword in her right.

That's how things stand, thought Jonathan. The question is, what can be done to put matters right?

His life had been full and satisfying until only a few weeks ago, when Braithwaite upset the equilibrium by voicing his threats and unleashing Jonathan's normally well controlled temper. But looking back now, it was clear to him that his reaction had not merely been excessive, it had been misdirected. He knew, as Braithwaite had guessed, that there were influences behind the scenes which favoured his upward climb at Dovedays, though neither of them could identify whose hand was at work.

Suppose, thought Jonathan, that Braithwaite's malignancy had been foreseen and allowed for; suppose that it had been deliberately provoked; suppose that any underhand plot to discredit me would have been turned back on Braithwaite, to get rid of him and clear the way for me? Then, by blasting him out of the way I did exactly the wrong thing. If whoever in the Order responsible for these arrangements ever finds out what I did, how shall I answer?

Even worse than the thought of being found out with a lack of trust for the Order was the damage he knew he had done to his own psyche by destroying another man's life for personal gain. Hired killers did it without a second thought, violent criminals casually shot down security guards who stood between them and the money. But in the thinking of the Noble Order, such people dehumanised themselves by their actions to the point where they could not be considered men any longer and their last state was unimaginable in its horror. Whatever their material gains, spiritually they were the walking dead, with worse to come. Though Jonathan had acted in such a rage against Braithwaite that his action was equivalent to a crime of passion, the hard fact remained that he had attacked deliberately and in possession of his reason.

There came into his mind a memory from his school days. The Greek myth of the Furies, the three sisters who hunted down men who committed unforgivable crimes. They had dogs' heads and bats' wings and in their hands they carried brass-studded scourges. Once they had the scent of wrong doing, they were implacable, untiring and inescapable. And they were more than an ancient Greek fantasy, they were an image of vengeance planted deep in the human mind. In the English Midlands where Jonathan had been born, the older people knew of a pack of spectral hounds that hunted the guilty by night on the Lickey Hills. Northwards, the same image surfaced in folk memory as Gabriel's hounds, baying on the lonely moors as they sought their prey. And down in Devon they were called the Wish Hounds and could be heard howling in the wind across Dartmoor by night for their quarry. Folklore that enshrined an imperishable truth – there is a hidden force in the human mind that punishes itself, whether the wrong doer knows it or not, or believes it or not.

Jonathan cleared the dismal thought from his mind and

stared at the mural of the life size naked man fitted into the five-pointed star. He pondered the statement the picture was making – man the measure of all things, man made in the image of God. The picture was more than a statement. By giving the naked figure his own face it became a great aspiration, a reminder to him that he had set his feet on the path towards becoming more than man.

What's done cannot be undone, he quoted to himself as he went back to bed. Before it was too late he must cross the Abyss that lay beyond the Seventh and so put himself beyond good and evil. Nancy Tait would be his bridge.

He arranged the ceremony for Friday evening. On a purely practical level, he might need the weekend to recover himself from his crossing of the Abyss, for he was under no illusion as to the perils and exertions he was facing. And on Tuesday next, Howard Bachrach was flying in from America to start the first round of negotiations with Jonathan and Trale, the finance director, on ways and means of setting up the New York operation called for by the new plan.

Yet there was another reason. Judith had taught him many years ago that Friday was a day of good omen for those who wished to approach the gods of life. The time must be right too, she had said, and the third hour of the night was when the planet Venus exerted its greatest influence on the earth. Jonathan checked and found that the sun would set at 8·12 that evening and rise again at 4·14 the next morning, giving a night of just over eight hours. In consequence, the planetary hours that night would be shorter than sixty minutes each. He calculated that the third hour of the night would begin soon after nine-thirty and end at about ten minutes after ten. Whether that would be long enough for what he planned, or whether it made any difference, was impossible to say, but he felt that he should at least start under the best omens and influences.

He picked up Nancy at her apartment at seven and drove her to his house in Chiswick. This was her first visit there and she was elated by the prospect, seeing it as a mark of progress in her imagined relationship with Jonathan. Between leaving the office and being collected she had changed out of the nondescript clothes she wore to work into a close fitting white jump suit and knee high shiny red boots. She had unpinned her hair and brushed it until it hung glossily down her back. The impression was still one of adolescence, Jonathan thought, but it was no longer little girl.

He had provided a bountiful cold supper for the two of them – smoked salmon to begin, cold roast duck, salad in profusion, four different cheeses and above all, plenty of good wine. Nancy soon became animated. While they enjoyed the meal and the music, Jonathan secretly gauged her drinking. He wanted her to be at precisely the right point at the right moment, not drunk and useless, but not quite sober enough to question whatever he suggested. She talked freely to him, opening her heart to his sympathetic listening. She told him of her moderately unhappy childhood in Guildford, with a mother who deferred in everything to her husband, to the point where she was hardly a real person any more. Her father had been kind enough in his way but never had much to say to his daughter. With these two as her models, she had grown up lacking in self esteem, as Jonathan read her, though Nancy put it in less analytic terms. Her sexuality had developed late and then timidly. She found it hard to form relationships with young men, though she had been engaged for a time to a budding accountant who used up all his energy playing squash. She was a perfect target for Braithwaite and he knew that from the moment he laid eyes on her.

Prompted by Jonathan, she related how after only a week as his secretary, Braithwaite had calmly pulled her onto his lap one afternoon in the office and put his hand up her skirt to stroke her thighs. To her blushing protests he said that he knew she was a naughty girl who needed her bottom spanked. She looked into his eyes and in a rare instant of self awareness she knew what he wanted her to be and found the idea more exciting than anything she had imagined before. They developed their fantasies together over several years, first in her tiny apartment and then in the much better one Braithwaite bought for her in Brompton Road, when he was sure that he had found what he had wanted for years. By then she had acquired an extensive wardrobe of schoolgirl clothes and skill in making herself appear to be fifteen years old.

'We never once did it naked,' she confided, 'not once in all those years. Derek didn't want me undressed – he said I was like every other woman when I took my clothes off. You are the only man who has seen me naked, believe it or not.'

Jonathan glanced casually at his watch and saw that it was a minute after nine. He had purposely left the wine cooling in an ice bucket on the sideboard instead of putting it on the table within easy reach. He took their glasses over to refill them and, with his back to her, deftly poured into Nancy's wine four drops of the potion he had prepared from plants grown in Judith's garden. It was a mixture of juices squeezed from thornapple root and henbane seed. The active ingredients, he knew well, were the alkaloids hyoscyamine, scopolamine and atropine, in tiny quantities, the natural products of the plants. Nancy took the wine and they chatted on, Jonathan observing her covertly. In ten minutes or so her conversation was slowing down, there were lengthening pauses between her remarks, though she was not aware of the change in herself.

At nine-twenty he suggested that they should go upstairs and she smiled slowly. He led her by the hand up to his bedroom, told her to strip naked and left her while he went to his chapel. He unlocked it, lit the four candles standing around the circle and the star and set the incense burning. That too was a special preparation for the ceremony, a mixture of musk, ambergris, aloes, dried rose petals and the pounded seeds of black poppies. From the cupboard where he kept his robes he took a white one for himself and an apple green one for Nancy.

She was standing by his bed, arms hanging loosely by her sides, stripped and staring blankly at nothing. Jonathan slipped the loose robe over her head and put her arms into the sleeves as if he were a window dresser dealing with a display dummy. In seconds he had his own clothes off and his robe on and led her to the candlelit chapel, closing the door behind them. She stood where he put her near the altar, facing the picture of the naked man on the wall, her attention caught by it.

For a Seventh as advanced as Jonathan there was no need to impress the symbolism of the protective circle on his mind by tracing it, unless he chose to. He stood at its centre and pointed round its entire circumference with his finger, visualising a wall of pale fire rising from the floor around him to cut off the outside world. Then once more he revolved, imprinting the fiery pentagrams on the air at the four quarters. Then once more, bowing each time as he summoned the Lords of the Watchtowers of east, south, west and north to be present.

He turned Nancy to stand beside him, facing east over the altar where the sweet-smelling incense burned, so that she was staring at the tree with ten fruits that covered the wall.

'Nancy,' he said, speaking slowly and clearly to get through to her, 'we are going on a journey together, up a ladder of lights, each one an emanation of God who made all and is all. You must trust me and not be afraid, even if you do not understand what is happening.'

Unless she consented, the ceremony would be void.

'Where are we?' she asked, turning her bemused eyes towards him.

'In a secret place.'

'You promised to look after me.'

'And so I shall.'

'Are we in a church?'

'We are in a sacred temple.'

She thought about that for some moments, looking from him to the painting of him in the star on the wall and then back to him, struggling to understand.

'Swear to God that you will look after me,' she said, her words slightly blurred.

Though she was physically pliant, some part of her mind was resisting. Knowing the value of symbolic gestures, Jonathan took her hand and put it flat on his chest over his heart, so that she would feel the beat through his thin robe. He put his own hand just under her tiny left breast.

'I solemnly swear to you that no harm will come to you in this sacred place.'

He waited for her reaction, watching her face closely. Her words startled him.

'Swear to Derek that you will look after me the way he wanted.'

'He cannot hear me. This matter is between you and me.'

'He will hear. I can feel him watching us.'

'As you wish. I swear to Derek Braithwaite that I will take care of you.'

There was a pause.

'Will you trust me now?' he prompted.

'I'll do anything you want.'

The heavy smell of the incense was all about them. He moved Nancy up close to the altar and stood just behind her. In his most commanding voice he began his opening prayer:

'Powers of the kingdom,
Be beneath my left foot and within my right hand . . .'

He felt the strength rising up within him from the deepest part of his being as he spoke the time hallowed words, until it seemed to him that he was nine feet tall and more than human. He pressed close to Nancy's back, put his arms round her and cupped her small breasts in his hands. The potion he had given her was not merely to numb her will – it also had the effect of arousing in her a non-specific and quenchless eroticism. The proximity of their bodies would stir her lust as never before and she would be unable to disperse it in sexual release. This was the inexhaustible fount of energy he intended to use to carry him across the Abyss.

'As above, so below,' he said, speaking to her, to himself,

and to the unseen listeners about their circle. 'As below, so above, to achieve the wonder of unity. We are going on a journey together, Nancy, a journey you will remember all your days. It is a journey inwards, and yet to make it possible for you to understand, you will experience it as a journey outwards, beyond the limits of the world that you know. Look at the picture of the Tree on the wall, look at its fruits and then concentrate on the bottom fruit.'

He reached past her to press the start button of the tape player built into the painted altar. A slow roll of drums, followed by a stately theme by a full orchestra, announced the opening of Bennick's *Gnostic Cantata*.

Since Hans-Martin Frick's day, the Order had been more fortunate in finding a composer to write music for its ceremonies. Randolph Bennick had already achieved international status as a composer before he joined the Order. After he had become a Fifth, he wrote the Cantata which Jonathan and many others regarded as his masterpiece, though it would never be performed in public, being the property of the Order.

A rich bass voice soared joyfully over the orchestra:

> 'The earth is God's, and the fullness thereof,
> The world and all they that dwell therein.'

Jonathan let the music take its effect on Nancy before he spoke quietly near her right ear.

'The bottom fruit on the Tree of Life represents Malkuth, which means the kingdom, the familiar world of people and things in which we live. It is a world full of wonder and splendour, made for the enjoyment and enlightenment of men and women, and only their own ignorance or greed hinders them from seeing that. Because we are here in this sanctified temple we are already moving onwards from the kingdom, up the trunk of the Tree in the picture, towards the next sphere on it. Look at it. That is Yesod, the foundation, a plane where there are no bodies of flesh, no time, no distance. We cannot see this world of the foundation with our physical eyes, but we see it with the inner eye. Soon we shall see it and enter into it and it will be as real as the solid kingdom we are now leaving behind us. Let your mind drift free from your body, so that I can take you with me to that place and show it to you.'

As his hands cupped her breasts, his thumbs moved gently over her nipples, fanning the flames that were leaping inside her. Her tiny nipples were stiff under the thin material of the robe and she was breathing in long sighs.

The deep voiced male singer had completed his celebration of the glory of the created world. A soprano voice of exquisite clarity softly heralded the vision of the hidden world beyond:

> 'Open ye the gates,
> That the righteous,
> Which keep the truth,
> May enter in.'

There was an unearthly quality to the music that made the hair bristle on the nape of the neck. The plane of Yesod lies very close to our everyday world, so close that most people at some time in their lives catch a glimpse of it in dreams or waking visions, for it permeates our being. Some accept that what they have glimpsed is as real as the world of men and women. Others, according to their temperament or understanding, think that they have had a ghostly visitation or have hallucinated. Mediums and psychics use it as their base of operations, interpreting it in their different ways. To Jonathan and advanced adepts like him, visiting this plane was no more difficult than stepping into the next room.

'What do you see, Nancy?' he asked.

He was checking to make sure that she was going along with him willingly. In her mind should be a reflection of what was in his, an interpretation of the indescribable transition from the conscious mind to the unconscious.

'Two dogs barking at the moon,' she said.

'Where? Describe the place for me.'

'There's a river and a path starting from the bank and going across fields, till it goes between two towers. The moon is big and low and the dogs are barking at it.'

'Be quiet, dogs!' Jonathan commanded briskly. 'Good! Now, we're going to walk along that path, Nancy. The dogs are friendly. They will lead us to our guide. There they go, trotting along ahead of us. Follow them with me. The towers mark the boundary of the material world we are leaving. The guide will be waiting for us beyond them.'

She was breathing through her open mouth as Jonathan's thumbs continued to rotate on her nipples.

'I can see him,' she said. 'Just past the towers, waiting by the path. The dogs are sitting at his feet and looking up at him.'

'Then we will go and speak to him. What does he look like?'

'He's not wearing any clothes at all. He looks like you – he's smiling at me.'

'He will guide us to where we must go. What is he saying?'

'He says we follow this path up over the hill to where it turns left and leads to . . . I can't understand the word.'

'I can. Thank him and we will be on our way.'

'Is it far?'

'There is no distance here, or time. Our minds impose these familiar concepts on what we experience in order to make it acceptable to us. Can't you hear the music from where we are going?'

'Yes,' Nancy gasped, pressing her small buttocks hard against him.

Jonathan held her tightly by her breasts as she writhed against him. Even as the quick throes faded, she was sighing again, carried along by the potion on new waves of mounting excitement.

'We are on the crest of the hill, Nancy. What do you see?'

The music rippled as she struggled for words to describe her vision. To its fast skimming theme, a tenor voice sang words of praise:

'Thou who art clothed with honour and majesty,
  Who coverest thyself with light as with a garment.'

'Do you see a man or a woman?' Jonathan said, to help her. He had been this way so many times before that he knew what figure awaited them.

'Neither . . . both . . . a woman with big breasts and a man's thing. I can't think of the word for him.'

'Hermaphrodite. What else do you see?'

'It must be an angel.'

'A god-form. Do not be afraid. This is part of your nature and mine and everyone's. Bow and acknowledge it. What else do you see?'

'A man and a lion and a bull and a big bird all in a circle round the hermaphrodite.'

'A man and a lion and a bull and an eagle,' he corrected her. 'They are the lords of the four quarters showing themselves to you in forms you can understand. They are also about us and they protect us. Call to them by their names – Raphael, Michael, Gabriel, Auriel.'

He saw her lips move as she silently recited the names. He had given the Lords of the Watchtowers these simple names out of respect for them and consideration for her. If he had told her their more secret names they would have assumed forms that might have frightened her – giant man-headed bulls with lion's paws and eagle's wings.

'They answered me!' she said. 'The bull dipped his head to the ground and the lion put his head on his paws! And the eagle spread his wings and the man opened his arms to me.'

'We are under their protection and we can move on. Do you see the path branching off to the right? That is the way we must go, over the grass.'

The sexual energy coursing through Jonathan from his sacred part held close against his body by the pressure of Nancy's buttocks was transformed into the vision that appeared, a naked young woman kneeling by a stream.

'Tell me what you see, Nancy.'

'The path runs down to a brook. There's a woman with no clothes on kneeling by it.'

The music had moved on to a theme of serene beauty and a contralto voice sang strongly:

> 'Who is she that looketh forth as the morning,
> Fair as the moon, clear as the sun?'

'What is she doing, Nancy?'

'She's got a sort of big jug in each hand and she's pouring water from them into the brook . . . she keeps on pouring and the jugs are never empty. Who is she?'

'She has a thousand names – Ishtar, Aphrodite, Miriam, Arianrod – I call her by the name the old Romans knew her by, Venus. She is very holy.'

'Why is she pouring water into the brook?'

'The brook is just an image for you to understand. In reality it is the great river of the universal consciousness we all share in. She pours into it unendingly the male and female essence which both differentiate men and women and draw them together. Do you understand this?'

By way of an answer Nancy moaned and shook against him in orgasm and would have fallen but for his supporting arms. And again she recovered quickly and was hot for more.

'I want to stay here,' she said in a sing-song voice, 'let me stay here forever in paradise.'

Jonathan pinched her nipples hard to shock her out of her incipient ecstasy.

'We must go further,' he said firmly. 'Follow the path, Nancy – there, where it turns away from the stream.'

A lengthy contemplation of the plane they had reached was part of the training of members of the Noble Order striving for the Fourth Degree, but they did so only with a guide of the opposite sex present. Afterwards they were totally spent, physically and emotionally, and they carried with them forever afterwards an unassailable conviction of the sacredness of human sexuality. It was no part of

Jonathan's plan to allow Nancy to linger here until she had exhausted herself through a chain of orgasms.

For a moment or two she resisted him mentally, but he had her mind under control and forced her along the path in front of him until she cried out.

'The sun! The sun!'

The golden orb of the sun was high in mid-heaven, shedding its life-giving rays down upon them.

The music was tremendous and remote at the same time, the voices were silent.

'What else, Nancy?'

'There's a lion coming towards us – don't let him hurt me!'

'Be calm, he will not hurt you. Is he being controlled?'

'Why, yes . . . there's a child on his back, a little boy. He can't be more than five or six. He's holding on to the lion's mane and riding him like a horse.'

'Can we go past?'

'No, the lion is barring our way.'

'He requires an offering before he will let us past. In the old days, long ago, when these things were understood differently, the child on his back would be sacrificed. That is, the life of a very young child would be offered back to the sun, who is the giver of all life on earth.'

'No, please, no!'

'Don't be afraid, there is another way. Lean forward.'

He arranged her so that she was lying with her belly on the wooden altar and her arms hanging limply down the opposite side. He pulled her loose green robe up round her waist, baring her buttocks and legs, stepped up close to the altar and hitched up his own robe to penetrate her wet slit quickly.

'The lion is waiting for the offering of a life,' he gasped as he drove in and out of her rapidly. 'Keep looking at him, Nancy!'

The long period of standing with her body pressed close against him had brought him to a high pitch of arousal. The act would be short, though of profound importance. In the lore of the Order, semen is composed of two parts, a visible substance and an invisible flame-like essence. The visible and material part is produced in the male body, but the fiery principle which is the basis of life itself descends into it from God, who is the source of all life.

Sprawled face down over the altar, Nancy was rocked forwards and backwards by the force of his thrusts, gasping loudly as her own passion mounted again towards climax. As Jonathan felt his seed surge within him, he raised his hands from her hips and spread them out, palms upwards, in the priestly gesture of offering. At the final instant, he pulled back sharply away from her and ejaculated over her back, forcing out the words *Igne natura renovatur integra*.

In English the words meant *all nature is regenerated by fire*, and were the formula for the offering. In that he had chosen not to plant his seed in her body, where it might grow into another human being, he had sacrificed a life. The lion, now without its child rider, moved away from the path. The offering had been accepted.

Nancy's orgasmic shrieks were drowned out by the full throated chorus, backed by the whole orchestra, raised in passionate praise:

'He hath set a tabernacle for the sun,
Which is as a bridegroom coming forth from his chamber,
And rejoiceth as a strong man to run a race!'

Jonathan eased Nancy backwards off the altar and held her upright against him, this time by both hands flat on her quivering belly.

'What do you see?' he asked urgently.

She screamed in fear.

'I can see God!'

'Be quiet,' he admonished her, in the same peremptory tone he had used to silence the dogs at the start of their journey. 'We are only halfway to God. The lion, who is the sun, is now enthroned in beauty in the form of a great king. Bow before him, for he gave you your life.'

'Dear God, forgive me for my sins,' Nancy sobbed.

'He is not interested in your sins. He is the giver of life, not its judge. What does he look like to you?'

'He has a gold crown on his head and a red robe and he's sitting on a throne made of marble. There are goats' heads carved on the ends of the arm rests.'

'Rams' heads,' he corrected her. 'What is he holding?'

'A long golden cross with a loop on the top.'

'The Egyptian ankh, the sign of life. Look at his face.'

'I can't . . . I'd die.'

'You will live, look at his face.'

As chorus and orchestra thundered out the mighty sounds of praise, she obeyed him.

'Is he Jesus?' she asked in a voice so hushed that he only just heard it.

'He has many names. Christians call him Jesus. Others have worshipped him as Apollo and Belin and Ogma Sunface. Feel the golden life he radiates! Can you feel it spreading through your body, through your veins, through your flesh? Feel it glowing here inside your belly.'

'Ah, ah, ah!' she gasped as his fingers plied the flesh around her navel through the thin material of her robe. 'I'm going to come again . . .'

She lifted her arms towards the enthroned figure of her vision as she climaxed spontaneously. But before she could dissipate the strength that had built up in her, Jonathan urged her further along the path, past the throne, bowing his head to its occupant. The chorus ended its hymn on a roaring crescendo and there was silence for a brief space. Then faint and far off, but approaching quickly, there came a very different music, the braying of war trumpets, the rattle of wheels, the high neighing of horses.

'What do you see now, Nancy?'

'A chariot galloping at us! There's a man in armour in it!'

'How many horses are pulling it?'

'One black horse and one white.'

The bass singer took up the theme, urgent and menacing:

> 'The horseman lifteth up the bright sword
> And the glittering spear,
> And there is a multitude of slain!'

The vision of the charioteer and the music swept them along in a torrent of destruction. They saw armies of men trampled under in bloody death, tall cities sacked and burning, captives led in bonds to the beheading and their heads piled into pyramids as high as trees, for they had touched upon the fount of the urge to live, which is the urge to conquer. Nancy screamed in delight at the chariot's wild ride, afire with blood lust, and Jonathan bellowed out the words of the cantata with the singer, until his training asserted itself and he pulled Nancy away from the scene and pushed her along the path branching off to the right.

The battle music faded behind them, not ending but rolling away into the distance. Jonathan held Nancy tightly against himself, waiting for her to sink back into the erotic semi-trance.

Out of hushed silence the clear soprano voice sang with absolute conviction, accompanied by the orchestra's strings:

> 'God reigns, clothed in majesty.
> He is clothed with strength,
> Wherewith he has girded himself.'

'But that's not God,' said Nancy, sounding puzzled.
'What do you see?'
'A man standing at a table . . . he's shuffling things on it.'
'What things?'
'He's got a knife and a stick . . . and a goblet and a round plate. What's he doing?'
'He is creating everything we know from these seemingly simple things.'
'But he looks ordinary.'
'He is an aspect of God, so ordinary in our eyes that we fail to see the endless miracle of creation that he is performing.

Do you understand this paradox?'

'No.'

Aloud, Jonathan declaimed the words of the singer in homage to the vision, using the Latin version he preferred:

> *'Dominus regnat, celsitudine indutus,*
> *Indutus dominus robore se accinge.'*

His hands had inched slowly down Nancy's belly to stroke her thighs and soft mound through the robe, preparing her for the ordeal she was soon to face. When her langorous sighing indicated that she was ready, he gently propelled her past the figure she did not understand, to where the path ended.

They were on the edge of a cliff. Together they stood at the brink and looked out and down. There was nothing, no landscape below, nothing ahead, however far they tried to see. Jonathan had travelled to this point often before. The route was so familiar to him that he had been able to bring Nancy with him, though it had been necessary to give her the potion so that her life energy stayed at a high enough pitch. To become a Seventh in the Order required that the adept should be able to reach and contemplate the man at the table with his curious shufflings of the elements of creation, and to understand this aspect of God at work in the universe and in the adept himself.

Beyond that vision lay the Abyss. To cross it was to pass into the world of emanation, to become identified with an aspect of God so high that the adept became a Master of the Temple, liberated forever from human good and evil. The Order said that it was possible to make the transition and survive, but it offered no instruction in the means of doing so. Only very rarely was the crossing attempted, for this eighth initiation could only be a self initiation. To make the attempt and fail was to destroy everything the adept had achieved until then.

Because of Nancy's uninitiated state, the approach to this point had been presented to her in the form of a journey, so that she could partly understand; the god-aspects had been revealed as figures in human form, so as not to terrify her. None of this was necessary for Jonathan and over the years he had experienced the ascent to this point in many guises; the ladder of lights, the spiral inwards from the conscious ego to the ultimate and enduring self, the seven steps up to the king's throne. He stood now on the seventh step, as often before, and was ready to make the last and greatest effort – to seat himself upon the throne of power.

Staring out into the Abyss, he prayed aloud to strengthen his resolve:

'What is man, that thou art mindful of him?
And the son of man, that thou visiteth him?
For thou hast made him a little lower than the angels,
And hast crowned him with glory and honour;
Thou madest him to have dominion over the works
　of thy hands,
Thou hast put all things under his feet.'

He took the neck hem of Nancy's apple green robe between his hands and tore it sharply. He ripped the thin material down the length of her back in one movement, so that it fell away from her body and she stood naked. She made no resistance as he turned her to face him and lifted her by the waist to sit her upon his altar. He tore his own robe down the front and let it slide to the floor at his feet, symbolising his resolve to conquer, when he would have no further use for these outward trappings.

The cantata was still playing, the woman's voice praising God in his majesty, as Jonathan stepped in between Nancy's parted legs and penetrated her again. He had chosen this position for connection with her because it was of high significance to him to experience the divine presence beyond the Abyss standing upright on his feet, not on his knees like a Christian or with his face in the dust, like a Moslem. Like comprehends like, he must be equal to God to comprehend God.

Nancy's legs curled slowly round his waist. He gripped her

childish breasts to steady her as he began a slow and strong thrust.

'No!' she whimpered when she saw that they were about to leap from the cliff edge into nothingness.

'Trust me and we shall not fall. We shall fly.'

'No,' she moaned, but the sexual tension that had been building up in her since the long ceremony began was nearing its peak, her previous orgasms mere plateaus on the way to the mountain top. Whatever the objections of her mind, her hot body clamped itself to Jonathan eagerly, and in seconds raging lust blotted out her ability to think or fear.

Out over the Abyss they soared, locked together, Jonathan's ferocious concentration enabling him to exclaim words of prayer and praise as his body performed the familiar act of copulation:

> 'He that dwells in the secret place of the Most High
> Shall abide under the shadow of the Almighty!
> I will say: He is my refuge and my fortress.
> He is God, in Him will I trust!'

Apprehended in terms of distance, from the cliff edge to the other side was further than the bounds of the universe. Seen in another way, there was no distance at all, only the thinnest of veils between the Seventh and the Eighth, a translucent veil, yet harder to break through than a wall of diamond. As the life energy roared up like flame in Jonathan and Nancy from their joined parts, it seemed to him that the void shivered and divided and very far off he caught a glimpse of such unbelievable splendour that his heart raced and he jabbed faster into Nancy, as a rider spurs his mount when the end of the race is in sight.

Nearer and clearer, until he stared in awe and exultation at a vision of the cosmic lord, the Cosmocrator, the maker and ruler of the universe. Not God, who is unknowable and unimaginable, but a manifest aspect of God which his mind could nearly grasp, almost apprehend. Since the human mind requires symbols in order to understand, what Jonathan saw was a being of blazing white light, so vast that he wore the entire zodiac as a crown. In his right hand he held the seven stars of the Great Bear and with them he turned the universe on its axis.

Dazzled by his vision, Jonathan no longer consciously heard the music and the chorus as it exulted:

> 'To him that overcometh
> I will give to eat of the Tree of Life
> Which is in the midst of the paradise of God,
> To him will I give the morning star.'

Nearer and nearer Jonathan approached the cosmic lord. Nancy was screaming in terror, but he no longer cared what happened to her. In another instant the life essence would gush up through his sacred part into her and he would be one with the mighty vision. He gasped out the words, timing them to his final thrusts:

> 'Praise God in his sanctuary,
> Praise him in the firmament of his power,
> Praise him for his mighty acts,
> Praise him according to his excellent greatness . . .'

He was all but there, under the shadow of the Almighty, when Nancy pulled away from him, breaking their sexual connection, her screams piercing and continuous. Instantly the vision vanished and a hurricane blast as cold as interstellar space knocked Jonathan to the floor. Nancy fell heavily from the altar and landed on top of him.

The journey was not yet over, though its direction was now out of Jonathan's control as they tumbled together into the Abyss. He saw that they had fallen from the top of a tower that had been struck by lightning. Down they rushed towards the sharp rocks below, a catastrophic helter skelter descent of the planes they had ascended. Before they were dashed against the rocks, a huge, goat legged devil, bearded and horned, reached out to seize them. He fixed chains round their necks and fastened them to a stone plinth on which he stood. Jonathan groaned aloud, understanding the meaning; he had misused his knowledge and made himself a prisoner of the evil inside himself. And he had chained Nancy to it with himself.

She had been screaming when they fell from the lightning struck tower of God, her shrieks became insane in their intensity as she was chained to the stone. Then that vision faded and they lay huddled together on the wooden floor of Jonathan's chapel. The final vision made its appearance and its horror struck Nancy dumb.

Inside his circle of protection, transparent as a wraith and yet real, there stood a grinning skeleton with a blood smeared scythe in its bony hands. It lurched towards them, swinging the sharp-pointed blade an inch or two above the floor. Then it was gone.

It was some time before Jonathan regained possession of himself. He rolled Nancy roughly off him and sat up. She was unconscious and her body felt cold. He left her lying while he stood at his altar and cautiously felt out the atmosphere. The Guardians were not there. The circle was no more than a painted line on the floor. There was an oppressiveness in the room that told him that it was no longer a sanctified temple.

Wearily he picked Nancy up and carried her to his bedroom. He dropped her on the bed and put on his dressing gown. He had never felt so cold and tired in his life. He left her where she was and went downstairs to pour himself a large glass of brandy and force himself to think about his position. As the brandy warmed his stomach, he wondered whether things were quite so bad as he had feared up in the chapel. Literal interpretations were very unsound, he thought. After all, he had very nearly reached out across the Abyss. It was only Nancy's fear that had precipitated the fall. Now that he knew the way, he could do it again, with a woman of the Order, and this time he would succeed. With Orline, of course. They would stand in the presence of the cosmic lord,

Masters of the Temple together, united forever in ways beyond mere mortal understanding.

The falling visions were merely fear phantasms induced by Nancy, and not to be taken at face value. After all, the tower struck by lightning could be interpreted as an erect penis at the moment of ejaculation, the falling people as drops of semen, flung forth to lodge and flourish or to perish. The meaning surely was that if he had reached the climax before Nancy collapsed, he would have completely crossed the Abyss. The method had been true, the partner unequal to him. Instead of making do with an uninitiated woman, he should have got on a flight to Los Angeles and made Orline his partner.

The vision of being chained to the stone plinth with Nancy only served to reinforce his interpretation. He had bound himself to her for the great ceremony and she had proved to be an inadequate vessel. The choice of her had been an error of judgment.

Damn the woman, he thought. It was a mistake to get involved with her because of that stupid letter from Braithwaite. And as for the final vision of the skeletal reaper inside the circle, only the very unenlightened would understand that as a portent of death and the end. Its esoteric meaning was an end and a new beginning. Applied to himself, the significance was that because of his mistake in using Nancy and so falling short of what he intended, he was for a time cut off from the divine light. But only for a time. There would be a new and more glorious beginning. With the co-operation of Orline he could regain the heights and move on to a plane of grace undreamed of.

When Jonathan had comforted himself in this way, he went back upstairs and got into bed with Nancy. Her eyes opened slowly and she said reproachfully,

'You promised to look after me.'

'And so I did. You're not hurt in any way and you gave every appearance of enjoying yourself for most of the time. If you'd held on for another second or two instead of going into a blind panic, things would have turned out very differently. You messed the whole thing up.'

'The devil came for me and chained me up!' she said, remembering.

'Don't be silly. That was all in your mind. You're not chained up.'

Her hand went to her throat as if feeling for a chain, her eyes bulged and she screamed hysterically. Jonathan smacked her face to stop her and the sting of his fingers on her face unleashed all the anger and resentment he felt towards her for failing him. Growling in his throat like a dog, he grabbed her by the neck with both hands and threw his weight on her, intent on killing her. Nancy fought back, wrenching at his fingers, struggling to get her knees up between their bodies to kick him off her. As they fought, Jonathan's rage flared into lust, as on the first occasion he had taken her by force. He got his legs between hers and pinned her arms to the bed while he raped her. She screamed non-stop. Her resistance served to drive him on until a murderous triumph flooded through him as he reached a furious orgasm. He was a conqueror who had killed his enemy and taken his woman by force. She had invoked Braithwaite's shade in the chapel – now finally Braithwaite was dead and done with and had no more power over him.

When he pulled brutally away from her, she lay as if crushed for a moment or two, then scrambled out of bed and was at the window. She had it open and was halfway out before he got to her and pulled her away. He flung her roughly on the bed.

'What the hell do you think you're doing?' he shouted.

'Derek is waiting for me,' she answered listlessly.

'You stupid bitch – he's dead.'

'I have to go to him now. He's waiting.'

Jonathan sat on the bed and looked into her eyes. He saw no sign of recognition.

'Nancy, do you know where you are?'

'I have to go now.'

'Who am I?'

She looked at him dully for a while.

'I can't remember your name,' she said eventually, 'but it doesn't matter. Derek's the only one who matters. He's outside, waiting for me. Can I go now?'

Alarmed, Jonathan wound one hand in her long hair to hold her pinned to the bed while he reached for the bedside telephone to call his doctor to come quickly.

CHAPTER 25
THE SCALES

JONATHAN'S CONTACT with the chairman of the board of Dovedays had been no more than fleeting in the time he had been with the company. The longest he had ever been in the same room with him was at the board meeting where he had presented his plan for the future of the overseas sales department. Innes was a non-executive chairman – that is, his only function in the company was to turn up once a month to chair a board meeting. His main business interests lay elsewhere, in finance and banking. The man who actually ran the company and took the major decisions was Peter Bennett, the managing director.

Innes had expressed a wish to have lunch with Dovedays' newest board member and so on the day arranged for their lunch, Jonathan sent for the office copy of *Who's Who* to check Innes's pedigree. In Nancy's absence, Jonathan's former secretary had moved in to work for him. Jonathan scowled when he thought of the reason for Nancy's unavailability. After two days of heavy sedation at his house with no change in her mental condition, the doctor had insisted on calling an ambulance and transferring her to a private psychiatric hospital. And there she still was, at Jonathan's expense, so scrambled by drugs that she was like a zombie on the one occasion he had visited her. She had not even recognised him.

The psychiatrist in charge of her took Jonathan into his office and put him through a grilling on the events that had led up her admittance.

'I can't understand it at all,' Jonathan lied. 'She came to stay with me for the weekend. We had a couple of bottles of wine over dinner and listened to music and went to bed.'

'At this point you had normal sexual relations with her?'

'If by normal you mean with her underneath and me on top, yes. After that she went crazy and tried to jump out of the bedroom window. I had to restrain her while I got hold of Dr Chesney.'

The psychiatrist looked doubtfully at Jonathan over the top of his spectacles.

'Did she take any drugs, to your knowledge, Mr Rawlings?'

'Cannabis, you mean, or LSD – that sort of thing? Certainly not. Not while she was with me. I can't answer for what she might have taken before she arrived.'

'I see that you can't help me much. I have to tell you that it's going to take some time to get to the cause of her condition. She's still heavily sedated to stop her screaming. Do you happen to know if she is a religious person?'

'I would have said not, on our brief acquaintance. Why do you ask?'

'In her coherent moments she asks to see a priest. Not once, but repeatedly. She's very disturbed and religion seems to play some part in it.'

Jonathan shrugged, and there they left it.

The massive blue-bound *Who's Who* arrived on Jonathan's desk and he leafed through the pages of professors, businessmen, service officers, writers, musicians, actors, landowners, politicians and other worthies until he found Innes. Conventionally distinguished, he thought, as he read the first few lines.

386

Innes, George James Robert, a Companion of Honour, chairman of Morgenroth Frères Ltd since 1972; a director of the Bank of England since 1974; a member of the Board of Governors of the British Broadcasting Corporation since 1976; born 1917, eldest son of James Edward Innes of Glebe House, Lower Haxton, Surrey, and Mary Charlotte, daughter of Sir Rugeley Stephens, baronet, of Hallerton Hall, Berwickshire; educated at Winchester and Balliol College, Oxford; served war of 1939-45 Scots Guards, final rank Major; Military Cross, American Bronze Star, Croix de Guerre.

Jonathan wondered briefly whether he would have achieved that kind of military recognition himself if he had been born twenty years earlier and had been involved in the war. Not having Innes's Scottish connections, he would not have joined the Scots Guards. Nor any other infantry regiment, he thought, to hump weapons through mud. Tanks or artillery – that would have been more interesting. He read on,

. . . married 1950 Ilse-Dorothea, daughter of H.M. Frick;

He read it again, his hands trembling on the page. Innes had married one of the daughters of Hans-Martin Frick! There it was on public record and he could have found it at any time if he had bothered to look for it.

He took a deep breath and forced himself to think clearly. If Frick had consented to Innes marrying Ilse-Dorothea, then Innes must surely have been a member of the Noble Order. It could hardly be otherwise. And he must still be a member, for initiation was for all time and not even death could terminate it. But Innes had not attended any Lodge meetings in all Jonathan's years of membership, nor had there ever been any reference to him or trace of his existence. Why had he ceased to be active in the Order so long ago?

The answer which formed itself in Jonathan's mind hardly bore thinking about. Could Innes, at some time before 1963, the year in which Jonathan was received into the Order, have crossed the second threshold, the Abyss, to become a Master of the Temple? If he had, that would account for his total withdrawal. Records of him would then be transferred to the secret archive which only the Lodge Master had access to. But was it possible?

Suppose Innes had joined the Order as soon as he came back from the war. That gave him about four years to progress from Neophyte to the point where Hans-Martin Frick was sufficiently impressed to allow him to marry Ilse-Dorothea. What would be enough for Frick? Innes would have to be a Fifth to qualify for that honour. And four years was not long enough to get that far – so Innes must have been accepted into the Order at an earlier date, sometime during the war, when he was still a serving officer. Could that be so?

Most certainly it could, in one of several ways. Back in the very early years of the Order, Frick was personally recruiting pillars of the establishment and looking to them to find young high fliers. That was how Jonathan's tutor at Cambridge had been recruited and had then in turn recruited suitable young men himself from among his pupils. Frick would certainly have had someone at Oxford to do the same, another respected teacher. And that someone could have sounded out Innes during a leave from the army. Or another way – Frick also recruited senior officers. One of them could well have selected Innes as suitable, when they were not too occupied with shooting the enemy.

In whatever way it came about, Innes must have been a Fifth, a Lord of the Threshold, when he married Frick's daughter in 1950. Some time after that he had risen to Seventh and had then gone on to cross the Abyss and move out of the active life of the Order before Jonathan even joined it.

What else, Jonathan wondered, could be deduced from the abbreviated record of Innes's life in *Who's Who*?

It recorded that Innes had joined Morgenroth Frères, a merchant banking company of international reputation, in 1946 and had become its managing director in 1965. That was well after Frick's death, but it was a reasonable bet that Frick had part control of Morgenroth and had actively propelled his son-in-law upwards to get him into a position of strength from which he could in due course take over the business.

Innes's other business interests were impressive. He was listed as chairman of United Commercial Assurance Company Ltd and of Dovedays Ltd. He was a director of Whitelands Credit Trust, Maxwell Property Development, Bourne Investments, Assam Plantations. And other companies, the book said, as if they were too numerous to mention.

The company names set Jonathan's mind working. One of the members of the London Lodge was a director of United Commercial Assurance. And another was the managing director of Assam Plantations. And at Dovedays there's me, Jonathan thought. And what about the other companies too numerous to list? It was plain to him that Innes had been secretly steering him through Bennett, who was not a member of the Order and therefore did not know that he was being manipulated. Innes saw to it that members of the Order rose to the top of the companies they worked for, and they were all companies in which he had a personal interest.

There was one more question to ask. Could Innes's long term plan for Jonathan be for him to succeed Bennett as managing director? Yes, he thought, it could surely be. Then he must remain very silent about what he guessed and, above all, about what he had done to advance himself at Braithwaite's expense.

There were four of them at lunch in the guest dining room that day, Innes, Bennett, Trale and Jonathan. Kenneth Trale had started by being a determined opponent of Jonathan's reorganisation plans and was now his staunchest supporter, having been through the figures and convinced himself that it was his own plan all along. Bennett was reassured about the plan by Trale's acceptance of it and was therefore well disposed towards Jonathan.

Innes was secretly pleased that one of his covert protégés had been appointed to the board on his own merits. At least, that was how Jonathan read the position. He would need some convincing, perhaps, that the promotion was not premature, but it had been on the recommendation of Bennett, who was no fool.

To look at, Innes was a sturdy, handsome man who looked fifteen years younger than he was. His back was straight and his face had the healthy glow of a man who spends much of his time outdoors. With his background, he would traditionally have been interested in foxhunting and game bird shooting. But killing for sport was inconsistent with being an adept of his level. He must do a lot of horseriding or skiing, Jonathan thought – though how he finds time with all those meetings of boards of directors and governors to attend is not easy to see.

'What do you do to keep fit?' Innes asked Jonathan, as if he had read his thoughts.

'I play squash and I swim regularly. It's not the same as outdoor sports, of course, but living in London limits the choice.'

'There's golf,' said Trale. 'That gets you out into the fresh air. I play twice a week, winter and summer.'

'Yes, but to me it seems such a slow game,' said Jonathan.

'Wait till you're ten years older,' said Trale, 'then you'll change your mind.'

'Did you row at university?' Innes asked.

'Yes, I enjoyed that. I wasn't extremely good, but I got as far as the college boat.'

'I was picked for the Oxford-Cambridge boat race of 1938,' said Innes, 'and would you believe it, three days before the race I sprained my ankle badly and had to drop out. That was the biggest disappointment of my life.'

'I've heard you say that before, George,' said Bennett, 'and I still find it difficult to believe that no greater disappointment than that has ever come your way.'

'All the same, it's a matter of fact. What was your biggest disappointment, Peter?'

'I think it was when my youngest son failed to qualify as a chartered accountant.'

'Was that your disappointment or his, though?' Innes asked.

'I think that I felt it more than he did.'

'Kenneth, your turn.'

'My biggest disappointment?' said Trale, 'not easy to say. Let me think about it for a moment.'

'While you're thinking, we'll ask our new colleague to tell us his.'

Jonathan blanked out from his mind the memory of his disastrous attempt to cross the Abyss. He was sure that Innes had not started this line of conversation by chance. If Innes were a Master, as he had speculated, then he would have the ability to interpret the vibrations which emotion charged images set up in the mind. He was probing delicately to see if there was anything unsound in Jonathan.

'It was years ago,' he answered lightly, 'before I joined Dovedays, when I was a bright young brand manager trying to get a new product off the ground. I did everything by the book, worked like a slave, day after day, late into the evening. The product was going to be a world beater. We were going to sell millions of cases of it in the first six months, and after that, the sky was the limit. The profits would have been splendid. And then less than a month before the launch, our main competitor came out with an identical product at two thirds the price. Ours was a dead duck.'

Bennett and Trale laughed sympathetically, but Innes was looking at him with his head cocked to one side, as if he were listening to something else, not the words.

For Jonathan it was an uneasy lunch. Innes kept the conversation going deftly to draw Jonathan out on a variety of subjects connected with the business, seeking his opinions, giving him every opportunity to shine. Bennett and Trale played along and Jonathan forced himself to rise to the occasion, working hard at putting across the impression that he was a shrewd, intelligent, hard working and trustworthy new director of the company. But there was a hollowness about it all.

At the end of the meal, when the port decanter appeared, Innes raised his glass.

'Let me take this opportunity of welcoming you to the board of Dovedays, Jonathan. You've been on Peter's promotion list for some time, as I'm sure you knew. From all that he's told me about you, I fully expected to toast your appointment before too long. Our pleasure in welcoming you here should not be diminished by the circumstances of Derek Braithwaite's shocking death.'

At the mention of Braithwaite's name and death, Jonathan instantly drew a circle about his thoughts to prevent any hint of his complicity communicating itself to Innes. In silent panic he saw Innes's eyes close for an instant and then stare hard, just as his own did in those rare moments of precognition when he knew which number to put his stake on at the gaming tables.

'Thank you,' he said formally. 'I shall do everything in my power to make sure that your trust in me is not misplaced.'

'I've got it,' said Trale. 'The biggest disappointment of my life was not being elected captain of my golf club two years ago.'

They all laughed and soon after that they said goodbye to Innes and went back to work. Jonathan sat motionless at his desk for a long time, the open *Who's Who* in front of him, thinking hard. If he was right about Innes, then it would be nigh on impossible to conceal what he had done or to evade its consequences. He would be compelled to make restitution in full, and what form that might take was beyond him to guess. Innes was powerful, he had friends and influence everywhere – it would not be hard for him to check back on what his intuition had told him and to reveal hard facts.

In the event, it took three days. Then Jonathan had a telephone call from the Marshal of his Lodge to present himself that evening at the Temple. When he tried to ask the reason, his caller hung up.

When he arrived at the Temple, he found only two people in the robing room, both already dressed in the Order's parade uniform, but with no badges of rank about their necks. There was Dorothy Mawson, who had been Jonathan's first teacher in the Order, and Harold Griffiths, who had been Marshal the previous year. Neither of them answered his greeting.

'Something wrong?' he asked, attempting cheerfulness.

'We are under orders not to talk to you,' said Griffiths. 'You must wear this.'

He held out a robe of a sulphurous yellow colour.

'What is it?'

'The penitential robe. Strip and put it on.'

Jonathan had never seen its like before, but he had heard of it. Members under any kind of suspicion were required to wear it while allegations against them were investigated.

'Someone has spoken against me,' said Jonathan as he started to undress. 'What's this all about, Dorothy?'

'I don't know,' she said miserably, 'and if I did, I'm not permitted to speak to you.'

Jonathan threw his clothes onto the nearest bench and stood naked while he slipped the ugly robe over his head. At once Griffiths stepped forward and put a noose around his neck.

'This is damned silly!' Jonathan exclaimed.

But Griffiths put the other end of the rope into the woman's hand, so that she could lead him to the closed door of the Temple.

'There is no point in being angry with me,' said Griffiths. 'Examine your conscience while there is still time.'

'My conscience is clear,' Jonathan answered boldly. 'Let's get on with it.'

Griffiths beat his fist twice against the door, bolts rattled on the other side and it opened just enough for the Knight Sentinel to look at them. After a moment of inspection, he stood aside and flung the door wide for them to pass through.

The Temple was in darkness except for the illuminated star in the middle of the floor. Dorothy went first, leading

Jonathan by the halter and Griffiths walked behind him. As they advanced, Jonathan glanced left and right at the rows of wooden chairs and though they were in darkness, he knew that they were all empty. At least, this was not a public examination in front of all the members of the Lodge, and for that he was grateful.

He stood in the centre of the six-pointed star. The woman moved to his left, the man to his right, taking up their positions half a pace behind him. The rope from the noose hung down his chest to the level of his knees, a reminder of the pain and fear of the Fifth Degree ceremony he had once endured, through which he had emerged into light.

The veil was drawn across the sanctum and there was no light behind it. But someone must be there, he reasoned, to tell him of the allegations against him and to hear his answers. It had to be the Grandmaster, surely, in a matter touching a Seventh.

Slowly he became aware of the music. It had started as soon as he had been led into the Temple, but so remotely that even the sound of his bare feet on the floor and the measured tread of his escort's boots had obscured it. As he stood silent, it forced itself into his consciousness, a low and desolate moaning of orchestral strings. For once he was at a loss to put a name to what he heard. He saw light glowing dimly behind the veil. It grew and spread, the veil parted and slid noiselessly away and the light blazed out full. Jonathan stared in amazement at the scene revealed to him.

In the middle, on his golden throne, sat Miles Brentwood, Master of the London Lodge and Grandmaster of all the Lodges of the Noble Order around the world. To each side of him sat five members, in tunics, surcoats and boots, their short swords drawn and lying across their knees. Half of them were men and half women, all of them were well known to Jonathan. Before the throne and a little to one side of it stood the Marshal of the Lodge and beside him, head on its paws, lay a great black Alsatian dog. To the other side of the throne stood the Guardian of the Grail, her chalice held before her in both hands.

The Marshal looked at Jonathan and ordered him to identify himself.

'I am Jonathan Rawlings, a Knight of this Order.'

'What is your rank?'

'I am a Seventh.'

The music spread spiritual desolation through the Temple as the Guardian walked slowly towards Jonathan and halted before him. She held out the golden chalice towards him and, as he reached for it to drink, she deliberately upturned it so that the wine spilled on the floor at his feet, splashing his yellow robe. While the significance of her gesture was penetrating his mind, she turned her back to him and returned to her position by the throne.

The Marshal spoke with force and menace.

'Knight of this Order, before you are your accusers. It is their will that you make the Profession of Righteousness. Is it your will also?'

'It is my will.'

'Then they are waiting for your words.'

Jonathan took a deep breath and spoke the familiar formula:

> 'I have done no wrong;
> I have not been covetous,
> I have not stolen,
> I have killed no man,
> I have not given short measure.'

He paused, summoning his courage to continue, blanking out from his mind the meaning of what he was saying so as not to weaken his position.

> 'I have done what is pleasing to the gods;
> I have given bread to the hungry,

And water to the thirsty,
And clothes to the naked,
And a passage to those with no boat.'

As he finished, there was a mournful roll of drums and then silence for the space of a minute, an eternity of oppressive silence in which Jonathan could feel the sweat trickling under his armpits.

'Mighty accusers,' said the Marshal, turning to address the men and women ranged beside the Master. 'You sit in this Temple as representatives of the gods. How say you?'

The first to speak was Cora Hamilton, who had been Jonathan's pupil when she was a Fourth.

'He is a liar,' she said loudly. 'He coveted another man's worldly position.'

'He is a liar,' said the man next to her. 'He stole another man's worldly position.'

'He is a liar,' said the woman after him, Susanne Greely, whom Jonathan had once seriously considered asking to marry him. 'He killed another man to steal the position he coveted.'

'He is a liar,' said Ronald Burgess, one of Jonathan's closest friends. 'He gave short measure to a man who charged him with a duty to protect a woman.'

'He is a liar,' said the next woman. 'He gave a stone instead of bread to the woman in distress.'

'He is a liar,' said the bass voice of John Andrews. 'He gave her vinegar to drink instead of water when her soul thirsted.'

'He is a liar,' said Ann Woods, with whom Jonathan had spent many memorable nights. 'Instead of clothing her with dignity he used her body for his own selfish ends.'

'He is a liar,' said the next man. 'He gave neither the man he harmed nor the woman he harmed a passage in his boat.'

'He is a liar,' said the next, her voice hard with indignation. 'He said that he did no wrong and he has done wrong in these things.'

'He is a liar,' said the last voice, 'for he has indeed done what is displeasing to the gods, contrary to his words before us.'

The voices had been like hammer blows on an anvil. Jonathan's head was reeling. The big black dog lifted its head to snarl, showing long fangs.

'You have heard the accusers,' said the Marshal, 'listen now to the words of Solomon the King, who out of his wisdom said:

> 'The treasures of wickedness profits nothing,
> But righteousness delivers from death;
> The memory of the just is blessed,
> But the name of the wicked shall rot.
> He that walks uprightly shall walk surely,
> But he that perverts his ways shall be known.'

The same long and mournful roll of drums was repeated, then for the first time in the proceedings the Grandmaster spoke.

'Knight of this Order, you have heard the accusers. How do you answer them?'

'I did not kill Braithwaite. He took his own life in hospital. That is a matter of public record.'

'What of the woman Tait? She too is in hospital and has attempted to take her own life. Is this coincidence?'

'I showed her a vision for which she was unprepared. In this I was at fault and should be reproved.'

'What vision did you show to a woman not of our Order?'

'I betrayed no secrets. All I did was take her up with me through the planes of God. She could have discovered this for herself if she had been interested.'

'If that was the full extent of what you showed her, why is she now mentally deranged?'

'I do not know. Perhaps her own fear and guilt made her unworthy to see these things.'

The Grandmaster stared at him in silence for a while and said:

'The heart is deceitful above all things and desperately wicked; who can know it? God searches the heart, even to give every man according to his ways and according to the fruit of his doings.'

He gestured towards the Marshal and the Guardian and they advanced a step or two and stood together between Jonathan and the elevated throne. The Guardian no longer held the golden chalice which was the symbol of her office, but a brass balance three feet across, with pans hanging on long wires from each end of the arm. She held it out in front of her at the length of her outstretched arm. The Marshal watched it until the pans were level and still, then in a stentorian voice he said:

'I summon the gods to be present and witness this act. In their sight I weigh the heart of this Knight of our Most Noble Order.'

He held up a pure white feather for Jonathan to see and placed it gently on one pan of the balance.

'Behold the feather of truth, plucked from the wing of a sacred swan.'

He held out towards Jonathan on the palm of his hand a wrapped bundle and then unwound the cloth to reveal a dark red lump the size of a fist.

'Behold the heart of this Knight, ready for the weighing.'

Jonathan watched open mouthed as the Marshal put the heart in the other pan of the balance. A brassy gong sounded crescendo through the Temple as the balance fell on that side. The black dog was up on its feet at the sound, its coat bristling, its jaws apart. The Marshal turned with upraised palms to face the Grandmaster and wait for his word.

'His heart is heavy with evil,' said the Grandmaster. 'Let it be cast to the destroyer.'

The Marshal took the heart from the balance and threw it to the waiting dog. Jonathan swayed on his feet, the yellow robe plastered to his body with sweat as the dog slavered over the meat, pinning it to the floor with its paws while it tore pieces from it and swallowed them. As soon as the hideous symbolic destruction was finished, the Marshal approached the star where Jonathan stood and on the three points on the sanctum side he set, respectively, a three-thonged whip, a thick black lighted candle and a double headed axe.

The Grandmaster addressed Jonathan, not accusingly or angrily, but remotely.

'One of our own, for greed's sake, threatens to make ruin of this Noble Order by his folly. Unrighteous is his mind and his pride goes before a fall, for he grows rich through the work of evil deeds and steals from others with no respect for possessions, either sacred or profane, nor has heed of the mighty foundations of justice. But in her silence, justice is well aware of what is and what has been and, soon or late, comes always to avenge.'

He paused for some seconds while Jonathan took in the words, then went on:

'Nothing is hidden from your accusers. Your dealings with the man Braithwaite and the woman Tait are known in full. You have coveted, stolen, destroyed and done what is displeasing to the gods. Make your confession now.'

'Who set you as a judge over me?' Jonathan shouted at him, suddenly angry.

'You are your own judge.'

'Then I am innocent of evil intentions, though mistaken in some of the means I have used. I confess to errors of judgment, though my motives were good.'

'That is your verdict on yourself?'

'Yes. Now tell me how I can make restitution and finish this charade.'

'It is finished. Before you are set the symbols of the oath you took willingly when you first were received into this Order. If you ever break that oath of silence, then your flesh will be torn with scourges, your life ended by the axe and your body consumed by fire.'

'There's no need to threaten me.'

'I made no threat, only reminded you, for your own sake. One last word before you leave this Temple forever.'

'Goodbye?' Jonathan sneered.

The Grandmaster rose to his feet and stretched out his arm

to point at him. The accusers stood and held their swords with the points towards Jonathan.

'You have judged yourself in our hearing and have found yourself to be without evil intention. Now by the power vested in me as Grandmaster of the Noble Order I pronounce the sentence of your peers upon you.'

He paused for the drums to roll menacingly.

'Jonathan Rawlings, you are cut asunder, your soul is shrivelled up, your cursed name is buried in oblivion and silence is upon it forever.'

The mighty discord of sound that followed the words drowned out any retort Jonathan might have made. Before it faded, the lights dimmed in the sanctum and the veil closed to hide the standing Grandmaster, the Marshal, the Guardian and the accusers. And at last Jonathan realised the full significance of the ceremony. He had been ignominiously cast out from the Order which had been so much a part of his life for nearly twenty years. At a stroke, he had lost its support, most of his friends, its certainties and its shared aspirations.

A quick rap on his arm brought him to himself. It was Griffiths.

'Leave the Temple now,' he said shortly.

Jonathan was still trying to grapple with the thoughts and fears seething in his mind as he turned and walked slowly towards the door where the Knight Sentinel stood. As he went, he heard his other escort, Dorothy Mawson, weeping quietly as she kept pace behind him. At least she felt something for him still, he mused miserably, though what the hell was the good of that?

The Sentinel stood aside, drew the bolts and waited for him to go through. He was no sooner past the door than it slammed shut heavily behind him and the bolts rattled home. He was alone in the robing room; his escort had stayed in the Temple.

So if I'm alone, I'm alone, he said to himself; who needs them?

He pulled off the yellow penitential robe and threw it to the floor, dressed quickly and left. On the way home, the delayed shock started to catch up with him. He could not rid himself of the image of the heart being taken from the balance and thrown to the black dog to tear and swallow. Yellow fangs set in red gums, ripping at the bloody meat. The destroyer, that's what the Grandmaster had called the dog.

In no sense had there been a trial or even a fair hearing – not when the balances and the hound were there. Heart weighed against feather – the outcome was determined before he had entered the Temple. His guilt had been established before they sent for him. He had been summoned to confess to what they knew already, that was all.

By the time he reached home, Jonathan's hands were shaking and he felt physically sick. The telephone was ringing as he went into the house. Automatically he picked it up and said *yes?*

'Rawlings? I've been trying to get you all evening.'

'Who is this?'

'Burney. Can you hear me – you sound very distant.'

'Bernie who?'

'Burney of Personnel.'

'Personnel?'

'Rawlings – are you drunk? You sound very strange.'

Jonathan forced his mind away from the image of the black dog devouring the heart. Ralph Burney, personnel director of Dovedays. What the hell did he want?

'No, I'm not drunk. What is it?'

'I'm afraid that something unpleasant has come up. That's why I've been trying to contact you. It's about your secretary, Nancy Tait.'

'God! Don't say that she's killed herself too!'

'Killed herself – what do you mean?'

'Nothing. Go on.'

'Yes, well, I had a call just before I left the office this evening. It was a doctor named Canning. He told me that she was a patient in a mental hospital. I had no idea until then, I thought that she was just unwell and off for a few days.'

'So?'

'Well . . . look here, this is a bit embarassing – I understand that you knew she was there. In fact, you've been to visit her. Is that correct?'

'What of it? I was trying to be discreet about her illness. I felt sorry for her.'

'The thing is, according to the doctor who called me, she's rational again. He got my name from her and called to let me know that he was getting in touch with the police. He sounded very angry.'

'The police? What about?'

'All I know is what he told me and that wasn't much. It seems that she's accusing you of all sorts of things. It sounds very serious. I expect the police will want to talk to you to get your side of the story.'

'But nobody will take her word against mine, surely? I mean, she's deranged. That's why she's in hospital.'

'It's nothing to do with me,' said Burney quickly. 'I gather from the doctor that it all happened at your house, whatever it was that unhinged her in the first place. I think you'd better get your story together before the law arrives on your doorstep.'

'Who else knows about this?'

'I had to tell Peter Bennett, of course. He was none too pleased at the prospect of a scandal involving the company. Just think what the gutter press could do with it if there were any charges against you. *Company director and secretary in drugs and rape orgy* – that's the sort of headline they'd print.'

'Drugs and rape?'

'I shouldn't have mentioned that. It was something the doctor let slip. Anyway, I've done my best for you by warning you what's on the way. Unofficially, of course.'

'Of course. Thank you, Ralph.'

'I've got another unofficial message for you from Bennett. I'm to make you understand that if there's any truth at all in what this woman is saying that you did to her, you're no longer a director of Dovedays, not even an employee of the company. Got that?'

'He could at least listen to what I have to say!'

'Let's hope it doesn't come to that. Naturally, I don't believe a word of what she's accusing you of. She's obviously raving mad. I'm sure you'll be able to sort it out quickly with the police. By the way, until it is all sorted out and your name cleared, you have to stay away from the office. Don't come to work, understand. Regard yourself as on leave.'

'I must talk to Bennett and make him see reason. Is he at home?'

'Don't bother to ring him. He's not available. Good night. And good luck.'

The line went dead.

Dumbstruck by the turn of events, Jonathan reeled to the sideboard where the bottles stood and poured himself half a tumbler of brandy. He gulped most of it down, topped it up with a trembling hand and slumped into the nearest armchair. He felt as if he were on a carousel that was running out of control, faces were flashing past him in his crazy circular ride, mouths open to shout warnings, but the words lost in the speed with which he was passing them.

Innes, he thought. He saw the truth when we met. He set enquiries going – he's had someone talk to that damned psychiatrist. And he's done something himself to clear Nancy's mind so that she remembers it all again. She knows she was drugged, she remembers what she saw in the chapel upstairs, she knows that I took her by force. She's told them about the letter from Braithwaite – and that's set Innes on the scent of how I engineered his downfall. But not his death – I didn't kill him. They knew it all tonight in the Temple because of Innes. And when Burney contacted Bennett, Bennett would have talked to Innes to get his advice on how to handle the situation.

What I have to do is to decide on the priorities, he told himself, swallowing another mouthful of brandy. The most immediate danger comes from Nancy Tait. I can convince the police that she came here willingly and that we got drunk and went to bed together. The rape accusation is neither here nor there – she undressed of her own free will, I can say. The drugs thing might be harder to talk my way out of. Not that they can prove anything – it was all out of her system by the time she went to the hospital. But there could be damaging doubts.

Suppose she stopped being rational again and became certifiably insane? Then Dr Canning could never establish that she was ever rational. Whatever she has told them would be dismissed as ravings. There would be no charges to answer. I must arrange a relapse for her. Look what I did to that bastard Braithwaite! Evidently Abaddon strikes at his victim's weakest point. With Braithwaite it was his guts, with Nancy it's her mental balance. If I go up into my chapel and summon Abaddon again, in twenty minutes from now Nancy will be screaming mad – for five months. That interfering doctor will have a lot of explaining to do then. I might even be able to sue him for defamation – that should be worth a fortune. He'd have to settle out of court because his only witness would be certifiably mad. A successful settlement against him would put me right with Bennett and Dovedays. Wrongly accused, totally vindicated, back in business. That's the way I'll do it.

It won't put me right with Innes. Nothing ever will. He knows too much. But, on the other hand, he can't show his hand. He can't tell anyone what he knows or how he knows it. So he will always be against me and he's far more powerful than I am. No – there's a way to beat him too! When I cross the Abyss I shall become his equal. Then there's no way he can harm me. And I know how to cross the Abyss. If I hadn't tried to use Nancy I'd have succeeded and they couldn't have done that to me tonight in the Temple. All I have to do is get on the next flight to Los Angeles and rise up through the sacred alignments with Orline. Burney told me not to go to the office until further notice, so they'll never miss me. By this time tomorrow evening I can be a Master of the Temple.

He drained his glass, hauled himself to his feet and was halfway to the stairs when the telephone rang again. Answer it? Leave it? It might be the police, he thought – what I must do is to sound helpful and put them off for half an hour while I get up into the chapel and do what is necessary.

'Jonathan Rawlings,' he said, making his voice confident.

'Jonathan – it's Arnold.'

A premonition tugged at his heart.

'Arnold, what is it?'

'I'm at Judith's. She's very near the end now.'

'What do you mean, very near?'

'I think she will slip away during the night. She has been asking for you.'

'Not now, please God,' Jonathan wailed, his control gone. 'Not now! Arnold, I can't begin to tell you what's happening to me.'

'Jonathan, pull yourself together. You are a grown man and an initiate. Where is your strength?'

'I'm sorry. I was overcome for a second. I'm all right now. Is she in any pain?'

'No, she's between sleeping and waking.'

'Does she know?'

'Of course she knows. What sort of trouble are you in?'

'It's far too complicated to explain in a few words, but it's worse than anything you can imagine.'

'Whatever it is, it must take second place. Judith wants you here.'

'Yes, I'll leave within the hour. There is something I must do first. My entire future depends on it.'

Arnold's voice hardened as he spoke.

'Jonathan, when you were only a boy you were received into a circle, where you spoke with the gods and were blessed by them. What you've done since then is a matter for your own conscience. But you have not been released from the vow you took then. I charge you to come here at once, without any kind of delay, or the blessing will be turned to a curse.'

'I'm beyond cursing,' Jonathan mumbled.

'You can never be out of reach of either the love or the anger of the gods of life. You know that.'

'I have already incurred their anger,' Jonathan answered slowly. 'I doubt if there is anything I could do now which would make things worse.'

'Then make them better.'

'Yes, you're right. I'm leaving now, Arnold. If Judith can understand, tell her that I'm on my way and that I love her.'

'I'll tell her. Hurry.'

Jonathan put down the telephone and went straight out to his car, not even stopping to turn off the house lights. He headed for the Chiswick flyover then round the North Circular road. It was just after nine, the commuter traffic was long gone and he made good time to the start of the motorway to Birmingham. Once on it, he put his foot down hard on the accelerator and went roaring north away from London, not even glancing at the speedometer. If a police patrol spotted him exceeding the speed limit, he intended to give them a hell of a run for their money.

He had heard or read somewhere that people dying a natural death tended to do so between midnight and dawn. Just as, before hospital obstetricians started to induce labour artificially for the convenience of hospital administration, babies tended to be born between midnight and dawn. He must be at Judith's well before midnight. At some point he would have to stop to fill up the tank, but with a clear road he ought to do the journey in not much over two hours.

He had eaten nothing since midday, but the brandy was sustaining him. By stages the feel of the hurtling car and the distant drumming of its engine had a calming effect on him. The successive layers of misery that had been dumped over him that evening were shaking down and settling. By the time he had pulled in to a service station fifty miles up the motorway to fill up with petrol, he was able to think rationally again. He felt like an earthquake survivor poking his head warily above the rubble to see what was left standing. The view was bleak. Nearly everything was flattened. He was cut off from the Order and all it had meant to him. His business career was about to collapse. Judith was leaving this life. And he knew that Orline would sever relations with him instantly when the London Lodge circulated a notice of his expulsion, even though it might pain her.

How in God's name did all this get started, he asked himself, well knowing the answer. He had allowed his dislike of Braithwaite to take possession of him, until he had smashed the man out of his way instead of letting the Order work secretly to resolve the problem and help him upwards in the company. Everything followed from his one act of blind rage in his private chapel – the maiming, the suicide, the involvement with Nancy Tait, and his present fall.

But was that so? The chain of events had really begun long before the day when Braithwaite threatened him and provoked his retaliation. He had harboured a growing antagonism towards the man for a long time, otherwise he would not have let himself be provoked so disastrously. In truth, he said to himself, I have been guilty of disobeying a fundamental rule of the Order: *give only good, expect only good.* That was where it started.

A calamity he did not care to think about was the price to be paid for his failed attempt to cross the Abyss. He understood now that it was not Nancy's fault that he had failed. It was because he had not been able to shed his earth-bound consciousness before taking the great step. He had tried to exalt his own ego to the throne of God. He would never have made so arrogant and self defeating an attempt in the days before he lost his head over Braithwaite and corrupted himself with malice.

Those who try to cross and fall into the Abyss set in motion within themselves a force of retribution as fatal as inoperable cancer. By trying and failing to become more than human, they become less than human. Jonathan knew all the precedents, right back to Gilles de Rais, Marshal of France, who went to his death on the gallows in relief when he realised what he had done to himself. And another French adept, the Marquis de Guaita, who headed the Kabalistic Rose Croix group in Paris, attempted the crossing some time in

1893 or 1894, failed and killed himself by a drug overdose at the age of twenty-seven. Aleister Crowley made the attempt in North Africa in 1909 by offering himself as a sexual sacrifice, Victor Neuburg being the active partner. And a few days later Crowley's presumption was rewarded when he became possessed by the force of destruction. Jack Parsons had hurled himself out across the Abyss, riding Marjorie Cameron, as Jonathan had ridden Nancy Tait. Parsons failed and his death was by fire. There were others Jonathan could bring to mind. Retribution took many forms, but it was sure, once the hounds were baying on the scent of wrong doing. Whatever men might think, God is not mocked.

Jonathan had been given the chance to make a full confession before his accusers in the Temple and he had spurned it. In retrospect, he saw that they were being merciful to him. It would have lightened his burden in part if he had made a full avowal of his motives and deeds. Not that it could have changed the judgment upon him. The Order invariably excommunicated a member who departed from its precepts, as doctors isolate a patient suffering from a highly contagious disease. But if he had made a confession and shown contrition, some small formula of comfort might have been spoken by the Grandmaster after the words of expulsion. There was a saying in the Order's rubric – no man, however vile, is eternally beyond God's mercy, if he seeks it.

He had thrown away his chance of hearing even that, through his unreasonable anger against the Grandmaster and the accusers, so that the last words spoken to him were those of the terrible sentence: you are cut asunder, your soul is shrivelled up, your cursed name is buried in oblivion and silence is upon it forever.

That was the word of the Order. Jonathan Rawlings was dead to it.

'But no man, however vile,' Jonathan said aloud, 'is eternally beyond God's mercy . . . if he seeks it.'

Being sorry for what he had done was not enough, not nearly enough. He had a debt to pay and there was only one way he could see to pay it. That was to call back to himself the blast of hatred he had aimed at Derek Braithwaite. The prospect terrified him, and he knew that unless he did it at once, he would never again find the courage to do so.

Beads of sweat trickled down his face as he reached down inside himself to touch the source of the red hatred, the sleeping volcano of destruction he had allowed to erupt once before – and which even that very evening he had been prepared to direct against Nancy Tait, to drive her insane. He let the molten lava flood up inside him, let it sear away all other emotions, thoughts, fears, sensations, until he was howling out a wordless chant of malice and pounding with his clenched fists on the steering wheel. He was unaware that the car was almost out of control, swerving from lane to lane as it pushed a hundred miles an hour.

As best as he could remember them, he began to scream out the words he had used before:

'He opened the bottomless pit . . . and there arose a smoke from it, as the smoke of a great furnace . . . and there came out of the smoke locusts upon the earth and unto them was given power, as the scorpions of the earth have power . . . and they had a king over them, which is the angel of the bottomless pit, whose name is ABADDON!'

Jonathan's eyes bulged blindly in his purple-flushed face as he roared out at the top of his voice:

'Abaddon, Abaddon, Abaddon – appear! I command you!'

It seemed to him that a black figure with blazing eyes and lanky hair to its shoulders was rushing at him from far away, sailing at him on leathery bat wings. He greeted the manifestation with ferocious joy.

'Abaddon – angel of the bottomless pit – I have corrupted my life and made it hideous. It is yours to take!'

The car careered off the motorway, its front end lifting as it mounted the grass verge and struck the central barrier. A wheel ripped off as the car skimmed over the barrier, twisting over as it flew. It crunched down on its side on the south bound carriageway and slid screeching in a sheet of red flame from the rasp of metal on road, towards an oncoming thirty ton truck.

From touching the barrier to the impact with the truck took seven seconds, an eternity of hard dying for Jonathan. When the car first lifted off, his legs were broken at the knees under the edge of the instrument panel. He felt the agony as Abaddon's first stroke, the stroke which maimed but did not kill. As the car hit the road on its side, his collar bone collapsed under his weight and the sharp end of a splintered rib tore through his lungs, as if a clawed hand reached for his heart to shred it.

He exulted in his suffering, knowing that he was making restitution at last and that he was dying the death of the just. Through the racking pain and the splintering of glass and the screaming of rending metal, he gasped out the Order's best loved words ' . . . *from God I am born . . . to God I return . . . what then shall I fear?*'

With hard-locked brakes, the oncoming truck skidded and turned sideways across all three lanes of the carriageway. The sliding car smashed into the truck's rear wheels and stood briefly on its nose, breaking Jonathan's neck, then fell back to the road upside down. Its newly filled petrol tank exploded and Jonathan's body, the spirit fled from it, was consumed in a great red-gold rose of fire.

A good word is as a good tree,
its roots set firm
and its branches in heaven,
giving its fruit at every season
by leave of its lord;
So God citeth symbols for men,
that they may remember.

NOTES

Though it is not usual to provide notes to a novel, most of the characters in this story were real people and since they performed the acts attributed to them, however bizarre, a little background documentation may serve to show the reader that a novel is not necessarily a work of fiction.

Prologue – Sand Devils
The account of Crowley's possession was first published in his own magazine *The Equinox*, two years after the event. It was republished as a separate work after his death by the Californian Lodge of the Order of the Temple of the Orient.

The translation by S.L. MacGregor Mathers of *The Key of Solomon the King* was published in 1888 by George Redway and subsequently by Routledge & Kegan Paul. It was from this that Crowley took his protective formulae. Mathers was not the first English translation. Another adept, Frederick Hockley, translated it in 1828 and his original manuscript, with hand coloured drawings, was bound into book form. There is no known Hebrew original of the work, but there are several Latin manuscript versions, including one dated 1634 in the Bibliothèque Nationale in Paris. In his *Memoirs*, Casanova mentions that the work was studied by Venetian adepts during the time he frequented their circle in the middle years of the eighteenth century.

Chapter 1 – Hans-Martin Frick
One of the links in the long chain of Orders and adepts between the original Templars and present day organisations claiming descent from them is, by secret tradition, Cagliostro. He became a Freemason in London in 1777 and later established in Paris his own Lodge of the Egyptian Rite, which is still active today under another name, in several countries.

An independent witness and participant in Crowley's goat ritual was British novelist Mary Butts. She was later described by Crowley in his *'Diary of a Drug-fiend'* as 'a fat, bold, red-headed slut'.

Chapter 2 – Advice from a Master
The Book of Esther in the Old Testament was written about 1500 BC and was based on earlier, perhaps verbal accounts, of events during the Jewish captivity in Babylon three and a half centuries before. In its present form it was probably written to justify the continued observance by the Jews of an otherwise inexplicable annual Feast, which originally in Babylon had been the confirmation in office of the King by his ritual marriage and coupling with the goddess Ishtar in the person of her high priestess.

Chapter 3 – Business Dinner
Although Mathers wrote to his benefactress Annie Horniman from Paris to the effect that he and Moina had never consummated their marriage, Crowley, who stayed in their home more than once, recorded in his *De Arte Magica*, published during their lifetime, that they practised sexual vampirism, by which he meant oral sex repeated to the point of total exhaustion. Crowley was at odds with his former teacher at the time and may or may not have been telling the truth.

Chapter 4 – The Rose and Cross
The words used in the ceremony as acceptance of the truth of the Profession of Righteousness are from Psalm 1 – *Beatus est vir ille qui non ambulat in consilio improborum*. The original is attributed to King David, father of King Solomon, and may be the work of his hand.

Chapter 5 – To Be A God
Austin Osman Spare, son of a London policeman, was a gifted artist who joined and then left Crowley's Order to

pursue his own exploration of the hidden world. He died in
1956. The best account of his beliefs and discoveries is
Images and Oracles of Austin Osman Spare by his friend
and literary executor Kenneth Grant, published by Frederick
Muller Ltd in 1975. Grant was for a period Master of the
British Lodge of the Order of the Temple of the Orient.

Chapter 6 – Sauna and Sibelius
Mozart's first contact with the hidden world was at the age of
twelve, when Dr Franz Anton Mesmer, then resident in
Vienna, commissioned from him a small-scale opera suitable
for performance at a musical soiree at his house on the
Landstrasse. Its theme is the union of two lovers through the
good offices of an adept.

John Ireland (1879-1962) was born in Cheshire, England.
He studied at the Royal College of Music. The inspiration for
some of his music was derived from the writings of Arthur
Machen, who was upgraded to Third Degree in the Hermetic
Order of the Golden Dawn (London Lodge) in 1900.

The dangerous Abramelin system was translated into
English by MacGregor Mathers from an eighteenth century
manuscript in the Bibliothèque de l'Arsenal in Paris, which
purports to be a French rendering of a Hebrew original dated
1458, though no such original is known. The system requires
the aspiring adept to segregate himself from the world for six
lunar months, starting at Easter. By following the prescribed
regime of prayer, meditation and fasting, he acquires such
self knowledge that many seemingly impossible things become
possible to him. Heseltine failed to complete the difficult
course, so did Aleister Crowley, who attempted it at his
Scottish home, Boleskine on Loch Ness, in the year 1900.
Though he tried for most of his life to acquire great wealth by
means of the Abramelin SEGALAH process, it never
worked for him, because of his failure.

The adept known as Georges Chevalier completed the six
month ordeal and his ceremonial diary was published in

1976 under the title of *The Sacred Magician* by Paladin Books.

In the Abramelin manuscript, the CASED square and five others are given in a section headed: *This chapter is only for evil*, and of the square itself, the work says *This symbol should never be made use of*.

Chapter 7 – The Earthly Temple

Alex Sanders, the best known and most publicised living British covenmaster, claims descent from a line of hereditary Welsh witches going back to Owain Glyndwr, the last independent Prince of Wales. He was initiated by his grandmother when he was seven and achieved such esteem by 1965 that he was elected Grandmaster of 107 separate covens. His follower and exegist, Stewart Farrer, makes it apparent in his *What Witches Do* (Peter Davies Ltd 1971) that Sanders had by then gone far beyond traditional witchcraft and had become a self-initiated adept.

Chapter 8 – Time Bomb Ticking

The mantra used by Rawlings to protect himself is from the *Wisdom of Solomon*, a work written in Alexandria, Egypt, about the year 50 BC, long after the historical King Solomon was dead and had passed into legend. The mantra is claimed to have great protective virtue.

Chapter 9 – The Bottomless Pit

The music chosen by Rawlings to accompany his ceremony was from Kurt Weill's *Bastille Suite*. The words used to summon and exteriorise the latent force of destruction within himself are from the ninth chapter of the Book of Revelations. The words serve only as a focus and have no power in themselves. Any carefully composed formula can be used. The ceremony itself has been established for as far back as written records go and is not for the merely curious to attempt.

Chapter 10 – Tower Struck by Lightning

Like popular astrology, numerology has fallen into disrepute through the incompetence of amateur practitioners. Its origin can be traced back to Pythagoras, who saw the universe as a series of numerical relationships, as do many physicists today. Though in the average person's mind Pythagoras is inescapably connected with school geometry, he was an adept who founded a closed Order at Crotona in southern Italy about the year 530 BC.

Chapter 11 – Seven Miles High

Works on tantric belief and rites by Western authors tend to over emphasise spirituality at the expense of carnality and are somewhat inhibited in their approach. One of the best available accounts in English is *The Tantric Way* by Ajit Mookerjee and Madhu Khanna (Thames and Hudson, 1977). It describes the ceremonial worship of the male and female sexual parts and their conjunction in an unabashed manner without losing the metaphysical aspect.

Chapter 12 – The Sacred Mountain

There are striking parallels between the lives of Dr Franz Anton Mesmer and Dr Carl Gustav Jung. Mesmer was born near Lake Constance, on the Swiss-German border, in 1734. He qualified as a doctor after six years at the University of Vienna, went into fashionable practice in Vienna and moved on from medicine to psychotherapy. After a stormy life, he retired to the region of his birth, by then an advanced adept. After his death in 1815, the members of the Berlin Academy of Science paid for a marble monument on his grave – symbolic in shape and inscription. Jung was born in 1875 near Lake Constance, on the Swiss side, qualified as a doctor at the University of Basel and became interested in psychotherapy, his inspiration at first deriving from Vienna, where Dr Sigmund Freud was alarming the medical world with his theorising and unorthodox approach. During the course of his long and successful life, Jung became a self initiated adept. He died in 1961. Yet by one of the ironies of history, Mesmer is remembered, if at all, as a fraud, and Jung as a near saint. Believers in reincarnation may be tempted to discern the same soul behind two masks.

Chapter 13 – A Deal
The esoteric significance of the number eleven is that it represents one added to ten. The numbers from one to ten are the essential numbers in the system of Pythagoras and from them all other numbers derive. That is, they stand for everything – the whole created universe. One, the beginning, stands for God. One (God) added to ten (the universe) is therefore the number of revelation, the beginning of the knowledge and understanding of God. People with this number are thought of as special messengers, whose words must be listened to carefully, for God may be speaking through them.

Chapter 14 – A Memorial on the Moon
Parsons wrote: Modern man, in half conscious reaction against the patriarchy and Judeo-Christian religion, seeks an escape to the mother in materialism and science, but these cannot really help him, since he is unable to face or understand their origins. On the other hand, the fear and hatred of the demon mother results in increasing components of homosexuality and its repressive corollary, the paranoid psychosis. The partialities in man fear nothing more than a move towards totality. Consequently, in secondary reaction we observe fanatic militarism, pseudo morality and dogmatic politics in their most violent aspects.

Chapter 15 – Unveiling
The ceremony described is not for the inquisitive to risk. A.E. Russell said that once at the apex of intense meditation he awoke that fire in himself of which the ancients have written and it ran like lightning up his spinal cord and his body rocked with the power of it. He seemed to be standing in a

fountain of flame and there were fiery pulsations as of wings about his head, and a musical sound not unlike the clashing of cymbals with every pulsation. The experience frightened Russell away from further experimentation, as well it might.

Chapter 16 – A View of Hollywood
It is highly improbable that the producer, director or star of *Deep Throat* had any knowledge of what adepts term *mors osculi*, which in English means the *death of the kiss*. This is taken to refer to the ecstasy brought about by prolonged sexual activity, usually orally performed, to the point of exhaustion. The point of orgasm is repeatedly attained without emission, bringing about a suspension of normal physiological functions and an ecstasy far beyond the normal range of human experience. Crowley practised *mors osculi* with many of his women followers and his term for it was eroto-comotose lucidity. It is also sometimes called sexual vampirism.

Chapter 17 – Earth and Sky
The link between Charles Manson and Aleister Crowley's Order of the Temple of the Orient was through the *Solar Lodge* of the OTO headed by the wife of a professor of philosophy at the University of Southern California in Los Angeles. The blood sacrifice of chickens formed an important part of the ceremonies and members were required to give up independent thought and let the Mistress of the Lodge direct their lives completely. Manson joined this group and learned their ways, before setting up on his own. He soon progressed from the sacrifice of chickens to that of human beings.

Chapter 18 – An Army with Banners
The exchange of formal liturgy in the ceremony is from the Book of Haggai, written about 520 BC after the return from captivity of the Jews.

Chapter 19 – Red and Black
Hieronymus Bosch painted the *Garden of Earthly Delights*

for initiates, as did his contemporary, Henri met de Bles. Much of the work of both painters is therefore puzzling to those who do not understand the symbolism. De Bles was probably an Adamite, an heretical religious group which worshipped naked in imitation of Adam and believed that the natural sexual act could take place in such a manner that it was equal in value to prayer in the sight of God. They were, naturally, persecuted by the orthodox Christian church, which held that Adam's original sin was in having sexual relations with Eve. It is possible that Bosch was a member of the same group.

The formula of words with which Rawlings possessed the land and identified himself with it were composed as a formula of sacred ownership by King Hammurabi of Babylon about 2000 BC. The words were carved on a stone column, at the top of which was Hammurabi receiving his authority from God in his sun-aspect named Shamash by the Babylonians. The column can be seen in the Louvre Museum in Paris.

Chapter 20 – Good Old Boys
The first Grand Lodge of England was formed in 1717 and from then on Freemasonry spread quickly across mainland Europe and to America. In Europe it was denounced by the Catholic Church and the first papal bull against it was issued by Clement XII in 1738.

Italian prime minister Arnaldo Forlani and his government resigned in May 1981 when the existence was revealed of a secret Freemasons' Lodge in Rome. The Lodge was reported to have over 900 members, including government ministers, bankers, industrialists, generals, admirals, senior police officers, journalists, broadcasters and other influential people. Grandmaster Licio Gelli proved to be absent on urgent business when the Italian authorities sought him in connection with their enquiries. The Lodge's banker, Roberto Calvi, met a violent death in mysterious circumstances in London a year later. Investigations revealed that there was a shortfall of about £750 million in the bank's funds and that there had been close relations between Calvi's bank and the Vatican's bank. Grandmaster Gelli was arrested by the Swiss police in September 1982 when he attempted to withdraw money from a Geneva bank account.

Chapter 21 – Gateway in the Mind
The *tattwa* symbols derive from Indian tantrism and there are twenty-five of them in all, symbolising the five elements in permutations – earth, water, fire, air and spirit, each with its own colour. They were used extensively as means of producing otherworldly experiences by the members of the Order of the Golden Dawn. No reader will come to harm by trying the experiment which Rawlings proposed to Braithwaite, and the results may well be enlightening.

Chapter 22 – Childhood Memories
Professor Jeffrey Russell of the University of California (Santa Barbara) makes a passing reference in his *A History of Witchcraft* (Thames and Hudson, 1980) to Isaac Bonewits who holds a Bachelor's Degree in Magic from the University of California. No similar academic course is as yet available in any British or Continental university. Present day British witches fall into three main categories, hereditary, Gardnerian and Alexandrian. Hereditary witches keep very quiet about themselves and rarely initiate outside their immediate family. The two other categories descend from the covens founded by Gerald Gardner and Alexander Sanders and his former wife Maxine.

Interestingly, Gardner claimed descent from a Scottish witch who was burned for her beliefs in the sixteenth century and in his later years saw his work as a revival, which it may have been, though much of his inspiration came from an Italian witch named Maddalena, whose liturgy was translated into English by Charles Leland at the turn of the century. Sanders claims descent from Owain Glyndwr through his grandmother who initiated him as a child by means of a ceremony in which she nicked his scrotum with a ceremonial dagger to make his blood flow.

Those interested in such matters are referred to my *The World, the Flesh, the Devil*, a biographical dictionary of witches (New English Library, 1981).

Chapter 23 – Old Photographs

Sexual congress between older men and very young girls results from deep springs within the mind. It was formalised in the Cult of the Ku, which originated in China and became established in London in the 1920s. During an elaborate ceremony the young woman became possessed by the fire-serpent goddess and, after copulation, the devotee underwent an experience which he perceived as a journey through the kingdom of the dead. In the *I Ching*, Ku represents 'arresting decay' and indicates great progress and success to the superior man who can deal properly with the condition represented by it. That is, the end purpose of the ceremony was rejuvenation by acquiring control of the physical and psychological elements within the devotee which produced ageing and decay. The same basic thinking lay behind the event recorded in the First Book of Kings: 'Now King David was old and stricken in years, and they covered him with clothes, but he got no heat. Wherefore his servants said unto him, Let there be sought for my lord the king a young virgin, and let her stand before him, and let her cherish him, and let her lie in thy bosom. So they sought for a fair damsel throughout all the coasts of Israel, and found Abishag, a Shunammite, and brought her to the King. And the damsel was very fair, and cherished the King and ministered to him, but the King knew her not.'

Evidently the matter had been left too late and for all the girl's ministrations, David was past rising to the occasion.

Chapter 24 – Sacred Alignments

The plants mentioned in this chapter and in chapter 22 are common in the English countryside and their extracts have the effects described. It is exceedingly dangerous to experiment with them unaided, since the amount ingested is critical and an overdose can have fatal results.

The images presented to Nancy Tait by Jonathan Rawlings are those of the Tarot pack designed by Arthur Edward Waite and drawn by Pamela Coleman Smith. Waite became head of the London Temple of the Order of the Golden Dawn and remained so until 1914. His revised Tarot pack was first published in 1910 and is still printed.

Chapter 25 – The Scales

The *Book of Coming Forth by Day* is mistitled in English the *Book of the Dead* because the hymns and litanies and prayers which compose it were found in ancient Egyptian tombs. The text is a manual for the benefit of the illustrious dead to guide them in their passage through death to resurrection.

The copy on display in the Egyptian Rooms of the British Museum came from the tomb of Ani, a government official. On it may be seen depicted the judgment before Osiris, when Ani was required to make confession of his deeds before his heart was weighed against truth. The righteous man was led to eternal life, but the wicked were cast to Amam, the devourer of souls.

Book Tokens

Give them the pleasure of choosing

Book Tokens can be bought and exchanged at most bookshops in Great Britain and Ireland.

NEL BESTSELLERS

T51277	'THE NUMBER OF THE BEAST'	*Robert Heinlein*	£2.25
T50777	STRANGER IN A STRANGE LAND	*Robert Heinlein*	£1.75
T51382	FAIR WARNING	*Simpson & Burger*	£1.75
T52478	CAPTAIN BLOOD	*Michael Blodgett*	£1.75
T50246	THE TOP OF THE HILL	*Irwin Shaw*	£1.95
T49620	RICH MAN, POOR MAN	*Irwin Shaw*	£1.60
T51609	MAYDAY	*Thomas H. Block*	£1.75
T54071	MATCHING PAIR	*George G. Gilman*	£1.50
T45773	CLAIRE RAYNER'S LIFEGUIDE		£2.50
T53709	PUBLIC MURDERS	*Bill Granger*	£1.75
T53679	THE PREGNANT WOMAN'S BEAUTY BOOK	*Gloria Natale*	£1.25
T49817	MEMORIES OF ANOTHER DAY	*Harold Robbins*	£1.95
T50807	79 PARK AVENUE	*Harold Robbins*	£1.75
T50149	THE INHERITORS	*Harold Robbins*	£1.75
T53231	THE DARK	*James Herbert*	£1.50
T43245	THE FOG	*James Herbert*	£1.50
T53296	THE RATS	*James Herbert*	£1.50
T45528	THE STAND	*Stephen King*	£1.75
T50874	CARRIE	*Stephen King*	£1.50
T51722	DUNE	*Frank Herbert*	£1.75
T51552	DEVIL'S GUARD	*Robert Elford*	£1.50
T52575	THE MIXED BLESSING	*Helen Van Slyke*	£1.75
T38602	THE APOCALYPSE	*Jeffrey Konvitz*	95p

NEL P.O. BOX 11, FALMOUTH TR10 9EN, CORNWALL

Postage Charge:
U.K. Customers 45p for the first book plus 20p for the second book and 14p for each additional book ordered to a maximum charge of £1.63.

B.F.P.O. & EIRE Customers 45p for the first book plus 20p for the second book and 14p for the next 7 books; thereafter 8p per book.

Overseas Customers 75p for the first book and 21p per copy for each additional book.

Please send cheque or postal order (no currency).

Name..

Address ....

....

Title ....

While every effort is made to keep prices steady, it is sometimes necessary to increase prices at short notice. New English Library reserve the right to show on covers and charge new retail prices which may differ from those advertised in the text or elsewhere.(7)